THE BLOOD PRINCE

AYLA MARIE

THE FOUR KINGDOMS
MAP

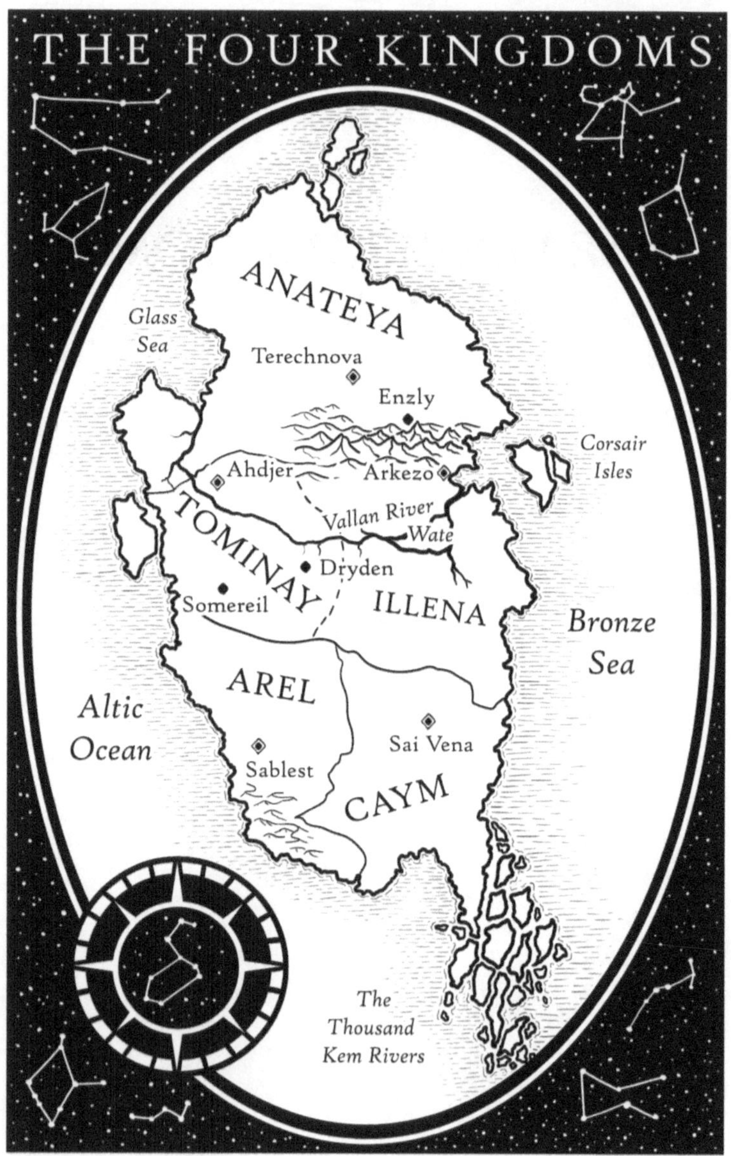

THE FOUR KINGDOMS
ANATEYA
Glass Sea
Terechnova
Enzly
Ahdjer
Arkezo
Corsair Isles
Vallan River
Wate
TOMINAY
Dryden
Somereil
ILLENA
Bronze Sea
Altic Ocean
AREL
Sai Vena
Sablest
CAYM
The Thousand Kem Rivers

To Laura,
For teaching me the ins and outs of being an author
And to Mum,
For learning it all with me, no matter how late I wanted to work
I couldn't have done it without you <3

PART ONE
TOMINAY

CHAPTER
ONE

LEO

I see every person passing by, but not a soul can see me. The hood of my usual midnight-blue cloak is pulled low over my face to keep me hidden from any wandering eyes. I pull my favorite dagger from the dark leather sheath strapped tight to my thigh. It has a thick blade and a pommel of old cedar inlaid with copper wire worn to the shape of my hands. I drag my fingers carefully along the edge, feeling the cold bite of the steel against my skin. It slices into my pinkie, drawing a single drop of blood. I don't flinch; the sight of blood stopped making my stomach roll a long time ago.

A door creaks open across the road from where I stand. My target emerges from the only completely dark shop along the lamplit street as the clicking of heels against stone bounces through the air. Two stalking shadows follow close to her sides, crouching low to the ground. I sneer at the sight of the dogs, snarling and snapping at the passing rats. They're going to make this interesting.

I keep to the shadows, blending in with the night as I stalk silently closer to my prey. She's a cunning con artist known for tricking even the smartest businessmen. They obviously weren't thrilled with being deceived.

"I know you're there. You're good at using the darkness, but my job is to find what is being hidden," she says. Her strong voice hangs eerily in the smoggy air.

"You're not afraid," I call, my voice sprinkled with amusement. I let my good conscience float to the back of my mind while the demon living in the depths of my being takes hold. "You should be when faced with a dangerous person," I say. *Keep her talking, let her think she can feel me out.*

"And why would I be afraid? The people who hired you are too cowardly to kill me themselves. The fact they want to kill me tells me that I am seen as a threat, and I consider their fear a personal compliment," she states merrily as her squinted eyes rove over the darkness.

"It shouldn't be," I say evenly.

A huffed laugh escapes from deep in her chest. "You sound like you've seen much in your days, why don't we find a way to make a deal? I can use an extra mercenary in my ranks," she says as a smirk forms on her lips. She's a rising boss then, interesting. "But if I'm going to take you in, I do need to see who exactly I'm hiring." A true snake.

I sheath my blade carefully back into its scabbard and step into the light. I glance up just far enough to reveal my face to the woman. She takes a couple sure-footed steps toward me. The mutts snarl as they pick up on my scent, baring their teeth. They seem to be the smartest ones in their little band.

Her eyebrows shoot up as she takes me in. As quick as the surprise hits her face, she stows it away and hardens her expression to stone. She scoffs to herself, eyeing me up and down. "You're but a boy. Oh, you must be lost! Do you want me to walk you home? Your mother and father must be terribly worried," she says mockingly, not trying to disguise the cruel smile playing across her face.

I let her words fly past me, keeping my expression expertly cold. She won't be speaking like this for much longer. She won't be speaking at all, for that matter. I take my dagger into my hand once more and spin it between my fingers.

"Do you recognize this blade?" I ask, staring right through her. She pales as her eyes stick to the weapon in my hand. "It's tasted the blood of many other arrogant fools exactly like you. You underestimate people you should not, like all those who have come before you. And like them, you'll end up dead; your corpse left propped against a wall for the body men to drag away." The hilt of my weapon sits snuggly in my hand as I hold her fearful stare. The body men are less like people and more like mindless monsters who've lost their souls. They never speak and are only seen lurking when they're dragging the dead to the morgue.

"You can't be the Blood Prince; your eyes aren't red," she snaps, but I can hear the shudder lurking beneath her words.

"Oh, you mean, like this?" My eyes flash crimson as I let my primal senses take hold. Everything I see takes on the hue of red I've come to know so well. My muscles tense and relax as power surges through my veins. I sheath the dagger at my side and reach behind my back to grab two long, thin slayers, twin killers perfectly crafted with hilts wrapped in a deep-navy-blue leather, the same leather as both my sheaths and the straps I wear across my body.

I take a step toward her as she stumbles over her feet. Without a second thought, she lets go of her snapping dogs with a high-pitched whistle. The first dog launches at me, its teeth set on the flesh of my throat. With a single move, I wrap my arm swiftly around the dog's neck and pull away. My blade slices through its soft flesh like air. The dog drops to the ground with a thud, drowning on something much worse than water.

The second dog jumps moments after the first, sinking its teeth deep into my arm. A frustrated growl escapes my chest as I hit the dog in the temple with the butt of my blade. It lets out a high screech and drops my arm like a scolded puppy. The dog shakes off the blow, giving me enough time to prepare myself for its next attack. It lunges for my legs, baring its bloody teeth. I swing my leg back and land a crunching kick to its ribs. Whimpering, it tries to limp away but falls to the ground before it can crawl back to its shaking master.

I meet the lady's terrified gaze. Nothing will stand between me and getting paid. I wipe the blood dripping off my blades onto the leg of my worn trousers and take a step toward her. Snapping into reality, the lady raises her arm, holding a small dagger tightly in her shaking hand. I place my slayers back behind me and take out a small steel throwing knife. I flip it once as I take another few steps closer, and let it fly. She drops her meager blade as my knife embeds itself deep into the flesh of her hand, a wild, guttural scream bursting from her throat.

Her stare burns into me. It's the last thing she has. The last weapon she can wield. A feigned confidence. The sad thing is, death doesn't care about wits, only how long you can survive and what price you're willing to pay for the time. "If you're going to kill me, you owe me a death wish," she says, her voice unwavering. "Kill my kids for me after I'm gone." I stop, my concentration slipping as my siblings' faces pass through my mind.

I narrow my gaze and let my instincts take the reins once more. As if she could sense that my guard was down, the lady launches at me with the dagger switched to her working hand. I pull back and miss getting slashed in the throat by no more than a hairbreadth. My shirt clings to my shoulder like it's been drenched as I regain my footing. I roll it slowly, feeling the skin over my collarbone move strangely, as if it weren't in one piece. She thrusts again, jabbing the knife at my stomach. I catch her hand before the steel embeds itself in my gut and twist her wrist hard. The knife clatters to the ground as I spin her around and force her arm behind her back. Trapping her against my chest, I pull my blade out of the sheath strapped to my thigh and hold it to her throat. With a swift kick of my leg, she falls heavily to her knees.

"I owe you a death wish," I say flatly. Emotionlessly.

"Go to hell!" she spits.

"Ladies first." I run the blade smoothly over her throat and just as fast as it started, it's done.

I wipe the blood from my hands and place my dagger back in its scabbard. I heave a sigh and drag her to the nearest wall, propping her up against it. I close her eyes and cross her hands over her lap. Grabbing her bleeding hand, I pull my knife free and put it back with its sisters attached to the bandolier running from my shoulder to my side. I pick up the blade she dropped and tuck it into my boot, the cold steel biting against my skin.

I stand and turn to walk away, not wanting to look at her corpse any longer than I already have. I freeze as the sound of thick boots hitting the stone street fills the air one after the other like an easy melody. I straighten as they stop behind me, far enough away I wouldn't be able to reach him if I turned.

"Why do you close their eyes after you kill them?" a deep voice asks. Even though he always shows up, I never quite get used to the way Mr. Vela lurks in the dark. "Why not run and leave them to bleed?"

"Do you have my pay?" I ask, keenly aware of his movements, even with my back turned.

"Yes, when have I not had it?"

I turn to face one of the most feared arena bosses in Tominay and close the gap between us in two strides. Mr. Vela tosses the small pouch in his hand, the sound of clinking coins filling the silent street. I reach my hand out to take it, but he pulls back, tilting his head to the side with a dark smile.

"You never answered me, boy," he chides, dangling the bag in front of my face like a master to his dog. Cold rage seeps through my bones. I'm going to do the world a favor by ripping his head off his shoulders one day. I keep my mouth shut and hold his dark gaze. "You're imagining what it would feel like to kill me, aren't you? Well, you know the minute you disobey me, you get put into the open. Your family will pay for your mistakes," he says with a cruel smile. I kick up the back of my boot, sending a knife flying into the air. I catch it and press the edge to his throat as my mind goes blissfully clear.

"Oh, no. Did I hit a soft spot? Poor boy," he says sarcastically, staring into my bloody eyes like there's nothing strange about them. My stomach clenches as he holds my stare and pushes closer to the blade, daring me to slit his throat. He's a lunatic, but a clever, filthy rich one, nonetheless.

"I have to say though, you're getting good at hiding your knives. Good idea with the boots," he adds, eyeing them curiously.

With a frustrated growl, I snatch the bag from his hand and place the blade back into the small compartment built into the sole of my boot. I back away slowly, my eyes lingering on his form. I'm bound to this man's word and I hate it. When I get far enough away, I toss the bag around in my hand, testing the weight. It's lighter than usual. I curse under my breath as I run a bloodied hand through my hair. This isn't going to be good.

CHAPTER

TWO

LEO

I breathe easier when the forest comes into view, a wall of darkness guarding the only people that matter. The dark might be a frightening place for most, but it's a comfort to me. A familiar entity calling me home. I slow to a jog, taking a second to breathe. The stillness of the night helps me forget about what I've done, even if it's only for a moment.

I pass the big oak I used to swing on as a child. I used to love coming to this tree, now I can barely stand to be around it. The only indication of my employment is a worn piece of red cloth wrapped tight around its lowest branch. I avert my gaze and force my feet forward. The red cloth is the call to action, the signal to kill. I don't remember when I discarded the slip of paper that was attached to it. I push the thought aside. I won't need to worry about the blood-colored cloth for another couple of days now.

I know I'm home when I catch light filtering through the trees. Blood drips from my arm, leaving a clear trail as I walk to the door. I did my best to cover it up, but I may need to go back and make sure I haven't marked the way to my home in red ink. I take a deep breath, step up to the door, and reach for the handle. Before I can take it, the door swings open, revealing a tense face sporting a clenched jaw and scrunched brows.

My brother-in-arms stares at me for a long moment, his dark, shadowed eyes fixating on my bloodied arm and shoulder. "I'm guessing by the fact that your eyes are still red and the blood dripping on the floor that you've been hurt," he says sarcastically. I nod, looking down to where a little red puddle has begun to accumulate. I step inside as he turns away and the slight warmth overwhelms my senses. I sigh as it wraps itself around me, chasing away the cold.

"Knives off!" Cael says over his shoulder as he stalks off to the kitchen.

I shrug off the straps running crisscross over my back, unbuckle the sheaths on each of my thighs, and pull off my boots. I haul open the old trunk stashed beside the door and toss in the blade I took off the lady. I stare at the hundreds of other weapons I've accumulated over the years, some still encrusted in blood. I close the lid softly and carefully place my own weapons on top of the old, fraying chest.

I walk into the next room where my brother disappeared, holding my hand to my arm to avoid leaving more of a trail along our already rotting floorboards. An old wooden chair left in the middle of the room waits for me. The table has been pushed to the side along with five other chairs. Cael's lock pieces lie hastily discarded across the table, along with mismatched cups scattered among the mess. The window on the side of the room is boarded up and framed by cracks running up the wall. As far as we know, the house was abandoned long before our parents took up residence. Shaking the thought away, I take a seat, the joints of the warped chair whining in protest as I drop my weight into it.

Cael comes into the room carrying a bucket and some old linens in his left hand and a large first aid box in his right. He puts the buckets down and shoves the yellowed linens at me. I take them and press them to my arm, going through our usual routine. "I'm not looking at your wounds until I see the silver of your eyes, Leo," he says as he lays out our meager collection of medical supplies on the table.

"I don't want to feel what happened as well as remember it," I grumble to myself, keeping my eyes trained on the floor. He tenses and turns to face me. I lift my gaze as his face twists with both annoyance and sympathy.

"Leo, you know what happened last time I let you stay like this while I stitched you up. I got a black eye and you ended up with an extra cut I had to sew back together," he says tersely, spinning the ring on his finger. He's had the habit for years. Since my father first gave him that ring and offered him the chance to become part of our family.

After a moment, I nod, giving in. I extend my hand to give him the small pouch of coins. "Here," I say simply before shifting my eyes back to the floor.

Cael stares at the bag for a long moment before taking it. His brows shoot up as he feels the weight of it. He slowly opens the pouch and dumps the coins into his hand. One silver piece and ten coppers tumble out.

"That's it?" he asks, already knowing the answer. I nod with a sigh. "You don't get paid enough for what you do. We won't get more than three days' worth of food from this, if that. And we all need new clothes." He smothers his face with his hands, his expression devoid of emotion as he thinks. "I don't know why you do this, Leo. You only get hurt and we barely have enough money to eat, never mind the fact you're the most wanted mercenary in Tominay."

I glare at him. "You know exactly why I do it. I don't have a choice," I say, my words clipped. He straightens, pulling his shoulders back.

"You say that, and yet, how many more people are you going to have to kill to keep us safe? They shouldn't have to die for the lives of six." I flinch and his eyes sharpen at the movement.

"I'm not letting anyone put a hand on any of you, and you know it. I don't care how many people have to die," I counter a bit too aggressively. He closes his eyes and takes a breath.

"I know. I'm sure I would do the same if I were in your position." He stares at me for a moment, reading whatever lies in my expression. "What put you on edge?" he asks, his voice softening. I shake my head and avoid his gaze. My brother simply waits, giving me time to straighten out the words.

"She asked for a death wish," I say, scowling at the memory.

"Lots of people believe in Lady Death as we do," he says, tilting his head to the side as if he were trying to figure out why such a thing would bother me so deeply.

"She asked me to kill her children." My brother goes still, his eyes blazing with worry. He's right. Many people do believe in Lady Death, that she gives us all a purpose and takes us away before we can live the worst moment of our lives. But there are many versions of her tale. Some people are convinced she is evil and wicked, stealing us away from our loved ones. I think she's good, a type of peacekeeper who induces change in our world.

"You won't do it though, right?" he asks, his voice low. I shake my head. I know many people believe that Lady Death is the one who delivers the killing blow, so they ask for a wish in exchange for their souls. I've never thought anyone but the one who held the blade is responsible for taking life, but I have granted death wishes before. Simpler ones: to burn their bodies or help their families get out of the city.

Cael takes a deep breath, pushing past the subject. He folds his hands over the bag of coins and makes his way to the corner of the room where he leans over and tugs at one of the floorboards. It comes clean out of the floor, exposing a small compartment. He stuffs the money in and carefully places the board back in its rightful place.

"I'm getting some water. When I come back, your eyes better be silver," he says as he picks up the bucket and turns away.

"Yes, father," I murmur sarcastically.

"I heard that!" he yells from outside. I roll my eyes and stare blankly at the wall. With all the will I have, I drain the blood from my eyes, red tears running down my cheeks. As the world loses its crimson sheen, pain bursts through me, burning and stabbing. I clench my jaw and swallow the screams that push against my throat. I take deep, hissing breaths as I try to quench the ache, but it does nothing to stop my shaking hands as my body begs me to let the numbness take hold again.

Cael walks back into the room, water sloshing in the bucket as he sets it down beside me. "Thank you," he says sincerely, offering me a tight smile. "Where did you get hurt?"

"Knife cut along my collarbone and a dog bite on my arm." I clutch the arms of the chair so hard my knuckles become a ghostly shade of white.

"Can you lift your arm?" my brother asks. I glue my eyes to the wall and shake my head. Even as worry overflows from his gaze, Cael manages to give me a sad half smile. He helps get my blood-encrusted, torn-up shirt off, revealing two deep gashes.

"These are bad, Leo," Cael says as he inspects the wounds. "Gashes like these would have easily killed anyone else."

"Yeah, I'm so grateful for my fantastical heritage," I say, sarcasm thick in my tone. His words send my thoughts back to the story of my ancestry I used to beg my parents to tell me. I am a descendent of a people who should not exist, a race of weaponized soldiers created to kill. During the Great War nearly a century ago, there were two fighting sides: the Allied Kingdoms and the Death Dancers. As the least gruesome tales go, the Death Dancers used to drink the blood of their enemies and walked into battle with red-stained mouths, growling like animals. They were ruthless, devious soldiers whose weapons were so advanced that one Death Dancer could take down ten of the Allied soldiers. Even with their supreme strength and wealth, they still wanted more land, resources, and power. They wanted to rule the continent. So, the Death Dancers created my people, an army of prisoners of all the kingdoms genetically modified to fight. We were made to be faster, stronger, able to resist pain. But with these strengths, we were cursed with endless sleepless nights and the ability to suffer and survive the most horrible injuries. The stories don't tell much more than that, and my parents never offered any more real insight either. Their only words were a warning to me that my people are viewed as unnatural, so the kingdoms hunt us, no matter where we try to hide.

"Leo, you know I didn't mean it like that. I just..." His voice snaps my attention back to the moment.

"I know, I know. I'm a bit rattled, that's all," I say, my voice unsteady. "Could you give me something for this?" I grind out, nodding to my shoulder. I inhale sharply from the sting of the movement. He raises a brow as he stays rooted in place.

"Please?"

"Come on, Cael," I say desperately, getting impatient. My brother pins me with a heavy stare. Damn him. "Please, my brother-in-arms, my very best friend, would you have mercy on me and give me something to ease the pain of these excruciating wounds?"

He grins wildly to himself, reveling in his win. He hands me a cup from the table, the brown liquid sloshing against the rim. I shake my head incredulously as I down it in a single swig, grimacing at the taste. I should have known he'd already made the numbing concoction when I saw the cups on the table. Cael never lets anything mix with the clutter of his lock pieces. The mixture smells like the Low Town of Somereil in the middle of a sweltering heat wave and tastes like it too. His grin widens further at the grimace blooming on my face. No matter how many times I drink it, it never gets better.

I hand Cael the cup and he quickly places it on the table, moving a couple of his mechanisms to make space. My brother spends hours bent over those locks, taking them apart and putting them back together, memorizing each gear and spring. It's a talent that proves useful when you have no money for expensive things like the ingredients needed to mix that awful drink.

A small creak bounces off the walls from the hall, pulling me out of my thoughts. We both tense, taking a moment to listen and ready ourselves for whatever may be coming our way. Cael lets out a sigh of relief as the sound of someone taking a step back reaches us.

"Altair, you can come in, we're fine." I relax immediately and slouch in my chair. My younger brother steps into the room with our baby sister in his arms. Out of the six of us who live in this house, Altair is the third eldest behind Cael and me. Antares is three years younger than him, and Cass was born another two years after Antares. Our little sister Saiph is only a few months past her second birthday. Cael and I are the same age, but I'm quite sure anyone who saw us would, without a doubt, think him older.

Altair stands nervously at the threshold, rocking from foot to foot. "What is it?" Cael asks, taking a step toward him.

"Saiph woke up," he says, his voice small. My brother has always been one to find the perfect excuse. I fight hard to hide the grin trying to push onto my face.

Cael gives him an easy smile. "Did she now?" He nods as his eyes fly between us. "Did you get a couple hours of sleep at least?" Altair nods again, his eyes lighting up.

"Seven," he says neutrally.

"Do you want to stay with us?" Cael offers. Altair watches us in disbelief, his silver eyes wide as he tries not to smile. He nods quickly as if afraid we might take it back. "Come here. Leo can hold Saiph and I'll show you how to do proper stitches. It's about time you learned," Cael says gently, motioning him over as he turns his attention back to my arm. Altair comes over and hands me our squirming little sister, his face turning a tinge of green as he takes in the wounds.

"Hey, Saiphy," I say with a small smile. She relaxes in my arm with her little linen doll held tight in her grasp.

I move my shoulder ever so slightly to test out the stitches. They hold, as usual. Cael and Altair help me into a new shirt before making their way back to bed, or in Cael's case, to bed for the first time. He doesn't sleep while I'm gone. He's never admitted it, but the dark crescents under his eyes are proof enough. I try to put Saiph back in her bed, but the moment I lower her down to the wilting mattress she starts to fuss. Not being able to stand seeing her upset, I let her sleep in my arms with her head resting on my good shoulder.

I start up the fire in the pit built into the floor of the kitchen, hitting the worn piece of flint against the dull end of a cooking knife. Antares is the first awake as always, pounding into the kitchen as the first plumes of smoke start rising through the chimney. He slams into the wall as he runs, righting himself before he can fall to the floor. I groan as Saiph stirs in my arm, whining at the commotion. I pass him a stern look, silently telling him to go into the other room if he's going to be loud. Knowing Antares, being quiet isn't within his skill set. I sigh as he moves to the next room, his footsteps shaking the entire house.

I start to serve breakfast as Cass makes his way silently into the kitchen. I slop the last of the gruel into his bowl. My stomach screams to be fed, but I give myself a little less so the boys can eat a little more. A straining sadness weighs me down as I stare at the unimpressive meal.

"Good morning, Cass. How'd you sleep?" I ask. He simply nods, his dark-gold hair sticking up in all the wrong directions. He offers me a tired smile as I smooth it out, trying to tame his sleep-stirred locks. He shares his features with Altair, Antares, and Saiph, with their round faces and muddy-gold hair. I barely resemble them; my hair is a flat brown and my skin a shade darker from the sun.

I give him a tight hug as he takes his plate from my hands. Saiph wakes in my arms as Cass turns to leave. I put her down and she walks on wobbly legs, following Cass into the dining room. My shoulders slump as they disappear silently into the next room. Since the day his twin Pollux died just over four years ago, I've hoped to hear my youngest brother's voice again. Despite my wishes, I've been met with nothing but a nod and a smile.

Altair makes his way into the room as I take a seat, grinning from ear to ear. He takes a plate and sits down, falling into an easy silence. Antares, unlike Altair, seems to think it's his duty to be as loud as possible as he chases Saiph around the room. He slips a few glances toward me, eyeing the bandages specked with spots of red wrapped tight around my bicep and shoulder. Altair is still beaming about being able to stay with us last night, but I don't think he exactly enjoyed learning how to sew me up. He gave it a try and ended up pulling the stitch so tight, it ripped right through my skin. He tried again, but Cael, thank the Goddess, took over after he almost lost the needle in my arm.

Cael slips in an hour later with sleep-stirred hair and half-open eyes. "Good morning," he manages between yawns, rubbing the sleep from his dark eyes. He takes the open seat between Cass and me, pulling over his bowl of cold gruel. He practically inhales the meal, not speaking another word until his plate is wiped clean.

"Morning," I say, tearing my eyes away from my book as he pushes his bowl away.

"How's the arm feeling?" he asks, nodding at the bandage.

"Like I was bitten by a dog and sliced by a dagger," I say blandly, a half smile playing across my face. He mirrors my expression and rolls his eyes.

"Where are the other two?" he wonders aloud, scanning the room.

"Antares was bouncing off the walls so Altair took him outside to see who could climb the big maple the fastest," I explain, a small smirk pulling at my face as I look back to the book laid on the table before me. Altair is and has always been an amazing climber. Dad used to say he could climb before he could speak.

Cael mirrors my smile, pulling over the pieces of the locks

lying on the table. "How many times has Antares complained that Altair cheated?"

"Five," I say casually, raising my eyes to my brothers. "I'm almost certain they've had at least sixteen rematches by now." Cael snorts as he leans back and crosses one ankle over the other. As if he heard us, Antares comes bursting through the door, covered from head to toe in leaves and twigs.

"Altair went before I said go!" he complains, breathing hard. Altair comes into the house, composed as ever and shrugs. Cael leans over and pulls a twig from Antares's hair.

"Well, you know the rules: whoever gets to the top first wins. If Altair got there first, then he wins," he says, trying and failing miserably to hide his laughter. I think I'm doing as good of a job.

"I know," Antares grumbles, turning toward Altair with a clenched jaw and fisted hands. "One day, I will beat you!" he swears, stomping off to sit in the corner of the room. We all explode, laughing wholeheartedly, and after a while, so does Antares.

***

Eight o'clock hits and I start to pack up my bag to make the trek into the city. Mum and Dad had started to teach us how to read and write, but after they were gone, I decided to take it upon myself to find a literacy class so I would be able to teach the rest of the kids. It's expensive and I have to take on extra jobs to pay for it, but it's worth it for my family.

"Do you have to go, Leo? Why can't you stay, just for today?" Antares asks. Cass and Altair both look up at me, sharing the same pleading expression.

"I can't today, but tomorrow's Saturday. I'll be home all day and we'll go into the city and get some bread pastries. How does that sound?" Cael stares at me, knowing full well we don't have extra money to be making any such promises. I ignore him. One bread pastry won't be too much if we get a day-old one.

They all give curt nods, not meeting my eyes. They always know how to get to me. Cael's glare warns me to be careful about what I say next. I think for a second, going through all the possible ways I could cheer them up. I can't stop the smile that pulls at my face when the idea hits me. "All right, how about this. If you finish your work, training, and chores before I get back, we can play Hunters tonight. But only if you want to," I say, already knowing the answer.

"Yes!" they yell in unison. Of course, Cass only smiles, but it's twice as bright. Hunters is a big deal in our family. If you win a game, not only do you get bragging rights, but respect.

"Wait, but only if Leo has to carry Saiph with him," Altair declares, his brows knitting together as he tries to level the playing field. They all turn their gaze on me, silently asking their question.

I roll my eyes and grin. "Fine, I'll carry Saiph with me. But when I win, you all have no excuses for why the lot of you lost."

"Yeah right. Who says it's a given you're going to win?" Cael challenges, a smile playing across his face. "I'll walk you out," he says as the amusement drops from his expression.

I sling my bag over my good shoulder and follow Cael outside. "You all right to play Hunters?" he asks worriedly. He keeps his face relaxed, but I can see the concern flash in his eyes.

I nod reassuringly and wave him off. "I'm always up for Hunters." He doesn't seem convinced as he spins that onyx ring around his finger. "Honestly, I'm all right. And before you ask, I did change the bandages on my shoulder and arm, and I did remember to bring extra wraps to cover the bands on my wrist. I'm all good," I reassure him with a smile. Cael nods, seeming unconvinced.

"Well, don't die, all right, brother? It's your turn to cook tonight."

I roll my eyes and clap his shoulder as he smiles warily. "I would never skip out on dinner duty," I assure him with a wink before striding away. I know he stays there watching long after I'm out of sight.

CHAPTER

THREE

LEO

I pass the marked oak and sigh with relief as I catch the faded-blue cloth hanging from the lowest branch. Blue means I can stay at home tonight. Blue means no blood. I take a long piece of cut linen out from my bag and wrap it over my left wrist, covering the numbers and the two thick, dark bands marking my skin above and below them, 43201006. The mark of a creation. Every member of my family, except Cael, was born with a similar mark. Mum, Dad, Saiph, Pleiades, and the boys all have numbers and a single band below it. While my sibling's digits start and end with the same six numbers, mine are completely different for reasons I can't explain. From a young age, my parents taught us the kingdoms fear us because they know the weapons we were created to be. We are hunted, and the only way to stay alive is to hide who we are, so I wrap my wrist day after day.

Somereil is a mediocre city, complete with crumbling buildings in the poverty-stricken areas and sprawling mansions with manicured lawns in the wealthier quarters. It's an entertainment and trade city with large stone buildings and brightly painted signs. The shops pull in wandering tourists, draining what little money they bring with them, to keep the city alive. It has everything we need, including a faceless, destitute crowd that allows us to slip in and out unnoticed. The only problem is the royal estate within Somereil's borders. Whenever the Tominese king is in residence, his soldiers swarm the streets, and that's never good when you're a wanted man.

I get to the small tailoring shop right on time. It's situated in one of the poorer districts closer to the heart of the city. I round the building and enter through the back door before climbing the narrow stairwell. Academic classes aren't encouraged by the wealthy, so it's better if they're kept out of the public eye. The rich don't like the beggars having the opportunity to do anything other than clean the streets and waste away until Lady Death comes to take them.

"Good morning, everyone. I'm glad to see you all here," Mrs. Ortaga, my instructor, says with a smile. Her accent isn't a common one, with blunt, choppy words and extensively rolled *r*'s, but it holds a strange sense of comfort between every syllable. "Let's start with a review of yesterday's lessons..." I stop listening. I remember exactly what we did yesterday. I have to if I'm going to regurgitate the information once I get home so that Cael and the boys can learn it. As the minutes pass, my gaze wanders to the map of the continent on the wall. It's divided into the four kingdoms. The isolated Kingdom of Anateya to the north, the Kingdoms of Arel and Caym to the south, and the vast Kingdom of Tominay between, stretching from coast to coast across the continent. The miserable country made on the backs of those who have nothing to give. The country that's had a bounty on my head for years.

The four kingdoms were founded over three centuries ago by the winners of the Great War. The Death Dancers, a people whose true name had long since been erased from the histories, had been bred on greed and pride. Their lands were rich and plentiful, but the Death Dancers couldn't settle with their great wealth. They had to have more, so they started a war with the four kingdoms to seize what was not rightfully theirs. As the stories go, they had the best soldiers, the likes of which the other kingdoms had never seen. They were merciless killers rumored to be made of metal and stone, indestructible living weapons. After a half a century of fighting, the Death Dancers thought nothing of the few survivors left, for no one could stop them. They were weeks away from conquering the world. No starved, beaten, or crushed rebel could fight back against the mightiest force to have ever gathered. But they underestimated the power of a people deprived of freedom. The four kingdoms joined together quietly in the shadows while the Death Dancers marched in the light. As they prepared to make the final attack, the four kingdoms fought back. Slowly, city by city, they reclaimed what was theirs. Strength not in numbers, but surprise, until every last Death Dancer had taken their final breath.

A large piece of Tominay's lands depicted on the map is colored in stark red ink. The Barren Lands. It's still a part of the country, but it's inhabitable, or so the king and his council say. My eyes trace the borders of the Barren Lands, the dense forest stretching for hundreds of kilometers east into the cities and fields of Tominay, the chain of mountains to the north, the Vallan River lining the south, and the Bronze Sea to the east. Before the Great War, it was Death Dancer territory, but was decimated during the battles.

A knock comes at the door, tearing my attention from the

map. Mrs. Ortaga slowly makes her way over, slipping outside the room. No one else seems to notice her disappearance as they bury their noses in their books, flipping back and forth through the pages. She comes back in, her face slightly tighter than it had been a moment ago. "Leo Hael," she calls. I watch my white-haired teacher as she starts toward my desk, her worn, wooden cane hitting the floor with a steady thump. She relaxes her face as she walks by the others, stopping to answer a question with a smile on her wrinkled face.

"How are you today, Mrs. Ortaga?" I ask, nodding to her as she stops beside me.

"Quite well, thank you," she says, in a soft way that calls for your attention. Her face seems to drop in concern as she places both hands on her cane, the shining silver bracelets clicking at her wrist. "Leo, there are some officers in the hallway who would like to see you," she whispers.

I keep my gaze steady, "Would it be rude to ask why?" Mrs. Ortaga straightens and looks down at me like I would imagine a doting grandmother. My heart twists as the thought circles my mind. "I was not given details, just that I should tell you they would like to see you." I nod and place my book back into my bag as I begin to stand, but she catches my arm, stopping me short. "They're searching for arena fighters." Her lips thin into a tight line. "You don't fight in them, do you?" she asks quietly, her concern genuine. I've known Mrs. Ortaga for years, and if I say yes, I know she would lie to the officers with a sweet smile and figure out a way to help me flee. This woman is known to have helped more than a few get out of precarious situations. When she hears of anyone going through a harder time than usual, she makes sure to bring them a full basket of good food the next time she sees them. She's helped house families and taken countless children off the streets. People say she has enough gold to compete with the wealthy living in

Somereil's northern quarters. Obviously, she can help, but even I can't explain *why* she does it. I paste on an easy smile and shake my head.

"They can't bring me in for something I haven't done in years," I admit quietly. I would bet a month's wages every person in this room has committed some kind of crime to get by. She nods, worry dancing along the lines of her face.

"Be careful, boy. You never know what those royal henchmen can pick up on." I think she's the only person who could call me boy and mean it as a term of endearment.

"I will."

"Good. Now go before they break down the door and I have to pay to get a new one," she says as a smile plays across her face.

I walk quickly to the door and step out into the cramped hallway, keeping my face neutral. The blade tucked into my boot seems to blaze against the sole of my foot. Two officers in deep-green uniforms stand in front of me, armed to the teeth. Both men seem like they want to be anywhere but in this cramped stairwell. Street officers, and low ranking from the unadorned blades they carry. The sharp edge of my worry ebbs. They wouldn't send these men after me if they knew who I was. The one closest to me has a strange eye that whirls in its socket, focusing anywhere but the same spot as the other, and his companion has a permanent sneer cut into his expression.

"Are you Leo Hael?" I nod, keeping a step away from them. They can't stand shoulder to shoulder in here. "The Council received a tip causing us to have suspicions. We would like to ask you a few questions." I nod numbly, waiting for him to continue. "You carry many visible injuries," he states.

"With all due respect, you do your rounds in some of the poorest quarters in Somereil, sir. It's not uncommon for people who work their fingers to the bone to have wounds," I reply bluntly. Mrs. Ortaga was right. They're searching for arena fighters. The arenas are illegal, as per the king's decree, though I'm sure he has his own personal arena hidden away in Ahdjer. Tominay's capital houses the king's personal fortress, one big enough to hold a city. The arenas are fighting rings where some choose to fight for glory and coin. Two people walk into the ring, but only one can come out. They were becoming so popular with the underpaid working class that the rich found themselves without laborers. Industries and businesses crashed, and that did not bode well for a greedy king. So, he passed a shoddy law and declared them banned.

After Dad died, we became desperate, with Mum sick and seven mouths to feed, pickpocketing, petty theft and unreliable street jobs weren't enough. So, I joined a fight. I started at the bottom in one of the most neglected arenas. I'll never forget the rotting bodies pushed into piles, the crimson-stained floor and squelch it made when you treaded on top. The most people could give was a copper toward the winnings, but multiply that coin by the ten fighters and with a win, you can afford a whole meal. That was just over three years ago, before I climbed the rungs to the arena boss's level. Up to Vela's level.

"Do you have any family? Brothers?" Sneer Face asks.

"Yes." The pair wait for me to elaborate, but I keep silent. There are more than a few families who live on the streets of Somereil.

"Do you have any tattoos or markings?" Sneer Face continues as he picks at his dirt-crusted nails. Arena winners usually tattoo their victories onto their skin like medals. It acts like a brand, marking them as feared champions and giving them a free pass with all but the king's law.

"Yes," I repeat. They exchange a knowing glance, their eyes lighting up.

"Do the markings hold any significance?" Whirly Eye asks

with clear excitement. I wonder if he's fantasizing about the rewards he'll receive after bringing in an arena fighter. He would be dancing if he knew who stood in front of him, and the bounty on my head.

"Yes. They signify each member of my family," I drone, crossing my arms over my chest. Identical ugly smirks pull at their faces.

"We're going to need to see them and search your bag," Whirly Eye says, making my stomach knot. A small ember of hope extinguishes inside of me. I can't let them see the blades in my boots or the band under the bandage on my wrist. These men are doing their jobs, and I don't want to have to do mine with only a door to separate me from Mrs. Ortaga's class. I used to fear they would recognize me just by looking at my silver irises, but people have proven to concentrate on only the most interesting parts of tales. I watch the officers for a long moment, reading everything written on their faces. They aren't going to back down, but they are human. Everyone has limits to keep their sanity and the guards who work the poor quarters choose to turn a blind eye to keep themselves whole.

"All right," I say, smoothing my expression to one of cool indifference. I slide off my bag and hand it to them, trying my best to hide my wince as I pull my arm the wrong way. They don't miss it.

"Do you have any weapons on you?" Sneer Face demands.

"No." He takes the bag from my hand and passes it to his counterpart.

"Where's this tattoo," Whirly Eye asks with raised brows.

"My back."

"Then you're going to have to take this off to show us," he says, grabbing the arm of my shirt. His hands hit the bite and pain shoots through me, making me grit my teeth as I swallow a scream. I beg my hands to still, but they seem to be set on making me look the part of a guilty criminal.

"What is that?" he asks, feeling the slight bulge of the bandage wrapping my arm.

"A bandage," I say through clenched teeth. I roll my hands into fists, swallowing the bile rising in my throat.

"Why are you shaking?" Whirly Eye asks.

"You touched the wound, it hurts. I'm trying not to scream, sir," I add bitterly. He nods slowly.

"Did you find anything in there," he asks his partner who scrounges through my bag.

"No. A few rolls of bandages, a book, and a few coppers," he says, clearly disappointed. Whirly Eye nods, but still seems eager as he motions again to my shirt. He's not going to find a cup, gold coin, or blade etched into my skin like the victors usually do. Sometimes it's even the names of the people they've defeated. After I won my first big tournament, the other winners that had come to watch hauled me off to get my victory inked into my skin. In their drunken stupors, they tried to convince me to get crossbones because I had crushed so many that night. The thought still unsettles me. I never understood why they would mark themselves as criminals, but most who walk away from an arena fight were not afraid of the king's law but of the rival bosses. The King of Tominay may rule the country, but the bosses rule the streets.

So as not to disappoint, I still got a tattoo. Something I once saw on the arms of an Anateyan ambassador. The Anateyans are a rare sight in Tominay, the northern people preferring their lives of solitude on the ice. When they are here—on the rare diplomatic trip to sustain alliances—they speak only to their own, so the surprise I felt one day when an ambassador visited an arena and *spoke* to me was inevitable. I never knew what to make of the few Anateyans I had encountered, but the warmth in the way that man spoke to me had me hooked in a conversation.

I slowly peel off my shirt, sweat beading on my upper lip as the officers stare me down with impatient eyes. I get it off and turn, giving them a full view of my back. I glance over my shoulder and have to subdue a laugh as their jaws nearly hit the floor. They wince as I face them, concealing their view of the nine star maps running up my spine and years' worth of faded scars. Most of them were wounds that would have killed anyone else, but after all this time, all that's left are pale lines of rough skin.

"Are those Anateyan?" Sneer Face gapes. I nod, clutching my shirt tightly in my hand.

"Each represents a member of my family," I explain, my gaze flitting between them. They stare at the blood-specked dressings wrapping my arm and shoulder, Sneer Face even going as far as to take a slight step away. They stand with their hands limp at their sides as they ogle at me. People get injuries from the arenas, but they're more the sort you expect from a brawl. Scratches, bruises, and broken bones, not gaping wounds. "Can I put my shirt back on now?" I ask dryly. Their mouths clamp shut.

"Um... yes... please do," Whirly Eye says. I slip my shirt back over my head, biting my tongue to keep away the pain. It does nothing to help, the taste of copper swirling through my mouth.

"Why would you get such a tattoo?" Whirly Eye asks, deep creases lining his forehead.

"Most of my siblings are named after stars or constellations. My parents and adopted brother are the only ones who are not, but I decided to get star maps that represent them as well." Revolt courses through me as I blab, but captivated people are easier to dupe. Dangle a piece of truth in front of their faces while you hide away the demons.

"What constellations are there?" Sneer Face asks, unable to contain his curiosity.

"My youngest sister is Saiph, then the twins, Castor... and Pollux, Antares, Altair, then... Pleiades, Perseus for my brother Cael, Cassiopeia for my mother and Cepheus for my father." My tongue feels like lead as I mutter their names. Words I haven't spoken for too long. I can't stop the memories pounding at the doors of my mind. My heart beats double time as I fight to push them away.

"Are you all right?" Whirly Eye asks, his good eye scanning me as if he could find a physical reason for my distress. I nod, breathing deeply. "Why did you hesitate when you said your sibling's names?" The walls feel too close and air too thick in my lungs. I need to get out of this stairwell.

"Because they're dead," I force through gritted teeth, daring them to press further.

"Oh," he blurts uncomfortably, shifting from foot to foot.

"Well," Sneer Face says, clearing his throat, "That will be all for today. Thank you for your cooperation." They nod and turn, making their way down the stairwell, muttering as they pass final glances back at me. I can see the pity in their eyes, and it makes my skin crawl. They think I'm no more than an unlucky soul born in the streets who'll die a bone-thin beggar. How little they know.

I count to two hundred, giving the officers time to get far away from the building. Mrs. Ortaga goes on explaining today's material in the class, oblivious to the war raging on in my mind. Guilt funnels through me as I think of the old instructor. She offered to help me; she has the right to know that I haven't been dragged away to a cell. I fist my hands so hard, my nails bite into my skin as I push the door open. Mrs.

Ortaga meets my gaze, her speech unfaltering. She nods once, smiling before I silently shut the door.

I take the stairs three at a time and burst through the back door as my mind reels. I run into a small alleyway hidden from the bustle of the street. I stand silently, my shaking hands braced against the stone wall as I force myself to breathe. I squeeze my eyes shut and allow the world around me to fall away. *My youngest brother weeping silently by his twin's cold corpse.* I press my forehead against the wall, and my lungs constrict in my chest. *My sister's steady golden eyes locking with mine as the floor dropped from under her feet, her hands scraping at the rope knotted at her throat.* I can't move. My mind is frozen in a loop as my entire body shakes. *My father falling to the ground, his hand flying to the blade skewered through his chest, his strained voice pleading for me to run. To live.*

Blood rushes to my eyes, and with it, a roaring wave of numbness. The moment the world gains a gleaming red sheen, breathing becomes easier. My muscles slowly relax as I tear myself away from the wall and my mind focuses back on the alley around me. I close my eyes once more, listening to my steadying heartbeat. My mind settles and senses sharpen as the memories recede. People walk by, oblivious to me watching them. I drain my eyes, letting go of the instinct as reality takes hold again. I wipe away the crimson tears, waiting for the memories to come back, to attack from the dark and take me down one more time. They stay away. I take a deep breath as my hands shake madly, and I walk into the street.

CHAPTER

FOUR

LEO

I cradle a cold loaf of bread in my hand and stand a little taller knowing how happy it will make the boys. I wandered into the richer quarters where people only buy fresh bread and the bakers use the unsold loaves to feed the chickens. The lady who ran the bakery was about to throw this one away when I stopped her. She wanted two coppers for it, but I talked her down to one. My mouth waters at the thought of tasting it.

I pass the marked oak and silently thank the Goddess that the cloth is still blue. Yawning, I jump over the stream as fatigue starts to weigh me down. It's been three days since I last slept. Tonight, I'll have to sleep. I dread nightfall, whether I have to face the night terrors that plague my sleep or lie awake alone and fend against my memories in the dark. I take in a ragged breath as my body tenses at the thought.

I hear sounds of my family before I see the house. Screams of joy float through the air, pulling me to the only place I dare to call home. Even though we live deep enough in the woods that no one can hear my brothers, my worry stirs. I push it away as I always do and jog toward the house with a smile. I quickly walk inside and place the loaf of bread in the dusty bread box before closing it tightly to fend against the mice.

Shutting the rusty door slowly to keep the squeaking to a minimum, I creep back outside. Crouching low, I watch my brothers assault each other with soaked strips of what used to be a blanket, a dented aluminum bucket sitting full of water between them. Cael and Saiph sit smiling on the side watching the others play, guarding a pile of dry shirts from the cross fire. Cael's clothes are soaked through, drawing a silent laugh from my chest. It seems my brother has fallen victim to a tag-team attack. Cael's eyes shoot to where I crouch, a question written clearly in his eyes. I raise a finger to my lips, making his smile stretch wider. He nods and turns back to the boys, lying back as he waits for the show. I watch silently, waiting for the perfect moment.

I jump out from my hiding place and charge for the bucket. I scoop it up and unleash the wave onto my stunned brothers. Screams of surprise resound as they abruptly stop running at each other and turn on me. I know I'm doomed as soon as their eyes see the empty bucket clutched in my hands. My brothers attack, tackling me to the ground.

I'm soaked by the time Cael finally decides to intervene. He jumps to his feet and walks over, Saiph waddling close on his heels. I take his outstretched hand and he pulls me to my feet, the ghost of a laugh lingering on his face.

"You seem happy," Cael remarks as Antares stalks behind him, a wet rag in his hand. As Antares lunges toward him, Cael turns quickly and picks him up off the ground, throwing him over his shoulder. My younger brother laughs hysterically as he kicks at Cael, trying to twist out of his grip.

"Well, it was… interesting," I admit, wiping my face as Cael puts Antares down. My younger brother falls to the ground dramatically. Cael meets my gaze and his face drops.

"Something happened, but you don't need to worry," I say, trying unsuccessfully to sound reassuring. His brows furrow as he looks me over with dark-brown eyes, twisting his onyx ring around his finger. With a sigh, I give in under his stare.

"Street officers asked me some questions and searched my bag. Quite sure they thought I was an arena fighter. Made me show them my tattoo," I explain, running an anxious hand through my hair.

"I'm guessing they didn't find anything. Where did you hide it?" Cael presses, intrigued.

"How did you know I had a knife on me?" I accuse, crossing my arms.

"Leo, I've lived with you for years. By now, if I didn't know that the only time you're not armed is when I tell you not to be, there would be something wrong with me." Cael scans my attire attentively. Someone who didn't know him might think he was analyzing my outfit, but I know my brother; he's working out the problem in his head, taking in all the information and drawing a conclusion with a stone-cold expression. "You hid it in your boot," he says with a smirk, knowing he's figured it out. "In the sole." I stare, dumbfounded. At this point I shouldn't be because his senses have always been uncanny.

"Did you go snooping around in my boots?" I ask in dismay. He laughs, shaking his head. "How did you know then?"

"For years you dragged whatever Goddess forsaken substance that got stuck to your boots all through the house and then suddenly, whenever I tell you to take your weapons off, you take your boots off too. Leo Hael is not one to simply start doing something that makes life easier," Cael explains, wearing a smug smile. I huff a disbelieving laugh. It amazes me how he knows exactly what's going on, even with the bare minimum of details. I follow his gaze to where Saiph stands, telling a story to her older brothers in the way of a two-and-a-half-year-old.

Cael looks me over and tilts his head slightly to the side. "You're not telling me something," he says almost to himself. I stare my brother down, silently asking him to drop it. Being the man he is, he throws me his own challenging glare. After a long moment, I give up and shift my gaze back to the boys as Altair takes Saiph into his arms, listening intently to her gibberish.

"I may have sunken into myself a little. Talking about... them. I shut down."

"And?" he pushes softly.

"I broke down in an alley. No one was there to see," I tell him. I feel him tense beside me, going completely rigid.

"What did you plan on doing if someone did see?" he presses.

"I don't know," I confess, crossing my arms tightly over my torso. "If someone went to the compound to report me, I doubt the officers would believe them. They'd probably think they were trying to get a piece of the bounty."

"How much is the price on your head today?" he asks as his posture eases slightly. The corner of my lip turns up at the thought.

"Fifty gold marks," I say smugly. My brother lets out a high whistle.

"Maybe I should sell you out." I huff a laugh and give him a good shove. "What?" he says, feigning innocence. "Come on, if we talk any longer, Antares will explode. He's been boasting all day about how he's going to win tonight." I pass a knowing glance to my brother; one he returns confidently. Even if Antares had the luck of Lady Death on his side, it would be a miracle if he made it to the final two and we all know it.

"You ready? First one out has to start dinner," I announce, a smug smile settling on my face as I take Saiph in my arms. She squeals with excitement as she waves her little hands through the air. I note the light in each of my brother's eyes. We may not have much, but this freedom is the only thing I'll ever need. "I'll whistle when I've got Saiph's pouch on, then it's game on," I declare, bouncing on my toes.

"Go!" I yell. We split off in different directions, my blood buzzing in my veins. I make a beeline for the house, pushing past the door and into the room Cael and I share. I spot the carrier sitting in the corner and quickly grab it. I slide it over my head and buckle it in place. Our mother had used this contraption to carry all of us when we were young, except for Cael. I give it a good tug to make sure it's stable before slipping Saiph carefully into the front.

"You ready Saiphy?" I ask as I dart out of the house. I let out a high-pitched whistle to let my brothers know that the game has begun.

I run through the forest for half an hour, tracking footprints and checking my shoulder. I come to a wide stream that makes me smile. Altair loves to hide by the water. He's an amazing swimmer, unlike Antares, and has used the waterways to hide more than once before. I crouch low, steadying Saiph against me with a hand. She goes still, watching as intensely as I do. The way the water runs by a patch of reeds is strange, unnatural. Altair will be one of the first out. I hesitate, weighing my options. Do I chance having to eat Altair's cooking or leave him be? I decide on the former.

I make my way toward the reeds, using the tangle of overgrowth as a cloak. I can hear him now; his shallow, controlled breaths are barely recognizable over the sound of the flowing stream. I spring up from the forest floor and launch myself into the attack. I land swiftly in the water, one hand firm on Altair's back. My brother scrambles, caught off guard. He throws his body into my legs, making me lose my grip. He's up in a second, knees bent and hands at the ready as we circle each other. Keeping one hand on Saiph, I easily deflect the circuit of jabs and hooks he throws. Altair is a precise fighter, but he's repetitive with his movements.

His silver eyes flash gold as he takes a quick step back, making me stumble. My parents had gold eyes when they died. Altair seizes the advantage and kicks full force right at Saiph. I turn to shield her, taking the hit to my side. I stumble backward and fall into the rushing water. Altair's on me in seconds, wrestling hard to keep the upper hand. Unfortunately for him, I'm stronger. I kick him in the gut, just hard enough to send him stumbling back. I jump up and press him into the water.

Altair's arms flail as everything starts to bleed red. Pleiades's eyes were gold when the life was stripped from her. I push him farther into the water, nothing mattering but my hammering heart and the memories flashing in my mind. Something moves on my torso. I look down into a pair of silver eyes. Saiph's eyes. The trees come back into view as I force myself to calm down, building up a wall against the memories. How long had I held him there? Panic surges through my bones as I pull my brother up, draining my eyes of blood.

Altair comes up out of the water with a gasp, staring at me with eyes of molten gold. I blink and within seconds, his irises return to a bright silver, the same glowing color as my own. Cael and I hoped he would be different, that he would not have the golden eyes that led to Pleiades being hung from a post and my father being run through by a sword. I study my brother, praying I saw wrong, but by the unease sitting heavily in my stomach I know deep down that I haven't. Altair stares back, his expression slowly melting from fear and surprise to disappointment and confusion.

"Damn it," he whispers to himself. Relief floods through me as the realization dawns. He lost, early in the game too.

I force a smile, one that doesn't reach my eyes. "You're on dinner duty, little brother," I force myself to say lightly. I stand and wring out my clothes as best as I can. Altair trudges over to the side of the stream and collapses onto his back, breathing heavily.

"One day. One day I will beat you and I will not be on dinner duty!" he vows, throwing his arms in the air.

"I'll love the day I don't have to eat a burned meal!" I throw back. "And you will not beat the one who taught you everything you know. You'd do well to remember every move was mine before it was yours," I chide, forcing my voice into an even smugness. I can practically hear Altair roll his eyes as I walk away.

I head back toward the house, having decided to bring Saiph in before it gets too late. I crouch low to the ground and survey the forested area swallowing up our ancient home. The wind carries the gut-wrenching smell of whatever creation Altair must have made for dinner. I have to stop letting him cook— no matter if he wins or loses—if only to protect our taste buds.

I make my way to the front door and silently walk inside.

Antares nearly trips as he sees me, his eyes going wide. I close the gap between us in one step and place my hand over his mouth.

"No, I'm not out. Who's still in?" I ask, pulling my hand from his face.

"Altair was first, then Cass got me, then Cael got Cass. He's the only one left besides you." I nod as I untie Saiph and set her on the ground. She plops to the floor as if her legs had lost their strength.

"Would you tell Altair to give her dinner, please? We might be out late," I say, grimacing at the smell wafting through the room.

"He burned it and then tried to fix it by adding some herb he refused to name. He said it was edible, but he ate some and his face turned green," Antares says, pulling the collar of his shirt over his nose. I huff a laugh, half listening to his explanation.

"How do you burn a soup that's mostly broth?" I ask. A devious smile pulls at my brother's young face. He shrugs as I walk to the door. "I'll fix it when I get back, just make sure Altair doesn't touch it again." Antares nods proudly.

"I'll tell him to wait for you," he says as he pulls his shoulders back and marches through to the other room, most likely to gloat about being given responsibility over Altair.

I take a moment to quiet my thoughts as a thousand variables race through my mind. I'm stronger and faster, but Cael's always been smarter and sharper. I have to figure out a way to catch him off guard. This game has gone on right through the night on more than one occasion.

Antares's words hit me with a sudden jolt. He said he would tell Altair to wait for me. I whip around, catching Antares and Altair peeking their heads through from the kitchen. Saiph waddles over to them as smiles bloom on their faces. "What did you say?" I ask.

"I can't say anything, but if I was going to, I would tell you to turn around," Antares says as his eyes sparkle with mischief. I pivot on my heels, my knees bending as the muscle memory kicks in, readying me for an attack. Two brown eyes so dark they look black stare at me from the doorway. Cael smiles, calm radiating from his body as he leans against the doorframe.

"Leo," he greets.

"Cael," I say with a slight nod.

"Ready to give in?" he asks lightly as he pushes away from the door. I smirk as I watch him.

"Never."

In the blink of an eye, we're punching and blocking, kicking and spinning out of the way. I push Cael through the door and force him outside with a swift kick to the gut. He reels backward but manages to stay on his feet. He wipes the blood now steadily flowing from his nose with the back of his hand and readies himself for another attack. I can feel my eye swell courtesy of a brutal jab to the face as I take a step toward him. I lunge forward as my brother steps to the side, landing a hard blow to my injured shoulder. I stumble and suck in a sharp breath. I take a second to steady myself as the urge to pull on the instinct simmering just beyond my fingertips rages through me. I won't bleed my eyes, not again.

Cael attacks, seizing his chance. He knocks me to the ground with a quick maneuver, but I tuck in my knees as I fall and easily roll back up to my feet. He lunges again, but this time, I drag him down with me. We exchange blow for blow as we fight through the dirt. We both pull our punches, but I can still feel the bruises blooming on my skin.

We find our way back to our feet, gasping for air that refuses to fill our lungs. Cael moves to attack again, flying toward me. I land a hard punch, but as my fist collides with his stomach, he sweeps my foot out from under me and pushes me to the ground, pinning me beneath his knee. I can feel his bones buzzing as he waits for me to try and get out of the hold. I could, but I don't, waiting the five heartbeats that declare him the victor.

Cael stands up as I shift into a sitting position. My brother extends his hand, clearly confused as he watches me. I grab it and pull myself up, meeting Cael's quizzical gaze. He knows I stopped fighting. Most times we'd be at this for half an hour before one of us would try and change the setting to gain the advantage. Breathing hard, I shake my head, silently telling him that I'll talk to him later. He gives me a tight nod as we trudge back to the house, our younger brothers gaping at us in awe from the doorway.

I eat dinner in complete silence, stuck in my own head. Altair's eyes won't stop pushing their way to the forefront of my mind. Cael shoots me worried glances throughout the meal, which I willfully ignore. I'll tell him when the boys aren't around.

"I can't believe you got Altair out first, Leo. I hate when he cooks," Antares whines as he drags his spoon through the thin soup. I tried to fix it as best as I could with whatever we had, but it was so far gone that it took more than a little effort to make it palatable.

"Come on, it's hard to measure the herbs!" Altair shoots back, throwing his spoon. It hits Antares square in the face. I feel a hand press onto my back, right where the tattoo of Altair's star map sits on my spine. I glance at Cass as he shrinks into his chair beside me. I meet Cael's gaze from across the table and not a second later, Altair lunges at his brother. I stand and grab the back of his neck, stopping him midattack. Antares moves to stand, but Cael wraps his hand around his arm, keeping him pinned to his seat.

"That's enough! If you're going to fight, go..." Cael trails off, stopping midsentence. He looks to the front door and stands. "Boys, take Saiph to your room," he demands, tensing as his eyes stay fixed to the door. We all still as the pounding of a fist against worn wood echoes through the room.

"Now!" Cael urges, his voice as sharp as a general's. Altair scoops Saiph into his arms and they file into their room, the argument quickly forgotten. I don't move until I hear the soft click of the lock from the room, a precaution we took long ago for times like these. I stand and head toward the door as Cael follows beside me, furiously spinning his ring. I grab one of my daggers from the trunk and hold it behind my back before opening the door.

A tall, broad man stands on the step. His eyes are feral as they rove over us. I lace my expression with irritation to resemble the mood of any person who has been bothered in the evening by an uninvited guest. He tries to conceal a blade behind his back, but he must be amazingly stupid to think he could hide it while he still wears an empty scabbard at his waist.

"Can we help you, sir?" I ask evenly. Cael swallows hard beside me. I know he wears the same expression I do, but I can feel the unease dripping off him in waves.

"You boys live out here?" the man spits, rage searing his words. I stand taller, nodding slightly as I make my annoyance evident. Like a king talking to his subject, I stare him down.

"You got any older siblings or parents in there. Someone with red eyes, likes to play with knives?" he snarls. His hands shake, drawing my attention. He's scared. He should be.

"Not that I know of," I deny, leaning against the doorframe to position myself in front of Cael. "Now I would ask that you leave my home," I order flatly. He sneers at us, rolling his massive shoulders.

"You call this a home? I would think Vela gave his Blood Prince better pay." Neither Cael nor I bristle as we stare him down.

"I don't know who you think we are, but we asked you to leave. I suggest you get on it if you want to walk away with the ability to see," Cael threatens emotionlessly. My brother must not feel good about this, because I can count on one hand how many times he's thrown out a threat.

"Well, a boss was murdered not long ago, and from the trail of blood left in the woods, the guilty little street rat lives here. And it's only fair that blood be paid with blood," he fires, not able to hide the grief flashing across his face. I push away my emotions, my head going blissfully clear as the monster starts to take hold.

"I agree, blood *should* be paid in blood, but it won't be ours. To answer your question, I don't have a family member with red eyes," I say, mimicking his tone. He flinches as I point back at Cael. "But he sure does." The man's eyes go wide as he brings a rusted short sword into my line of sight. How could he have thought he would get a scratch on me with that mangled blade? I let the red curtain fall over my vision, and with a quick step and flick of my hand, I have him unarmed. I bring out my own dagger from behind my back.

"You should take better care of your steel. It irks me to see people with blades like these," I state, staring right through him. He turns to run, but before he can take a step from the house, my dagger sinks perfectly into the flesh of his neck. Cael barely flinches, but I know he turned away before the man's body hit the ground.

"Don't say a word. Don't come back in with a drop of blood on you. Don't bury him by Mum and Pollux," Cael whispers defeatedly, not caring to face me.

"Cael, I would never…"

"Don't. Not now, because I need to go tell the boys we aren't dead, and not later, because I'm not letting them think someone is going to murder them while they sleep. If you need to speak, wait until they've gone to bed." I watch him walk to the boys' room, murmuring as he places a hand on the wall. He waits until the click of the lock sounds from the inside and pushes the door open, then disappears into the room. I hear Altair's whispered voice speaking frantically before the door closes. I press my palms to my eyes. All I do is put them in harm's way. Every day we stay here I endanger them. But where could we go? My eyes wander over to the closed door beside the boys' room. A room that none of us have dared to open since the day our mother died.

"What should I do?" I ask out loud. A smooth whistle of wind through a crack in the roof is my only answer as I walk out the front door.

CHAPTER

FIVE

LEO

I come back into the house with heavy eyelids and covered in dirt and sweat. Cael sleeps hunched over in a chair with his head propped up in his hands. I watch him for a moment, curling and unclenching my fists. I've gone four days without sleeping before, I can do it again. I yawn as I tiptoe past my brother, desperately trying not to wake him.

"You're sleeping tonight, Leo," he mumbles, exhaustion slurring his words. I stop dead in my tracks and turn to face him. My brother sits up, cracking his neck with a wince. Dark crescents lie under his half-open eyes. He's human and only human. He needs sleep, and it pains me that I'm the reason he can't have this simple thing. Cael tosses me a cloth as I take a seat.

"What happened today?" he asks. I watch him for a long moment. I can tell he doesn't want to talk about the man I just buried, or the fact he's not the first, but the fourth this year. I take a steadying breath, pulling at a loose thread in the rag.

"I almost lost control when I fought with Altair today. I saw... I don't know what I saw," I confess, my voice so small it's a miracle he hears me. I start wiping the dirt off my face as the need to keep my hands busy becomes overwhelming. He stares into space for a long moment before his eyes meet mine.

"Then we won't play Hunters for a while. Your terrors are getting worse at night. That could explain it," he wonders aloud. His eyes darken as he spins the ring around his finger. In the candlelight, his skin looks almost as dark as the shining onyx. "But that's not it, is it? Something else happened. You've had flashes where you lost control before, and you've dealt with them. Whatever this is, I can tell it spooked you, Leo."

I inhale deeply and stare at the floor. "Altair's eyes were gold. They *turned* gold." Cael's breath hitches, his eyes going wide as I meet his stunned gaze.

"Dad, Mum, and Pleiades had gold eyes." he sputters, his brows creasing.

"I hoped it wouldn't happen," I breathe, running my hands down my face. "I asked Mum and Dad and they said they wouldn't be like me." I stare at the number and the band on my wrist as pained memories threaten to resurface. Over the years, we wondered if the boys would grow into who we were created to be and prayed they would escape such a fate.

"Mum and Dad said the boys weren't like you, but they didn't say the boys wouldn't end up like them," he says, and it makes sense. How naive have we been to believe they wouldn't become like our parents? My heart skips a beat as my hands fall from my face. If he's like them, that means he could become like me, a monster with blood-stained hands. I can't let that happen.

"What are we going to do? Altair could be dangerous. I had Mum to teach me how to maintain control and I still ended up killing people. Too many people," I whisper, despair clawing at my throat.

"I don't know," Cael says, mirroring my dismal tone. "We'll figure it out tomorrow. We both need to sleep on this." I nod, running my hands through my hair as I let out a long breath. I wipe the last of the dirt off my hands and stand. We walk to our bedroom, the one directly across from the boys' room. Saiph would normally stay with us, but it's better if they don't see me when I sleep. They live through enough. I lie down and close my eyes, silently hoping to get eight hours of peaceful rest. It's an empty wish, like all the rest.

Cael ties my hands and feet to the rusted bed posts. I've been getting terrors for so long, I've forgotten what it feels like to not dread the night. My parents used to tell me it was a punishment delivered to my ancestors from those who created us. A punishment embedded in my blood and passed down through generations.

I have to hand it to the Death Dancers, they perfected the art of torture. They found a way to implant the last memories of fallen soldiers into my mind. I relive their deaths over and over in my dreams, feel their pain as if it were my own. The terrors only got bad after Pleiades died. Before that, they were a rarity, like nightmares triggered by a bad day. But ever since my sister's murder, they've haunted me relentlessly every night, so terrible I shred my own skin trying to fight off the invisible threats. They found a way to make me die silently every night. I couldn't scream for help if I wanted to, no matter how painful it is. I inhale deeply and count the seconds as the darkness takes hold.

I wake with a start, my throat dry and palms clammy. My entire body shakes as I gasp for air, pushing down the lingering flashes from the terror. Cael puts a hand on my arm, steadying my reeling mind. When breathing becomes easier, I drain my eyes as he starts untying the restraints binding my hands to the bed frame. I always wake up with my eyes bloodied. It's the only thing my mind can do to escape the pain. "How bad were they?" I croak, my voice like gravel as it scrapes through my throat. I rub the raw skin on my wrists as they come free.

"Worse. You didn't stop struggling, and you only got seven hours. I don't know if that's a good or bad thing," he admits, yawning as he rubs his eyes. I don't know either. I've spent countless hours mulling over it, do I want more sleep or shorter terrors? I've yet to decide which is better.

Cael drags himself into the small bed on the other side of the bare room as I unlatch my ankles and stand up. The sun should be coming up soon. I glance toward my brother before I walk out. He barely made it onto the bed before falling asleep, his leg hanging off the edge.

I watch as the sun slowly grows over the horizon from the front step. If I had to be grateful for the terrors, this would be why. While most sleep, I get to watch the world turn in all its glory. When the sun rises fully over the horizon, I walk back into the house, putting the dagger I brought with me back in the trunk. I walk to the boys' room and knock softly on the door. Altair opens it with Saiph in his arms. Cass is slowly waking up behind him while Antares is still fast asleep, sprawled in his bed with his threadbare blanket strewn across the floor. I make a mental note to get him a new one when we have enough money.

"How did she sleep?" I ask Altair, taking our sister from him as he rubs his eyes.

"Good, she slept all night." We stand in silence for a

moment, letting the void absorb all the questions I know he wants to ask.

"And you?" I ask, willing him to say anything other than ask me about my night.

"Cass had a nightmare again and Antares wouldn't stop talking about bread pastries, but I slept well once I fell asleep." I give him a small smile.

"Is Cass all right?" I ask, my voice low. Sadness flashes across his face.

"Cael came in when he heard him and helped him get back to sleep. He um... he didn't shut the door." Altair winces, avoiding my gaze. The boys all know about the terrors, but I still hate the idea of them having to see them. I nod, forcing myself to take even breaths as I look away from my brother. Cass got back to bed, that's all that matters. I turn and head toward the kitchen with Altair close on my heels.

By the time Cael wakes up, it's almost midday. Antares pounces on him the minute he comes into the room. "It's Saturday! Town day! Can we get bread pastries now!" he asks, jumping on the spot. Cael smiles, but the grin doesn't meet his eyes.

"Yeah, give me a couple minutes to get changed, then we'll go," he says.

Twenty minutes later, we're walking through the forest, Cael's eyes darting back and forth from me to Altair. I stop dead when we get to the oak. The strip of cloth marking the tree is red. The tag tied below it blows in the slight wind, taunting me. "What is it?" Cael calls, stopping a few paces ahead to look back at me.

"Nothing, keep going. I'm coming." My eyes stay fixed on the tag. I walk over and rip it off. I turn it over in my hands, not allowing myself to glance at the inked instructions. I hold it tight and with a deep breath, I shove it into my pocket. *I'll worry about it later*, I think to myself as I jog to catch up with my family.

"One bread pastry, please. Do you have any day-old ones?" I ask the raven-haired girl standing behind the counter of the bakery. She nods, giving me a once-over before glancing over my shoulder to Saiph and my brothers as Antares pushes his face against the window. He takes in all the delicacies—most of which he'll never get to try—with bright eyes. She gives me a small smile and disappears into the back room. She comes out with a fresh bread pastry in hand.

"I'm sorry," I say, my forehead creasing. "I don't think I can pay for a fresh one."

"It's all right," she says quietly, opening and closing the register. "My father owns the shop. Take it, please," she insists, extending her hand. I force a smile to my face. I hate that she thinks my family needs charity, that to her we are people she feels the need to help. But regardless of my pride, we need every spare coin. I take the warm pastry and mumble a thank you that leaves a sour taste in my mouth. I walk out the door to find Antares practically drooling at the sight of the steaming pastry.

Cael walks toward us from up the street, his face stricken as he stares at the dessert. "Come on, brother, do you not trust that I can make a good bargain?" I ask, hooking my arm over his shoulder. He rolls his eyes and takes Saiph's hand from Antares.

"She gave it to you for free after she saw Antares in the window, didn't she?" I nod with a mischievous grin and shove him away.

"You make out all right with the apothecary?" I say,

knowing very well that it isn't open at this time on Saturdays. He nods, the corner of his lip kicking up.

"He needs to change his locks," my brother drawls. I bark a laugh as his smile drops. "I couldn't find any thread for stitching, but we should have enough to last us until he restocks." Cael says tightly as he steps ahead of me as the crowd thickens. Cass walks beside me along the narrow street, wedged between myself and the wall. People rush past, trying to push through us. When we finally turn onto a wider street, I look down to see Cass wiping his face furiously.

"Are you all right?" I ask. He shakes his head, scratching at his face hard enough to leave a mark. I catch his hands, stopping him from gouging his eyes out.

"A kid coughed on him," Antares explains from behind him, taking a step away from us. I turn back to my youngest brother, my expression softening. "Wipe your face with your shirt." He does so feverishly. Cass shivers as he slides behind me, using my body as a shield against the oncoming traffic. I extend a hand he gratefully takes and holds like a lifeline.

We take up a space along one of the quieter streets, the boys huddling around as I divide the pastry between us. We eat in silence, savoring our meager morsels. Not a moment after Altair finishes his bit of pastry, a group of boys runs past playing kickball, the ball flying between them. Altair watches them for a long moment, his eyes filling with yearning. He turns to us, unable to keep still.

"Can I go?" he pleads, watching the group play up the street. Cael and I turn to each other at the same moment, sharing identical weary expressions. I glance at my younger brother and sigh as his eyes gleam with hope.

"Don't go farther than we can see," I say tightly. His face lights up with a smile as he runs to meet the group. Cael watches him like a hawk. While he's distracted, I reach into my pocket and pull out the tag, swallowing the bile rising up my throat. I take a deep breath and read the inked words. *Fortieth Avenue, east side, midnight. Illegal weapons trader, middle-aged male. Yellow eyes, blond hair, pale skin. Kill order.* Those last words leave me uneasy no matter how many times I've read them. Kill order. Altair pulls me out of my thoughts as he comes running back, grinning from ear to ear. I crumple up the tag and shove it back into my pocket.

"What are you smiling about?" Cael asks, his gaze sharp.

"They invited me to play a real game of kickball with them tonight. Can I go? It's in a back alley a block that way," he asks excitedly, pointing to the next street. I know the place; I've passed through it dozens of times. There's a vacant lot behind the buildings the kids in the city have claimed as their territory. I look to Cael, pleading with him to take the lead on this one.

"Maybe not tonight," he says reluctantly as he spins his ring. Altair's face drops, his hands going still at his side.

"Why not? I train every day and I'm getting better. I take care of Saiph and Antares and Cass when you can't. I do all my work and chores. I've almost finished reading the novel Leo gave me. Why can't I stay out one night? I promise I'll be fine; I know the way home," he pleads. His words hit me like a punch to the gut, and one glance at Cael tells me they've done the same to him. I study Cael's face, wondering if he'll break. If I open my mouth to speak, I'm afraid I might.

Cael sighs, his shoulders tight as he spins his ring around his finger. "Fine, but you have to be back at the house by dark and not a second later or else we're coming to get you." He gave in. My jaw goes slack as I gape at him. I can't believe it. He shrugs tightly when he catches my dismay. Altair's face lights with joy, a kind I haven't seen him wear in a long time. I melt at his smile. This will be fine, he's a month away from being fifteen. I was taking care of him when I was his age. He can manage himself.

"Yes! I promise I'll be back before then," he shouts over his shoulder, sprinting back to the group of boys. They gain their own smiles when Altair tells them the news.

"Are you sure it'll be okay?" I ask Cael, not sure what to do with myself. He shakes his head.

"I have no idea, but I want to give him a chance to have this kind of freedom in case it's his last." Unease settles in his gaze as he watches Altair go. "We've left him alone before and we were both coming in and out of the city when we were younger than he is. He needs to learn how to take care of himself," Cael amends. His words are strained, like he's trying to convince himself of that very thing. I close my eyes and pray the Goddess will keep him out of trouble.

I sit on the doorstep, watching the sun sink under the horizon. We came home three hours ago, and I haven't moved from this spot. My stomach pulled in all the wrong ways the moment we left Altair and it's only gotten worse as the skies turn dark. The door opens and Cael takes a seat on the step next to me. If it's possible, I think he might be more concerned than I am.

"I don't feel good about this," I tell him, straining to see further than possible. I take out the piece of paper from my pocket. "He needs to come back soon. I don't have the time to go find him and bring him home," I whisper, not meeting my brother's gaze. I can feel him eye the tag held between my fingers.

"I could go look for him," he offers, sitting straighter. I shake my head, heaving a heavy sigh.

"I don't want any of you near Somereil when I'm on a job.

There are too many people out to get me who would love to get their hands on any one of you." I grimace and push myself upright. "I'll go, but if I don't come back by the time the sun comes up..." I don't know what would happen if I didn't come back. We don't talk about it because it's not an option.

"That won't happen," he states with finality. I nod, checking the blades strapped into the sheaths on my body. I've had them on since the moment I got home. A dagger at my thigh; a longer one at my hip; small, thinner blades in and under my boot; twin slayers crossed on my back; and throwing knives strung diagonally across my chest. I fit the part of an assassin. I stand without another word and walk off into the trees, Cael's eyes burning through the back of my head well after I'm out of sight. When the feeling finally fades, I sprint, pushing my legs as fast as they'll go as fear narrows my thoughts.

I almost miss the dark form sitting by the oak as I fly past it. I slow, stopping a few paces past the tree as my lungs heave. I slip the dagger from the sheath at my thigh to spin it between my fingers. I turn slowly, knees bent, and hands slightly raised. Mr. Vela leans against the tree, the grin smeared across his face freezing my blood. "What do you want?" I ask evenly, smoothing my expression into stone-cold indifference.

"Am I not allowed to pay a visit to my best employee?" he challenges lightly, waving his hand through the air. I clench the dagger in my hand as disquiet rages through me. *You can't kill him. Not yet. He's here for a reason.* "Well, tonight I do have an ulterior motive." He chuckles and my senses narrow to the sound. "I believe you have a little brother who went into the city," he says, his sneer of a smile growing impossibly wider. I snap, launching at him. I press my blade against his neck, trapping him against the tree with my other arm.

"What did you do with him? Where's Altair?" I demand

breathlessly, a mixture of fury and fear flashing across my face. He doesn't miss it.

"Why do you assume I had anything to do with this? I've been nothing but generous to your family. You should take care in seeing how you treat me." I seethe, shaking my head as I inch the blade away from his throat. The only good thing he's ever done for my family is hang their lives over my head as collateral instead of sending word to Somereil's guard.

"Where is he?"

"Always so eager to get the job done," he chastises, exhaling a deep sigh as if this were a normal conversation, as if I'm not holding a dagger a breath from his jugular. "Let me enlighten you. Your little brother, Altair, was it? Strange names your siblings have. So at odds with yours…" I push the blade closer, making Vela laugh deeply. "Don't rush me or I might change my mind about graciously delivering you this information." I ease the tension, shaking as I wait for him to continue. "He was caught by the king's officers about to kill someone, blood smeared all over his young, little face." I let go and take a step back as my heart beats in my throat. "They say his eyes glowed gold. Still are, last I heard. You know, he doesn't resemble you at all. Your hair's a dark brown, like old mahogany. His is more like a soft gold, maybe even some brown in there to match his eyes on that round face. Is he your brother by blood? Maybe you took him when he was young. Oh, now that would be interesting." I shake my head as his eyes gleam. *He's trying to get into my head.*

"Stop playing with me, where is he?" I demand, blood boiling under my skin. This is my fault. I shouldn't have let him go, not with what I've lived through.

"I don't run a charity. You must give me something in return." A dark smile grows on his face as his eyes light with cruel expectation. I shake my head, not believing that my brother's life depends on this monster. No, it depends on me making a deal with him.

"What do you want?" I'm almost scared to hear what he has to say. Almost.

"Well, if this boy of yours is as good a killer as you are, I want him to join me. He will be compensated, of course," he states with a deadly calm. My eyes widen. This can't be happening. This man always gets his way, but I can't bring Altair in, I won't. "And you would get a promotion for allowing your brother to join my ranks. Four guaranteed jobs a week. I picked you out of the arenas when you were just a little older than him. I'm sure he'll be a fast learner, especially with an experienced mercenary such as you by his side." I can't do this. I don't want this. "I will give you your brother's location and you will be permitted to miss tonight's job if you agree to these terms. Now." My arms hang limply at my side. I can't let Altair end up like Pleiades or Dad, dead because he messed with the wrong people. "You would do well to remember that you don't have a choice here. I know your secrets. The lives you've taken. The family you hide. I know about your brothers, even the one who shares none of your blood and—"

"Fine! Fine! I agree! Tell me where he is! Tell me now!" I shout desperately, the image of my brother hanging from a post filling my mind.

"Good boy. You will meet me here tomorrow at midnight to discuss the conditions. Be sure to bring your brother as well, I want to meet my new mercenary." I nod, grinding my teeth. *Don't think about it. Get Altair first, deal with the rest later.* "Your brother is being held inside the royal guard edifice. He's being kept in a solitary room in the innermost ring where they keep their most wanted criminals. The guard would keep *you* there too if they didn't kill you on the spot."

"Focus," I press, baring my teeth. He raises his hands in

innocence, but I can see the joy in having ruffled me flash in his dead eyes.

"It's under heavy guard at all times. Thick walls, ceiling, and floor. No windows. The only way in is using the master key, which should be on one of the officers. You're going to have to hurry, they have a protocol for people like you. I'm quite sure you know they will only hold him until the king gets word and declares his sentence," he whispers with eyes bright. The urge to gut him where he stands is unbearable, and the only thing keeping me from ending him is the image of my brother.

"You're sick," I spit before turning and running as fast as my legs will carry me toward the city, bursts of his cruel laughter chasing me through the trees.

CHAPTER

SIX

LEO

The behemoth of a facility that is the royal guard edifices is so elaborate I can't help being taken by the sight. Four circular buildings with sparkling windows evenly spaced along each sand-colored wall stand in an interlaid pattern of rings. But by far the most impressive part is the king's sprawling estate planted in the middle of it all, flying the royal flag printed with its green circle and hammer.

There are soldiers of all ranks patrolling the grounds, each dressed in ghastly green uniforms with blades peeking from under long coats. The king himself will be out for my head after this, if he isn't already. I creep past a group of drunken grunts stumbling outside the main building. I'm going to have to make it past three rings of buildings bursting with guards before I can start searching for the cell. I pull my hood low over my eyes and keep pace with the drunken soldiers. I count seven as I follow, enough to start a good brawl. I walk up behind a man whose stench makes me gag and give him a good shove, sending him crashing into his mates. Three fall to the ground in a tangle of limbs. I hide behind a corner as the sweet sound of anger fills the air. I glance around the wall in time to catch the first fist fly, hitting its target square in the jaw. The guards standing watch at the main entrance crane their necks to get a better view, blatantly placing bets on who will be left standing. Finally, they leave their posts to watch the show, buzzing for a good brawl. Tominay's soldiers are known for one thing: being terrible at their jobs.

I slip behind them and clear the entrance of the first ring. Now comes the hard part. I scan the area and find a stack of crates with bright-green circles painted on the fronts. I slide behind them, taking a long moment to survey the soldiers and officers. I'll have to run through the open if I'm going to get to the innermost building.

"What are you doing?" a high voice rings. I pivot behind the crates, an idea unfolding before my eyes. A boy maybe two years younger than me stands steps away with a dagger held incorrectly in his shaking hand. I pull my sleeve over my fingers and lunge, clamping my hand over his airways. He struggles as I pull him to the ground and passes out in less than half a minute. Leave it to the Tominese to prove how little they care for their people, putting a runt in a uniform and calling him trained.

I strip off his clothes, exchanging them with my own before replacing my blades under the thick overcoat. The pants and sleeves are far too short, but they'll have to do. I wait until a bigger group of soldiers passes then slide out from behind the crates.

The sentries at the second gate take no notice as I approach. "I have a letter to deliver," I announce, patting my empty pocket. A woman with fire-red hair looks up from where she's sharpening a rounded bronze sword. The curve of the blade as well as its color marks it as the craftmanship of the infamous Areli smiths. I can attest to the perfection of their weapons, though I always preferred my own.

"You new or something? They don't usually care as to tell us when there's a letter passing through," she says, eyeing me curiously. I wring my hands together and shuffle uncomfortably.

"Yes. I was transferred a couple days ago. This is my first task," I say, patting my pocket again. She snorts and goes back to her work.

"Let me give you a tip. No one in Tominay's army cares about anyone else. Stop walking like you're of some importance or someone will gladly beat the pride out of you." The older woman next to her with graying hair and lined brown skin glances up with little interest, focused completely on picking at her dirt-crusted nails. I force fear into my movements as I nod, continuing on a little faster than before. I walk right through the third gate, not one of the four sentinels batting an eye. The gate in the fourth ring makes my muscles tense as soldiers clad in light gray watch with sharp eyes. The King's Elite. They're only one step down from the Obsidian Guard, the personal sentries of the royal family. I scan the yard for the distinct black-and-dark-green uniforms, exhaling gratefully when none cross my sight.

Few souls walk in the yard between the third and fourth ring aside from the King's Elite loyally manning their posts. Swallowing hard and transforming myself from nervous to fearfully lost, I approach the half-open gate. "Business?" A gruff man with bright-blue eyes asks as he studies me with visible distaste.

"I have a letter to deliver," I reply, tapping my pocket. I can feel their scrutiny even with my gaze lowered as they try to see through my disguise.

"We'll get someone to take it in," his counterpart states evenly. She's a tall, long-limbed woman with the stoic face of a general. She strokes the bow strapped across her back; it's a motion I know she means for me to catch.

"I was given orders to take this directly to its recipient," I say, searching for the right words. She tilts her head to the side and narrows her eyes as the blue-eyed man goes deathly still.

"You're not from here, are you?" he says. If I mutter the wrong answer, I know they won't hesitate to try to put me down.

"I was transferred from Dryden a few days ago," I reply. A sneer pulls at each of their faces. Dryden is the most crime-ridden city in Tominay. The people who live in that hell are either high in the crime chain or tied to the predators running the city. If you want to hire a kidnapper or mercenary, see the best arena fighters, or die, you go to Dryden.

"You were stationed in Dryden?" I nod.

"We were ordered to try and clean out one of the better quarters. To shut down some of the smaller arenas and set up various checkpoints. I was the messenger." They exchange a knowing look. I said the wrong thing. "I do need to deliver this letter; I was told it's urgent," I lie, veering away from the subject.

"Only King's Elite or His Majesty's personal guests go past this point. Give me the letter and we'll make sure it gets to where it needs to go," the man assures me, reaching out his hand. This isn't going to be pretty. I allow myself one second to check over my shoulder and take account of the few people loitering in the area. The man takes a step toward me as I plunge my hand into my pocket. I move forward and strike, crushing his jaw with my elbow. The lady behind him sets into action and reaches for her blade as I pull out my own. She barely has time to take a breath before my dagger is deep in her stomach. I catch her before she can fall and drag her into the small guard house standing beside the gate. I turn back around as the man stumbles to his feet.

My eyes turn bloodred as I step forward. He swings his sword madly as tears fog his eyes. With two easy swipes, he falls in a heap to the ground. I drag him into the gatehouse and set him beside his partner before patting them both down. The woman pants with blood-stained teeth as I search for the master key. Nothing. "You're the blood-eyed mercenary. You're the one the child called for when they threw him in the block," she says with a wet rasp, laughing slowly. I glance behind the gates toward the third ring. No one seems to have taken notice of the exchange. I turn away and quickly change into the man's gray uniform. Letting some of the desperate rage leak into my eyes, I grab the woman's face in my hand and force her to meet my gaze.

"Where is the master key?" I demand as my fingers dig into her jaw. She continues to laugh hysterically. Death acts in strange ways, but never helpful ones.

"You won't get that monster out. The guards at his cell will tear out your heart. You're going to die," she wheezes as she grins, blood dripping from her mouth.

"Death would be a mercy, but not one I will accept today," I whisper before dropping her face. She goes quiet, realizing she's given me exactly what I needed. I stand, her string of curses fading as I stride past the gate.

I consciously ignore the gardens leading to the king's home as I keep close to the wall and scan the grounds to find the entrance to the circular building. The door closest to the right side of the gate holds a constant flow of gray-clad officers. *That must be the barracks.* I spot another door to my left. Tucked under the overhang bracketing the building, two guards step out of the doorway wearing full armor and tired expressions. They acknowledge me with a simple nod as I pass. I wait until there is no one close enough to notice the dagger in my hands before I force open the lock. I silently thank my brother and his dexterity as I check over my shoulder before sliding inside.

There must be dozens of cells, all windowless and separated by thick iron bars. The numbers marking the cells are difficult to read by the dim light of the sconces illuminating the passage. I march down the hall and swallow hard as I take notice of the inmates either sleeping or clawing at the bars, spewing mouthfuls of madness. The air is thick and damp, causing chills to run up my spine. Two guards walking their rounds come into view and do a double take before advancing toward me. I continue forward, painting a purpose with each step and hoping that they'll walk by. Unfortunately, they make the mistake of trying to stop me and although I spared their lives, both will wake up with terrible headaches in a locked, dank cell.

I flatten myself against the curving wall as a second set of voices echo through the hall. As I continue past the cells, a long gray corridor stretches before me. I take a slayer in each hand and hide the blades behind the length of my arms.

I quickly close in on the droning voices, angling my head down to shield the crimson sheen of my eyes. The three sentries guarding an iron door go silent as they watch me approach.

"The rounds aren't supposed to come this far," the woman to the left says, her voice low. I don't stop as they pull swords from their scabbards in unison.

"You shouldn't be here," the man in the middle reiterates.

"You have something of mine," I accuse, my steps

unfaltering. I lift my eyes and like a monster unveiled to children, the three sentries gape in fear and recognition. The first man falls in three easy motions. The second and third lunge at me as a unit, but rage fuels my attack. Strike, block, parry, thrust, lunge, block, pivot. They are skilled fighters, their steel gliding dangerously close to my flesh, but they are no match for the demon I let loose. The second man lands a shallow gash across my forearm before I disarm him. The third is taken out just as quickly, falling to the ground in a heap. I sheath one slayer behind my back as I fumble for the master key, pulling their pockets inside out. I search the man who spoke to me first and release a relieved breath as warm metal meets my fingers. I pull out a ring of old iron keys..

I shove each key into the lock of the iron door with shaking hands. The third glides in with a soft click, granting me access to what lies beyond. I expect the sound of torture as I push through the door, only to be met by a deafening silence. Wooden doors line the length of the hall. I open the first to find a small room with a table and chair sitting in the middle of the floor. My nostrils burn as the smell of smoke invades my senses. I tense as I take a closer look at the room and realize that the table and chair are scarred by burn marks, the ceiling stained with the remnants of a flame. I tear myself away from the eerie sight, the hands of the dead seeming to scrape down my arms. I walk into the next room a few doors up. A small window high in the wall sheds a dim light on a table surrounded by four cuffed chains lying in neat piles.

I rush out of the room, my stomach flipping as panic sets in. "Altair!" I yell, striding toward the metal doors near the end of the hall. The sound of shuffling feet from behind one of the doors makes my knees wobble. I knock on the first and a growl —more animal than human—answers through the slit barely wide enough to fit a hammered coin. I bang my fist against the cool steel of the next door. "Altair?" I try, desperation closing around my throat. What if he's not here? What if Vela set me up? I peer through the slot as something moves in the back corner of the pitch-black cell.

"Leo? Leo! Help me! Get me out! I didn't mean to hurt them, I swear!" Altair sobs, his voice thick with tears as his hands pound against the door.

"I know, I know, don't worry. I'm going to get you out, hold on." I ram key after key into the lock with quaking hands as my brother begs me to help him. I growl in frustration as I near the end of the ring, fear clawing at my mind. The second to last key slips in seamlessly, turning with a loud click that makes my heart skip a beat.

I pull on the door and it swings open with a groan. Altair stands in the middle of the cell with blood splattered over his hands and face. Tear tracks snake down his colorless cheeks as he stares at me. He takes three steps toward me before falling into my arms, shaking so hard I can't stay still.

"I'm sorry," he whispers over and over into my shoulder.

"It's all right, it's going to be fine. We'll figure it all out later, but right now, we need to get out. Do you understand?" I ask, pulling away to make him look at me. He nods, wiping his face on his sleeve. I take the keys out of the lock and throw them into the cell before closing the door. I take my brother's arm, willing him to come with me. The world slows as the door to the main hall swings open. Dozens of the King's Elite block our only exit. I push Altair behind me as soldiers clad in gray pour through the open door, knocking their arrows and drawing their blades. I can feel their surprise as they come face-to-face with the mercenary whose stories are not just tales, but nightmarish warnings muttered on the streets. The ruthless, red-eyed Blood Prince. What a sight this must be, the monster so many fear protecting a bloodied child in a dark corridor with nowhere to run, surrounded by the King's Elite.

"Drop your weapons!" one of them yells from the other side of the doorway.

"Altair, when I say run, you stay behind me," I whisper. He presses closer in response as I raise my hands in front of me.

"If I drop my blades, you put down your arrows," I say confidently, my voice carrying over the tense hall.

"If you drop them, we won't fire," the same voice replies. I nod slowly, my mind piecing together the impossible way out. I let the slayer drop.

"Go!" I yell, flicking my blade back into my hand with my foot a second after it hits the floor. I ram through the door on my right, dropping my shoulder as the hinges shake. It swings open, Altair smashing into my back as we move through. I shut it behind me and replace my second slayer back with its sister. I hold the door shut as arrows embed themselves into the wood.

"Push the table under the window!" I order as the soldiers work to force the door open. Altair is petrified, but he does as I say. He drags the table across the floor, his eyes glued to the chains glinting in the moonlight. "Stand on the table, pull your sleeve over your arm, and break the window," I tell him urgently, gritting my teeth as the door begins to splinter. He jumps onto the table, his eyes flying between me and the glass. "Do it, Altair!" His hand flies through the glass and the shards shatter around him. The voices on the other side of the door go silent as the pounding momentarily ceases. I let go, pulling the table over and jamming it against the door. I lift Altair over my shoulders and push him through the opening as fast as I can, doing my best not to cut him on sharp edges. I jump up after him and fly through the opening, catching a glimpse of the moon as it blazes like a beacon in the starless sky.

I take Altair by the arm and run, pushing him ahead of me. Boots pound behind us as shouts rise from all around. Arrows fly by as we sprint past startled soldiers clad in green. We get past the second to last gate before an arrow hits me, embedding itself in my thigh. I stumble but don't stop, willing my feet forward, one after the other. The numb tear of muscle weighs me down as I snap the shaft and drop the wood without a thought. The soldiers form a blockade at the gate while others close the iron fence with drawn weapons. Altair runs toward the middle of the yard, but I grab his arm and pull him away from the exit. "Leo, the gates are the only way out!" he pants.

"There's always another escape," I force, dragging him toward the crates I hid behind when I came in. "Climb and run across." He nods, his eyes lingering on the boy still lying unconscious on the ground. I give him a boost before hauling myself up after him, gritting my teeth against the pull of flesh as another arrow slices my ear. The whizzing sound stops suddenly. I look down, breathing hard as I try to keep my head from spinning. Soldiers begin to climb the crates with weapons in hand. They're gaining fast, but I manage to send the first tumbling down with a swipe of my blade, then another with a kick to the face.

I pull myself over the final crate and make the slight jump to the roof; Altair grips my arm to help me up. I yank him out of the way as an arrow flies by where his head had been a moment before. I send one of my throwing knives at a soldier who starts to clear the last crate. The steel embeds itself in her eye, making her fall backward, screeching. I limp across the roof as Altair stumbles beside me. I hurl myself to the ground when I reach the other side, my bones shaking in objection to the impact. Altair drops just as the gates start to scream open, the guards desperate to push through. My breathing comes easier as I scan the area and take in the yard outside the compound. We're in my territory now.

I lead Altair through the back alleyways, hiding among the shadows as soldiers run past, some on foot, others on horseback, all with arrows nocked and blades drawn. I drag us to the poorest quarters of the city, stopping at every corner to watch and listen. When we get to the crumbling houses, we climb our way slowly to the disintegrating roofs, the height making my head spin. Altair slows many times, but I urge him forward, needing to get as far away from the city as possible. When we're well into the woods, he trips over his own feet and lands face-first on the cold ground.

"Are you all right?" I ask frantically, kneeling beside him. The head of the arrow still embedded in my thigh scrapes against my bone. He sits up and nods, wiping tears from his eyes. I lift him up from the ground, taking his arm as we slow our pace. We're almost home.

"Altair!" a familiar voice calls. Cael comes flying through the trees, stopping dead when he sees us. "What happened? Your eyes!" he whisper-yells, fear lacing his voice. I stare at Altair, noticing the golden color of his irises for the first time.

"I'll tell you when we get inside. We need to snuff out any lights and pick up anything we've left outside," I say quickly. Cael nods and helps me haul Altair to his feet before hurriedly herding us into the house.

Cael pulls out a chair for Altair and disappears outside to do as I had asked. Antares and Cass come running in with Saiph and skid to a stop when they see us. Antares stares, eyes wider than I've ever seen them as Cass walks over to me hesitantly and places a hand where Altair's star map lies on my back before sliding it over mine. His fingers come away smeared with blood. He shakes it as panic creeps into his gaze. I grab his hand and wipe it against the cleaner part of my shirt.

"We'll be fine, just got into a little bit of trouble," I explain as he takes a step back toward Antares, holding his hand to his chest like it had been mauled. "I need the three of you to go put out any lights and lock all the doors. Antares, you're the oldest, watch Saiph and entertain her for a while. I promise I'll explain, but Cael needs to clean us up a bit first," I add, my gaze bouncing between them. Antares stands frozen in place with a pale face, his mouth moving as if he's trying to speak but the words refuse to come out. Realization hits me as I follow his gaze to Altair. I forgot my eyes were still bloodied and that Altair's are shining golden. I force myself to drain them as I shift to my uninjured leg. I have to clench my jaw against the bursts of pain. I wipe the crimson tears from my cheeks, leaning stiffly against the chair as Altair takes a seat.

Cass nods slowly, his eyes fixed on Altair as he takes both Saiph's hand and Antares's arm and drags them to their room. "Did you get hurt?" I ask, scanning Altair as he shifts uncomfortably. Small cuts litter his hands from the glass, but I can't tell if the rest of the blood on his clothes is solely his or belongs to someone else. He hesitates, then shakes his head.

"I don't think so, I don't feel anything," he whispers shakily. Cael flies back into the room with his arms full of medical supplies. He disappears again and comes back with clean water and the box of thread and needles. I nod as he finishes laying everything out, lighting a single candle to help him see.

Cael scans Altair with a flat expression as he tries to figure out his best course of action. He moves to touch Altair's arm, fresh blood still soaking his sleeve. I should have noticed that before. Altair flinches and in the span of a second his fist flies directly at Cael's face. He somehow dodges it, taking the impact to his shoulder instead of his nose. Altair's mouth drops open as tears start to well in his eyes.

"I'm sorry, I didn't... I," he stammers, staring at his hands. Cael passes me a glance and winces as he rolls his shoulder.

"It's all right, don't worry about it. I've done the same thing more times than I'd like to admit," I say, sliding down to sit against the wall. I regret it instantly as the torn flesh on my thigh pulls in the wrong way, my muscles screaming and joints cracking. "But I got him square in the face." The side of Altair's mouth kicks up through the grime. Cael grunts at the memory, spinning his ring with a grin. I shift my attention back to Altair, any semblance of ease melting away. "You need to take a deep breath and push against the instinct. Think of a happy memory. Something that makes you feel like you're in control, then grab the reins and lock the numbness up," I say, holding his fear-filled gaze. He nods and closes his eyes, clutching the arms of the chair. His screams bounce off the walls before Cael can push a hand over his mouth. Altair's silver eyes shoot open as tears flow over Cael's hand. I let out a sigh of relief as Cael pulls it away.

"It hurts! Why does it hurt?" Altair cries, tensing against the chair. My heart strains at the sight of him. Cael moves to the table, his brows knitting together as he scans the supplies.

"It's going to be fine. Where does it hurt?" I ask, pulling my eyes away from Cael. He points to his arm as Cael turns to him and peels away his sleeve, revealing a long, shallow gash running from his elbow to his wrist. "Is that the worst one?" Cael asks. Altair nods, swallowing a new sob. "That's good, you're lucky," Cael says with a tight smile. Cael gives him a thick cloth to bite down on as he stitches up the wound, taking longer than usual. He frowns at the box before tying each stitch a little farther apart. Black-and-blue bruises bloom all over Altair's face, but bruises are better than broken bones. I wrap my own wounds as best as I can until Cael can help me cut the arrowhead out of my thigh. Cael watches me closely as I breathe through the pain, monitoring my every movement.

Altair goes to change once he's cleaned up. I heave myself into the chair, leaning heavily on Cael as he helps me. Altair comes back into the room with Cass, Antares, and a heavy-lidded Saiph on his heels. "They wanted to hear what I have to say," he explains, as if he had forgotten I was still in need of being patched up. Cael and I exchange a hesitant look.

"None of you so much as glance this way while Cael fixes my leg, all right?" I rasp. Cael tenses at my side. They nod, Antares dutifully turning Saiph away, though I doubt she's awake enough to register anything she sees. They each take a chair and sit, patiently waiting as Cael unwraps the haphazard splint I had tied around my leg. His lips fold into a thin line as he stands up straight and walks over to the chest at the door. He comes back with a dagger and cleans it off with some alcohol. "What's that for?" I ask, my stomach sinking as the answer hits me.

"We ran out of thread," he says numbly. "And the arrowhead has spines." I curse under my breath, leaning my head back on the chair.

"I hate Tominay." I've been hit with a spined arrow once before, and it took Cael an hour to get it out. It was one of the few times we'd worried about the amount of blood I'd lost. I wonder what would happen if we left it in there? "All right, I need something to busy my mind, so please start explaining exactly what happened," I beg Altair. Sympathy pools in Cael's eyes as he hands me a murky drink and a cloth. I down the vile mixture in one gulp and place the cloth in my mouth before gesturing for Altair to begin.

"I did play with those boys, for a long time, and it was fun. When I left, the sun was still up. I got about halfway home when I heard yelling. Then someone pushed me to the ground before running off. I got up and started to turn around to walk the other way, but a man came out and screamed at me. I think he thought I had stolen something from him. He came after me and caught me by the neck," he breathes out, his eyes glazed. I wince as Cael starts prodding at the wound. "He kept saying bad things. Calling me names. Telling me about how this was the last time. He started pressing harder on my throat. I couldn't breathe." My breath hitches as Cael uses the blade to start digging out the arrowhead. Altair stops, his eyes shooting to me as I grind my teeth against the gag.

"Keep going," Cael orders softly, his unfaltering attention stuck on the wound. Altair nods, if not reluctantly. "Then I felt this strange... power, I guess. But... I was afraid. I wanted to kill him. I wanted to tear his throat from his neck. I was going to. I beat him to the ground, so bad I couldn't make out the shape of his face," he says, his voice a shaky whisper. "He had a blade and cut me, but I took it and was about to, to..." He swallows hard, tears welling in his eyes. Cass and Antares both watch him, stuck in a trance from which I'm not sure they can escape. Their faces shift with emotion as he continues. "Then an officer tackled me. I hurt him too, but within seconds there were four, and they bound my hands. They said I was gold—"

A deep, guttural scream escapes my chest as my brother pulls the triangular arrowhead from my leg.

"Sorry," Cael mumbles as he stuffs a bandage into the wound to stop the bleeding.

"I'm fine," I force through the cloth, squeezing my eyes shut as the pain eases. Cael cleans my blood off the dagger and sets it over the candle. He holds it there until it glows a reddish orange. My brothers all hold their breath as Cael presses the burning metal to my thigh. I feel my eyes roll in my head as my good leg bounces against the floor, begging the burning to stop. When Cael finally peels the knife away, the smell of burning flesh floats through the air, searing my nostrils. The boys pull their shirts over their noses, but I stay put, willing the pain away. Whatever concoction Cael gave me was nowhere near strong enough and by the sympathy in his eyes, he knows it too.

"Keep going," I grind out as Cael moves to a smaller wound on my bicep.

"Then they threw me into a cell. They kicked me before they closed the door, but I couldn't feel anything." We all stay quiet for a long time, rage boiling my blood as Altair stares at the wall. None of us speak as Cael seals up the rest of my wounds. He drags the boys and Saiph to bed, telling them to come get us if they can't fall asleep. I don't hear what they reply, but Cael's grim expression says enough. I help him clean up the bloody rags, murky water and supplies strewn across the floor. My thoughts race and the words I need to say sear my tongue, and though I try to keep them in, they push back with double the force.

"I found Altair because Vela told me where he was. I told him Altair would work as a mercenary and that I would take more jobs," I blurt out. He drops the bloody bucket, the crimson water spilling across the floor. His gaze burns through me, hotter than any heated knife. I sink back into the chair, feeling like a scolded child. "I'll figure it out," I assure him weakly. "He won't be doing any jobs and I won't be working more than I am now. I'll figure it out," I repeat, trying and failing to sound confident.

Cael spins his ring furiously, shaking his head as he glares. "Leo, you can't say no to the one person who holds all of our lives in his hands, and you know it," he says shakily, breaking under the weight of my words. I nod.

"I know," I admit, at a loss for words. I smother my face in my hands, wincing at the various injuries stinging from the movement. "We will find a way out of this. I don't care if I have to kill Vela. I'm not letting Altair become what I am," I whisper as my head spins. Raw desperation shines in my brother's eyes. He nods solemnly, understanding that the boys following the same path I tread is the only thing scarier than losing them.

CHAPTER

SEVEN

LEO

I hobble through the hall, my muscles screeching in opposition as I take each step. Cael went to bed with heavy shoulders a half hour ago. He gave me direct orders to stay seated, going as far as to threaten to tie me to the chair. He should have. I sat in the silence for as long as I could before the darkness started to whisper things I didn't want to hear. I stare at the rotting door across the hall. It hasn't been opened in over two years. Mum and Dad's room. I place my hand on the cold handle and turn it. A shiver runs down my spine as it creaks open. For some reason, I imagined when I finally had the courage to enter the room, it would be locked.

I step over the threshold, careful to avoid the broken floorboards. Plants grow savagely through the room, piercing and strangling both the roof and walls. A small animal skitters across the floor, disappearing into a crack in the wall. Spider webs hang from the ceiling like winter decorations. I sit on the half-sunken bed and close my eyes with a wince. I imagine them sitting next to me, telling me what to do next. Telling me that everything will be all right. That I did something good, even if I can't name what it is.

I can't go back into the city, nor can any of my siblings. They've seen my face and Altair's. My brother has gold eyes, which I have no idea how to control. As a successful mercenary, several people would love to see me bleed onto the concrete. Not to mention Vela is sniffing around for Altair now. I open my eyes and stare at the old bedside table, the drawer hanging open. A single envelope sits inside. I'm sure we emptied everything from this room, but I don't remember much of the night Saiph was born but my mother's blood. There was so much blood. I pick it up and turn it over. I nearly drop it when I see Mum's faded handwriting. *My children.* How did we miss this? It's been sitting here for two years, and we never knew.

I open it carefully, trying my best not to destroy the yellowed envelope. I take out the letter inside, half eaten by whatever creature was hungry enough to resort to the thick paper. I slowly unfold it and start to read.

To Leo, Pleiades, Cael, Altair, Antares, Castor, and the new little one.

I'm sorry. I know I should tell you this in person, but I can't find the right way to do it. I won't be with you much longer. I can feel it. I won't make it after the little one is born. Just know I love you all and your father did too. You all need to take care of each other now. I know you'll all amount to great things. Keep going and remember that I love you all, no matter what. That your father and I will forever watch over you. I'm sorry I couldn't say a proper goodbye, but I hope this will bring you comfort. Goodbye, my dears.

Love, Mama.

Tears roll down my cheeks as I read it again and again. Over and over. She knew she was going to die. She knew. She left us, knowing she wouldn't make it through. She chose not to say goodbye, to warn us. She let us name Saiph by ourselves when she could have given her daughter this one simple thing to hold on to. So much grief and anger courses through me as the old wounds rip back open. I try to put the letter back into the envelope, but it won't go in. I throw it to the ground and grimace at the sudden movement. Another letter falls out of the envelope and floats to the floor. I pick it up, the shaky, crooked script lining the page. I gasp when I see the three letters written on the outside. Leo. I turn it back over with shaking hands.

Leo, there are so many things I wanted to tell you in person. Who you are, who you are meant to be, where you come from? Your real story. I wish I could tell you all about your past, but I have no strength, so this is one you must figure out yourself. I promised your father two things when we ran away together. The first was that I would take care of you forever, and I'm sorry I couldn't keep that promise. The second was a vow I wish I had never made. I promised him that I would not tell you about where you were born, who you were meant to rule and the people who should have raised you. Your blades were your father's, and they may be the key to convincing them of who you are, the key to understanding who you were born to be.

I'm afraid that when I leave, you will only find trouble in Tominay, so I'm asking you to find your way home. To the hidden country meant only for us. To Illena. Follow the Vallan River to the Bronze Sea; you'll find people before you get to the ocean, but do not stop until you reach the bay. I don't know if they'll have you, but you need to make them see who you are and take what was meant to be yours. I love you as my own and always will, remember that no matter what you discover.

—Mama.

I'm lost in old words meant to be read years ago. What does she mean by my true story? Who I am? I know who I am, but she makes it sound like I have no idea. My true home? But across the Vallan River toward the sea... She wants us to go to the Barren Lands. "Illena, a country meant only for us," I recite softly. There isn't anything in the Barren Lands but forest and savage animals. There couldn't be a hidden country hidden among the bush, could there?

I sit there for a long time, my fingers curling the withered paper. The door creaks open. Cael stands in the doorway, his face grave. I know he wants to scold me about moving, but as he takes in the crumbling room, I can see the strength drain from his body. He walks in slowly, as if this room were a forbidden place. He sits down next to me and stares at the floor. After a long moment, I hand him the first letter.

"I found them in the drawer," I croak, my voice thick with emotion. His eyes go wide as he recognizes the script.

"She wrote them, didn't she?" he asks weakly. I nod, avoiding his gaze. He reads the first letter written for all of us, tears streaming down his face by the time he gets to the last line. He wipes them away before they get a chance to drop.

"There's more." I hand him the other letter.

"She wrote one for you?" he asks, his face contorting as he flips it in his hand. I nod.

"It will help all of us though. She's given us a way out." Cael stares at the back of the page, his shoulders rigid. "Read it," I push. Hesitantly, he flips the page around.

"That's not possible. There can't be..." he says as he finishes. His eyes rove over the paper again and again, memorizing the inked words, as well as the ones in between.

"So much of what she's written doesn't make sense. But we can't stay in Tominay, and she told us to find Illena. Mum wasn't one to lie; it has to be out there," I say, my voice strained. Cael's expression is stricken, stuck between a whirlwind of emotions and level-headed thoughts.

"Leo, look at her handwriting. She knew she wasn't going to make it. Maybe her mind wasn't all there when she wrote this. It could be nothing, something she constructed in her mind while she was dying." We both wince as his words hang in the air.

"She may have been dying, but her mind was sharp." Though, as I say it, I can't deny the doubt sowing itself in my mind. She was so sick those last days, barely strong enough to speak. He nods hesitantly, spinning his ring. "It's a risk, but what other choice do we have? We can't stay here. Altair is probably getting a death sentence written by the king's own hand as we speak. Never mind the bounty on my head. Vela is expecting me to meet him at midnight tonight with Altair by my side. This is the only way out, however impossible it may seem, we need to try. Even if Illena doesn't exist, we could live in the woods for a while, then pass the mountains into Anateya. We'll keep out of the farmlands as we go to stay hidden. No one goes to the Barren Lands. They won't expect us to hide there. And if they do, they won't find us," I say, my voice becoming stronger than it had been before. I know Cael sees the promise in the idea.

"That's it then, we're leaving," he says as I finally meet his gaze. I give him a slight nod. We've spoken about leaving before, but the idea was but a passing thought born of fear. "We should go tell the boys," Cael mutters, helping me stand. He grabs the letters and tucks them tightly into his pocket. I follow him out, pausing at the door to take in the room. We're going somewhere better. Somewhere where the walls won't let in a breeze, and we don't have to fight for food. Somewhere where we'll be safe, where we'll be free.

Cael and I rally everyone into the living room and sit down, Saiph bouncing on his knee. Altair stands beside my chair with stormy eyes. Antares and Cass lean against the wall, the former unusually silent as his foot bounces against the ground. "We're leaving," I blurt. Cael winces, averting his gaze as he spins his ring. Antares gasps, jaw dropping. All three boys look to Cael as confusion plays across their faces.

"We're leaving?" Altair repeats, taking a step away from me to stare at Cael. He dips his chin in confirmation.

"What!" Antares yells incredulously. Cass walks over to me, face scrunched. He places a gentle hand over Altair's star map. I shake my head.

"No, Cass. This isn't because of Altair. We're not safe here anymore, we haven't been for a while. We should have left a long time ago," I explain, giving him a tight smile that doesn't reach my eyes.

"Where are we going?" Altair speaks up from beside me, his voice wary.

"The Barren Lands," Cael pulls out Mum's letter, clutching it as if it were the key to life itself. "Mum called it Illena."

"Do the people from Mama's stories live there? The people made of blood and gold. People with numbers on their wrists like ours?" Antares asks, fidgeting with the hem of his shirt.

"We think so. That's why we're going," Cael says, wearing a flat smile. "We should be safe there for at least a little while, if not forever." Hopeful smiles light their faces.

"All right. Each of you get a pack and fill it with anything you'll need. Only the necessities, we don't want them to be too heavy. A blanket, extra clothes and one personal item each. The other things we all need, like medical supplies, get piled here. We'll divide it among each other later." They nod, faces grave and yet somehow still hopeful.

I stride to the door and throw open the chest. I dig through the blades, placing eight of the most suitable weapons on the floor. "You each get two," I declare. Cael's expression darkens as I disappear and come back with an old sheet. I rip it into strips and start wrapping the blades. I hand two to each of the boys, their eyes wide as they hold them. I stop in front of Cael, the two long daggers I hadn't bothered to wrap shining in my hands. His fiery gaze meets mine defiantly. "You keep one on you at all times, the other in your pack. You don't take them out unless you're going to use them, understand?" I ask as I watch Cael's reaction with my hands still outstretched. They nod slowly. Cael finally relents, taking the blades from my hands with a withering glare.

Cael walks into our room as I rip out my old pack and stuff it with my change of clothes and a blanket. "You had to break out the knives?" he asks, putting Saiph down on his bed. I knew he wasn't going to be happy about me giving them weapons, but by the look on his face, I underestimated his reaction.

"I'm not taking a chance. They know how to use them. If they ever need the skills they've been taught, they should have weapons at their disposal. I will do everything I can to keep them safe but they need to be ready to protect themselves." Cael opens his mouth as if to retort but thinks better of it and clamps his lips shut. His piercing glare is enough to cripple me anyway.

"You didn't have to give them *two*," he seethes, and I swear I can see smoke rising from his skin. I shrug, his tone making me wince. Cael doesn't miss it, stepping back as he wills his fury away.

"I don't know what's waiting for us out there, Cael. By the Lady, I have no idea if we'll even make it to the woods. But you can believe I'm not going to pass up a single advantage we have," I persist, my voice breaking. The exasperation in my brother's eyes melts into understanding. I didn't give them the blades because I was being rash. I did it because I'm afraid I won't be able to protect them when the time comes. And we both know that time will come. He nods slightly, moving to stuff his own meager collection of wares into his pack. In less than a minute, I've shoved all my belongings into the bag.

I pack anything Saiph will need and my bag is still only half full. Cael hands me the letters, his expression pained as I take them. "You don't want to carry them?" I ask, folding them neatly between my clothes. He shakes his head and gives me a sad smile.

"They're not for me to carry, Leo."

I nod, seeing the flash of yearning in his eyes. I saw him melt when he read his name on the first letter, when he was included in the family. Even after years of living with us, he still feels apart, an outsider in a close-knit circle.

"You know Mum wrote your name on there for a reason, right? You are family. You always have been," I say, nodding to his ring. "And that proves it." He stares at the ebony band our father had given him so long ago. It used to be Dad's, but he gave it to Cael after we took him in to convince him to stay with us. My brother was skeptical, since only hours before he had escaped from the cage where his parents kept him. He rarely speaks of it, but I can tell when his mind goes back to those times, his eyes glazing and his attention impossible to grasp.

We all noticed the way he scanned the room when our parents brought him home. He didn't sleep and watched us with distrustful eyes. He didn't know what it was like to be safe, to live with people who did not want to hurt him. Our father decided not to press him and after a time, he gave him the ring along with the option to leave and sell it or keep the band and stay with us. The trade would have bought him enough coin for lodging and more than a few good meals. I remember listening from another room as my parents gave him the choice. I don't think he ever gave them a real answer. My brother simply put on the ring and stayed.

"Ready?" I ask, stepping outside with my pack slung over my shoulders and Saiph secured to the carrier on my chest. They nod, their own bags strapped tight to their backs. I catch the weapons peeking out from under clothes and inside boots. Even Cael wears his, appearing much more warrior-like with the shining steel hung at his hips. My own blades are in their respective scabbards, cleaned and sharpened for the journey.

We round the house and head toward the little clearing flecked with wildflowers. Four stones roughly engraved with names sit up in the earth. Pleiades Hael, Pollux Hael, Ada Hael, and Kerin Hael. Only two mark real graves. I lean down and wipe the dirt away from the headstones one last time.

"Say goodbye to the family, Saiphy," I whisper, waving her tiny hand. Cass steps away from Cael, touching his twin's gravestone with a sad smile. He closes his eyes for a long moment before heading back to stand behind me. No one says anything as we turn to leave, but I swear I hear Cael whisper a thank you before following behind us.

CHAPTER

EIGHT

LEO

We walk for two days, only stopping when we find a decent space to sleep. We chance only small fires to cook whatever food we manage to kill or scavenge. At least there's an abundance of hare in these woods. Last night was not a good one for any of us. I had to sleep, and my brothers had to watch. They were awake when sleep took me and sat pale faced and wide eyed when I awoke. It's going to be that way for a while and my stomach roils at the thought of putting them through it again, let alone for the rest of this journey.

It's after midday, the sun descending in an arc to the horizon. A couple more hours and we'll have to set up camp for the night. Cael stops suddenly, his head whipping around and his body going rigid as his hand inches toward his dagger. We go completely silent, listening to what lies beyond the rustling wind. I strain my ears to hear an inconsistency in the natural forest sounds. A branch subtly cracks ahead of us, as if someone had walked over it. We're not alone.

"Behind the tree!" Cael warns suddenly. I turn on my heels as an arrow flies through the air. I dodge it before it hits the tree with a thunk, splintering the wood beside my face. I drop to the ground as more arrows fly past, pressing my back against a wide tree trunk. I untie Saiph and roll over to where Altair is huddled on the ground. I pass her to him as she wails. Altair takes her without a thought, shielding her with his body as he tries to calm her down.

I rip off the pack and free my slayers. "Leo, six of them, two in the trees. I can't get eyes on them!" Cael calls, pulling out his own daggers. I can see the dread build in his face as he pushes away the instinct to tell me not to run into the jaws of the beast. This time there is no option but to fight our way out.

I take a moment to think. The King's Elite could have sent out parties to find us. I shake my head. The Tominese are not naive enough to send only six and hope to walk away alive. The king could have raised the bounty high enough that people would risk venturing into the woods, but Somereil is a city of people who either travel in luxury or do not have the means to travel at all. That means it could only be one man: Vela. These are trained mercenaries.

Cael orders the boys to stay down as he tries to draw the fire away from them, cursing as an arrow nearly hits his head. I pull out a throwing knife and hold it between my teeth, my twin blades clutched tight in my hands. I climb up the tree and disappear into its crown. Careful not to shake the branches more than the breeze, I move swiftly from tree to tree, passing unnoticed above our attackers. Cael was right, there are six of them, two in the trees ahead. I take a deep breath and let the red sheet fall over my vision. My senses sharpen and my pulse races with the steadying surge of adrenaline. I set my eyes on the first man, pull my blade from between my teeth and cock my arms back the way I've done hundreds of times. They're smart, trying to take us out from a distance. I throw the knife and a moment later, the man gasps and falls limp from the tree. The shooting stops.

"He's in the trees!" one of them calls.

"I can't see him!" another replies frantically as I continue to move. Their feet shuffle through the brush as they scan the skies. I come up slowly behind a woman positioned in another tree. I take a breath and let the monster take the reins on my actions, banishing my conscience. I jump onto the branch where she lies on her stomach and the wood immediately snaps under our combined weight, sending us plummeting to the ground. I land on her back, her bones snapping on impact. Her screams are silenced in seconds as my slayers make quick work of finishing her off.

Arrows fly at me as I flatten myself behind an oak. I move swiftly to the next man and lop his head clean off his shoulders before he can blink. Within seconds a woman comes up behind me as Vela's fighters lock onto my position. Recognition flashes on her face. I engage her as another attacker stalks toward me. I slice and block, advance and turn, defending myself from two angles at once. The first blow I take is a cut threateningly close to my head, slicing from my temple to my ear. I repay it quickly with a blade through her gut. They may be good hit men in Somereil when they have surprise on their side, but they lack the experience of a real fight.

My unhealed wounds strain as my lungs work to the steady rhythm of my movements, my mind clear and at ease. A third fighter joins and tosses them both another blade. While the first woman moves to catch the flying steel, I slice her unprotected thigh, sending her sprawling to the ground.

Two now stand before me, visibly tired as they bare their teeth. The man hurtles forward, blades lifted as he leaves his entire stomach unprotected. I duck, my blades flowing through the air before finding the soft flesh of his gut. I turn, hearing the woman I cut down nock an arrow. She releases it and the arrow flies out of sight. I walk up to her, cracking my neck as I dodge arrow after arrow. She pulls her last one, hyperventilating as I continue toward her. With a steady breath, I bring my blades up as she releases it, and catch the whizzing arrow between the edges of my slayers. It hovers a breath from my face, and the woods seem to go silent. She stares wide eyed and drops the bow from her shaking hands. She stumbles backward, desperate to get away. I toss the arrow away, and with a slight of my hand, her last breath comes easily. I don't linger, turning on the last man. I know exactly how I look, blood soaked and vicious. *The image of a monster.* I grin, spinning my slayers in my hands. He turns and sprints through the thick woods. I pick up the bow the woman had dropped and take my time scanning the arrows strewn across the ground. I nock it with ease, pulling my arm back until the bowstring goes taught and my muscles strain. He runs like a scared animal, tripping over every bump molded into the earth. I aim, feeling the direction of the wind, and let the arrow fly. I lower the bow before the arrow bites into its prey, knowing it will. A feral scream followed by a thump signals the sixth fighter's fall.

I set my focus back on my family and scan the tree line behind me. Relief hits me when I see movement among the brush. "Is everyone all right?" I call. One by one, they crawl out. Antares, Cass, Altair, and Saiph are crusted in mud with leaves and twigs sticking out of their hair, but they're all right. I close my eyes, my conscience taking back control as I allow myself a moment to breathe. I sheath my slayers and take a step toward them, readying myself to drain my eyes.

Cold metal presses to the back of my head, a sharp point pressing hard against the soft spot between my skull and spine. "Poor boy, how I'll hate to do this," the voice sings. I shudder at the words, my mind fighting against the thought that he came. Mr. Vela left his den in Somereil and stands at my back. "You could have had everything! You were the best, but you tried to run, and when I had been so good to you! Then you kill *six* of my best mercenaries. Annelia was showing such potential for the arenas. You owe me a debt I'm all too happy to collect," Vela sneers in my ear, his snake's tongue working as the blade presses harder against the base of my skull. A second dagger appears and pierces into the skin above my kidney. "If I remember correctly, there are six in your family, including yourself, of course. A life for a life sounds quite fair to—" The sound of steel cutting through flesh rings in my ears. I tense, waiting to feel the numb sensation of pain. It doesn't come. I open my eyes and touch the back of my head as the steel drops away from my neck and side. A struggling gurgle sounds from the ground.

Vela's body lies crumpled in the dirt, his eyes permanently open as blood flows from his neck. I look up to Cael's stunned face, his hands wrapped around a dripping dagger. Air rushes out of my lungs as I drain my eyes. Pain pounds at the edge of my mind, but I push it away as I study my brother, his eyes stuck on Vela. He allows me to pry the dagger from his hand, too shocked to protest. I throw it to the ground and gently grab his shoulders, pulling him away from the body. He's never killed anyone before.

"Cael?" He meets my eyes. Confusion flashes in his gaze, like he has yet to absorb the last moments. I watch as it solidifies in his mind, becoming reality.

"I killed him," he mutters, color draining from his face. I shake my head.

"Don't think about it like that, it makes it easier to carry," I say, watching him skeptically. I remember my first kill. I hadn't had time to mourn the frail man from the arena before I was pushed in front of another and forced to do it all over again. I found his family a few days later and gave them most of my winnings. I didn't have it in me to tell them who murdered the man, all I could do was hand them the coin I told them he had won. "You saved my life. Thank you."

"I saved you," he repeats shakily. I nod and let go of his shoulder as he takes a slight step back. My brother's face goes completely slack. He only gets a couple steps away before doubling over and throwing up his last meal. I avert my eyes, cringing. I walk over to where he had discarded his pack, take out his bottle of water and throw it over to him when he's finally emptied his stomach. He stands and wipes off his mouth before taking a long sip.

"Better?" I ask, noting his movements.

"Yes," he rasps, taking another swig from the bottle. "I don't think I'll ever get that image out of my mind." He shakes his head as if he were trying to physically rid himself of the memory. My face sobers, a tight smile pulling at my lips.

"You learn to block out your conscience when you kill, like turning off reality. If you don't, your mind starts to do torturous things," I explain as I pick up my lost throwing knives and put them back in their rightful places, reassembling my armor as my thoughts start to go hazy. I remember those nights when I would let myself sink too deep. The year I spent enjoying the fear and craving the power like a starved man craves food. There was so much blood staining my hands. Still staining my hands...

"Leo?" Cael's voice startles me back into reality. I wince at the sympathy in his eyes, my brother knowing exactly where my mind had gone. Within seconds his gaze turns hollow. It's a look I've seen too many times on people before they tear themselves apart from the inside out, their guilt the spark of the forest fire slowly burning away at their souls.

The boys come out from behind the trees, their expressions a swirl of fear and wonder as they gape at us. Antares drags my bag through the dirt and drops it at my feet before taking a tentative step back. I pick up my pack, hesitating when I see my hands. I scan my arm, then wipe my sleeve across my face. Blood. I'm covered in blood, my own and others. I walk over to one of the corpses and tear off a bit of clean material from his shirt. I can hear the others cringe behind me, but I'm not going to waste our own clothes and blankets.

I clean up fast, wiping away any blood and shrugging off my shirt to stanch my bleeding wounds. They had been tracking us for a long time, so they must have had supplies stashed somewhere. Sure enough, we find four full bags hidden in the overgrowth. Two are filled to the brim with food, while the others are packed with clothes, blankets, and medical supplies. There's more here than we ever had at the house. Cael fixes me up as he ogles at the sterile white bandages, proper stitches with shining needles, and vials of mixed medications. There's even a book on sicknesses and injuries that I shove into my bag. We pull out new, crisp clothes and put on everything we can, helping the boys fold up their oversized pants and sleeves. We fill our packs until they're bursting and quickly set off again, not wanting to be anywhere near this place when the scavengers show up.

As the sun begins to sink under the horizon, we find a flat spot to sleep between a couple of trees. I light a small fire, the heat warming us enough to be at ease. I warm the cans of stew, the smell of venison filling the air. I serve myself last as usual, and Cael helps Saiph with her portion. More than once he has to stop her from shoving her hand into the can. At one point, my brother makes the dire mistake of glancing away, giving

Saiph the perfect opportunity to make a mess. She takes full advantage of the moment, giggling madly as her meal spills onto Cael's lap. Even I can't help a smile as he swears, trying to salvage his food while wiping off her tiny hand and cleaning his pants.

"Is there any more, Leo?" Antares asks as Altair looks up, licking the spoon he carved out of a fallen branch.

"Have mine, I've eaten enough," I say, handing them my can. "Share it. Equally." They nod quickly as matching smirks appear on their faces. Cael passes me a disapproving glare, one I blissfully ignore. A familiar pessimistic feeling overwhelms me at his heavy gaze, but as I watch Altair and Antares, it all seems worth it. Cass extends his can as well, having barely taken a bite of his food.

"Does yours taste all right, Cass?" Cael asks, noticing his lack of appetite. Antares takes his food, greedily shoveling the stew into his mouth. Cass smiles weakly as he nods, his face taking on a green tint in the firelight. Cael and I exchange a worried glance.

"Not hungry?" I ask, my voice soft. He dips his chin slightly as his eyes slip to the ground. That makes two of us. I have no appetite after what happened, and even as my stomach rumbles, I have to force down every bite.

It doesn't take long for the boys to get huddled against each other as their fatigue starts to take hold. They nod off faster than Saiph, who's sleeping soundly between Cael and me.

"How're you doing?" I ask into the fire. My brother stays silent for a long moment. He's drowning against the tides of his memories, his eyes void and cold.

"I don't think it's completely sunk in yet. I know I killed him, but it doesn't feel like it. I thought I would feel different," he says, staring out into the darkness.

"Different as in how?" I wonder aloud, genuinely curious. He shakes his head, his eyes settling on the whispering flames.

"I don't know. I thought I would be more... upset? I feel numb," he explains emotionlessly. I turn my head to watch him. My brother may know my tells, but I know his too.

"What else?" I push. I'll give him space if he wishes it, but sometimes, it's better to get the weight off his shoulders. He stays silent for a long moment. I lean back against the tree, wrapping myself in a thick wool blanket nicer than any I've ever felt.

"This doesn't make me like them, does it?" Cael asks quietly, lifting his scared eyes to mine. My brows crease as I realize who he's talking about. His parents, the ones he was born to. "They tortured me for years. Kept me in that room because they got sick of me. I was where they directed their anger. How they felt powerful... What if I'm becoming them?" he asks desperately, his hands shaking beneath his blanket. "They never felt a lick of regret when it came to me. I don't regret what I did either."

"Cael, you're *nothing* like them. Death is strange, and it doesn't hit any two people the same. Some will be scared by what they've done, unable to live past the moment, while others won't feel a thing. Though, I know you aren't completely numb. I can see what you're hiding." *The fear and regret you don't want to show.* Cael stares into the dark, his face twisted with grief. "You are not your parents. I do everything I can to keep my family alive and safe, Cael. If I thought you were even a minor threat, I would have left you in the streets a long time ago. *Our* father would have done the same thing," I say, emphasizing the fact that in my father's eyes, Cael was his son. He seems to break through whatever thoughts were keeping him trapped in his head as he nods. I give him a half smile, my relief palpable.

"Do you miss them?" he whispers. I nod slowly.

"Every day. Each more than the last," I admit as memories begin flowing thickly in my mind. Pleiades's eyes stare at me as they haul her up the post, the rope ripping at her neck. She holds my gaze until the end, her eyes still finding mine when it gets dark... A sword pierces through my father's stomach as his plea to run bounces off the buildings in time with my pounding footsteps. Guilt weighs on my bones as I run away instead of fight. But I'm so scared, too scared... My mother's tears and sweat drench the sheets as Cael and Pleiades try to wake her. I cradle Saiph in my arms. My hands, the first to ever hold her, covered in blood... Pollux's withering body lies in bed as the disease slowly tears him away from us. It took his sight, then his movement and finally his voice. Cass stays by his side until the end. He eats when Pollux eats. Sleeps only when his twin sleeps. When Pollux's heart stops beating, Cass stops speaking. He has nothing left to say...

"Leo!" My name drags me out of my thoughts. I blink, regaining my bearings. "Are you all right?" Cael asks, scanning me worriedly. I nod shakily.

"Yes. Sorry," I say heavily. His eyes are somber as he gives me a tight smile, knowing exactly where I went. I clear my closing throat. "You should sleep."

He sighs, a whisper of a laugh escaping his lungs. "Don't do anything stupid until I wake up," he says before lying down and pulling his blanket over his head. The corner of my lip kicks up.

"I wouldn't dream of it."

CHAPTER
NINE

We hike from dawn to dusk for two weeks straight. Our feet blister and cramp with each step. When we finally set up camp, the first thing we do is pull off our shoes. The boys are barely able to stay awake long enough to fill their stomachs. I've had to sleep four times, and when I wake, I always catch the boys gaping as if I'd risen from the dead. In a more literal way than is pleasant to believe, I do.

We've found two people mindlessly wandering through the woods so far. They seemed to have been walking for days, hitting the trees as they passed with wide eyes as if they'd seen ghosts. We tried to point them in the right direction, but I doubt they'll make it back to civilization. Even if they do, they'll simply be lost in another kind of forest, just one with more visible predators.

Cass is slowing and it hasn't gone unnoticed. I carried him on my back so he could get a few extra hours of sleep after barely being able to open his eyes before we set off. Altair helped with Cass's bag while Cael took my pack with him.

"Can we take a break and set up camp early?" Antares pleads, eyeing the wide stream we've been following. "We could go swimming and wash our clothes." I study my brothers as they drag their feet, walking with worn spirits. One afternoon won't hurt. I nod, my own need for rest weighing heavily on my hunched shoulders.

We set up camp and everyone but Altair and I head into the water. I nod to Cael, silently telling him that I'm taking Altair for a walk. Once we get out of earshot of the others, Altair slumps as the shield he's held up for days starts crumbling away.

"How are you holding up?" I ask as I sit on a low-hanging branch. He takes the spot beside me. "That's not an easy thing you went through, and you haven't said anything about it," I add, glancing his way. He's been getting nightmares, his breath catching in the middle of the night before he wakes with a start.

"All right," he whispers, ripping apart a leaf. I don't say anything, giving him time to straighten out his thoughts. "Do you feel it eating at you? Like it's trying to get you to yield to it?" A deep shiver runs down my spine.

"At first, it felt strange. Unnatural. But the more you call on it, the more it becomes a part of you. Something you can control instead of something that controls you," I explain, watching him carefully. He mulls over my words, the leaf forgotten in his still hands.

"What if I don't want it? What if I'm scared I'll succumb to the...?"

"Instinct?" I finish for him. He dips his chin in a shallow nod.

"You don't have to be scared. Not of yourself. Are you afraid of me?" I ask. He meets my gaze and shakes his head furiously as if he were worried he had offended me. "Right now, it's a reaction to a threat. You see it as something big and wild that could swallow you whole. But once you allow yourself to get closer, you'll realize it's at your mercy," I explain. Something seems to click inside him as he nods along with my words.

"I don't know if I can. I don't know if I want to," he says cautiously.

"I'll help you. We'll walk right up to it, and you'll see how easy it is to control," I say, standing up. He follows, his brows creasing. "If you're going to learn how to control what I call an instinct, you first need to figure out how to call on it." I take a couple of steps back and pull on the familiar feeling, letting the crimson curtain fall over my sight. Power courses through my veins, readying my muscles and sharpening my senses. A glimpse of a smile flashes on his face, seeing how easily he could call upon the same instinct lying restless in his blood. "Try and remember the emotion you felt when your eyes shifted." He nods as his lids fall shut. After a long moment, his hands curl into tight fists and his eyes fly open, his irises shining their usual silver. His shoulders slump down as he reads my face.

"I'm sorry," I say as an idea sparks in my mind.

"For wha—" I charge at him as fast as I can, shoulders down before he can even finish his sentence. His eyes flash gold as he turns out of my way and elbows me in the jaw. I skid to a stop and watch him. He seems dumbfounded, the gold fading from his eyes.

"Stop! Concentrate on the feeling. Hold on to it," I order quickly, throwing my hand out. He straightens and looks around, as if realizing for the first time that he called on the instinct. He meets my gaze and the gold fades back to silver. "Good," I sigh, wiping the crimson tears running down my face. I touch my jaw and wince.

"I'm sorry, Leo, I didn't... I never..." he stumbles, his hands tight to his sides. I flash him an easy smile and shake my head.

"At least you know how to give a good elbow," I point out, gesturing to my face. "Let's try it again."

We work at it for another hour before he's panting and I'm rubbing away more bruises than I can count. As we head back —Altair walking a little straighter—we pass Cass coming out of the water, shivering so hard I can hear his teeth chatter. He doesn't acknowledge us as he passes. Altair runs ahead, chasing Antares and Saiph through the shallow water. Antares doesn't go in deeper than his ankles, running back to shore when the water comes up his shins. He knows how to swim, but it's been such a long time since he's been in deep water, I wonder if he remembers that he can. Cael smiles when he sees me, smirking as he catches the bruises blooming on my skin.

"Seems like Altair gave you a beating worthy of the Goddess," he drawls with raised brows. I shove his shoulder, my brother making a show of exaggerating how hard I hit him.

"He's doing better than I did. He can almost call on it without threat of danger," I say, seriousness creeping into my voice. Cael straightens and nods beside me.

"What is it exactly?" he wonders, his eyes trailing Altair in the water as he dunks Antares.

"I'm not sure," I admit. "It's always been there, like a natural instinct. You know how you can extend your arm, well it's the same type of thing. I will it to take away the pain and sharpen my senses and it does." Cael watches the water, pondering on the Lady knows what. I let him think, not wanting to try and understand what goes on in his head. I watch Saiph slip in the water and right herself with a laugh. A smile pulls at the corner of my lip as I stop myself from getting up to help her.

"Did you see Cass as you came? His nose started bleeding after you left. It stopped, but he seemed off," Cael says, swaying his feet through the water.

"Yes, we did. I only glanced at him, but he kept his eyes down." Now that I think of it, Cass walked by like he hadn't noticed us at all.

"Something's up with him," Cael says worriedly. I nod in agreement.

We don't spend much longer in the stream, heading back to make sure Cass is all right. When we get back, Altair, Antares, and Saiph are dripping from head to toe. Cael walks up to Cass, who's curled up sound asleep, too close to the fire. I crouch down and lay my hand on his arm, recoiling at the heat radiating from his skin. I bundle Cass into my arms, pulling him away from the flames. He's shivering madly. Cael meets my eyes, seeing the fear etched on my face. I give my youngest brother a little shake, quietly calling his name. He cracks open his eyes before quickly shutting them again, whimpering as he curls into me. I swallow the bile rising in my throat as fear starts to creep in. His eyes were black; his pupils were dilated enough to block out the color of his irises. Cael and I stare at each other for a long moment, not having a clue what to do.

"What is it?" Antares asks from behind me. We don't move, rigid in place. I sit down, holding him tightly against me.

"He's sick," I breathe. The silence is thick between us as dread weaves its way into my thoughts. We all know what happens when someone gets sick. None of us can forget what happened to Pollux.

"But..." Altair starts, yet no other words manage to pass his lips. Cael jumps out of his crouch and strides over to his pack, pulling out the book we took from one of Vela's bags. He flips viciously through the pages, taking extra care to read over the words before turning to the next page. He stops abruptly, reading the same lines over a couple times.

"Good or bad news?" Cael offers, his face grave. My stomach sinks. I know that look, and it only makes an appearance when we're in trouble.

"Bad first," Altair says from behind me.

"It seems like it's Rackers. Extreme fever, languor, dilated eyes, nosebleeds, and lack of appetite. It's contagious and transfers in bodily fluids." His arms hang at his sides, the book all but forgotten in his hand. "I read a paper on it in the apothecary once. It's serious, his chances are slim," Cael whispers, voice breaking.

"Of dying?" Antares dares, hope blooming in his voice. Cael shakes his head as the air flies from my lungs.

"And the good news?" Altair presses, needing to know if there's a way to save him.

"There's a medication that cures it," he says, his face dropping. "But it's hard to get, and if you find someone who can actually procure it, it's extremely expensive. It's made from a plant that grows in the Anateyan steeps." He spins his ring, squeezing his eyes shut as he slides to the ground.

"How expensive?" I ask. I can get money. A few well-placed hands in unknowing pockets of the wealthy shouldn't be too difficult.

"More coin than I've ever seen," he says, lifting his eyes to meet mine. "Ten gold marks for six doses. We'll need to give him twice that to kill the disease. Twenty gold marks, Leo. We can't get that," he breathes defeatedly as his eyes drift to Cass.

"And if I could?" I challenge. He meets my gaze, his own filled with skeptical hope. I hold Cass a little tighter.

"We shouldn't be too far from Dryden. If I win an arena fight there—"

"We are *not* going to Dryden, Leo. The one place we will not go is Dryden. You know better than I do those who go into that city end up either killed or enslaved. People go there when they want to *die* Leo, not to find help," he fires, his voice ringing with finality.

"I have an old friend who lives there, Fumbles. When I get the coin, he can find someone who can get us the medication. Dryden's citizens may be murderers, cheats, and thieves, but they're rich ones. Win the right arena fight and we'll be drowning in gold. Enough to buy extra medication," I coax, my voice begging as I hold his stare. He needs to agree because I don't want to consider the alternative.

"And if this friend doesn't help you?" Cael pries, worry painted across his face. Even concerned, he can't hide the hope pushing against his cautious nature.

"He will. I got him out of Somereil a long time ago. I've saved his life twice over. He owes me more than we'll ask. Plus, we'll have no need for the whole prize, so we'll give him the rest. Fumbles was a dirty cutthroat who had a taste for gold. People like that don't change," I say, remembering how he used to hoard whatever money he made, picking a fight with whoever would put up a wager.

"Do you even know where to find him?"

"Last time I went as Vela's second, we paid him a visit."

Cael nods slowly as his eyes go far away. Finally, he sighs defeatedly, watching Cass with desperate eyes. "We go to Dryden, get the medication, and leave. We stay no longer than we have to," he acquiesces, his head hanging low. He turns his attention to Antares and Altair as they round the fire with

Saiph between them. They sit on the far side of the flames, away from Cael, Cass, and me. "You two make your own food, take care of Saiph, and don't come near the three of us," Cael directs, his grief replaced by stern conviction. They nod solemnly.

"Then it's settled. Tomorrow, we head for Dryden."

CHAPTER

TEN

LEO

We walk all day and at times well into the night. Cass's state only deteriorates as the days go on, his eyes barely fluttering when we try to wake him. We made a stretcher to carry him, weaving blankets around two thick branches. He won't wake up at all anymore and his clothes are covered in blood from the constant nosebleeds. We can hear his labored breaths getting shallower by the minute and I'm slowly losing the spark of hope that had ignited when we first set out. Altair and Antares walk behind us with Saiph, heads hung and shoulders slumped. Making them stay away from us is only adding to the cloud of dread floating over our heads. Altair had to hold Saiph down as she tried to come to us, screaming until she passed out from exhaustion. Cael looks as dejected as the rest of us, his cheeks sunken and eyes tired from so many sleepless nights.

When we finally see the first light of the city, it feels like a miracle sent from Lady Death herself. We stand there, staring at the faint lights filtering through the woods. We stop short as the forest begins to thin. Any relief we felt is quickly drowned by the hard truth of our reality. We're in Dryden, and it doesn't take long to realize the glow is not the light of streetlights, but raging fires, consuming entire buildings on several streets. We drop the stretcher at the forest line, and I take Cass into my arms. My heart clenches as I realize how much weight he's lost.

I lead my brothers through the streets, praying that we are the only ones lurking in the winding alleys. I've been to Dryden but a handful of times and every second I've spent in this city is branded into my memory. Maybe it's because Dryden feels like death. Cael moves stiffly behind me, and I know he can feel the heavy eeriness too.

The only people we pass are oblivious drunks and the homeless curled along the street, straining to keep warm. We pass at least two bodies the rats have claimed, hissing at us with sharp yellowed teeth. Fumbles's house blends in perfectly with the rest of the rotting city. The brick walls are painted black with Dryden's filth; the thatched roof is peppered with holes and bars that lie across the windows and door. I lead my brothers around the house and knock once on the back door, taking a step away to slip my dagger from its scabbard at my thigh. I bleed my eyes, holding Cass tightly in my arms. A hatch at eye level slides open on the door.

"I worked yesterday boss, you told me I had today off... Who the hell are you?" an ignorant voice booms. He hasn't changed one bit.

"You don't remember your good friend the Blood Prince, Fumbles? You owe me your life twice over," I say dryly. I hear his breath catch as I speak the nickname I've called him since the day we met.

"Hael?" I count the click of four locks before the door creaks open. A tall, lanky man dressed in black, holding a lit cigarette between his teeth, stares me up and down. A gruesome scar stretches from the corner of his mouth to his left ear. I remember how he got it. It was the first time I saved him from a situation that could easily have been avoided if not for his selfishness and tendency to make rash, angry decisions. He tried to play people who always won, cheating in games designed to make him lose. The men he tried to swindle figured out what he was doing, but when they confronted him, instead of denying and leaving, Fumbles sat back in his chair and ignored them, then proceeded to tell them all the ways their games were flawed. He's only alive because I showed up at the gambling house right as the owners started cutting him up.

"I thought you stopped smoking," I drone, pulling a veil of calm over my expression. His mouth pulls into a strange, one-sided smile, stretching his jagged scar.

"My memory doesn't do justice to your eyes. You're even scarier than I remember, a demon straight from hell." He shrugs and leans against the doorframe. "Now, if my memory serves me, you never much liked Dryden. Whatever you want, I won't help. Now you can all get off my step before the neighbors wake up and try to come slaughter me again," he says, crossing his arms loosely over his chest.

"You ever figure out how to use a blade, Fumbles?" I ask sarcastically, tilting my head to the side. He tenses as his eyes darken. I deemed him Fumbles the day I met him because of his skills with a dagger. He dropped every blade I handed him; his hold was so awkward I cringe at the memory. I was taking back all the criticism the moment I saw his skill with a bow though.

"What do you want, Hael?" His tone is light, but there is no warmth in his words as he throws his cigarette to the ground at my feet. I keep my face blank and my gaze unfaltering.

"I need to get into an arena fight. A good one. You're going to help me," I say, keenly aware of his movements.

"Why would I help you? Besides the fact that you've saved my life and all that nonsense, what makes you think I would get you into an arena? By the way, you all look terrible." He grimaces and waves his arms through the air with disgust. I sheath my blade, ignoring the intense urge to run him through.

"We only need enough coin for medication. You can take all the rest." He watches me for a long moment, weighing my words.

"You know how much they're offering for your head? One hundred gold pieces. It would be much easier to kill you and take the reward," he wonders aloud, his tone more serious than I would like as he quirks a brow. *They doubled my bounty.* Surprise bubbles through me. I'm not sure if I should be flattered or enraged. I hold his stare, letting the monster I keep buried deep inside flash across my face. He flinches as his ease falls away.

"Do you really want to push me, Fumbles? My patience is on a tight leash, and I doubt you've forgotten what happens when it snaps," I say, my voice low and serious. He swallows, training his features into a false tranquility.

"Why don't you come in," he offers, stepping back into the house.

"Do you have weapons inside?" I ask, already knowing the answer, but wondering if he would lie.

"Always." He winks, flashing me a smile. I lead my brothers inside the cramped hellhole, limiting the amount of space between us as the smell of smoke overwhelms my senses. I have to breathe through my mouth to stop myself from gagging. Somehow, Saiph and my brothers manage to keep quiet. Fumbles stands across from us in his dilapidated kitchen. It only holds the essentials: a dented table kept standing by a rock wedged underneath a leg, a cracked oil lamp sitting in its center, cupboards with doors hanging off their hinges, and an old rusty coal stove. There are two quivers lying on the table filled with sleek dark wood arrows and cans of food and dirty pots lying scattered all over the room. Cael's hand hovers dangerously close to his blade as his eyes pin to Fumbles. "I'm guessing you don't want the kids to hear our conversation," Fumbles says dryly, surveying the boys closely. "You always were..." He waves his hand through the air as he rolls his eyes. "Protective." I nod and he opens the door to a wide, bare storage room. The rusty stains on the tile tell me enough about the use of the space. I nod once to the boys and direct them into the room. I set Cass up on a pile of blankets, taking an extra moment to listen to his shallow breaths. We still have time.

I come back out and let crimson tears fall from my eyes to allow our host to relax. Fumbles goes to close the door, but I stop him short, grabbing his wrist before he can wrap his gnarled fingers around the knob. His other hand shoots up in surrender as I force myself to let go. He takes a step away, smirking. "Haven't lost those good senses of yours, have you?" I glare at him as I take a seat, Cael sitting to my left.

"New hostage, Hael?" Fumble asks airily, nodding to Cael.

"You remember my brother," I introduce dryly. He used to love to play these games. So did I. Not anymore.

"Ahh, right. The adopted one. Shame you don't resemble them even slightly," he says, feeling around for a soft spot, somewhere to wound if the need should arise. We remain unfazed, wearing twin blank expressions. He sighs, displaying his unnerving one-sided grin as he gives up on his attempt to rile us. "What exactly do you need me to do?"

"We need medication, and the money to purchase it. I need you to get me into the biggest arena fight you can find, along with someone who can get their hands on the drug," I state plainly as I cross my arms, the cold steel strapped across my chest grounding me.

"You were always a little messed up in there," he says to himself, tapping his temple. "But I didn't think you were that far gone. Too much internal bleeding. That or Lady Death's becoming too good of a friend." When we don't say anything, he shakes his head incredulously, becoming serious. "Hael, you're the most wanted man in Tominay. Even Miss Mares heard about what you did. Your bounty's become so big, the bosses are declining big jobs to send men after you. Anyone sees you here and you're dead on the spot."

"I've walked away from worse odds," I assure, meeting his gaze. "And you know arena rules. No one gets killed unless you're in the ring. I plan on getting in, grabbing the money, and getting out of Dryden before the bosses have even noticed I've won."

"And if someone notifies the king's army?" he tries, brows raised.

"Don't waste my time with questions you already know the answer to. Anyone leads a sentinel to an arena and they forfeit their lives. Everyone roped into the fights has too much invested to chance losing it," I dismiss, though the thought had crossed my mind before. I doubt anyone would be stupid enough to break the rules and try to kill me outright, but with the bounty in play...

"Fine. I can get you in, but I want forty percent of the cut," he demands, his eyes hard.

"Done," Cael says easily, his expression stoic. Fumbles's stare travels between us as disbelief crosses his face.

"And if I asked for fifty?" he pushes hesitantly.

"As my brother told you, we only need enough to pay for the medication. You get us into a fight with a prize big enough to buy out the King of Tominay, you'll get all the coin we don't use," Cael states, looking bored as he spins his ring. Fumbles leans back and props his feet up on the table.

"What's the medication for? You finally going to let yourself have some fun?" he asks, not bothering to hide his smirk.

"Cass has Rackers." Fumbles jumps out of his seat as his wide eyes fly furiously between us and the storage room. Now that, I wasn't expecting.

"Why would you bring him here? If he's sick, why would you bring him to me?" he spits urgently, his face tight with fear. I forgot about the only thing that truly scares Fumbles. Disease. His mother died from an illness and since then, he couldn't stand being around anyone who so much as coughed. He must have thought Cass was just asleep when we showed up at his door.

"You'll be fine. The disease only attacks young children. Leo and I have been taking care of him and we're both fine," Cael drones, unimpressed. My brother might be a better actor than I am.

"Why couldn't you get the medication from a surgeon or apothecary or somewhere— *anywhere* else?" he stammers, voice quaking with terror.

"Take a breath, will you? You aren't thinking straight." Fumbles passes me such a disdainful glare I smile. "One, we don't have documents. We're not registered anywhere, so we can't walk into a royal apothecary and no regular doctor carries the drug we need. Then there's the fact that, as you said, I'm the most wanted man in Tominay. We also don't have the twenty pieces it—"

"Of gold?" he balks. I nod as he peels himself from the wall. His hand runs over the patchy stubble covering his chin. He slowly starts smiling again, sliding back into his seat.

"All right, I can do it. There's a fight happening in two nights. All the big bosses will be in attendance. No street beggars or worthless bags of skin and bones. I can get you in, but Vela is expected to be there. I don't know how you think you'll be getting much more than coppers with that cheat around," he chides, his eyes brightening with anticipation.

"He won't be there," I state matter-of-factly. Cael freezes beside me, his hand stilling over his ring. A terrible grin appears on Fumbles's butchered face as he lets out a strangled laugh, throwing his head back.

"You killed Vela! I was wondering how you got this far with the whole family. To tell you the truth, I never thought you would do it! I should be mad because he was my boss, but by the Lady, I hated him. Thank the Goddess you killed him, Hael," he howls, his face twisting with laughter and an emotion I can't place.

"I didn't." Fumbles pauses, his delight wavering. He looks between my brother and I and realization dawns.

"You killed him?" he asks, pointing at Cael. "Well, all hells, congratulations! Welcome to the real world! How'd it feel? Amazing, wasn't it? Watching the light fade from a man's eyes as he bleeds makes the world seem right," he all but squeals. Cael jumps out of his seat, his gaze set on Fumbles. I catch his arm and pull him back down before he can tear my old coworker's throat out. He's shaking madly, fury burning in his eyes. I don't think I've ever seen him get this mad. And to think Fumbles used to be the sane one out of the two of us. My mood darkens at the memory.

"Oh, you're easy to rile!"

"Do we have a deal?" I ask, bringing us back to the task at hand. Cael takes in deep, measured breaths, watching Fumbles like a hawk as he laughs hysterically. He wipes his eyes, calming himself down as the amusement lingers on his face.

"Come on, Hael. When have I ever turned down a paying job?"

CHAPTER

ELEVEN

LEO

I sit with my back pressed against the wall of the storage room. I keep my hand on Cass's wrist, counting his sluggish heartbeats as his chest struggles to rise. Antares, Altair, and Saiph are lying almost on top of each other across the cramped space, seeming exhausted even in sleep. They've been so tired; I doubt they can even dream. Though, no dreams mean no nightmares. Cael turns over beside me, muttering as he takes in a sharp breath. The nightmares never cease to find Cael, no matter how many tiring days he fights or sleepless nights he's survived. I don't think he's had a full night's sleep since he killed Vela.

He screams as he shoots up and wildly searches the room. He backs up frantically against a wall, his chest heaving as he takes quick short breaths. His eyes fly around like he's still in a dream, the nightmare unwilling to relent. I move in front of him, placing my hands on either side of his shoulders. "Cael? Cael! You're awake. Look at me. You're awake! It's done," I say rapidly. He meets my gaze, his eyes slowly coming back into focus. I let go, giving him space as he rests his head against the wall. He pushes the palms of his shaking hands to his face as I slump to the ground, sitting between Antares and Altair. I glance at the boys, but they haven't moved, immune to the noise in their deep slumbers. Cael pulls his knees to his chest, wedging his forehead between them. I move over to sit beside him, leaning my head back against the cold stone wall as I place my fingers on Cass's wrist.

"They keep getting worse. The details keep replaying in my head, each time slower than the last," Cael says softly, his voice raw. "I see his face, but they're making me do it. In the room. They make me kill him over and over and over," he breathes, tears trailing down his face as he raises his eyes to watch the open door and the kitchen beyond. His parents would lock him in a dark cellar when he was young. They tortured and neglected him for years. I go cold as I think of the few times he's told me about it. I wish I had known who they truly were, but I know ridding them of life would not tame my brother's monsters. "How are you okay with it? All this death," he says, his voice trembling. Cael has always been the one to put us back together, unworried about Lady Death's will. Now he's not only carrying his past, which he could have done nothing about, but his kill, which he could. I take a long moment to put the right words together, knowing they could either help him, or hurt him even more.

"I'm not, but I hold on to the hope what I did will have an impact. People die and the world changes after them. For better or worse, I have no idea, but we need things to change. Lady Death is said to take us away before our worst moment... before we can be hurt too deeply or undertake our greatest atrocity. Vela has done... unthinkable things, and I would hate to think of the outcome of the worst he could do," I say, repeating the words I'd heard so many times. Cael nods, the ghost of a smile pulling at his lips.

"Do you believe in the stories? That she gives us a purpose and once it is complete, Lady Death takes us away before our worst moment?"

"Why not? It makes it easier to believe that what you're doing is for a reason. And imagining someone else is beside you, even if it is a goddess, helps." Cael closes his eyes, his breathing becoming easier.

"Remember when Mum used to pray to her every night," he mutters. I almost smile with relief as the tension lifts from his tone.

"I'm not as pious as she was. Not even close. Lady Death was a warrior I believe people painted into a Goddess to give themselves hope. And we could all use a little hope." He nods again as we fall into an easy silence. I know Cael won't get back to sleep, but he'll try and put on a show, if anything, to give me peace of mind.

I stare at the wall beside Antares as he finishes off the last of his meal. Fumbles came back late yesterday with a smug grin painted on his face and told me I was in. He used Vela's name, but seeing as the boss is incapable of collecting any winnings, we'll take the entire payout. Fumbles is to wait outside the arena when we go in to keep watch from afar. We agreed it would be better for him to stay out of sight to prohibit anyone from coming to the house. Cael decided he would come, disregarding my plea for him to stay back. I still don't want him to see the place where the monster stirring restlessly inside me was created.

"You ready?" Fumbles asks, leaning against the wall of the

kitchen. I nod, tearing my eyes away from the spot on the wall that surprisingly hasn't crumbled under my gaze. I check my blades before shrugging on the threadbare cloak Fumbles hands me. I step out of the small room after giving the boys a solemn nod, not daring to say goodbye. Cael exchanges a few hushed words with them before coming to stand beside me, daggers shining at each side of his hips. He also has blades tucked into his sleeve and boot, courtesy of our younger brothers. Fumbles straps a simple quiver of arrows to his back and slings a bow over his shoulder. He had been terrible with a blade, but with a bow, Fumbles was the best. He leads us out the door and locks a series of mechanisms before stepping into the street.

"What did you tell them?" I ask Cael as I pull the hood low over my face. Cael does the same, his own cloak one we had found in Vela's packs. It's past dusk, but you never know who can see in the dark.

"What I always tell them. That you'll be fine, we'll be back before dawn, and they should stay put no matter what," he says easily. We keep our focus on the street ahead of us, following Fumble's steps in complete silence.

"What am I walking into?" My brother asks evenly.

"I don't know if telling you will make it easier or harder to see," I say, a chill running through me as memories shoot to the front of my mind. Cael walks in silence for a time, as if he were weighing the question.

"Tell me," he demands, though the conviction in his voice wavers.

"All the big bosses will be there. Men and women like Vela and some even worse. They put their prized fighters in the ring, wagering as much coin as they can carry. Two people walk into the ring, one comes out with their heart still beating. Those are the rules. If you stay alive, you fight again until every other competitor has been slain," I whisper, putting more effort than I should need into keeping my emotions in check.

"What are the odds, of us getting out alive with the money?" he queries.

"About as bad as Cass's, worse if you factor in the fact that we'll have some of the most dangerous bosses in Tominay painting glowing targets on our backs the second we leave the arena. If we leave the arena," I say, trying not to emphasize the *if*. I glance at my brother, catching him shaking his head as his eyes stay glued ahead.

"I don't like this, Leo."

"I'd rather take Cass's odds than let him try his own hand at them." My brother doesn't argue with that. We wind through sparsely lit, grimy streets, covering our noses to escape the smell of sewage and decay. At first, we keep to streets I'm familiar with, but after navigating through the tangle of roads, I quickly lose all sense of direction as Fumbles marches ahead. Only the rats and dogs chance being out here this late, snarling as we pass. I don't dare look at what they could be feeding on.

I can feel people watching from all around and it sets me on edge. There are too many watching eyes for us to not be getting close to whatever sodden building they use to hide the arena from patrols. Fumbles turns suddenly, leading us into a dark alley. He stops in front of a wrought iron door, one extremely out of place in this crumbling quarter of the city. I stand shoulder to shoulder with Cael with my hand hovering close to my blade as Fumbles pounds roughly on the door.

A small hatch slides open noisily, revealing a pair of muddy-green eyes. They glow with excitement as screams filter through the slot. "Business?" The man asks gruffly.

"We're here to make a story but tell no rumors," Fumbles states as he sticks his hands in his pockets. The man behind the door nods before sliding the slot closed. *The passwords only get more ridiculous with time*, I think to myself.

"This is my cue to disappear. You're Vela's Blood Prince," he points at me, stepping away from the door. He turns to Cael as a wicked smirk grows on his face. "And you're his new pet. Here in his place because he had better things to do. Don't act like you care too much about your brother or they'll know something's up. Those bosses are hounds, don't leave anything for them to track or they'll be out for your blood," he says rather excitedly to my brother. We stay silent as he disappears from the alley, leaving us to the mercy of the arena.

My stomach flips as the door opens and a man with a neck the size of my thigh stares at me. He stands with crossed arms the size of tree trunks and twin axes hanging at each hip at the threshold. "Names," he demands dryly, all business. I pull a murderer's mask over my expression, falling into a state of false ease and confidence.

"Do you want my real name, or the one people like to call me?" I ask airily, forcing an arrogant grin as I pull down my hood. The man rolls his eyes as he studies me, the picture of a pompous child blinded by years of victory.

"Name and boss," he repeats, disinterested.

"You don't recognize my face?" I challenge as Cael follows suit and pulls down his hood. He stares, waiting for an answer. I huff a laugh and tilt my head as the amusement drops from my face. The man skips over me and scans Cael.

"The spectator doors are around the other side of the building," he spits.

"He's with me, new to the business. Vela got rid of his last representative. His son seemed to be a fair replacement. Personally, I think he could have done better. This one vomited last time he saw a man's eye out of its socket." The man sneers at my brother, disgusted. One thing people high in the chain don't condone is weakness. Or any show of humanity.

"You aren't Vela's usual guy," he counters, studying me more thoroughly.

"No, I'm better," I say, letting the corner of my eyes bleed for a flash of a second. The man stumbles back in shock, his eyes wide.

"Blood Prince," he murmurs, his hands beginning to shake as he pulls an axe from his belt. *Good to know my reputation precedes me*, I think to myself as my stomach turns leaden. I don't let my unease show as I allow the monster that stirs inside take hold. The man steps aside, flattening himself against the wall as we pass.

The arena is nothing like the others I've seen in Dryden. It's a pit dug around a cage, built to keep monsters with human skins captive. The ring is dug down into the ground to form three levels: two for spectators and the deepest for the fighters and their respective bosses. Men and women yell on the top and middle levels, held back from falling into the pit by thick black bars running from the roof to the stone floor. A withered old man watches me as we come in, particularly out of place in the screeching crowd. He seems to be well into his seventies, but his eyes are sharp, staring me down like a predator locked in on its prey. Strange, I could swear I've seen him before.

Two women fight in the cage, baring their teeth as they rip into each other. They move so fast it takes my eyes a moment to adjust and catch exactly what they're doing. Around the cage, the bosses sit in their designated places, some seeming pleased while others look like they're close to snapping some poor soul's neck. They sit unmoving in their seats with their fighters to their rights, recognizable by their smug expressions and the multitude of garish scars and tattoos. Not a trace of fear can be found in their expressions as they carry all types of brutish weapons at their sides. Though they are trained fighters, they all prefer bats and chains to a clean knife, choosing brutality over efficiency. There is no place for fear when only one person is walking out alive. The bosses' advisers sit to their lefts, murmuring hushed words into the ears of their masters. Some may be friends, trusted colleagues, partners, enemies... It's all in the game they choose to play.

The real fights haven't started yet, the women in the ring simply warming up the crowd. I remember Vela dragging me to arenas like this and placing me in the seat to his left. He would tell me this was where he pulled me from, so I would watch and be grateful for the life he allowed me. I did as he said, but I was anything but grateful. He told me that during the warm-up fight, the fighters pulled their blows and exaggerated their pain. It was their job to engage the crowd, keep them riled up until the real action began, and they were compensated greatly for it.

Cael and I walk to the ladder and stop before the heavily armed woman guarding it. Her skin is pale as snow and her face is covered in a motley of tattoos. She spits a few well-rehearsed rules before stepping aside with a bored expression. There is no killing unless you're fighting inside the arena. There'll be a weapons search before you go in. The moment you step out of the arena, the rules of fair play no longer apply. The crowd quiets to whispers as we descend into the pit, all eyes finding me. *Blood Prince*, they gawk. I keep my gait even, ignoring the dozens of disbelieving stares.

I take the last open seat, sitting beside a woman Vela had introduced me to last time I was in Dryden. From what he said, I don't want to find my way onto her list of enemies. She is the woman who single-handedly turned Dryden into the city it is, or so the stories go. Her grandfather founded Dryden's arenas, but she was the one who made them flourish. Her stare follows me as Cael and I take a seat, leaving the middle chair closest to the cage vacant.

"So, Vela finally had the good sense to let the famous Blood Prince fight in my arenas," she says, her voice quieting the entire crowd. The fighters stop sparring in the cage as their gazes find me, still in their stances. Cael shifts uncomfortably in his seat as every pair of eyes turns to me. I shrug off my cloak and lean back, putting my blades on full display. Gasps sound from the crowd as they finally realize who sits before them.

"Miss Mare, it's a pleasure to see you again," I say politely, inclining my head in greeting. Cael follows suit, his eyes narrowing on the feared boss.

"The pleasure is all mine," she sings as she smooths her ruby dress cinched tight around her waist. She's in her late forties, her hair the color of fire contrasting her cold cobalt eyes. "You've been up to quite a bit since I last saw you. Breaking into a royal base to break out a boy and surviving. The king himself is out for your blood. I'm impressed," she says airily, waving her hand through the air. No one speaks, waiting for me to respond, to deny or confirm my latest escapades.

"That means much coming from you. It wasn't my best moment, I must say. But this is my payment to Mr. Vela for going against orders," I say, tilting my head to the side. "He told one of his men it was impossible to get into the deepest cell of the king's compound and out with your heart still pumping. He was wrong."

"You speak quite openly about your boss, Little Prince," she points out, surveying me carefully. I need to show confidence, especially with Vela missing from the circle of bosses.

"Mr. Vela keeps giving me the same task. I needed something bigger, so I took my chance. This," I say, motioning to the arena, "is the next best thing." Miss Mare grins, nodding as the crowd exchanges outraged murmurs. I blatantly disparaged the place said to have the toughest competition, houses the best fighters and most esteemed killers in front of its founder. Unease sits heavily in my gut as a sense of foreboding washes over me. I've done one of two things, either unsettled my opponents with my disinterest, or given them all more reason to rip out my throat. I pray to the Goddess it's the former.

Miss Mare raises her hand, instantly silencing the crowd. With a slight twist of her wrist, the two fighters leave the cage and take their positions as guards by the ladder.

"Marianna Dariel. Your fighters will go first. Everyone knows the rules. You will each be searched for weapons by the bosses' chosen second. Two go in, one comes out until only one victor stands. The winning boss will take their prize and have the chance to leave first. There will be no fights among the bosses or their fighters, nor the spectators in the arena. The moment you step outside, feel free to do as you wish. Everyone is fair game after all," she says, a wicked smile lighting her face as her eyes gleam. Clearly, the fighters are not the only ones scheduled to die tonight.

Two fighters step up from behind their bosses. Before making their way to their opponent's seconds, they exchange a few words as they slide off their boots, weapons, and extra layers of clothing, each revealing a tapestry of tattooed skin. One wears a cap of thick ruddy hair, his face pierced with countless bits of metal. The second fighter stands slightly taller than the first, his skin a light brown with cold amber eyes. They both stand like stone statues as they're searched for weapons, their numerous tattoos of prior victories stark against their skin. A frail girl who can't be any older than Altair searches the shorter of the two men, his frozen expression one of nightmares. A dark grin that should not belong to a child appears on the girl's face as she rips open the arm of his shirt. A long pin clatters to the floor. I almost laugh at the attempt; it's one I've seen done in a variety of ways over the years. The girl picks up the weapon and turns it over in her hand. I take a deep breath as the red-haired man straightens, tensing under her gaze. Everyone stares as the girl winds up and punches him in the face with impressive force, his nose spurting blood as he stumbles back a step. Not as frail as she appears. Cheers go up around the higher levels, whooping as the fighters—one already bloodied—make their way into the ring.

"I thought they weren't allowed to spill blood outside the cage," Cael whispers beside me, crossing his arms.

"He broke the rules. They found weapons, so to even the field they get to wound him." As I say it, Miss Mare raises her hand, and the cage is sealed. With a tilt of her head, they begin to dance around each other, waiting for the perfect moment to strike.

"But didn't she say they could have a blade in the cage?" Cael asks, his eyes stuck on the fight.

"You can bring whatever you want into the ring as long as you aren't caught with it outright. I could bring an entire army if I found a way to smuggle it in. They could both have weapons on them right now, it's just a matter of when they want to reveal what they carry." Cael nods with a clenched jaw beside me as he spins his ring. "Don't look so spooked, these people feed off fear," I warn, doing my best to keep my expression blank. He relaxes instantly, leaning back against his chair.

The shorter man with the piercings and bloodied nose gains the upper hand, pounding his opponent into the floor. I see his mistake as it happens. He's forgetting the man he's beating could have a weapon on him. Cael tenses, confirming my suspicion. A flash of steel catches the light and rips into his stomach. A wet rasp escapes from the man's throat as he falls to the ground. It ends quickly enough as cheers ring in my ear.

"I don't like this, Leo. Even criminals have rules," Cael says, his eyes flitting everywhere but the body being dragged away. Mr. Dariel seems to be considering killing the entire arena as his second hands over a clinking bag of coins to one of the women who had been guarding the door to the cage. She places it inside the beginning of what will be the winner's prize.

"They have laws, ones with extremely severe punishments. But these people live between the rules, finding loopholes even in their own."

CHAPTER
TWELVE

LEO

Two more fights pass before Miss Mare calls Vela's name. The silence held by the crowd is total. No one dares to breathe as I take off the blades strapped across my body and hand them to Cael. He can barely hold them all when I'm done, wrapping the various weapons in my cloak so as not to cut himself on the lethal edges before depositing them behind his chair. I place my boots at the foot of my seat, feeling for the hidden compartment before slugging off my shirt. I scan the outer ring and my eyes land on the snarling fighter standing in front of Miss Mare. He towers over me, a braided leather circlet sitting on his brow. He's Caymen then. The people of Caym wear the bands to honor their God, who was said to have blessed the people with knowledge. As the legends go, he led the Caymen people to prosperity, so they wear the circlet as a sign of their faith. The man in front of me resembles the opposite of a peaceful, pious citizen. Lady, help me.

I walk over to Miss Mare's second as my opponent stalks

over to my brother, snapping at me with yellowed teeth that match his discolored eyes. Her second stands and searches me for weapons. I remember the first fight Vela dragged me to long ago, right after he plucked me from the low arenas. There was a woman there who managed to hide a throwing knife in plain sight, spinning it in her hands so deftly it became invisible. It was a trick of the eye, her hold on the blade changing depending on the angle of the onlooker, and it mesmerized me. That trick was the only good thing that came out of my visits to the arenas. The woman was Vela's fighter, and I only realized what she was doing when he pointed it out. The second does not find a single piece of steel on me, grumbling as he sits back down. I turn as Cael throws four weapons to the ground. Two small blades hidden in my competition's belt, another in the cuff of his pants and the last under a layer of false skin on his arm. My brother always knows what's there without having to see it. I don't think I've ever been more thankful for his gift. I give him a slight nod before he slugs my opponent, hitting him in the eye. The man barely moves, the only tell the crunching blow did any damage at all is the slight clench of his jaw. He hits him three more times with and intense accuracy, each blow more devastating than the last.

Miss Mare waves us into the cage and the gate seals tight behind us. I track my opponent's every movement. The twitch of his neck, the way he puts slightly more weight on his left leg. His eyes are beginning to swell shut, Cael's punches having been extremely effective. With another wave of the boss's hand, we start to circle as the crowd roars. I keep my knees bent and hands in front of my face. I follow his movements, feeling the anticipation in the room rise with my adrenaline. Not just anyone gets to see the Blood Prince in person, let alone in the ring. I'm a rumor they're dying to see come true. I let the monster loose, feeling a grin pull on my face.

The Caymen lunges first, his cackle the sound of nightmares. I dodge him easily, landing a soft blow to his temple. He rocks backward but doesn't stumble. He rolls his shoulders and advances again. He lands a bruising blow to my side, my ribs remaining intact thanks to my quick reflexes, allowing me to pull away. We go back and forth, exchanging blow for blow. I use his swollen eye to my advantage, moving out of his line of sight as he twirls, desperate to keep up. He is built as solid as a statue but moves with the grace of one too. I hook my foot behind his knee and use my momentum to try and bring him down, knowing my efforts will be futile. If the people want a show, they'll get a show. He spins, righting himself and catching my ankle. I feel a smirk pull at my face as the crowd quiets with anticipation. I bleed my eyes in a blink and my opponent goes still as death.

I jump into a horizontal twist, wrenching my foot from his grip and delivering a swift kick to the side of his head with my heel. He rears back from the force, but I'm on him before he can hit the floor. I wrap my arm tightly around his neck and press my foot into the crook of his knee to steady myself. He wheezes, turning purple under my hold. He claws uselessly at my arms, his nails leaving tracks as I pull tighter. I take a labored breath, focus on the barren wall, and finish him with a quick twist of my arms. I send up a prayer to both Lady Death and the Caymen God to allow him peace as he crumbles to the ground. The crowd stays silent as I straighten, the man lying still at my feet. My eyes fall on Miss Mare as a chill runs up my spine. She isn't watching me with fear or hot anger as I would expect, but eyeing me curiously. Her head tilts to the side as she claps slowly, standing out with her calm disposition as the crowd begins to rage.

As I exit the cage, Cael pulls out a strip of cloth from his pocket and hands it to me as I sit. I wipe the drops of blood from my arms and stretch out my legs as I sit. Relief floods through me as I test my body for injuries and nothing seems broken or strangely out of place. Cael scans me quickly and comes to the same conclusion before turning back to watch the cage. We sit in silence for the next fight, dissecting their strategies and fighting styles. Cael comments on a few tells my next opponent shows in her fight. She has a weak arm and she pulled a blade to win. She hid the small knife behind her teeth, spitting blood after she felled her competitor.

She's tall and can't be much older than me. Her obsidian-colored hair is shorn short to her head and her eyes are like bottomless pits of black tar underlined by tattooed scorpions to match the ones wrapping her arms. She fights like she can fly, floating from one movement to the next. She's the best I've fought in a long while, but she is no match for what I unleash. Her movements slowly become hurried and sloppy as fear sets into her mind. I block out her shaking and whispered pleas as I grab the back of her neck and smash her head into the cage. The crowd roars as her boss throws his seat before depositing his lump sum into the growing pile of winnings. I ignore them all, walking out of the cage in a state of numbness. Cael hands me the cloth again as he points to his brow. I touch my forehead and my hand indeed comes away bloody. I wipe the sweat from my face before putting pressure on the wound.

"This next one is better than her. I hope you have something good up your sleeve, Leo," Cael whispers, intently watching the ring. I place a hand on my belt.

"We'll be walking out of here with the prize in a matter of minutes," I reply, leaning back against my chair. I allow myself a second to shut my eyes, letting the darkness block out the death hanging in the air before it works its way behind my eyelids, flashes of the night replaying in my mind. I force them open and the world floods in again.

Cael nods as Miss Mare motions for the last fight. My opponent looks like the living dead. His eyes are bloodshot as he stares me down with an unfaltering glare and his tanned skin is filled with tattoos. Trophies, coins, monsters of myths, swords, and axes all inked to mark his victories. A gash gained in his last fight stretches from the top of his head to his nose. The steady flow of blood and the bruises only add to his undead appearance. His boss's second checks me for blades as Cael does the same to my opponent, shifting uncomfortably under my competitor's stare.

I walk into the cage with my eyes locked on my adversary. Miss Mare waves her hand and he advances. As we circle, the crowd hushes, the air alive around us. I glance at Cael. He places his hand over his left rib before his eyes go wide and shoot away from me. I lunge away before my opponent lands a crushing blow to my head. He strikes quickly again, leaving me with a half second to deflect it. I hit him back as I turn away, my elbow pounding into his side. The air wooshes from his lungs as he's forced to take a step back. We go back and forth, breathing heavily as we move. I dance around him, keeping on my toes as I wait for the moment his guard slips and use it to pummel his ribs. He grimaces with each hit, stumbling as he struggles to gain his footing. My opponent is relentless, gritting his teeth against the pain and panting with wet rasps as he continues to attack. Blood and sweat dribble down my face as my muscles strain.

I keep my breathing deep and even to exploit every opportunity. I force him closer and closer to the cage, working through several combinations, one after the other. I glance at Cael for a split second as he shakes his head, anticipating my next move. I block him out easily as I watch my opponent's gnarled expression. Taking a breath, I brace myself and drop my hands to my sides. The surprise crossing his face is fleeting as he wraps his hands around my neck. I take in a struggling breath and hold his stare as a smirk pulls at my lips. I pull the small knife from beneath my belt and shove it into the side of his neck. I push him away, taking my blade with me. Blood spews from the wound, an artery severed. Raw fear plasters across his face as he collapses to the ground, blood pooling beneath him as he chokes.

The crowd roars as I turn, avoiding my defeated competitor as my chest heaves. My gut twists as they chant the name they fear. Blood Prince. I keep my face cold as I step out of the ring, placing my knife back in the sole of my boot. Cael stands, his expression the mirror of mine. I slip on my shirt before strapping on my weapons and shrugging the cloak over my shoulders. Cael and I freeze as Miss Mare steps in our path, the sizable bag of coins swaying in her hands. "I'm impressed," she praises as the crowd buzzes. My ears ring as I block out the chants.

"Mr. Vela is expecting us," I say matter-of-factly, holding her gaze. She nods but doesn't hand over my winnings.

"I heard a rumor he lies dead in the woods outside of Somereil, along with all his best mercenaries. Yet you were his prized possession and here you stand," she wonders aloud, shaking her head. "You know the rules, Little Prince, you can't play if your boss doesn't pay. And since he isn't here, well, I need to see the money before I can let you take the rest." Those aren't the rules. I don't have to pay because I won, but there is no rule against having to show what your boss would have paid if you lost.

"You'll have to take that up with Mr. Vela. We were given strict rules to abide by. Win and return the prize," I reply calmly. "And I saw him last week when he told me of my task, so unless he died during the short time I've traveled, I'm sure he's alive." She nods, watching me through slitted eyes as she extends her hand. I take the heavy pouch and toss it back to Cael. My brother slides it smoothly into his pocket. We step past Miss Mare and make for the ladder. Cael climbs first, the women guarding the exit keeping a step away.

"Oh, and Little Prince, I suggest you don't go running off, because I could use your talent," she dares ask, stepping closer. I want to shudder at the thought of working under Miss Mare. Vela was a monster, one I enjoyed seeing die. But even he is nothing compared to Miss Mare. You don't get to the top of the chain by being fair or kind.

"With all due respect, I have a boss and I don't think he would take kindly to you trying to buy me," I reply dryly, my stomach turning leaden. I pull myself up the first rung, moving as fast as I can without revealing my unease.

"Very well. But I suggest you consider my offer. Think on it for a day and maybe you'll come to your senses." I swallow hard as I climb, ignoring the numb pull of my injuries. Cael reads my face as we head out to the hall, keeping close to my side as he slides his blades into his hands. The big man standing like a sentinel at the door moves to the side as we pass, his face ghostly pale. I hit him quickly over the head and his eyes roll back as he falls to the ground.

"What is it?" Cael asks, fear rising in his voice.

"Miss Mare has men out there waiting for us. She knows Vela's dead." I fill him in quickly and unsheathe my slayers. My brother nods stoically, squaring his shoulders.

With a deep breath, I push open the door, blades raised. Fumbles leans on the alley wall, running his fingers over his bow. The quiver at his back hangs empty, not an arrow in sight. He stares at us for a long moment, his brows creasing as if he didn't truly believe we would make it out.

"By the Goddess," he whispers in disbelief as we rush out of the doorway. "Lady Death does like having you around."

"We need to move. Now!" Cael orders, shifting from foot to foot as his eyes scan the rooftops.

"Don't worry, it wasn't hard to take out a couple grunts stuck on guard duty," Fumbles assures, waving his hand through the air in dismissal. I shake my head.

"Were any of them Miss Mare's people?" I ask urgently. His jaw drops as he glances between us. Cael passes me a questioning glance. His surprise seems... forced. Exaggerated.

"Miss Mare is after you? As in *the* Miss Mare, the most gruesome boss in Dryden," he asks incredulously. I nod, watching him carefully. "We need to stay out of sight. I took out the regular guard. They all worked for Miss Mare, but so does half of Dryden." He shrugs and turns away. Fumbles leads us through the back alleys, climbing between buildings and over fences. I'm sure we pass the same row of houses twice, but it's dark and I can feel my body shutting down. So I follow my old friend through the tangle of streets, pushing on.

THIRTEEN

LEO

I grit my teeth against the pain as Cael finishes off the last stitch above my brow. My side throbs and muscles scream. I cracked a few ribs along with three knuckles during the fights. Add the pounding headache and I remember why I left the arenas to become a mercenary. Well, that and Vela's blackmail techniques. I silently thank my gift to heal twice as fast as the average person, or we'd be in an even more precarious situation than we already are.

Fumbles walks through the door and shuts it silently behind him. He went out minutes after we got back, telling us he had to meet the chemist about the medication. It's been two hours. "What took you so long?" I ask, staring him down as he throws his bow on the crooked table. Cael stares at him with a stone-cold face beside me as he wipes my blood from his hands.

"He wasn't there when I arrived. It took me a while to find him," he says, shrugging as he pulls over the other chair to take a seat. Cael passes me a distrustful look. Something isn't sitting right. Before he left, we asked about who this chemist was and where he was going. Fumbles told us he knew his whereabouts and assured us this man was *always* there.

"Right..." I say skeptically. "So, when can I go to get the medication?"

"Doc says he can get it in three days. We'll meet him at midnight." He pushes off the wall to scrounge through his pantry. He pulls out an old roll and scarfs it down before sitting back in his chair.

"You don't die, do you?" he asks suddenly, finishing off his bread. He's diverting the conversation. Cael folds up our supplies and tucks them back into his pack.

"No," I say flatly. "Lady Death likes to watch me from a distance instead of taking my hand." Fumbles nods slowly. I wonder if he's remembering how I used to say that death liked to shadow my steps.

"I would have loved to see those fights. The show you must have put on." He lets out a long whistle, shaking his head with a lopsided grin. "I don't think I've ever seen anyone who's had the skill to kill you."

"What are you suggesting?" Cael asks, putting his pack down. My brother crosses his arms across his chest as he spins the ring on his finger, his eyes hard as stone.

"Nothing. All I'm saying is that I've never seen our Blood Prince fight anyone better than him," he dismisses casually, motioning toward me.

"They weren't better, they're dead," I state dryly, my voice colder than a winter storm. His hands shoot up in forced innocence.

"You two seemed riled up all of a sudden," he says lightly, sneering at a loose thread in his shirt. "The little ones get on your nerves or something?" He points his thumb back at the small storage room where they're all sleeping soundly. They were awake when we came back, but when they saw we were safe, it took all of a second for them to start snoring. Well, all of them but Cass, who didn't stir. The thought that he might not make it three days hits me like a punch to the gut. I go to stand, wincing as searing pain rattles through my bones. Cael takes my arm as my vision comes in and out of focus, pulling me up. We walk to the next room without another word to Fumbles, settling in on either side of Cass. Cael falls asleep almost immediately, unable to keep his eyes open another moment. At least I can rest knowing a night's sleep will do some good for one of us.

I stretch my shoulder as I walk, testing out my side. The pain hasn't let up, but I've run out of time to let it heal any further. I can walk and wield a blade, so it'll have to do. I keep my eyes locked on Fumbles, tracking his movements. Cael and I weighed our options yesterday. We could attempt to go out alone, but there's no time to search.

"I know I'm a pretty sight, but I'd rather you stop watching me like I'm about to kill you," he says smugly from in front of me, peering over his shoulder. His tone is light, but his expression is strained, his eyes jumping at every sound.

"I'm staying on my toes," I reply, matching his steps. I should put more attention into making sure no one's stalking us. Walking Dryden's streets in the dark is no laughing matter.

"Come on, Leo, you can trust me. Like you said, I owe you my life, twice over. A blood debt," he explains airily, staring ahead as his shoulders bunch. I tighten the straps of the harness keeping my blades fastened to my body. I slip my dagger with copper inlaid in the hilt into my palm and hold it tight against my wrist.

We walk in a tense silence through the maze of streets, the black sky spitting cold drops of rain. Most of the streetlights are unlit and broken, condemning us to travel through damp darkness. Finally, we stop in front of a weathered building. The roof is caving in and the windows are smashed and boarded up. The little remnants of paint left on the outside are cracked and flaking, the wood underneath rotting as the mortar holding the stone together falls away. Fumbles walks up the crumbling steps and opens the door without knocking. It feels like there are dozens of eyes watching me as a sense of foreboding urges me to turn around. I take a moment to quickly scan the area. Cass doesn't have time for me to waste, making sure every corner I pass is safe. I push my rising dread away and follow Fumbles inside.

FOURTEEN

LEO

The small room is lit by a single oil lamp and the walls are lined with vials of all shapes and sizes. There's another door on the far end of the room behind the serving counter left slightly ajar. I clutch my dagger tightly in my hand as Fumbles locks the door behind me.

"Doc! I need the medication I asked for," he calls, picking a vial from the shelf and reading the tag before throwing it to the ground. A string of bangs ring from behind the door, sounding like an avalanche as more and more things tumble to the ground. An old man trips into the room, bottles rolling at his heels. His sharp eyes lock onto me as he wipes a layer of dust from his sleeve. I nearly gasp when I see him illuminated in the faint light.

"You're a child," he drawls, rolling the *r* off his tongue in the same uncommon way Ms. Ortaga did. The choppy words seem to bounce around in his mouth before leaving his lips. He scans me over with all-seeing eyes, making me shudder. "Too young for what you do."

"I was told you have medication for my brother?" I ask evenly, holding his gaze. He's the man I noticed at the fights who seemed much too old to frequent the arenas, and yet there he was, watching me like a predator. Now here he is again, those same eyes locked on mine. He nods quickly, plunging his hands into his pockets. He takes out a small bottle and cradles it in his palm. I step a few paces away from Fumbles, take the glass bottle, and hold it up to the light. The old man steps away suddenly, his face grave.

Fumbles moves at my back as the sound of a bowstring being pulled taught rings in my ears. My eyes bleed red as I duck and spin to face him. An arrow flies past my head, making a loud thunk as it hits the wall. I hold my dagger tight to his throat before wrenching the bow from his hands.

"No one's that good," Fumbles gawks, shaking his head.

"I trusted you with my *family*. What did you intend on doing?" I spit, my words dripping with cold contempt.

"The moment you killed Vela, you destroyed the only life I had, Hael. Killed *everything* I've worked for, begged, and scraped for. You didn't expect me to be happy about Vela being gone did you? Sure, he wasn't fun to be around but he got me good jobs. You *made* me go to Miss Mare. She was all too happy to talk after I informed her of your betrayal. Miss Mare told me she wanted to test you, so she let you in the arena. She wanted you on her team, or dead with the bounty in her hands and I needed a new boss, so we made a deal," he squeaks, his voice strangled as my blade bites into his skin.

"You never took out those guards, they let us pass," I realize aloud, the pieces shifting into place. "And when you went out after we had come back, it was to see Miss Mare."

"I should thank you. She gave me a prime mercenary position. Plus, I get twenty percent of the bounty on your head," he gloats, his eyes glowing. He'll do anything for coin. I hit him on the temple and his eyes roll back into his head as I fume. I stare at his crumpled body on the ground, reeling in my anger. I turn on the old man leaning slightly against the wall. He doesn't look scared, just... curious.

"Is this real medication, or a fake?" I press, taking a step toward him. He doesn't blink, seeming perfectly at ease.

"It's not real."

"Do you have the medication for Rackers?" I pull the pouch of coins out of my pocket. He nods, crossing his arms over his chest. "Go get it," I demand. He turns slowly and makes his way into the back room once more. He doesn't come back for a long moment, dropping and breaking at least a dozen things before he reappears.

"Give the child a spoonful every day. He'll get better in two weeks," he says, passing me a slightly larger bottle. I shake it, feeling the thick liquid slosh inside. I pocket it quickly and turn to the door. I hesitate as dread pools in my stomach. My hand hovers over the handle as the old man shifts behind me.

"Say what you're thinking." I order as my feet stay locked in place.

"If you go out there, you'll become another corpse for the body men to drag to the pits," he says easily. I catch the warning in his tone, hidden under a blanket of indifference. He's a withered old croon who has no reason to look out for me, and yet, my hand drops to my side. He wants to help me, and the Tominese are not generous, not without a reason.

"Who's out there?" I demand, turning back to face him, and indeed, find his face tight with worry.

"Who do you think, Prince of Blood?" he asks, nodding to

Fumbles on the ground. The answer hits me like a pound of stone. Miss Mare, and probably half the city who are sworn to her. I yank the bag of coins from my pocket and lob it through the air. He catches it deftly, as if he's done so hundreds of times before.

"How do I get out?" I demand, my nerves firing with adrenaline. The old man tosses the small bag in his hand before taking out a couple of gilded coins and holding them close to the lamplight. He nods slowly as he slips the pouch into his pocket.

"Upstairs," he says as if it were obvious, pointing to the roof. He's definitely a strange little man. He turns away, picks up the oil lamp, and walks toward the next room. I expect him to disappear, but he stops at the threshold and waves me forward, "Come now, heir of Blood. It won't be long until the arena beasts come knocking."

I follow him through the cluttered room, slipping through a tight passageway between piles of junk. There are strange metal devices, small piles of powders, bundles of bottles, and candle stubs stacked on top of it all, adding to the disorderly clutter. It's no wonder he made such a ruckus.

"Why are you helping me?" I ask skeptically as we come to a winding set of stairs hidden by the back wall. I have to duck to keep from smashing my head on the higher steps.

"I don't have a choice. Your life is important to many people you have yet to meet." At my confused expression, he sighs and waves a hand in dismissal. "I was a mercenary for many years, Blood Prince. Good people showed me there was still something inside of me to salvage, I just had to find it. Lady Death is merciful, and you still have time to prove yourself," he explains, his voice scraping something raw inside me. No one else has ever called the Goddess merciful.

"How do you know that?" I ask, my voice unwillingly

revealing how much I want to believe his words as the truth, even if I know they can't be. He shakes the bag of coins and continues up the stairs.

"You gave me everything you won to save another. You may do bad things, but there is good in there too. Let yourself see it, Blood Prince. There are people who will soon depend on you." He pushes through a hatch built directly into the roof. The stout man nods one last time as he steps aside. "But I'll give you some advice. You may be hard to kill, but you can die. You bleed like the rest of us, Prince of Blood."

"Thank you," I say, meaning it to my very core. It's the most kindness I've received from a stranger since I last saw Mrs. Ortaga.

I pull myself up onto the roof, silently easing the hatch shut. I lie on my stomach and crawl over to the edge of the building. After my eyes adjust to the bleak darkness and my stomach stops swirling from the height, it takes me all of a moment to detect the men and women positioned on the ground. The longer I watch, the more I see. There are people crouched along the street, hidden in shadowy corners, and peeking out from neighboring windows. There must be at least fifty fighters poised to attack. Thank the Goddess for whatever luck she decided to give me today.

I take a deep breath as I move to the far side of the roof. I ease myself onto my feet, breathing deeply as I keep my eyes trained ahead. I roll my shoulders, trying unsuccessfully to ease the tension building in my bones. I jump to the next building, my stomach twisting as my feet leave the ground and hit the wooden shingles soundlessly. I repeat the cycle over and over, pinning my gaze to the next rooftop. Even though the danger is behind me, with every step I feel the noose tighten around my throat.

I burst through the back door of Fumbles's house with so

much force I almost fall over. "We have to go, now!" I order urgently, my head still spinning from taking the roofs. Cael's face darkens as he catches my expression. I drain my eyes quickly and stare down at myself. My side throbs from the climb, but for once, there isn't blood splattered on my clothes.

"Did you get the medication?" Cael asks, his face stern. I nod and hand him the bottle. "Fumbles tried to kill you?" he guesses, voice tight as a wire. I nod, hate washing through me at the mention of his name. It's not only directed at the person I once called my friend.

"He planned to sell me out after I told him you killed Vela. He went to Miss Mare." My brother's jaw tics, his eyes on fire. "Her people were waiting outside. I got out through the roof." After a moment, his expression slacks in relief.

"Let's get out of this wretched city," he mumbles, running a hand over his face before heading toward the storage room where the boys sleep.

I give Cass his first dose of medication, sliding the thick serum down his throat. He doesn't flinch as I get him to drink a spoonful of water afterward. Cael wakes the boys and starts packing up our few belongings. Altair is up in seconds, yawning as he tries to pick Saiph up without waking her. I step over Cass to stand before Antares. I shake his shoulder, and with all the grace of a frog, my little brother groans, and slaps away my hand. I grab his arms and pull him to his feet, holding him upright.

"Up, Antares," I order, forcing myself not to lose my nerve. He nods slowly and finds his balance before starting to roll up his blanket. As they finish up, I raid the rest of Fumbles's house, scrounging through cabinets and drawers. Stealing his food, medications, and clothes barely takes the edge off of the betrayal still pulling at my insides, but I can't disappear without leaving him a message. When we're all out of the house, I hit my dagger against a piece of flint, throwing sparks onto a pile of letters I found in the cabinet. I throw them into the house once they catch and listen as the wood floors start to burn. No one deceives the Blood Prince.

CHAPTER

FIFTEEN

LEO

We get out of the city as fast as we can, taking the main roads. The air seems too heavy, like it's trying to slow us down. Thankfully the stretcher we left at the forest line is still there, covered in leaves and stained with mud. We place another blanket down before laying Cass on top, Cael taking the front as I hold the rear. We move in silence throughout the night; the only sound is Antares's occasional complaining as he drags his feet.

We finally stop when the boys' legs start to shake and they are no longer able to hold themselves up. Three days after we leave Dryden, Cass starts to regain consciousness. I've never been so relieved as when he turned his head away when I tried to get him to swallow another mouthful of the medication.

A week later, my youngest brother managed to walk half the day before lying back down on the stretcher and falling asleep. I hold on tight to the slight smiles we get out of him,

Antares, Altair, and Saiph. Cael rarely smiles anymore, his nightmares and memories sitting heavily on his shoulders. Hunger silences our every need to talk as food starts to become scarce the closer we get to the Barren Lands, draining our energy. Seeing a glimmer of happiness or glimpse of a laugh has become as likely as finding any sign of civilization in this unending wood.

We walk for two more weeks before the chirping of the birds vanishes completely. I don't register the intensity of the silence until Cael stops, staring up at the trees. The sound of silence so complete that I can hear my heart beating in my chest.

"Why does it feel like... nothing?" Altair asks too loudly. I wince at the rasp of my brother's unused voice.

"I don't know," I whisper as a shiver of unease runs down my spine. We continue forward hesitantly, listening to the brush crunch under our feet. Even the wind is missing from this stretch of woods. Everything in me screams to run, to turn and leave this unsettling place, but we push on. The trees get bigger as we continue, the leaves a green so deep they blend in with the dark at night. I walk right into the empty stretcher as Cael stops suddenly, his eyes pinned forward.

"What's wrong?" I ask him softly, unease settling heavily on my shoulders.

"I don't know," he breathes, shaking his head. "Let's keep going." I nod once as the boys wait for us to take the lead. Something cracks behind us and a scream cuts through the hollow air. I turn on my heels and drop the empty stretcher to take my slayers into my hands. I sigh as Antares pulls himself up shakily.

"I'm fine," he whispers, wiping off his knees. Cael comes around him and stares at the spot where Antares tripped.

"What?" My brother's eyes go wide as he crouches down

and starts digging in the dirt. He pulls out a long shard of white wood. No, not wood, bone. He drops it and jumps away as he wipes his hands feverishly on his shirt.

"Bones," he confirms, meeting my gaze. I look around and my stomach drops. Thick shards of sun-bleached bones lie strewn across the forest floor as far as I can see. Cass jumps and runs to my side after seeing a half-buried skull lying beside his foot.

"That explains why it feels like we're in a graveyard," I force, my voice hoarse. The bodies of the enemies who died in the war were left where they fell in the woods. *These were the Death Dancers,* I realize with a start. I squint as I try to take in how far the bones reach. Thousands died and were left here to rot. I can feel death hanging in the air, weighing me down.

We tread carefully, maneuvering through the ancient graveyard. The further we push, the more remains we find. Sometimes the bones are in piles stacked high enough to graze the leaves while others lie alone, half buried in the ground, cracked and weathered.

We have food, but none of us are hungry. We sleep fitfully in the trees, not wanting to rest among the dead. After four days of travel, the bones finally become more sparse and the woods come back to life with the rustle of the wind and chirping of the birds. It becomes easier to breathe, the eerie feeling of death slowly fading. Still, none of us speak, becoming as silent as Cass.

The sound of flowing water stops us in our tracks after hours of hiking. Cael looks back at me as relief plays across his face. We drop the stretcher holding Cass's pack and move toward the sound, desperate for a sign that we're getting close. Cael lifts Cass up onto his shoulders as I unhook Saiph's carrier and hold her in my arms. We all make our way toward the susurration sighing through the trees like a ghost calling our names.

When the wide expanse of blue comes into view, all I can do is stare. I let out a sigh as a cool breeze plays in my hair. It's beautiful. The sparkling fresh water stretches for kilometers and reflects the cloudless blue sky above. It's been too long since we've seen more than a pinprick of the sky through the trees. I drop my bag and put Saiph down, Altair taking her hand. I shrug off my shirt and throw my boots to the side. The icy water bites at my skin and my teeth clench to stop from chattering. I didn't plan on going all the way in, but I continue walking until I'm deep enough to completely submerge myself under the easy current. Layers of dirt, blood, and grime peel off my skin with each wave, leaving me feeling better than I have in weeks.

"What are you all staring at?" I ask, turning back to my brothers. Within seconds, they've discarded their bags and are running into the water, Antares throwing off his shirt only for it to land in the wake. For the first time in a long time, we all smile, and I tuck away the glimmer of happiness deep within me.

We spend the better part of the afternoon soaking up the sun and lying in the waves, splashing each other with fistfuls of water. After more than an hour of spotting and stalking fish in the river, Cael and I manage to catch three with our bare hands. I would rather have stayed in the river all day, but the prospect of having a good meal lures me out. Cael follows me as I head to our camp, trusting the boys to watch Saiph and come in soon.

Cael quickly lights a small fire as I gather the tools to clean the fish. After adding a few thicker branches to the flames, we move back to the rocky shore. Cael takes on the task of cleaning a small fish with dark-red scales while I start on an opalescent one the length of my forearm while a third one sits between us. Every few minutes, my brother stops to watch the forest, his eyes flashing as he tenses.

"What?" I ask after the fourth time. Cael's knife hovers over a filet, the meat momentarily forgotten.

"I feel like someone's here," he breathes as he turns to scan the forest, squinting to see further than possible. My stomach twists as my grip tightens around my blade.

"Doing what?"

"Watching. Waiting and watching. Like they're hunting us," he says as dread rolls off him in waves.

"I'm sure it's an animal," I dismiss hesitantly, following his gaze to the woods. Cael is never wrong. The senses he learned when he was young have proven themselves time and time again to be correct. But he can't be right. Not here, not now.

"Maybe," he admits as he shakes his head slowly. "But I don't think so... I can't put my finger on it, but it feels like there are eyes on us. Not like a predator stalking, or hunting. They're just... observing." Goose bumps roll down my arms. I turn around and try to push away the rising dread, but the feeling of being watched is impossible to shake.

We decided it would be best if we took a day to recover before pushing on. The sun is almost at its peak in the sky as I walk through the dense greenery with Altair by my side. I weave my throwing knife through my fingers, searching for the game that will serve as a well-needed meal. We are all thinner than when we left home, our bodies slowly stripping the muscle from our bones. We didn't have a lot in Somereil, but at least we had some diversity in the food we ate. Here, we eat whatever meat we hunt and fruit we can scavenge. We usually have enough small game to keep us fed, whether it be hare or squirrel, but edible plants have been particularly challenging to find. We used to know what plants were safe to ingest and where to find them, but here we've forgone eating different berries more than once because we couldn't tell if they were poisonous.

"There's a nest," Altair points out, staring up the tallest tree in sight. My stomach rolls as I follow his gaze. A bundle of leaves and sticks sits perched at the top of the towering maple.

"You are not climbing that, Altair," I warn, my conviction wavering as I swallow. We need food, and as much of it as we can get. Who knows how much longer we'll be traveling.

"Come on, I can do it. Dad used to tell me that I was climbing before I could speak," he insists. After a long moment of weighing my options, I nod, giving in. Our father used to love telling stories of Altair's fearlessness. My brother flies up the tree and cheers as he pockets several eggs before turning to come back down. He pauses, leaning into the air to survey the horizon.

"Leo, you need to come up here," he shouts.

"Altair, I'm not climbing the tree," I reply, hoping he won't persist.

"Come up, I want you to see this," he says, not bothering to glance down at me. The longer I watch him, the taller the tree appears. I take a deep breath to steady my racing heart and start to climb. My breath comes in short gasps the higher I push, my chest constricting with every step. It takes me almost twice as long to get to the top as Altair, but I make it, clutching tight to the tree trunk as it sways in the slight wind.

"What was so important I had to..." The words get lost as I take in the thrilling view. The Vallan River seems to stretch for days, its waters sparkling like a path of cut diamonds. Along the northern horizon stretches various chains of mountains so tall they pierce the clouds. I squint toward the east and trace the Vallan with my gaze. I imagine seeing it from even higher above and watching the river merging into the bay and then to the Bronze Sea beyond. I think of the letter tucked away in my pack and almost laugh. My mother's last wish for us was to get to the bay. We're so close I can practically feel the sense of true freedom closing in around me.

"Is that where we're going?" Altair asks, leaning dangerously into the air. I nod, reaching out to pull him back toward the thicker part of the branch. "There's a meadow not far ahead. Looks like berry bushes on the outskirts," Altair says, pulling me from my thoughts before I can actually scan the land. He points to a clearing adjacent to where the river thins and something stirs in me as I survey the area. It's perfectly round, like it was carved out of the woods by a skilled hand. As I continue to scan the area I catch sight of a line of trees jutting south from the clearing and I can't help but feel as if a path had been laid out for us beneath the canopy.

"Come on, we need to tell them!" Altair says, shaking out of his trance. I glance at the ground and catch a flash of something out of the corner of my eye. I grab my brother's hand before he can begin his descent, his brows creasing with confusion.

"Did you see that?" I whisper, scanning the brush. He freezes and follows my gaze. "Let me go first," I order, taking a blade into my hand. I climb down silently, the pressure on my throat easing from the descent. I jump to the ground as I spin my throwing knife through my fingers and hold a slayer in my other hand at the ready. Someone's here, I can feel it. Within seconds something moves from behind a bush and I let my blade fly. A small gasp rings through the trees. I signal Altair to stay put and the sound of steel being drawn comes from where he sits perched in the tree. I push aside the branches and stop when I see my throwing knife embedded in the grain of a gnarled oak, dripping blood. I pull it free and curse under my breath.

"Do you think it was an animal?" Altair asks warily as he creeps up behind me and takes in the blood-spattered trunk. It's a possibility, one I want desperately to believe. I wipe off my steel and place it back with its sisters as a small voice rings in my ears. *Cael's senses are never wrong. You are not alone.*

CHAPTER
SIXTEEN

"Did you see any cities?" Cael asks as we walk, crossing his arms over his chest. The coils of his hair are pulled in all the wrong ways and his eyes are hollow and sleep-lined from the nap Altair had woken him from. But underneath it all, I know our tale has ignited a new spark of hope in him.

"No, but I didn't exactly look for any." My brother stares at me incredulously.

"So, you're telling me you swallowed your irrational fear of heights only to stare at the big mountains and a shiny river?" he jokes, trying not to smile. I shove him but can't think of a retort worth saying. I had the jab coming.

"The more I think about it, the more it occurs to me that the Barren Lands are the perfect place to keep a country hidden and protected. It's almost as big as Tominay and it's protected on all sides," I say, changing the subject. I think of Mum's letters tucked away neatly in my pack. *Follow the Vallan River to the Bronze Sea; you'll find people before you reach the ocean, but do not stop until you reach the bay.* Cael nods, his face turning grave.

"And you're sure the blood you drew belonged to an animal?" he asks, staring into the woods. He shakes himself and focuses back on me.

"No one could follow us all the way out here. And if it wasn't an animal, it can only be the people we're searching for," I say with less conviction than I mean to.

"Then the first thing we did to the people who, may I remind you, we're supposed to align with, is attack them. We may have unknowingly destroyed our chances of them being hospitable," he observes dryly. I wince. Maybe once I would have laughed, but my nerves are wound so tight even trying to smile seems like asking a horse to fly.

"You're unnaturally chipper today, brother," I say sarcastically, my voice sounding oddly deflated. "Maybe eating some of the berries from the clearing will cheer you up. Are you sugar deprived?" Cael rolls his eyes and huffs a laugh.

"We could all use a treat." I nod. Spending a day at the river was nice, but it failed to provide any of the foods we need to keep us away from scurvy.

It takes us another two days to get to the clearing. When we arrive, the wind off the Vallan rustles the tall grass, only adding to the peaceful feel of the space. I take an easing breath, allowing myself a moment of calm instead of worrying about what our next threat will be. No one says a word as we take in our new surroundings, the sweet, cloying smell of summer berries and flowers filling the air. It seems so tranquil, and yet Cael looks like he's ready to jump out of his skin, his hands hovering at the ready by his sides. I nudge him with my elbow and his fingers flinch instinctively toward the dagger at his hip.

"Sorry," he mutters, following the boys as they run into the field. Saiph pulls on my hand, wanting to join them. I let her go and watch as she runs through the overgrown meadow, her dark-gold hair appearing and disappearing in the tall grass. I make my way after them as the urge to smile overwhelms me.

The sweet fruits taste like childhood happiness. Their tanginess strips away the pain of weeks of peeling meat off leftover bones and eating whatever edible plant or roots we found. We devour the berries as if they were air to a drowning man, our faces and fingers stained red with the juices.

"I don't think I've ever eaten anything so good," Antares says, rolling onto his back. I bark a laugh, unable to speak. We ate way too much. I push myself up, thinking of the letter carefully stowed away in my pack. I'll give them a place where they can have this every day.

"Yeah, I…" The words die in the air as Cael scrambles to his feet with his dagger in hand.

"What is it?" I ask, pulling out my own blades. Something moves across the forest line. I zero in on the spot as I catch a glint of light reflecting from the other side of the meadow. The longer I watch, the more movement I see. I scoop Saiph into my arms as the fear sets into my bones. "Run."

Together, we sprint toward the forest line. Arrows begin whizzing past our heads and landing in the dirt at our feet. Cael pulls Cass beside him, forcing him to run faster.

"Don't run straight!" he yells. At his words, we all move in a zigzag, running from left to right as each step brings us closer to the woods. Suddenly the arrows stop, Cael halting in time. I don't have to turn to him to know why. Dozens of soldiers stand like a wall in front of us, some clad in a thick gray livery, others dressed in black and dark green. The King's Elite and Obsidian Guard. Half of the line hold nocked bows and the rest have their blades drawn. We're surrounded by the king's best warriors.

I try desperately to think of a way out, but with every

second that passes, my panic only grows. I reject every idea for escape that comes to mind, all of them too dangerous. I can't risk my family, but there is no way that all of us are getting out of here alive, not this time. This is it. This is how it ends, and just when I thought we had gotten away... but maybe they still can. I straighten as I decide on a plan, one I know they'll resent me for forever.

"Don't move!" a high voice yells from the line. I put my hand holding the knife up and instinctively angle my body to protect Saiph. "Drop your weapon!" I do as they say. Cael does the same behind me, his dagger falling to the dirt. I glance back at him as he steps in front of Cass and Antares.

"I am the Blood Prince. You want me, not them." I project my voice, forcing my expression into one of cold calm. I bend slowly to put Saiph down.

"Don't move!" they demand. I freeze, not wanting Saiph to get hurt.

"I'm putting my sister down." They stay silent. I gently let Saiph's feet touch the ground as tears run down her face, her cheeks still stained with the remnants of the berries. Cael calls her over, but she clings to my leg. My brother slowly comes to my side with his hands raised. He takes Saiph—screaming and kicking—into his arms. He holds my gaze, his worry bone deep. "Take her away," I urge him, but he stays put.

"Leo—"

"You must stay silent!" One of the soldiers demands. We both flinch.

"Go," I whisper under my breath. He hesitates, shaking his head as he holds his free hand in the air. I close my eyes in relief as he finally moves backward.

"If I come, you have to leave them alone," I demand more calmly than I feel.

"We can do no such thing; the boy is wanted as well. Leo

Hael, under the decree of His Majesty, Sovereign of the Tominese People, King Uldrus, you are sentenced to immediate death without plea for your crimes against Tominay." I nod solemnly in response as their words hang in the air.

"Will you honor a death wish?" I ask, my blood chilling with foreboding. One of the boys tries to move toward me, but the arrow that lands at his feet stops him short. They don't say a word, yet I can feel them begging. "Will you?" I repeat.

After some rustling in the lines and a hushed conversation, a deeper voice calls out, "What do you ask of the Lady?"

"That you leave them alone," I don't dare gesture my sibling's way, keeping deathly still. "I made them come with me, they have done nothing wrong. I made the other boy you look for do what he did. He is a child I commanded to stir up trouble, nothing more. I wish to take the penalty for his crime and for them to continue on to Anateya without being brought back to Tominay." The whispers start again as my hands start to shake.

"We will uphold your wish and they will not be harmed." A deep voice this time. I nod. I can't say I don't deserve this. Maybe it won't be such a bad thing if I'm not around to burden them.

"How did you find us?" I ask, taking a step forward.

"We tracked you," the high voice says eerily. Liar. What are they doing out here? Does it even matter? My brothers call out for me at my back. This is the first time Cael won't tell them it's going to be all right. I take another step forward. I can hear Cael fighting the boys, struggling to stop them from running to me.

"Leo, stop!" Altair sobs.

I don't turn to face him as I speak. "Altair, stay where you are! You have to be safe. You have to survive," I say, confidence sown deep into my voice. I stand taller and take another step forward.

My courage disappears in seconds as Cael calls my brother's name and I catch a flash of gold out of the corner of my eye. Altair runs in front of me, his face set. My eyes bleed red as I hear arrows released from their bows. I grab Altair and pull him against me, forcing him to turn away as I use my body as a shield. I feel my skin tear and bones crush, but no pain arises as the arrows rip mercilessly through me.

When the firing stops, I open my arms. Altair looks up, tears streaking down his face. "Are you hurt?" I ask, taking in the splotches of blood covering his shaking body.

"No..." His words get lost in a sob as he watches me. I breathe wetly as I realize that the blood covering him isn't his, it's mine. It's all mine.

"I need you to keep living," I say. Altair shakes his head as I start to stand, his eyes overflowing with tears as they lose their gold sheen. I raise my eyes and see Cael pinning Antares, Cass, and Saiph to the ground. No growing splotches of red appear on their clothes. *They're safe.* I take a deep breath as I pull Altair to his feet.

"No..." he repeats, struggling against my wavering strength.

"I'm not asking you to do this, I'm telling you. You'll never forgive yourself if you ignore me and it's my last wish." He stops struggling, sniffling. I can see him fighting against the will to stay with me, but in the end, he does as I say. I don't turn, not wanting to die looking at the soldiers who will cause my family so much pain.

I take a shaky step backward, keeping my eyes on my siblings as tears run down their faces. "Shoot!" An arrow crushes into my shoulder. I waver but keep on my feet. I won't let my family see me fall. "Shoot!" Another hits my arm. I smile sadly at my brothers as Cael pulls Altair down, protecting him under his arm. Let them see I'm all right, that this is for the best. This is the time Lady Death chose for me, to save me from performing my worse deed. "Shoot! Shoot! Shoot!" I don't fall. Lady Death will have to do better than a few arrows if she wishes to fell me. I can feel her hovering over me, wondering if I'll reach out and beg for her mercy. She feels like she does in my terrors when I die like those soldiers long ago. "Shoot!" The final arrow hits me square in my spine, seizing my body. I look to my side as I collapse, hoping to finally see Lady Death's hand reach out to take mine. People surrounded by a searing white light stand across the river, their voices blurring with the rest. They aren't Lady Death, her soothing shadow's nowhere in sight. I fall for years and seconds, time twisting and breaking. The moment my head hits the ground, like a star crashing to the earth, my vision goes black, and the light burns out, leaving only the scarring wails of my brothers to haunt my dying thoughts.

PART TWO
ILLENA

SEVENTEEN

CAEL

It's so dark. I hold my head in my hands as I try to calm my thoughts, but they whirl faster than a storm. We finally find a place where we should be happy and Leo's not here to see it. Worst of all, they've locked me away in a windowless, dark room. A *cage*. It brings back too many haunting memories of my childhood. I push away the excruciating flashes as I rock back and forth on my squeaking cot. No matter how many days they keep me imprisoned here, the walls keep closing in, suffocating me. My mind imagines my parents walking through the door with a belt or a bottle or a pair of shining brass knuckles, their eyes glazed and smiles cruel. But the worst was when they'd walk in with nothing at all, spinning their words into my mind and creating monsters out of the darkness. I close my eyes, reminding myself of the good to fight away the demons.

It was a miracle sent from the Lady when the gold-eyes

found us in the clearing. They made the soldiers stand down with nothing but a wave of their hands. I thought them a threat when they came toward Altair. My mind was shattered into so many pieces I couldn't figure out what to think, my instincts were only to protect. I pushed the boys behind my back, picking my dagger up from the ground in one hand as I held Saiph tightly in the other arm. It took three moves for the gold-eyed man to disarm me and another two to send me sprawling to the ground. A gold-eyed woman tore Saiph from my arms as another took Altair's face in her hands and examined his eyes, which had gone back to glowing the same gold as theirs. My breathing wouldn't settle as I tried to make sense of what was going on. They grabbed my sibling's wrists and spoke between themselves as they stared at the bands the kids have carried since birth. The boys calmed as the gold-eyed people spoke to them, but I couldn't hear their words through the ringing in my ears.

"Cael, we found them. They're like us," Antares said as tears flowed freely down his flushed cheeks. I don't think I said anything as more of the gold-eyed people crossed the river and amassed on the shores. My shock was so thick it was palpable. One of them had taken Cass by the hand while another was speaking with the soldiers that had been shooting at us mere moments before. Their faces blurred together as I looked around, but all I could think about was Leo. Leo... Altair tried to pull me up, but my eyes shifted to my wounded brother lying facedown in the dirt. A gold-eye went to him, flipping him over without a sliver of care. A sob escaped my throat as the arrows snapped under his weight. I let Altair pull me up and stumbled over to him. The gold-eye picked up Leo's wrist, examining the bands and numbers as they had done with Saiph and the boys. Confusion was stark on the man's face as he stared. He threw Leo's hand to the ground and walked away without care, calling to his companions. I didn't ask him for help, my voice couldn't have scraped its way out of my throat even if I had tried. I fell to my knees before my brother and shook his shoulders furiously, hoping by some miracle he would swat away my hand and make a joke about how I was worrying for nothing. But my brother didn't move, his shattered bones grinding against one another at the movement.

My heart sank so deep I could no longer feel its racing beat. When Leo passes out, he has terrors. Even when he was hurt, he struggled in unconsciousness. But he wasn't moving. I tried desperately to find a pulse, but there was so much blood. Too much blood. I couldn't tell if his chest rose and fell. I couldn't tell if he was alive. I tried to find where he was bleeding the most, but he was swimming in a pool of red. For once, I didn't know what to do. I stared and tried desperately to think of something, anything to help him. I didn't believe, couldn't believe he was dead. Leo always survived. It didn't matter if he'd been stabbed, gutted, or shot, he always made it back to us.

"Cael, do something," Altair had begged. All three of the boys stood over me, fear etched deep into their faces. I slumped onto my heels, not knowing what to say as I raised my blood-covered hands. I shook my head slowly. "Do something," Altair repeated weakly. I looked to the side and my eyes caught on the Tominese soldiers. The boys' gazes followed mine.

"They killed him," Antares whispered, his voice broken. I stood up, pulling him toward me as he sobbed over Leo's lifeless body. Cass shook against me as I pulled them away.

"You killed him. You killed him! You killed my brother!"

Altair screeched, the sound so guttural it sounded like his vocal cords had snapped. He started toward the soldiers, catching their attention. The King's Elite, Obsidian Guard, and gold-eyed people watched stoically as he screamed, blaming them, cursing them for what they had taken from us. I pulled Altair toward me by the shoulder and took his face in my hands, forcing him to meet my eyes. His words caught on sobs as he crumpled, the anger and hate falling away to sharp grief. I took Saiph from his arms and held him while he wept, held all three of them tightly as we stared at our bloodied brother. I couldn't tear my eyes away from him and the arrows sticking out of his back.

Minutes later, a man with shining silver eyes came to talk to Altair. I tried to speak, but he wouldn't listen, barely glancing my way.

"You, your brothers and sister are going to come with us," the man said to Altair. He put his hands out, finally meeting my gaze. "You may return to your kin. We thank you for bringing these children home." He did not bother to hide the scowl smeared on his face as he spoke, like it disgusted him to have to deal with me.

"These are *my* siblings. If I'm not going then they aren't either," I rasped, my voice low and rough. His brows knit together in confusion as I held Saiph tighter. He took a step toward me, but Altair stepped between us.

"We aren't going anywhere without him," he asserted, his voice ringing with finality. The man watched us for a long moment, noting the way Cass hid behind my leg and how Antares clung to my side. He left and furiously conferred with a woman standing close by. She couldn't have been much older than me. Her upturned eyes were cold as ice and her blue-black hair was severely cut above her shoulders. I didn't miss the sharp glare she gave me before the man came back and sat us down by the river. Her presence demanded respect and radiated power, but I didn't care, my brother was dead.

The girl with cold eyes spoke to the Captain of the Obsidian Guard. It quickly became a one-sided screaming match, the captain raging about taking the body. Leo's body.

"You are the ones who violated the treaty by killing a blood-eye on Illenian soil. By that action, every one of your soldiers' lives is forfeit," the girl said, her eyes like raging rivers of gold. "You should be quite lucky if I decide not to call in my warriors waiting in the city to rid you of your heads. The treaty clearly declares that we have all the right to kill you while you are on *our* lands." Her voice was calm, but it cut deeply and the captain paled in response. He backed off quickly with his head inclined in respect. The captain froze as she took a step closer and whispered into his ear. His eyes immediately went wide as his face paled to a ghostly color. The girl grabbed his arm and twisted it behind his back before pushing him toward his lines. The gold-eyed people snickered as the King's Elite and Obsidian Guard snarled openly. "As a reminder of who you're dealing with, captain," she purred before turning away.

The gold-eyed people huddled around Leo, some working to stanch the bleeding while others argued and pointed at his wrist. They all wore gold armbands around their left arms, marking them as people of importance. They moved crates across the river as I watched them dispute over Leo's body. I didn't pay attention to what might have been in the boxes. My brother was dead. Suddenly, their conversation stopped as a man with jet-black hair tied at the nape of his neck and golden-brown skin approached. The group lowered their gazes in respect as they placed a hand over their hearts. He was unmistakably their superior, his posture pin straight and gaze piercing. With three words the group dispersed, brought back a stretcher, and carried my brother away. They loaded him onto a barge with little care and set off across the river. I tried to get up, to stop them from taking him, but two gold-eyed soldiers forced me back to the ground with hateful smirks. I begged them to let us go to Leo, but the soldiers stood as sentinels and ignored our pleas, leaving us in the dark.

CHAPTER
EIGHTEEN

CAEL

After what seemed like hours, a silver-eyed girl with long wavy black hair brought us water and bread. She distinctly resembled the man who had ordered Leo be brought across the river, her skin the same golden tone and high cheekbones to match. But where his demeanor was rigid and cold, hers seemed warm and kind, her round face wearing a welcoming expression. She smiled as she walked over, her eyes showing equal sadness and intrigue. She spoke to me, asked who we were and where we came from. I could not respond. The boys were in no better condition when she tried to speak to them either. Cass had fallen into a restless sleep minutes later as Antares sat heavy-lidded beside him, their cheeks still stained with tears.

The sky turned orange as they led us to a rowboat, as if the world was burning in time with the growing hole in my chest. It scorched everything that had once brought me joy, turning the bond I cherished to ash. Nothing looked quite as bright. As the boat approached the shore, one of the gold-eyes rowing told the boys that our destination was a city called Wate, on the western end of the island. Surrounded by forests, fields, and small farming towns, this was to be their new home, a place filled with people like them.

A group of people with silver eyes bright against the darkening night waited for us where the wide trail we trekked ended and a city began. The man who gave the order to take Leo away was the one to make the introductions, of course, after introducing himself. He was the High Lord of Wate, and we were to address him as so. Among the people waiting for us, we learned were Saiph and the boys' grandparents. Their father's parents, so we were told. Their resemblance to the boys and Saiph was uncanny, the shape of their faces and noses identical. The kids' grandparents were cold, seeming to be hewn from stone, but they managed small smiles when they saw the boys. They kept quiet as I held Saiph, ignoring my presence altogether. The boys grinned wider than I've ever seen, laughing and crying as a whirlwind of emotions took over. I was as happy as I could be for the boys and Saiph, but I felt nothing but hate from their grandparents as they watched me holding their granddaughter and standing among their grandsons.

We walked together through the sprawling city composed of hundreds of buildings arranged in neat lines. It was hard not to balk as we continued through the pristine streets. The shops and homes were nothing special, each identical to the next, but I couldn't believe a society this size had been kept secret for over a century. The Barren Lands were supposed to be abandoned, left to the ghosts of the Death Dancers. I don't know what I imagined, but it wasn't this. I expected a few villages, but nothing so... permanent. A new wave of grief hit me as I realized that we didn't have our packs. We left everything across the river.

The grandparents explained all sorts of things about the city as we walked. They pointed out the extensive complex made of large buildings connected by sky walkways named the Council building, the various markets, the Academy the boys would soon attend, and everything in between. Antares asked question after question as Altair and Cass gaped.

The first words the grandparents spoke to me were a command before we entered their beautiful house. "Give us the ring." I didn't know what to do, what to say. "It does not belong to you." I froze as my mind reeled.

"The man who raised me gave me this when I chose to become part of their family," I explained, my voice low. The ring was the only thing I had left, the only thing that brought me comfort, but they didn't care. The soldiers shadowing the High Lord grabbed my wrist and yanked it off, nearly pulling off my arm. The High Lord grinned victoriously as the grandfather sneered at the ring he held in his palm. I hated them in that moment, we'd not been here a day and both my brother and ring were gone, stolen away.

The Hael house was bigger than the others, made of gray stone and white wood paneling. I handed Saiph over to Altair as their grandparents showed the boys their bedrooms and ordered me to stay in the foyer. I thought they wanted to speak to me, maybe take some time to learn who we were. How wrong I was. When they came back, there was no room for pleasantries. The grandparents immediately directed me to the kitchen through a door on the far wall of a sitting room. As we walked by, they barely passed a glance at the withered lady laboring over a boiling pot, her graying hair tied into a tight knot at the back of her head. The grandfather pried open a heavy door joined to the kitchen with a sizable lock sitting below the handle. The walls of the closet-sized space were made of thick slabs of stone, not a window nor furniture piece to be seen. I was staring into a pantry. A small, dark pantry. I turned as my heartbeat picked up and my hands began to shake with fear. I tried to retreat, but he shoved me in, the door slamming shut behind me. The click of the lock bounced in my head as my mouth went instantly dry and my thoughts started to swim. I pounded on the door for hours as my head screamed in the strangling darkness.

They gave me food scraps and a cup of murky water at night, only opening the door enough to slide the tray through. I jumped up from my corner, racing to get to the opening, but it closed before my eyes could catch the light. I rammed my shoulder into the door until my entire body throbbed, the sound of my pleas echoing off the walls. The room smelled stale, but it was the sharp tang of blood and waste and the sound of chains ringing in my ears that overwhelmed my mind.

The door opened again hours, maybe days later. I didn't move from my corner, my body frozen in place and eyes closed tight against the light filtering in. The scraping sound of the trays being swapped filled the room. The door shut and the lock clicked into place, but this time the light remained. Dimmed, yes, but it was still there. When I opened my eyes, a sob escaped my throat as I beheld a candle burning at my feet. I picked it up and drank in the warmth, using the light to chase away the monsters. I stared at the flame until the candle was nothing more than a stub, not caring as the scalding wax burned my skin.

I dreaded the moments those small flames would begin to flicker, but whenever the light would finally fade, another lit candle would appear. Finally, I convinced myself that I would face the darkness and keep my eyes open to see who left the candles. But the memories felt too real as I waited. I could feel the chains binding my wrist to the wall. Brass knuckles pounding against my body, steel and glass slashing my skin apart. I relived it all until the moment the door opened and little hands slid the new tray along the ground. Another pair of familiar hands placed the candle down and took the old one away. I raised my eyes and met my younger brother's gaze.

"They wouldn't give you light, and we know you don't like being alone in the dark. Grandmother and Grandfather don't know," Antares whispered, his voice soft as he analyzed me. I realized how terrible I must have appeared, because both him and Cass seemed to break as they watched me. I pushed myself up, my legs screaming in protest and wrapped them both in my arms.

"Thank you," I rasped. I pulled away to study them as my throat began to close. They both looked better than they had in, well, forever. They had obviously been eating three good meals a day and getting decent sleep. "You're both doing all right?" I asked. They nodded. Antares vividly explained how they each had a bed and had already made friends at the Academy. Footsteps sounded outside and without a goodbye, they were gone, leaving me with nothing but the sound of my uneven breathing and the light of the flickering candle for company.

After a few more days, the grandparents barged into the room. I quickly snuffed out the flame and hid away the evidence of my only weapon against the darkness. I squinted against the light that poured through the open door as they shoved in two rusty cots. No one said a word as the grandfather took my shoulders and hauled me off the ground, unexpectedly strong for such an old man.

"You will be let out for one hour," he sneered, wrinkling his nose as he dragged me out of the room. It was the first time I had seen natural light in over a week. Every sliver of fear festering inside like an open wound melted away and left a gaping hole of grief in its place.

After that they let me out of the pantry cell for a single hour a day. I counted the seconds until I was dragged out of the shadows. They started leaving a bucket of water and a washcloth as well. I laughed at the thought of how bad I smelled that they would give me water to wash but not a lamp to see. They found the candles my brothers had been leaving me and took it upon themselves to bring my food personally from then on, leaving me vulnerable to the darkness once again. This was supposed to be a safe haven, but it felt more like a living, breathing hell. I held on to the thought of the next time I would see my siblings, and used it to keep away the demons, shining an invisible light. The boys and Saiph spent all the time they could by my side, recounting stories of their new home and friends. Something broke inside me even further when I heard the chorus of their voices together, Saiph even chiming in. For the first time in a while, I felt at ease, maybe even happy.

The girl I had seen who resembled the High Lord was named Byrne and I soon learned she is indeed his daughter, second in line to his throne. She's come to see us outside a few times, her easy smile unfaltering. She took her time to explain everything, the first person from this place to give me the courtesy of knowledge. I asked her questions of my own, mostly about the boys and what exactly happened when they found us. Her answers danced around the truth, like she wasn't allowed to respond, but was still trying to be polite. When I finally asked the question burning inside me, she went rigid, her shoulders pulling back. She would not give up anything regarding Leo. No matter how I changed what I asked, she never budged, sorrow sown deep in her eyes. It seemed like she wanted to tell me, but the words kept getting stuck in her throat and so instead she would give me the same unhelpful response. "He was hit with eight arrows. I don't know where they took him. I'm sorry." The hole in my chest only grew.

The last time she came to visit she gave me a small pouch stitched with intricate gold swirls. It was filled with perfectly round silver coins stamped with a sword. She came with an order from the High Lord to allow me the freedom to explore the city for the hour, and if I wanted, I could buy anything I fancied from one of the markets. I gaped at the shining coins. The Tominese don't give their scraps to the starving, let alone hand out silver. The boys jumped with excitement at the chance to show me around, dragging me through the city as they pointed out all the different places they had discovered. It felt strange to do something so normal with them, though the unkind stares of the people we passed were anything but regular.

The little embroidered bag pulls on my pocket as I stand up from my cot and press my palms to my eyes. I take a deep, shuddering breath as I stretch out my limbs, needing to do something other than let my mind wander to places I would do anything to forget. I pace the small room, which ends up being less walking and more like turning in continuous circles. When my head starts to spin, I move to sit back down, but stop right before I hit the cot. Someone's outside the door. The warning system I developed when I was a child chained to a bloodied wall goes off in my mind. I stand as my bones beg to get away from the unrelenting tortures of the room. The door creaks open, and to my surprise, Cass peeks his head in. "Cass! What are you—" He catches my hand and pulls me out of the room.

I shake my head in confusion as he drags me past the kitchen and through the hall. What is he doing? "Cass, you know I'm not supposed to go... out..." I breathe, the air emptying from my lungs. Every thought passing through my mind comes to a screeching halt as I stare at the person standing before me. It's not possible. It's the light tricking me, or maybe it's a nightmare. But he's standing right there. He looks terrible, like he's gotten the life beaten out of him, but he's here, breathing mere steps away from me. "Leo."

CHAPTER

NINETEEN

LEO

My eyes shoot open and air fills my lungs with a gasp as the sound of a door slamming shut bounces hollowly off the walls. Flashes of the soldiers from my terrors linger behind my bloodied eyes as I stare at the ceiling. When the images finally fade, I go rigid with fear. I'm dead. I always imagined death to be an escape, but I feel more weighed down than ever. I look around and my neck cracks with the slight movement. I'm in a windowless room, one I don't recognize. The sterile smell burns my nose, pulling a hacking cough from my lungs. A stack of paper and a barely used candle projecting its light along the wall sit on a small desk beside my cot. Across the room, there's a pile of old linens thrown haphazardly in the corner. My muscles protest as I force myself to sit up. My head spins as I try to swing my legs over the side of the bed, but they snag on the thick rope binding them to the frame of the cot. I pull at my hands and realize they too are tied down tight. Why does death have to feel so much like being alive? Maybe it's punishment for everything I've done. It's an odd type of retribution, but Lady Death works in strange ways.

I need to get these restraints off. As I turn my head to stare at the flickering flame, a plan that could go extremely badly forms in my mind. I throw myself to the side, making the cot rock and hit the desk. The rope cuts into my wrists as the candle sways in its metal dish. I push myself as hard as I can one last time, sending the candle lurching forward. I breathe a sigh of relief as the wick drops over the lip of the desk. I stretch my hand toward it and the flame starts to burn through the rope. I can feel my blood start to pool as I pull harder, pushing the rope closer to the flame.

The smell of the singed fibers fills my nose as the rope weakens enough for me to pull it apart. Relieved and eager, I grab the candle to burn through the second binding. When I finally get my hands free, I carefully place the candle back in its dish and run my finger over the burns and blood beading on my wrists. I thought when you died, it meant the end of pain.

I free my ankles as I've done hundreds of times before and swing my bare feet over the cot, hesitating when I see my trousers. These aren't the threadbare, stained pants I had been wearing, but instead clean, gray trousers that are a size too big. As I touch the crisp brown fabric of my shirt, I realize that it's new as well. My feet meet the floor and blood rushes to my toes as the feeling of pins and needles jabbing at my skin takes a moment to fade. I stand and barely manage to get myself straight before my legs give out, sending me plummeting to the ground. I catch myself on the wall, breathing heavily as my head spins. It must take time to get used to walking again after you've died.

I can still hear my brothers' screams bouncing in my ears as I drag myself to the door. My hand hovers over the handle. I wonder if Pleiades, Pollux, Mum, and Dad are standing on the other side, waiting for me with open arms. The side of my lip pulls into the beginning of a smile as I open the door, my chest filling with warmth.

The feeling instantly disappears as a red-tinted hallway greets my eager expression. Maybe they're further along. I push my feet forward, slowly feeling the strength return to my muscles. After walking a few paces, I let go of the wall and my legs grudgingly hold my weight. I continue forward, scanning the identical doors I pass. This hall seems to stretch on forever, forking off in different directions every so often. I wonder if I'm walking in circles, if this is some type of torture.

Steps bounce off the floor behind me, then come to a sudden stop. I turn around slowly as a short lady facing me lets out a loud gasp, her silver eyes wide with fear.

"Don't move blood-eye!" she orders, her voice wavering. Blood-eye? That's a new one. Two people come bursting out of a room across from where she stands shaking. The men exchange panicked glances and immediately charge. Lady Death officially hates me. I turn on my heels and push my legs into an unbalanced sprint, my joints creaking as I trip and right myself in the same stride. It feels amazing to run, my lungs heave as adrenaline courses through my veins. My body slowly gets used to the motion as my steps begin to even out. More join the chase at every corner I blindly turn. Suddenly, the corridor opens to a larger hall, the ceiling stretching up two stories. People loiter all over the wide room as I come bolting through, quickly halting their oblivious conversations. I sprint toward the sky-filled windows that stretch along the wall above the double doors in front of me.

I barrel forward, knocking over a man coming through the door. The sun is blinding as my bare feet hit the rough ground, rocks piercing my skin as I run. Fresh air dives into my lungs, and if not for the people chasing me, I would have dropped to my knees to cherish the feeling. I weave through the growing crowd as people flock to the streets, coming outside to investigate the commotion. I need to get away, and then I can figure out where by the Goddess I am. I curse through panting breaths as I realize that I'm completely weaponless. Lady Death has a cruel sense of humor.

A group of people form a barrier in front of me as they figure out what's going on, forcing me to a screeching stop. I sink into a fighting stance without a thought, muscle memory quickly kicking in as my fingers curl into fists. I turn in tight circles, watching all those surrounding me and the flashes of steel peeking out from under coats or held in steady hands. There isn't a single gap in their formation. One word tumbles through my head, making my jaw clench tight. Soldiers. These people are trained fighters. I can see it in their resolve and from the lack of fear in their eyes.

A man clad in a black uniform steps away from the protection of the line with two short daggers cradled in his hands. I stumble back a step as his eyes shift and his irises shine gold. My eyes fly to his wrist where a number is embedded in his skin with a single dark band inked between the digits and his hand. It's nearly identical to the ones Antares, Altair, Cass, and Saiph carry on their own wrists. Another man and woman, both wearing identical uniforms, step away from the wall of bodies as their eyes lock on me with cool confidence. The silver of their irises shift as the others did, flaring a deep gold. I must have taken an arrow to the head because this can't be real, though my bloodied eyes and stiff joints would tell me otherwise.

When the first man launches at me, my instincts take over and my muscles move before I can think. I dodge the deadly steel and land a few punches as I weave in and out of his blows. Power courses through my veins, as if it had been sitting dormant for weeks and I've just slammed open the flood gates. I can feel the skin on my arm tear as one of their daggers finds its target. I watch the others as they continue to circle through a comforting crimson haze. I catch my opponent's fist as he goes for my stomach and twist his wrist at a sharp enough angle to make his blade drop. I kick it up with my foot and catch it as I throw out an elbow that crushes into his jaw. He falls in a bloody heap, grip loosening on the second dagger. I take it without a thought, turning in time to deflect the woman's nimble attack. The other man joins her, fighting in perfect tandem. The woman caries a short sword while the man wields a thin metal staff, spinning it effortlessly through his fingers. Who by the Goddess are these people? I've never fought anyone like them. Their techniques are flawless and their attacks ruthless. I'm bruised and bloody, and I doubt I'll be able to walk away from this. I wonder if you can die in death?

The woman dances easily around me, exploiting any weaknesses or missteps. My first dagger drops from my hand as she performs every combination to perfection. The man creeps up from behind and traps me between him and his staff, crushing my airway. I manage to get my hands on the inside of the rod, my shaking arms the only thing keeping my throat intact. I struggle but manage to bend my knees and hook my foot around his heel. I flip him over my shoulder, sending us both sprawling to the ground. I slam my fist into his face and raise my dagger to finish it, but the woman hauls me off and elbows me savagely before I get my chance to finish him. I roll on the ground with the single dagger clutched in my hand and regain my footing as my lungs heave. I size her up again and bring my fist back up in front of me. I roll my neck as I watch the stern-eyed crowd in my peripheral vision and wait for the fight to resume.

"Stop!" My thoughts halt and my limbs grow heavy. It's not possible. "Leo!" I haven't heard that voice in years. A strange, wheezing breath scrapes from my lungs.

"Cass?" I scan the crowd as I search desperately for my youngest brother while making sure to not turn my back on the woman and her raised weapon. She doesn't take a step, though hate and rage radiate off her in waves. The confidence running in my veins melts away as my gaze lands on my wide-eyed brother.

"Leo!" He runs to me and I drop to my knees, never daring to take my eyes off the fighters. Only when the woman finally sheaths her sword at her hip do I let myself fully return Cass's embrace. I hold him so tight that I wouldn't be surprised if he couldn't breathe, but he doesn't move, hugging me back with the same emotion-fueled strength. I pull away from him, keeping my hands on his shoulders.

"Are you dead too?" I ask, my voice strained. He smiles warily as tears prick his eyes. He shakes his head once. But then I'm... "I'm not dead?" I say almost to myself as hysteria creeps into my voice. I lock my gaze with my brother and my jaw drops. "You spoke!" I'd given up on the hope of ever hearing his voice again, and yet here he is, standing in front of me with a smile on his face while his words hang in the air. Cass grins wider, looking proud of himself. He should be. "Where are the others?" I ask anxiously, the thought suddenly pressing to the front of my mind.

"Home," he answers with sparkling eyes. Home.

CHAPTER

TWENTY

"We made it," I say breathlessly. I don't know what to do with myself as Cass helps me up. A strangled sound escapes me as the weight on my shoulders eases in time with a wave of relief. I can still feel it hovering above me, but for now, I can walk a little taller.

I scan all the unknown faces surrounding me, their eyes glowing gold. Some wear black uniforms sternly cut with a gold circle embroidered on the left arm. They carry various weapons, some with short swords hanging at their waists, others with a simple band of throwing knives strung across their torsos. No one speaks as they tend to those I left wounded. I cringe as I realize how terrible I must look. None of my injuries are serious, but I feel my skin swell as bruises bloom. I wipe my hands over my shirt, the once clean material now stained and ripped beyond repair.

Cass grabs my hand and drags me through the ring as the sneering, gold-eyed people hastily clear a path. When we're a dozen feet away from the deadly stares, I drain my eyes and let the crimson tears fall down my face. My legs immediately give out and send me plummeting forward. I catch myself on Cass's shoulder, my brother grunting as he battles to keep me standing. The pain works through my veins like spreading venom, slowly increasing as my joints freeze up. Cass pushes against me, doing his best to hold me straight. I grit my teeth and lock my knees, forcing myself to move. My muscles quickly get used to the strain and my mind clears enough to think through the pounding ache. Finally, my surroundings sink in, and it's a struggle not to show my shock.

Towering trees stand like sentinels around the streets. Sturdy stone homes line the roads in neat rows, each identical to the next except for the uniquely manicured gardens decorating the front lawns. We walk by shop-lined streets, and it takes me a moment to process just how clean it is. There is no peeling paint around the doors or crumbling bricks falling from dilapidated walls. I recognize a bakery only by the small wooden sign hung out front and the sweet, mouthwatering smell of fresh bread. A butcher's shop stands a few buildings down, indistinguishable from the bakery in every way but the sound of buzzing flies and its cleaver-shaped sign.

Black-clad soldiers follow us from a distance with their hands hovering over their weapons. I tuck the dagger I stole into my belt as we walk down the peaceful streets, my own hand staying on the hilt over my bloodied shirt. The people walking in the streets hurry into the shops and pull their children behind their backs as we pass. Every soul stares me down, their gazes conveying their message with complete certainty. I am not welcome here. I glance down at my brother, but he smiles innocently, oblivious to the scowling citizens.

Cass leads me past an intimidating wrought iron fence composed of bars three fingers thick. It stretches in a wide circle, isolating dozens of brick buildings and dirt fields. The closest clearings are filled with children moving in tandem as they learn fighting combinations. On another field older kids are sparring brutally, racks of wooden and steel weapons alike lining the area.

"That's the Academy," Cass says, following my gaze. "We train there." I blink as surprise washes through me.

"You fight with these people?" I ask, worry suddenly creasing my forehead.

"Classes and training," he explains as he eyes the grounds with reverence. I look again at the blood-spattered dirt clearings and the square buildings surrounding them. What my brother sees in this place, I don't know. He points out the mess hall and their classrooms, and explains where they go on their runs during the day. My stomach turns to lead as I listen. Hundreds of children must attend this Academy, training as soldiers before they can even read.

I silently thank the Lady when Cass leads me down a street of homes. My lungs are seconds away from giving out. The home we approach is bigger than most of the others. It's three stories tall and almost twice as wide as the houses we saw in the heart of the city. There are shrubs planted tastefully on either side of the stone walkway that leads to the tall, dark wood entryway. Cass helps me up the steps and pushes open the door. I feel uncomfortable walking into such a nice home covered in dirt and blood. He leaves me in the foyer, making sure I steady myself on the wall before disappearing through a door at the back of the room.

A settee sits along the far wall with two deep velvet chairs angled inward on either side of it. On the floor is a thickly woven cerulean rug, the color so vibrant it hurts my eyes. An intricately carved wood staircase on my left stretches up to the next floor, the balusters engraved with winding roses and wisteria. The dark doors directly on my right and on the far wall are all carved with a similar flora. In the same direction, an archway allows me to glimpse the shining dining room, the table already set for the next meal.

There are two overflowing bouquets of carefully arranged irises and purple roses sitting on a thin table beside me, framing a large portrait. The flowers bring back the memory of Dad trying to plant a garden years ago. The efforts we put into growing our own food and flowers was futile as the plants never survived more than a few weeks. I take a few steps forward, doing my best not to leave dirt on the floor. My eyes find the portrait hung in the middle of the wall and a sense of familiarity washes over me. A tall, stoic man and stern woman stand together with a young, pink-cheeked boy between them. There is no joy in the piece, the frigidness of the family too easy to feel. I lean in to stare at the boy, his face eerily similar to Altair's...

Hurried footsteps pull me away from the portrait, the image still lingering at the borders of my mind. "Cass, you know I'm not supposed to go... out..." Cael says, stumbling as he sees me. We stare at each other for a long moment, his breath catching as he lets out a disbelieving sound. He looks horrible. His eyes are bloodshot as he blinks at me, his skin gray and cheeks gaunt. "Leo?" he breathes, tripping over his feet as he moves closer. My brother throws his arms around me and wraps me in a tight embrace. I hug him back, wincing from the lingering pain. Cael eases his hold as he senses my discomfort. Cass smiles brightly and rocks on his feet before disappearing once more. Cael finally pulls back with tears welling in his eyes. "How? I mean, you're alive! You're standing! How are you alive?" he sputters, astonished. He shakes his head as he struggles to put sound to his thoughts. His smile drops as he notices my state. "You look terrible." I let out a small laugh that takes me by surprise, folding us both into a momentary silence before a grin appears on my brother's face, crinkling the skin around his eyes.

"I looked better an hour ago," I admit, wincing as I run a hand through my hair. "I don't think these people like me. They started chasing after me and I got spooked."

"So, you started throwing fists?" Cael asks, raising a brow sarcastically. He already knows the answer. "And you have a dagger?"

"I'd rather not be taken weaponless again. But if you think I'm a mess, you should see what I did to them." I bark a laugh, rubbing the back of my neck. I meet his eyes and his face drops as he takes in my expression. "I thought I was dead until Cass told me I wasn't."

"So did we," he whispers, his hand going to where his ring usually sits. Confusion sweeps through me as I watch his hands drop awkwardly to his side. I make a mental note to ask him about it later.

"Good thing the Tominese are terrible shots." The corner of his lip kicks up.

"Maybe you should sit down. I don't understand how you're standing, and I don't want to push our luck." He leads me through the door on the far wall into the steaming kitchen. An old, withered woman doesn't even pass us a glance as my brother pulls a stool from the corner and orders me to sit. His eyes jump at every sound as if he were afraid of getting caught.

"What did you mean when you said you were surprised I was standing?" I finally ask, leaning my back against the wall. I close my eyes and savor the moment as the pain eases. When I open them again, Cael's taught expression makes me sit up as warning bells go off in my mind. "What do you mean you don't know how I was standing?" I reiterate. Cael has never said such a thing, even after my worst fights when I was half dead, flesh hanging off my body and blood pooling at my feet.

He hesitates as his fingers graze his bare hand. "Leo, they told us you took eight arrows. Three to your legs, one to your shoulder, one to your arm, three to your back... I was told one went through your spine. We thought you were dead. Not near death. Dead. I couldn't feel you breathing," he whispers painfully as his eyes search my face. It takes a long time for his words to truly sink in. No one survives eight arrows, but I did. I shouldn't be alive, let alone fighting.

"How long was I out?" I ask, my voice hollow.

"Three and a half weeks. You were gone twenty-four days, Leo." Twenty-four days? He takes a step toward me as my head starts to spin. That's too long. I've never been out for more than a day. Cael puts a hand on my shoulder to steady me. "Leo, when you went down, the people here came from across the river and saved us from the King's Elite and Obsidian Guard. They made a deal and brought us over after they saw Altair's eyes and your wrists. They picked you up on a gurney and took you away. She told me you shattered your spine, punctured a lung, were suffering from extreme blood loss and that your leg was beyond repair. They told me you were dead, but I wasn't allowed to see... to know where they took you. I had no idea you were... That you could have been—"

"Alive?" He gives me a shallow nod. I can see him trying to stop the tears from falling. I was ready to die, but as I watch my brother's pained expression, I don't know how I could have ever been all right with letting him, all of them, suffer through that grief and pain.

Suddenly Antares, Altair, and an old scowling woman carrying Saiph burst through the door. The woman puts Saiph down with a frown, staying on the opposite side of the room as my sister runs toward me. I recognize her instantly: she's the lady from the portrait. The boys run at me so hard my back crushes against the wall and the stool nearly falls over as they jump on me. Saiph squeals as I pick her up and I wrap them all in my arms.

"I'm sorry, if I... if I hadn't..." Altair chokes out, tears streaming down his face. I push them back so I can look him in the eyes.

"Don't say that. You have *nothing* to be sorry for."

"But if you had died, we all thought you were..." I pull him in again, my brother's words turning into muffled sobs as Cass and Antares join in.

"It doesn't matter. I'm not dead and that's the only thing you should be thinking about. You can't blame yourself for something that didn't happen. Do you understand? You didn't hurt me." He nods against my chest as his entire body shakes.

Once the boys pull away, wiping tears on their sleeves, Cael pulls Altair into his side and throws a comforting arm over his shoulder. "And you are?" I ask the woman still standing cross-armed by the stove. Saiph pulls away and turns to her.

"You will not speak to me," she spits with a high-pitched voice before averting her gaze.

"Gama!" Saiph squeals, making grabbing hands at the woman. Her face seems to thaw at my sister's voice, though it ices back over almost immediately as her eyes meet mine. I glance at Cael as confusion washes over my expression. His hand moves once again to where his ring usually sits only to fall back to his side. It hits me how strange it is to see my brother without the onyx band. I can't remember a time when he ever took it off.

"She'll only speak to the boys. She's Dad's mother. This is her home," he explains numbly, a strange mix of anguish and anger twisting his expression. The woman, my grandmother, flinches when he mentions Mum and Dad, staring at my brother with ice-cold rage. That's why I recognized the boy in the picture, it was Dad. This was his home. This is Illena.

"Cael is family, why wouldn't you speak to him? Why won't you speak to me? I'm their son as much as Altair and Antares are," I ask my grandmother, my expression near identical to Cael's puzzled look. Her eyes narrow as she stares me down.

"You are no kin of mine, blood-eye," she snarls, a slightly lilting accent woven through her sharp words.

"They treat me the same," Cael huffs as his eyes darken. "Only one person in this entire city has spoken to me without seeming like she's going to rip my head off."

"Do they treat you like that?" I ask the boys, my words clipped.

"No, not at all," Altair says lightly. "They treat us like gods. Like we survived the impossible." A smirk lights his face as he gets lost in thought.

"Impossible? What do you mean 'survived the impossible'?"

"Us. They survived living with us," Cael clarifies irritatedly. My brother wouldn't say such a thing without reason, but my mind won't accept it. I let out a heated breath as my gaze roves over my family. Saiph and the boys seem happy, but I've been awake for no more than two hours and I've already been chased, attacked, and told I was a danger to my family. There must be something I'm missing, because this place is starting to feel like a living nightmare painted as a dream.

TWENTY-ONE

LEO

My brothers recall countless stories as we sit in the kitchen, Saiph even joining in with half-comprehendible sentences. Cael watches, smiling to himself when Antares exaggerates so extremely it sounds absurd. I keep an eye on Cael with one thought circling through my mind. *How can he look so beaten?* The boys and Saiph seem healthier than they have in years, but he looks starved and scared, the fear set into his flinching features. My grandmother doesn't say a word, keeping a keen eye trained on both Cael and me as she refuses to leave while we speak. Altair raids one of the pantries and pulls out two handfuls of fresh rolls. The cook sighs defeatedly, but doesn't refuse him, simply passing a flitting glance toward my grandmother.

"Altair, those are for family only," she warns sweetly, her tone like the suffocating scent of a roomful of roses.

He grins uneasily and lowers his eyes. "I know. But I can gift mine to them." My blood boils.

We all freeze as a fist pounds on the door. My stomach grumbles as Altair steps away with the roll to see who's at the door. I force myself to stand, grimacing at the movement. Cael watches me closely as he places a hand under my arm to keep me standing. I put Saiph down and take her hand as she fidgets with curiosity, itching to run to the hall as my grandmother moves into the front room. She opens the door and bows her head, placing a hand over her heart as Cael becomes extremely still beside me. "My Lord," she greets respectfully, motioning a tall man inside. A girl that can be no older than me walks in on his heels. They must be father and daughter. They share the same gilded skin, jet-black hair, and cold expressions.

When the girl looks at me, my breath snags in my throat. Her eyes are like raging oceans of silver. An unmistakable power lies in her frozen glare, calling to those willing to see and demanding respect. The top of her long, charcoal hair is braided back while the rest falls in wavy curtains over her shoulders. She wears black breeches and an ebony sleeveless vest over a gray tunic tucked in at the waist that does nothing to hide the corded muscles unmistakably carved from her years of training.

The man in front of her wears an immaculate raven-colored suit with a gold leather band wrapped tight around his bicep. I've never seen boots shine like his. He must float above the ground to keep them so spotless. I can tell he's used to reverence by the way he watches us down his nose, his gaze even more intimidating than the girl's. The way he instills fear in equal parts to awe from my brothers and grandmother sets my nerves on edge. The boys bow their heads and place their hands over their hearts, unlike Cael, who regards him with open distaste. The man meets my gaze and clearly wonders what path I'll choose. I can be submissive and grateful, or I can stand beside my brother. No matter who presents themselves before me, king or beggar, they do not have the right to look down at me and demand my servility. Unless it's earned, no one deserves such respect, especially from someone who's seen as much as I have.

"So, this is the man of the day. The immortal blood-eye," he addresses, his voice carrying high over the room. His words —spoken with the same accent as my grandmother—send chills down my spine. "I suggest you both bow your heads in my presence."

"And who are you to us?" I ask, hiding the genuine curiosity as I train my expression into plain indifference and lean back against the doorframe. The boys stare at me wide eyed as Antares's mouth falls open.

"I am the leader of this city, blood-eye. I am the High Lord of the gold-eyed lands."

"I don't bow to people I could kill," I state blatantly, motioning to Cael. "And neither will he." The High Lord forces a laugh, his posture easy as his gaze burns through me.

"This is why my people don't get along with yours," he asserts, motioning to my grandmother, then to the Saiph and boys. I clench my jaw as Cael's grip tightens under my arm.

"Those are my siblings. Cael and I raised them." How dare he tell me my own blood doesn't respect us and what we've given up for them. The girl hides a laugh under her breath, catching herself before the High Lord realizes she's made a sound.

"Do you think they are your family? By blood?" Confusion slips past my mask of calm. He laughs as a smirk spreads like a sickness on his face. "Your parents were blood-eyed." He points to the boys without breaking my stare. "Think about it, if their parents both had gold eyes, how do yours shift crimson? Blood-eyes and gold-eyes are two different peoples. These children aren't your siblings, and those you believe were your parents are nothing but two misguided souls who took pity on an orphaned infant." Every word he utters cuts deeper into me, leaving a new, gaping wound in my chest. I can't breathe. It must be a lie, but then why don't his words ring false? *I promised him I would keep you in the dark... The people who should have raised you... I love you as my own and always will.* Those were my mother's words, my mother telling me I was not hers. I glance at Cael as realization dawns on his face.

"Well, now that we're all on the same page, follow us, we have other issues to discuss," he announces, nodding his head to the girl at his back. She steps around him and throws a worn pair of boots to the ground in front of me. I had forgotten I was barefoot. I slip them on, leaning more on the wall than I would like to admit. "And do hand over the dagger you took from my slayer."

I freeze, meeting his steady glare. "Slayer?"

"Our fighters are ranked as slayers, phantoms, commanders and soldiers depending on skill. You fought a slayer. Now, the blade." His face remains stoic as the girl extends her palm, waiting.

"And if I don't want to?"

"We can finish what was started when you first awoke. I have no problem calling in my personal guard from outside," he says airily. I take the dagger into my hand and turn it over. *This place is going to be our home,* I remind myself. *For Saiph and the boys, I have to give it a chance.* I tilt my head to the side and lob the blade into the air. The girl catches it without hesitation before wiping it clean on her pants. She's skilled with a blade as well then. I keep my head high and make for the door as Cael follows close behind.

"Ah, how interesting. Let me be clear, I said *you*, not the getic," he says, his eyes slitting as he motions at Cael and I.

"Getic?" I repeat as my brows crease with confusion. The High Lord grins, delighted with himself.

"You are blood-eyed, we are gold-eyed, your... friend—"

"Brother," I correct sharply. He doesn't skip a beat, ignoring my lethal tone.

"Is a getic. He will stay here until after we've gone through the rules." I glance at my brother as he shifts his weight from foot to foot, his eyes flitting between the High Lord and me. Finally, he nods and steps away. The High Lord and the girl grin openly as I sway on my feet without Cael's steadying hand. Cael's jaw clenches as he nods to me before pinning a heavy glare to the High Lord. I'm already regretting giving up the blade.

The High Lord leads me out with the girl walking closely behind us like an escort. I watch them carefully as we step into the light. She has at least two blades on her in addition to the one I handed over: a dagger strapped on her thigh and another at her hip. She walks with the gait of a warrior: light on her feet and aware of every sound and movement. My gut tells me she's got at least two more weapons hidden under her clothes, and I have the good sense to know her scarred hands are likely just as dangerous as any piece of steel she could wield. I feel bare without my blades, missing their familiar weight like an old friend.

The High Lord, from what I can see, carries not a single weapon. He walks with his head high like he owns the very dirt in the street, a sense of authority floating around him. By his sharp eyes and calculated movements, I doubt he relies on steel, especially with the four soldiers clad in black-and-gold livery following just paces away. I can feel their protective gazes boring into the back of my head with each unsteady step.

We continue past the same identical homes I had passed with Cass, each one made of gray stone walls with thick overlaid lightly colored wood shingles covering the roofs. He leads us deeper into the city, making our way through the market and shop-lined streets. The High Lord stops in front of the sprawling iron fence Cass had looked at with glowing eyes. "This is the Academy training ground. You and the getic are forbidden to enter unless accompanied by me. You may bring your younger brothers to the gate, but you will not go any farther," he says, gesturing to the long field of buildings with a bored expression. I nod, not daring to say a word. This place makes my skin crawl. I feel like Lady Death is beside me, shaking her head as she stares out onto the training fields.

We come to a street filled with tents and carts. The sound of barter and the smell of spices wafting through the air hits me suddenly. It feels strangely... welcoming, although the way people watch me is anything but. "This is the Daeta's market. You may frequent this street *only* when the Haels allow you leave. You may come here and buy anything you can afford," he says, smiling wickedly as if it were a cruel joke.

He points out a few landmarks as we move on, not deeming them important enough to stop when he speaks. A system of giant interconnected buildings come into view as we turn a corner. It's constructed of multiple undecorated square structures connected by second-story walkways free floating in the air. The towering walls are made of shining white stone complete with windows of varying sizes disrupting the otherwise monotone surface. The complex casts shadows that eerily make it feel like it would swallow me whole if I stepped too close. "These are the Council buildings. Unless we bring you here in chains, you will not come near this place." In other words, it's where they kept me while I was unconscious. The tall doors bracketed by two high windows loom before me as I take in the center building, one story taller than the rest. I pull my eyes away and force myself to scan the area.

As we continue walking around the Council buildings, I realize they're set up as a hollowed-out square surrounding a green courtyard in its center. People dressed in black—some wearing gold armbands—carry handfuls of documents and speak in hushed tones as they walk hurriedly in all different directions. My gaze snags on the middle of the clearing where a tall stone post stands on a raised platform. The wood is stained a copper color I know too well. Thick chains hang from the top of the post and the memories of my sister hanging from a similar apparatus burst to the forefront of my mind. I stop dead in my tracks as my heart pounds in my chest. I can't stop myself from staring at the blood on the boards. It's a warning, left up to keep those who want to stray in line. My breathing becomes uneven as my throat tightens.

"That is where you'll end up if you break my rules, blood-eye. You should already be chained up for the display you put on today. You gave our amateur fighters a good challenge, but you won't do it again," he assures smugly as he catches me staring. He watches me with an easy smirk, seeming pleased I noticed the blood-soaked post, as if it were something to be proud of. I force myself to breathe and push against the flood of memories threatening to drag me down. My mind clears enough for his words to sink in and my stomach flips with dread. The skills of those fighters were flawless, and to think they were not the best this city has to offer...

"We're done here. You know the rules. If you choose to abide by them, we won't have any problems." He turns to the girl and her fingers twitch as if she were caught off guard by his attention. "Elana, take the blood-eye back to the Hael house," he orders, his entire entourage close on his heels as he makes for the main doors of the tallest building. The girl, Elana, tracks him like a predator until he's out of sight, the tension in her shoulders releasing when the doors close behind him. She starts to walk away, so I follow, deciding she will be easier to question than the self-absorbed High Lord.

"Where am I?" I ask after a few minutes. My head spins as I push myself to keep up with her long strides, my entire body throbbing as I limp. She doesn't look back, nor does she relent her pace.

"You are in Wate. The biggest gold-appointed city in Illena," she says ahead of me, her words cold and clipped. She has less of an accent than the High Lord; her words are smooth and lilting. I become strangely aware of the way I pronounce the rough syllables in the manner of the Tominese, like running in a zigzag pattern through each sound.

"We aren't in Tominay," I mumble to myself in awe, the notion suddenly feeling too real. She almost stumbles, her hands curling into fists. Still, she does not face me.

"We are *not* in Tominay. I don't care where you came from, but you are in Illena now. You are in Wate. I suggest you learn the name," she bites out, her words like the crack of a whip.

"What do they use those buildings for?" I ask, queasiness rising at the thought of the bloodied post. A muscle feathers in her jaw, but she does not answer. "Can you not hear me?" Her steps quicken. I curse as I struggle to keep up, the victory clear on her smug face. I scowl and open my mouth to repeat myself, but she beats me to it.

"The Council buildings are reserved for the work of the Council. They create laws, make decisions, keep records, praise the heroes, and condemn the monsters." She sends me a pointed look at that.

When I don't reply, Elana smirks victoriously. After a couple blocks, she begins to slow, realizing how far I'm falling behind. I consider bleeding my eyes to take away the pain, but I doubt the people would react well, considering my last experience. I fall into step beside Elana, panting and wincing with each stride. I nearly jump out of my skin when she speaks.

"Did you really believe you were a Hael?" She says, her eyes staying trained dutifully ahead.

"Why would I question it? We only discovered this place existed a few months ago in a letter written by my mother. How could I have known there were this many people like me?"

She turns on me then, her expression twisted with disgust as she stands a breath away. I barely manage to stop myself before I run into her. "I am not like you, and you are *nothing* like me. Blood-eyes don't belong with gold-eyes. I should be doing more important things than showing one its way back like a lost child," she spits, her words dripping with venom. As she turns around, I catch a shadow of a bruise on her jaw. It seems like she tried to cover it up. Elana continues forward without another word, fuming. I tuck the thought away and take a deep breath before pushing my aching body after her.

"And why are you so above showing a broken boy his way home?" I wonder out loud. I don't know why I ask. It's clear the last thing she wants to do is speak to me, but I can't help myself. Maybe this place is making my curiosity and boldness grow.

"This is *not* your home. My name is Elana Cassien. I'm the eldest of the two Cassien daughters, heirs to Wate." I was right, she's the High Lord's daughter. Yet no soldiers shadow her as they do her father. Maybe she's simply dangerous enough not to need protection. Unease sweeps through me at the thought. We walk in complete silence the rest of the way as I'm too out of breath to speak. I swear she watches me from the corner of her eye, lengthening her stride and smirking as I fall farther and farther behind.

CHAPTER
TWENTY-TWO

LEO

I walk in the door as the sun starts to set. It's a strange feeling as I catch a final glimpse of the glowing sky, half painted in an array of rich pastels while the rest is covered in dark storm clouds. Even the sky can't figure out what to think. Grandmother—Saiph and the boys' grandmother—sits on one of the prim upholstered couches, her back straight and hands laid neatly in her lap. She stands when she sees me, her face unreadable. She motions me forward without a word as she walks through the door leading to the kitchen. I follow mindlessly as I scan the room for Saiph and the boys, but there are no signs of children living in this house. My eyes catch on the staircase before I step into the kitchen, remembering how Antares had told me their rooms were on the second floor. My heart squeezes as I think of them. Do they know I'm not their real brother, their blood?

The grandmother lugs open a heavy door to what I assume is a pantry, the one I sat beside while I spoke with my siblings.

She doesn't say a word as her piercing eyes track my every movement. Even the cook watches as I take a step forward and glance into the strange room. Cael's frantic gaze meets mine from the corner. His hands are shaking as he raises his head from between his knees. There's fear deeply etched into his face as he holds himself tightly like he's trying to fade into the darkness.

Hands push at my back, but I lock my knees and spin away. The grandmother stands behind me, dread flitting across her face. She tried to shove me in. I meet Cael's frantic eyes again as the crushing feeling of the room claws at my mind. This is his childhood. They're forcing him into the one place that will break him without even knowing it. The grandmother flinches at my expression when I turn to her.

"We are not staying in there," I seethe. She stands straighter, seeming to remember herself.

"You will be grateful, as we can take the *privileges* we have gracefully gifted you away. Your kind do not deserve the kindness we have shown." I take a step toward her, but a hand stops me, holding my shoulder with a sure grip.

"They won't let us see Saiph and the boys if we don't listen. I'll be fine. Everything will be easier if we abide," my brother says from behind me, his tone tight and shaken. I see red as I watch the grandmother, the monster roiling inside me. Cael's fingers dig into my shoulder as if he can sense the violence sparking in my bones.

"I won't forget this," I swear, allowing him to drag me into the cramped room. I keep my eyes pinned on the grandmother as the door shuts and the locks click into place. Cael swallows hard behind me as his breathing audibly becomes labored. I can't see a thing. When my eyes adjust, I can barely make out the outline of my shaking brother in the sliver of light filtering through the cracks between the door and its frame.

"Are you all right?" I ask, knowing the answer but bringing up the question nonetheless. If I make him speak, it will draw his attention away from the too-close walls.

"Fine," he breathes, his voice a gravelly rasp. I hear him sit on the cot as it squeaks under his weight. I do the same, turning to sit beside him. "How'd Cassien treat you?" he asks, desperate for a distraction.

"I don't think he likes me." Cael scoffs, but the act is half-spirited. I can feel him reach for his ringless hand as the habit resurfaces again.

"Why did you take it off?" I ask, voicing the question simmering in my mind. My brother goes still as death.

"I didn't." His voice is cold, devoid of emotion. "It's an heirloom, the Hael family ring. It was supposed to be passed on from generation to generation. It was the symbol of the head of the family, the representative, the one who made all the familial decisions. The minute they saw I had it, they ripped it from my finger and told me I wasn't *worthy*. I have no idea where it is, but neither of the grandparents wear it."

"We should get it back, it was given to you," I point out, my confidence slowly building like an iron wall to contain the flames of rage rising in my soul. He sighs heavily beside me and I feel him curl impossibly further into himself.

"Leo, don't you get it? This place... there's something wrong with it, its people. We're trapped while they hook the nooses around our necks, threatening Saiph and the boys to keep us compliant. You can't say you don't feel it, Leo. The way they look at us, the way they speak to us only when they deem us human enough to hear their blessed words." My wall of confidence blows away like dust in the wind as the truth of his words sinks in. I can sense the monster inside of me roiling and whispering in my ear in time with my outrage.

"I can feel it," I snap. Cael doesn't acknowledge the anger I let slip into my voice as his own simmers under the surface. We stay silent for a while, letting the fury burn away the fear.

"What did they tell you about your parents?" Cael asks. He unknowingly may have brought up the one thing I'm not willing to speak about. He might as well have shoved me into the freezing Vallan and held my head under the water. I face him in the dark and my entire being seems to contract. I forgot about the news after I saw him in this room. The High Lord's words cut back into my memory like a searing knife. *Think about it, their parents both had gold eyes, so how do yours shift crimson?*

"I don't know what to believe," I admit, staring down at my hands in the darkness. "The only thing I've ever been sure of feels like... like it slipped through my fingers and turned to ash." I bark a laugh of desperation as my soul sinks past my feet. "How is it my family now isn't my family? I don't want to believe it, but it makes sense. Too much sense. I don't look like them at all, and my eyes... I can't deny it. And Mum and Dad were different with me, cautious."

"You don't have to be blood to be family, Leo," he reminds me softly, as if he was talking to himself.

I speak without thinking, blurting the first words that cross my thoughts. "But it's not the same. Family is a bond as strong as blood. It is blood." The minute the words leave my mouth, I realize how deeply I've cut into an already open wound. Cael goes still beside me as the sound of his breath halts. He was trying to console me, trying to tell me this is the way he fit in with us. He is family by choice instead of blood. My mind works as I try to find the words to fix what I said, but none come fast enough.

"We're sharing this cell, Leo. I would appreciate it if you didn't point out how the family I was given didn't treat me as such," he says, his voice a numb whisper.

"Cael—"

"No, it's all right. You're in shock, I understand. I don't hold it against you, nor do I believe you meant it to be painful."

"I didn't." I sigh, rubbing my hands over my face. "I'm sorry, Cael. You know you're more of a brother to me than anyone could ever be, blood or not." He relaxes slightly beside me, taking slow, shallow breaths.

"I'm going to try and sleep." My stomach knots with regret as I nod. I move to the opposite cot, his own creaking as he lies down. He goes still, but I can feel his quiet panic rise. I turn my head toward him. I have no idea how he isn't completely falling apart.

"Do you remember the time when Antares thought he caught himself on fire and dumped a bucket of water over his own head," I say, the memory bringing the shadow of a smile to my face. I hear him laugh silently, the sound more like a shiver.

"It was a leaf," Cael adds, his voice floating with ease. I sigh, the gloom lifting slightly.

"Antares does like to make a show." I fill the time with memories until I hear his breathing even out, sending my brother into a reminiscing sleep as I struggle alone to keep the darkness at bay.

Cold air bites at my skin as I climb the side of the house, tensing with every step higher. I swing my legs up and sit on the roof, breathing heavily. I can't see through the thick trees lining the back of the Hael house, but when I close my eyes, I imagine the Vallan flowing restlessly before me.

I spent the last forty-five minutes speaking to the boys and playing with Saiph. Cael was more silent than usual, so I decided to let him have his space before being cramped back into the pantry. I apologized again twice this morning and though he told me it was bothering me more than it was him, I could still see the hurt lingering in his eyes. On top of that I immediately understood why Cael looked so sickly when they delivered our food this morning. It was two plates of meat more solid than an oil-quenched blade and a half-rotten roll, but at least the water seemed clean. I limited my consumption to half my plate, dumping the rest of its contents onto Cael's. He protested, but only halfheartedly. He needs food more than I do, even considering how I've only recently woken from the dead.

"What are you doing?" a stern voice demands from below. My eyes shoot open. I glance down and my gut twists at the height. Elana glares at me from the ground, her silver eyes duller than they had been yesterday. She wears a long, dark cloak over her clothes with the hood pulled back to reveal her face. The cloak seems like it's been patched more times than it's been worn, a strange choice considering her immaculate clothing underneath.

"Fresh air," I reply simply. I'm so focused on my primal fear of heights that my mind has no time to think.

"You aren't allowed to be up there," she snaps, crossing her arms over her chest. I stare up at the sky and ignore her, refusing to move a muscle. "Blood-eyes are idiots," she mumbles under her breath. My gaze cuts back to her.

"Maybe to you. But you don't know why I am who I am, why I do what I do. It makes sense you don't understand when you never could." She stares at me as she becomes increasingly livid. "Why do you care what I'm doing up here? You made a point of not taking a liking to me yesterday, so why bat an eye if I get strung up on a post for sitting on a roof?" Her eyes blaze as she sneers at me and I falter when I feel the smirk growing on my face.

"Get down. You will obey before I drag you down by your throat," she commands heatedly. I paste on an uncaring grin and roll my eyes dramatically as I lean back.

"You can try." Her fingers curl and straighten as if she were forcing herself to remain calm.

"Why are you up there?" she asks, her hold on her frustration clearly slipping.

"To clear my head." I close my eyes and turn my face to the wind. I can feel the raw disdain radiate off her from all the way up here.

"That's what sleep is for," she coos, her voice deceivingly soft. I deserve the I'm-wiser-than-you tone, but I won't let her take away the few minutes of peace I can procure.

"I don't sleep." She doesn't respond. I open my eyes, wondering if she left, but there she stands with her gaze locked on me. The ground comes in and out of focus as I hold her glare. I press my hands to the roof to steady myself and Elana doesn't miss the stiff movement.

"Everyone sleeps, blood-eye," she argues, speaking to me like I might speak to Saiph.

"Not me. I sleep once every three nights." Her stony expression wavers but it's gone before I can blink. I wonder if I wore the same look when the lady I murdered asked me to kill her children, a crack in the mask. An ember of hope fizzles out inside me. "You don't get terrors?" I ask softly. Her brows knit together as she studies me with bewilderment. With a sigh, I climb down, jumping deftly to the ground.

I've got three inches on Elana, but somehow, she makes it feel like she's the one looking down at me. I cross my arms as her lips thin and her eyes narrow. Her hair is coming out of her simple braid, the dark strands framing her face.

"I've never heard of a terror," she says, the words a challenge. Other than my family, no one knows about the memories I relive while I sleep. But if I explain, maybe she'll laugh and say they're a common occurrence, easy to be rid of. The notion of figuring out a cure makes hope bloom in my chest like a spark to kindling.

"When I fall asleep, other people's last thoughts play out like nightmares in my mind. It's never good memories or even random ones, it's always their last ones. Eight different final moments. When I close my eyes to sleep, I become them, take on their body and soul. I've watched people I don't know, but am sure I care for, die before feeling a knife slash through my throat. I've been struck in the back of the head by an arrow and felt an axe split me in two. I've been tortured and interrogated for information I don't have. I've slowly drowned in a sea of blood under the bodies of unknown friends. I've watched Lady Death stare down at me as my heart stopped from sickness, a small portrait of the person I thought I would have an entire life with held before my eyes by a weeping friend." I take a deep breath, trying my best to push the memories down, but they drive back with double the strength. "I don't sleep, I die, over and over again. I have to be tied down or I will rip the flesh from my own bones, desperate to rid myself of the agony." My eyes beg to flood with blood, the pull pleading me to fall into numbness. I battle to keep control. It only takes one glance at Elana to know I've said too much. Her face is pale as snow and her eyes are wide as she digests my words.

"You were silent while you were... recovering." Her face pales as she wraps her arms around her torso, then drops them to her side as if realizing what she was doing. My parents had the same reaction when I told them the first time. Still too numb from escaping his birth parents, Cael didn't treat me like I was something to fear or someone to pity when I told him.

Instead he had laughed and said, *then I'm not the only one who dreads the dark.* That was the moment we became brothers.

"I can't make a sound. It's a cruel joke played by whoever embedded the memories into my blood. Let him die every night, but make sure he's alone and unable to call for help." A chill runs down my spine as my words hang in the air. I meet Elana's gaze, and the tiny spark of a fire that had caught, the hope that had flared, hisses out.

"You're cursed," she breathes, shaking her head. "Blood-eyes aren't natural."

"And you are? You and your gold eyes?" She doesn't respond as her cheeks redden.

The grandfather and grandmother come around the house with their jaws clamped shut and eyes narrow. They spot Elana in tandem and stumble in surprise before quickly bowing their heads and placing a hand over their hearts. Her eyes rove over them in a predaceous manner. They stand frozen in place, not meeting Elana's eyes. They fear her. I almost laugh at the thought of the Haels, as cruel as they are, cowering under Elana's stunning glare.

Finally, the grandmother remembers herself and clears her throat. "My Lady. We've come to bring the blood-eye back."

"Where is the getic?" Elana asks coldly.

"In their room, my lady." She nods as her eyes meet mine. The look burns right through me. A vicious smirk grows on her lips as her arm sweeps out before her.

"Welcome to Wate, blood-eye."

CHAPTER
TWENTY-THREE

LEO

I walk beside Cael as the boys fill the silence with their stories of the Academy. They've been attending since we arrived, and though my unease has yet to subside, my brothers spew nothing but praise. Even Cass throws in a few words laced with reverence. Cael and I were grudgingly informed yesterday that we are now allowed out for two hours, something we greedily agreed to. Cael basks in the sunlight like it is the last time he will ever see the sky. For him, even a minute in that cell of a room is an eternity.

I still have a slight limp, but the full movement and strength of my legs are slowly coming back. I reach to touch the scar where the arrow shattered my spine. It hit right below Saiph's star map, something I was extremely grateful for. I wonder if the scars will ever stop being added to my skin and whether I'll truly get the chance to heal here. By the withering glares of the passing citizens, a voice inside tells me it's an empty, foolish wish.

We arrive at the metal gate and Cael and I stop before the threshold. Antares and Altair walk on as if they had been alone, but Cass turns around, coming to give us one last hug. He wraps his arms around Cael, then quickly around me, pressing firmly on Antares and Altair's star maps.

"They say bye too." I give him a tight-lipped smile before he runs to catch up with our brothers, already deep in conversation with another group of kids. Even with his few words, he told me exactly what I needed to hear.

Not far from the Academy gates, Cael and I find a shady tree and claim the roots bursting through the soil as our seats. We settle into an easy silence, content with listening to the purple-tinted leaves rustle in the wind. Cael leans back against the trunk as he closes his eyes and I swear I hear the clinking of coins ring from his pocket. I look over at him, the question sitting on my lips.

"Byrne gave me some money to use when we feel like it," he says without opening his eyes. My forehead creases as another question passes through my mind, but of course, my brother answers before giving me the chance to speak. "She's Elana's sister, Cassien's second daughter. The only person in the whole bloody city who doesn't seem to care we're not gold-eyed." I scoff.

"You need to stop reading my thoughts like that. It's terrifying," I tell him sarcastically. Instead of retorting as I thought he would, my brother's eyes shoot open. He sits up quickly, his gaze locked ahead.

I follow his stare and immediately understand why his spine straightens and expression evens out. High Lord Cassien, Elana, and another girl, Byrne, with features identical to the High Lord and his eldest daughter, walk toward us with four armed guards at their heels. Byrne has a much softer appearance than her sister, the waves of her midnight-hued hair flowing unbound over her shoulders. Her eyes are bright and her lips are set into an easy smile. She wears a light-blue chemise, with loose gray trousers. Beside her, Elana couldn't be more different with her hair braided into three tight plaits that join at the back. She's dressed in black, her formfitting long-sleeve shirt neatly tucked into leather breeches. A simple sheath holding an unornamented dagger is strapped to her thigh, but the way she wears it somehow makes it seem like a centerpiece. A pang of grief courses through me as I remember my lost weapons. It may be strange to most, but the familiar weight of the steel was a comfort, one I miss terribly.

Byrne's smile glows as she walks toward us, throwing me off guard. Cael was right, she does look, well, she looks... friendly. It's a sentiment I haven't seen from a stranger in months. I feel strangely warm at the thought as she nods to Cael and me in turn. We return the gesture with tight smiles.

Elana angles herself in front of her sister, and as if Byrne had been snapped back into reality, she wipes the smile from her face and passes her elder sister a distasteful glance. I scan Elana's face and her eyes catch my gaze. Her brow and eye seem bruised and slightly swollen, but strangely, there's no discoloration. She glares at me so fiercely I turn away, switching my focus to her father.

"Come," he orders, the single word nothing less than a command. The High Lord pivots and begins to walk away, but both daughters stay stuck in place. *They're waiting for us,* I realize. With a heavy sigh, Cael stands. I follow suit as my mind screams that nothing good will come of whatever Cassien has planned.

"I don't like this," Cael whispers, voicing my thoughts.

"Neither do I." We follow them through the iron gates of the Academy, trapped between the sisters and the High Lord's entourage. As I look around, I notice there isn't a single color in this entire place. Everything is plastered and painted gray with only the rusty dirt for contrast. There are no trees, grass, painted doors, or flags, and it puts me on edge. This is a prison yard.

Children train in dirt rings chalked into designated clearings between the long buildings. They work through the combinations with ease, each one in perfect sync with the next. I would expect wooden spears and swords, but even the students no older than Antares wield steel weapons. A small girl stumbles over the movements, catching herself so quickly I question what I saw, but there's unmistakable fear flashing in her eyes. An instructor with a similar gold band tight around his arm to the High Lord's stalks toward her. I don't know what I was expecting, maybe a lecture or scolding, but what he does makes both Cael and I halt. The instructor asks her a heated question, and when she doesn't respond, he backhands her across the face so hard she falls to the ground, blood spurting from her nose. When she doesn't move, the instructor orders another student to take her away. The young, emotionless boy doesn't hesitate to grab her foot and drag her to the side of the field before returning to his training. I shift my gaze to Cael, his shocked and scared expression a mirror of mine. My blood boils as I think of the boys... did this happen to them? These people are going to be sorry if they thought they could hurt my brothers.

"We do not tolerate missteps. Mistakes allow the students to become hesitant, unfocused. We train weakness out of our youth, and if they do not right their ways, we beat it out of them," Cassien drawls as a smile spreads wide over his face.

"You're going to regret if you put even a finger on my brothers," I snap as that sense sizzles at my fingertips, begging to take hold. I grudgingly push it away. Elana steps forward, her face drawn tight. Her sister catches her arm and holds her back. To my surprise, she abides and doesn't move further.

"That sounds like a threat. I believed you to be more intelligent, even for a blood-eye." My nails dig into my palms as my entire body shakes from holding myself back.

"Take it as you will, but know we are not ones to make empty promises," Cael says coldly, keeping his voice calm even as his eyes burn. Cassien laughs. The man *laughs,* tilting his head to the side as if he only now truly sees us.

"I find it interesting you believe you hold any power here, how you think you could control what happens to those Hael boys." I'm going to kill him. Cassien turns away with his daughters following close behind. Elana's face is trained into cool indifference, but I catch a flash of sadness in Byrne's eyes, a silent apology.

We follow them along the straight main road. As far as I can see, it separates the grounds in two, leading from the gates to a large dome. Four barracks line each side of the road about halfway to the circular building. Every building is marked by a single word painted in black above the entrances. Puppet on the first, phantom on the second, soldier on the third and slayer on the last. Kids of all different ages stand around them, but I can tell who belongs where. The puppets are the smallest, frail children marred with cuts and bruises. They walk with a hunch and a limp, their eyes trained on the ground and arms slack by their sides. They don't loiter, giving the rest of the students a wide berth before disappearing into their barracks. The students outside the slayer's barracks argue loudly, shoving each other and laughing incessantly. The kids outside the largest barracks, deemed for the soldiers, are the most numerous and watch the rest with visible envy and respect. But it's the students outside the phantom barracks who unnerve me. They watch us pass with a disturbing stillness. I understand immediately where they get their name. I doubt they would make a sound if they had to trudge through a muddied battlefield. If there were such a thing as cold fire, it was what burned in their eyes. The puppets seemed to be by far the youngest here, a visible age gap between them and the rest of the students. I wonder which group the boys would join.

"The students spend their last three years of training living at the Academy," the High Lord explains, following my gaze. I hadn't realized I'd stopped, or that Cael's eyes were filled with helplessness as he stares at the puppet barracks. I know it's a feeling that runs deep, derived of his past. "But the Puppets, they stay here until they can learn to keep up with the others in their age groups. They do extra work to make up for their failures. Children who fail are seen as a type of... disappointment, so their parents send them away to avoid embarrassment," he beams with a crazed edge to his words. My gut screams for me to run, that the man in front of me is nothing but a suit of skin hiding a monster more dangerous than those I've ever dared to face. The High Lord is the type of person even I stay away from. A man worse than Vela with a mind rotted with years of exposure to the worse types of cruelties. The edge of my unease abates as he turns, but the gnawing dread remains.

I scan the training fields for the boys and sigh in relief when I don't see them. Cael continues beside me with his jaw clenched tight as his eyes fly over the Academy grounds. We walk up to the large gray dome and head toward a curved arch carved with intricate depictions of Lady Death and the Great War. Above the opening, words are hewn into the stone. My blood goes cold as I read them. Thieves of blood. Heirs of gold. Never merciful.

Cassien finally leads us through the arch as dread grinds at my insides. Dozens of people spar in rough circles marked into the hard ground. Some train in hand-to-hand combat while others fight with blades, staffs, and shields. The High Lord nods to his daughters and the sisters quickly move away at his signal. Byrne watches us for a long moment with an apology set into her features. Cael's face is blank as he takes in the open space. His eyes go wide as Cassien moves to grab my arm. I pull away, his fingers catching air as a vicious smile prowls onto his face.

"Don't be afraid, blood-eye. We simply want to see what you can do." By the Goddess herself, he wants me to fight. No, he's going to *make* me fight.

"I'm not sparring with anyone," I snap, grounding myself. I doubt spilling someone else's blood will make these hateful people like us.

"You will fight, and we will watch. You do not have a choice. You would do well to remember what you saw out there and who holds the power over your beloved siblings." He steps closer and drops his voice so only I can hear. "I would hate for an accident to befall the eldest, leaving the young ones to fend for themselves. Or maybe the one who does not like to speak?" My eyes meet his as fire rages in my blood. I shake as I struggle to remain in control, but how I would love to see him bleed.

Those in the rings stop fighting and walk toward us with eager eyes. My gaze locks with my brother's, the resolve of his expression at odds with the panic buried in his eyes as he searches uselessly for a way out.

I force myself to calm my nerves and step into the nearest circle. I roll my shoulders, keenly aware of the growing crowd. They stay a step away from Cael as he takes his place on the outskirts of the ring. He nods once and I flood my eyes with blood, letting a crimson haze fall over my vision. My mind calms and sharpens like a dagger sliding over a whetstone as the wave of numbness falls over my body. The surrounding people make no clear reaction to my eyes like the Tominese had in the arena. I blink as a thought hits me. *There is no one like me in Wate, yet they all know what I am and do not fear me...*

My mind empties of thoughts as Elana walks into the circle. Her eyes lock on me like a predator on the hunt. I look over to my brother as his face contorts with terror, his hands hanging slack at his sides. Byrne comes before me, holding two long strips of fabric. Her face is colorless as she carefully wraps my hands and wrists. Instead of watching Byrne, my eyes stay on her sister. Elana's hands are already wrapped, and I wait impatiently for Byrne to finish with mine. I swallow the bile rising in my throat and banish my conscience once she finishes, letting the monster free.

"We only have one rule when it comes to blood-eyes," the High Lord booms, his voice bouncing off the domed roof. Elana's eyes flash golden as she starts to circle. "What is it?"

"Never merciful," they chorus in unison. A smirk rises to my lips as my blood begins to buzz. Elana advances on me within seconds of having uttered the words. She strikes perfectly as she flies over the ground. I block and duck, bobbing through her movements. I strike fast, stringing together one blow after the other. She's the best adversary I've ever fought. Adrenaline pumps through my veins as my mind goes blissfully clear. I don't see anything but the next move, her next step, my next breath. She maneuvers away from several bone-crushing hits and without missing a beat, she lands a hit of her own. She takes a moment to regain her breath and wipes her face on her shoulder. Her bronze skin smears onto her shirt, revealing a deep-purple bruise along her jaw. I don't allow myself to think about it, grinning slightly as I breathe through my nose.

Her combinations are flawless, never allowing me the opportunity to get past her guard as she tries to bait me again and again. As I block her attacks, I see her irritation starting to build. Frustration makes you act without measure. It blinds even the most skilled fighters to deceit, and clearly, she is not used to losing.

I let my hands fall slightly and make my movements sluggish to allow her an opening. Her eyes flash as she catches it and jabs at my face. My brain shakes numbly in my skull, but my body does what is needed without being told. I move my arm as her fist collides with my face and catch her recoiling hand in my elbow to sweep it aside, allowing my left fist a passage to find its mark. Her nose cracks under the impact and blood spurts as I hook my foot behind her knee and sweep her legs out from under her. Even bloodied, she's still quick. Elana twists as she falls, bringing me down with her. Fire rages in her eyes as we scramble to pin each other. There's the crack in her armor, all I need to do is hit the right spot and she'll shatter.

I throw blow after blow, putting all my strength into each hit. Elana manages to spin out from under me and jumps to her feet as her lungs heave in time with mine. I pull on a smirk that used to make the arena bosses curl into their seats. Her last string of control snaps and she lunges, her good senses pushed aside as she sees red. I fake to the left, drawing her near before swinging my fist at her temple. She reels back from the shot and falls flat on her back. The gasps ringing through the dome smash into the foreground of my senses and allow my conscience to take hold once more.

I sort through the faces of those making the tight circle, searching for my brother. When my eyes fall on him, my stomach sinks. His face is pale and his eyes are wide with terror. Byrne bursts out of the crowd and runs for Elana. I think she's going to help her up, but her expression gives me pause. I watch as she rips a small, crimson knife out of Elana's grip and throws it aside without care for the bystanders. Byrne mutters furiously as she stands over her sister, breaking the furor in Elana's eyes. Her face smooths over to one of steely indifference as she moves to stand, swaying on her feet. I feel a thick warmth trickle down my neck as the taste of rust fills my mouth. My gaze snags on the ordinary blade covered in dark blood. I touch my neck carefully and my fingers come away slick and red.

Cael runs at me from the circle, the spell keeping him rooted in place broken. He rips a strip from his shirt and presses it to my neck as I breathe a wet rasp. Before I realize what I'm doing, I step away from him and throw out my fist in primal defense. Somehow, he dodges the blow and steps out of my range. He takes a deep breath and holds the strip of material out for me. I take it before opening my mouth to speak. "Don't! Don't say anything, it'll make it worse," he urges, holding his hands in the air as if he stopped himself from helping me. I press the cloth to the wound as blood runs freely down my hand.

Byrne turns to walk over to me, but Elana catches her arm as fear sets into her eyes. She shakes her elder sister off easily.

"Can you breathe?" she asks me, her voice strained. I take a deep breath, filling my stinging lungs until they feel like they'll burst. By the luck of the stars, Elana didn't hit my trachea and from what I can feel, narrowly missed the main artery running along my neck. I nod, and my brother lets out a relieved sigh. His eyes flit over the crowd still watching us closely as wariness sets into his features. Byrne moves toward me, not a trace of fear visible. I try to step out of her grip, but she grabs my arm and gently leads me through the gaping crowd.

TWENTY-FOUR

ELANA

I pace the length of the sitting room as I wait for Byrne to come home. It's well into the night now, the stars having appeared hours ago. If she's still with that blood-eyed rat, I'm going to lose it. How could she run to him when I was on the ground? How could I let him knock me down? I rub the new bruise on my jaw, the only evidence of Cassien's disappointment.

Byrne walks through the door and avoids my eyes as she strips off her cloak.

"Where have you been?" I ask quietly, my worry and anger merging. The adrenaline from the fight has yet to wear off.

"Where do you think, Elana?" she replies dryly, not daring to look at me. "Where is Father?" Byrne walks past me as if I were a ghost, trekking into the kitchen. She steals a roll from the counter and immediately tears into it with the grace of a starved animal.

"Sleeping," I rage-whisper. She sits down at the table the

cooks use to knead dough and finally dares to meet my gaze. We used to spend hours watching Mother cook at this table, standing on our toes to get a peek of her scarred, skilled hands at work. Byrne and I would giggle when she would throw flour at us, the powder floating in the air like a blizzard. We would run around the room like leaves in the wind, trying to step close enough to get a decent handful of the powder to take our revenge. My anger ebbs to the sorrow and grief still fresh all these years later.

"What were you thinking? You could have—would have killed him!" she scolds. I took an extra beating on her behalf when I got home. Cassien was not pleased with her little display. I'll have to figure out a way to keep them separated until he forgets her betrayal.

"Why is that such a bad thing, Byrne? He's a blood-eye! He deserves to be burned for all he is!"

"He doesn't even know there are other blood-eyes across the river, Elana! He has no idea *who* he is! He believes he's the only one of his kind because no one thinks it right to tell him he has people." She shakes her head incredulously as fury burns through her whispers. "How could you be so cruel to a person who wants only peace for his family? All they want is to have a home, Elana. A place where they don't have to worry about getting sliced in the throat!" The words become a tangible entity around me, strangling the air from my lungs.

"You can't be serious, Byrne?" She crosses her arms, telling me she is very much so as she dares me to push her further. Blood-eyes are the reason we're confined to this island. Why we are deprived of knowledge and freedom. Decades ago, the gold-eyes tried to gain what we were denied, only to be crushed by a blood-eyed king who banished us to three gold-appointed cities, restricting our every move... our very lives. The blood-eyes trapped us in gilded cages and yet Byrne feels the need to help one, even after all they've done.

"Have you ignored what Cassien has told us all these years? All of the history they shoved down our throats at the Academy?"

"Elana, those stories are one sided and you know it. We started a war with them because we wanted power. They vanquished our forces to *save* theirs. This is our punishment for killing *hundreds*. And what does that have to do with Leo and Cael? They've been through more than you can comprehend. Maybe if you took the time to open your eyes and stopped sucking up to Father, you would see." My heart skips a beat as the air filling my lungs becomes too heavy.

"Take it back!" She shakes her head steadily, her expression one of resolve. "I'm not a scared child who runs to her father at the first sign of trouble, Byrne. They are the foolish children and so are you." She snorts, her eyes bright with fire.

"Yes, Elana. I am. I am a child who is terrified of the people I'm supposed to trust. They are scared children who have been running from Lady Death's grip for so long they've all but given up their souls! We are all scared, Elana, because there is no place where we can be safe. Until you take off the blinders Father placed over your eyes, you will never see." Her voice is soft and low as disappointment molds her expression.

"You're wrong," I whisper helplessly. The words sound like I've given up and curled into myself. I hate that she has the power to argue with me.

"You know what I learned from all those years at the Academy, Elana? You can't win an argument with someone who won't see the other side." She turns without another word, the heat of our dispute following her up the stairs, leaving me cold.

I stand, unable to move. I replay our whispers over and

over, searching for something, anything to prove that what I was saying held some semblance of the truth. The more I run through the conversation, the more I realize Byrne was right. I acted rashly, without common sense. I allowed my frustration and hate to take the reins. I shouldn't have pulled the blade, but I couldn't be knocked to the ground, not without leaving a mark. His face replays in my mind, staring at me with old, sad eyes on a young, scar-flecked face. I can't stop thinking about his expression when he realized what I had done. He looked... broken. He's naive if he feels betrayed by someone he doesn't know and shouldn't trust.

I take a deep breath and focus on the image of his blood-boiling, arrogant smirk and the shadows that darkened his face as he fought. He's a blood-eye, selfish and vain, just like his forefathers. Byrne can believe what she wants, but nothing will change who he is.

My reflection stares back at me in the gold-trimmed mirror, framed by dried wild daisies stuck between the glass and the mundane wooden frame. I know I'm looking at myself, but the girl in the glass is a stranger, with all too-sharp angles and bruised skin. Deep tired eyes and a face hiding behind a mask of strength sit on slouched shoulders too worn to be bothered to straighten. Indigo spots run across her jaw and up to her eye, marring her legs, arms, and torso. She's pathetic, too weak to hit back the way she was taught. I pick up the cream on my table and turn it over in my hands. The itch it causes is insufferable, but it hides the marks well. I may be a fighter, but I refuse to parade around with bruises not gained in a match. I won't let them see how my mind shuts down when he lifts his hand. No one can be allowed to think of me as anything but made of unwavering, cold strength. I may have fallen in the ring, but I will not allow myself to take on the part of a defeated soldier. I apply the irritating concoction generously over my tender flesh, declining myself the luxury of wincing, even alone.

I silently stalk out of my room and make my way down the stairs, avoiding all the creaking boards out of habit. My mouth waters as the smell of cinnamon wafts through the halls. Spices are scarce in Wate, seeing as the blood-eyes control our trade and we can't grow it ourselves. But when we do use them, I'm reminded of good times, of childhood, and it makes the world seem a little brighter. I push through the doors to the kitchen and my steps falter as my eyes land on Cassien seated in his old chair at the weathered table. I almost smile, thinking of him as the father he used to be, the one who used to tell us stories as Mother would make the pastries. But as his predatory glare locks on mine, my blood freezes in my veins and reality comes crashing back. My body tenses as it prepares for an attack. He isn't supposed to be here in the mornings. He should be seeing to his lordly duties in the Council building, far away from us.

"Father," I say by way of greeting as I slip on a mask of calm. Byrne stands by the charcoal oven, cooking the source of the familiar smell: cinnamon toast. She places the drenched bread onto the heated pan as her sweet smile hides the primal fear in her eyes.

I sit down across from Cassien as my attention is drawn to his hands. He's wearing a ring, one I've never seen before. The band is jet black, but reflects the light like a diamond, the color sown deep into the stone. Small sweeping engravings adorn the otherwise simple ring. The gold ring Cassien keeps locked in his room holds the same patterns, as do all the original family rings. He hasn't worn ours since the day Mother died.

"It's the old Hael ring. It's beautiful, isn't it? Their family always did try to outdo the rest. They passed down this ring as a show of strength. To give the person who wears it the clarity of mind to make the right decision and the will to carry it out," he explains, moving his hand in the soft light filtering through the window. "The Haels took it back from the getic. They replaced it with a new one ages ago when Kerin disappeared with it on his finger, but the family could not stand to see their heirloom disgraced. They gave it to me for... safekeeping." Byrne drops a fork, the metal clattering loudly on the ground. My sister swallows hard but keeps her eyes on the pan.

"They have names, Father," Byrne says quietly. Panic rings in my mind. Why would she provoke him?

"Byrne, my daughter, getics are the people who created us. The people who cursed and tortured us. The weak idiots who think they can control us. They don't deserve the gift of recognition." He leans back casually in his chair, but I can see the violence sparking within him. "And the blood-eye is a blood-eye, I should not hear any contradictions from your mouth. They are *all* vicious beasts and can not be trusted. They do not deserve names, either of them." My sister flinches, shaking while I become impossibly still.

Cassien's eyes slowly shift to me as his face remains flat, emotionless. I wish I could read him to know what to expect. He's most dangerous when he has a clear mind. "Elana, you and your sister have spent time with our *guests,*" he drawls, the evenness in his tone making me recoil. I swallow the fear pushing up my throat. "Have you heard anything interesting from them. Anything I could... use for protection?"

"No, nothing of interest," I answer immediately, hoping he'll drop it but knowing it's a foolish wish. He stands slowly and I watch him step toward Byrne as my hands start to shake. He grabs her wrist and holds it over the searing pan as her body goes rigid. She swallows a scream as her hand floats a breath away from the burning metal. Sweat builds on my lip as I rack my brain for something, anything to give him. Byrne would rather be burned at the stake than cause others harm. I would face Cassien's wrath until the day I die before letting her suffer.

"Are you sure, Ella?" he presses gently, his use of the old nickname sending me into a full panic. He used to call me Ella before Mother died, before the grief carved out his heart and stole his gentle touch. He inches my little sister's hand closer to the heat. She presses against him as her eyes plead for mercy, but Cassien places his other hand on the back of her neck to keep her rooted in place. I know she doesn't want me to speak, but I won't let him hurt her.

"He can't sleep," I say quickly, the story slowly assembling in my head. Byrne goes deathly still beside him as her eyes bore into mine, begging me not to continue.

"And why would his insomnia be of interest to me, daughter?" He pronounces my title as if it were to be stepped on and forgotten.

"Because he gets terrors. The blood-eye hasn't slept soundly in years. He is haunted by dreams of past soldiers' deaths from the second he closes his eyes and sleeps only every three nights because of it. I don't doubt he would do anything if it were to allow him a single minute of peaceful sleep," I explain quickly, forcing the words out in a single breath. Cassien's thoughts go far away. His face curls into a smile as he looks back at me. He throws Byrne's hand at the pan and a loud sizzle erupts at the contact. She yelps as her palm bounces off the burning iron and pulls it to her chest as if to protect it from further damage. My shoulders slump with relief as Cassien steps away from her.

"That wasn't so hard to tell me now, was it?" he asks in a

disturbingly calm tone. I force myself to keep my chin high as I shake my head.

"I want you to tell him we have a drug that could help him. If what you say is true, he'll be desperate enough to take it without question. He's to inject it into the side of his neck when you give it to him. I want you to watch him do it and report back on the effects."

"Father," I start, my voice low as I struggle to keep my words composed. "I sliced open his throat, I can't imagine he'll trust me."

"Then gain his trust, Elana. Do what you must. Byrne, you will accompany her. You are trained as a phantom; your skills may be needed," he says as he folds his hands behind his back, the embodiment of a High Lord. Byrne backs away, jumping when she hits the wall. She starts to shake her head and opens her mouth to oppose, but I take a step toward Cassien, drawing his attention to me.

"It will be done, Father." His cold gaze stays locked on me as his eyes rove over my unblemished face. I can feel Byrne's disapproval burning into me. She knows exactly what I'm doing, how I'm shielding her.

"That's my dutiful daughters, doing the right thing. Wait for me outside the Council building when the sun starts to set. You have until then to convince him to take it," he dismisses, done with the both of us. Before he can walk out of the kitchen, Byrne calls to him. I freeze with fear, then shame at the childish reaction.

"Could it hurt us, this drug?" my younger sister calls. The beginning of a smile pulls at the side of Cassien's face as he looks over his shoulder.

"You will not be taking it, so there is no need to worry about such a notion." His words do not sit right, like a duvet spread over crumpled sheets.

"Father, what is this drug? What are we supposed to tell him?"

"Ruby Tar. It will be our salvation." He exits without another word, leaving Byrne and me to nothing but the sound of the smoking cinnamon toast and our dismembered thoughts.

"Why would you agree?" Byrne breathes as she clutches her hand to her chest. Stunned out of my silence, I walk over to the charred bread on the stove. I pull it off the heat and dump what would have been my breakfast into the wastebasket full of eggshells. Byrne tracks my movements with sharp eyes as I pour water into a bowl and leave the kitchen to get some salve. When I return with bandages in hand, she continues to watch me as if she had been doing so even while I was in the other room. She dips her injured hand in the water without breaking my gaze. I place the salve and the dressing on the table and reach for her. She quickly pulls away, spilling the water over the table and floor.

"I asked you a question," she says sternly. Her eyes narrow and her chin lifts, telling me that she won't back down no matter how long I stay silent.

"I wasn't going to let you walk into the cross fire, Byrne. He burned your hand for not answering. And we both know that he is capable of much worse," I say as the covered bruises on my face begin to burn. She squares her shoulders, her expression and stance at odds with the tenderness with which she cradles her hand.

"Elana, he could be handing us poison. This drug could be incapacitating, or deadly! What happens to his brothers and sister if he dies, Elana? How would *you* feel if you gave up everything to escape Wate, only to have them kill me with a poison disguised as a remedy?" she scolds, her voice raw and low. I want to break something, shatter every dish in this room to snap her out of these thoughts.

"We are not the getic and the blood-eye, Byrne. I promised Mother I would keep you safe. I don't care who has to get hurt or die, I'm not subjecting you to pain we could avoid. Ruby Tar could very well be the miracle to end his misery," I say, forcing myself not to shout. Somehow, I keep my words strung tight and even. Her lips form a thin line as she shakes her head, disgust and disbelief flashing across her face.

"Father would never do such a thing and you know it. He is not a peaceful man nor one who will change his beliefs," she says as tears cloud her eyes. "If something happens to Leo, we are going to help him no matter the cost. Promise me we will," she begs, holding out her burned hand as a peace offering. "My life is not worth the infinite suffering of others. I can't live knowing the price is someone else's pain, no matter who they are or what we're supposed to think of them. I won't let you burn the world for me."

I nod, relief flooding my mind even as I disagree with her words. I would do anything to keep her safe, no price is too high. I close my eyes and open the tin of salve. "I promise," I whisper, not knowing if it's a vow I'll be able to keep.

TWENTY-FIVE

ELANA

I head back toward the Hael house with Byrne by my side. We both watch the small wooden box in my hand, waiting for something to happen. It feels like I'm holding a deadly weapon capable of bringing an entire people to their knees.

Earlier today, Byrne and I managed to convince the blood-eye to take the drug. Well, we convinced the getic to let him take it. They were in the old pantry closet when we arrived. The Haels brought us to them, unlocking the sturdy door before swinging it open. The brothers' eyes blazed as they glared at us from the tiny room. The space was so small the two stacked trays and a wash bucket had to be shoved under the beds in order for them to walk in and out. The younger boys were already off to their first classes, their sister held tight in her grandmother's arms as she tried to run to her brothers. Mrs. Hael had to leave the kitchen when Saiph started crying, evidently desperate to be away from her grandmother's iron grip.

The blood-eye and getic did little to hide their bitterness, but just as their fury showed on their faces, so did their longing. The blood-eye caught himself in a second, melting his features into the picture of arrogance and ease. A murderer's mask, slipped on in times of need to hide what he does not want others to see. His brother was less successful at masking his unease and simply wiped all emotion from his face, leaving nothing to read at all. I made sure to stay behind Byrne as the elder Haels left us alone after quickly dismissing the cook. When my sister shakily proposed the idea to the brothers, the blood-eye's eyes lit up, ready to do whatever we asked if it meant the end of his terrors. I'm sure if we had told him to jump into the Vallan and sing to the high heavens, he would have done it without a second thought. It was his brother who posed a challenge. He seemed comfortable around Byrne but had nothing but wariness and displeasure reserved for me. The fact we had done nothing but help to keep them in a cage and draw their blood did not help the matter.

The blood-eye's neck was wrapped in crisp white bandages, but I could imagine the gruesome line of stitches underneath. My eyes had snagged on it more than once, regret pooling in my stomach. I gave myself an internal slap every time the emotions surfaced. I should not feel bad for a wound he deserved.

Neither brother spoke to me, though I caught the blood-eye staring several times. The getic asked about Byrne's hand, and for a moment, I thought she might tell him. Thankfully, she explained that she'd simply made the mistake of touching a pan too soon after it had been used. The blood-eye showed no signs of sensing our lie, but his brother seemed skeptical. The leery expression he wore still grated at my soul. He seems to catch every detail left unsaid. It's unsettling to say the least.

In the end, the blood-eye was the one to convince the getic as he pleaded his case with the notion of peaceful, restful sleep. The hope in his eyes slowly chipped away at his brother's reluctancy. It was strange to witness the love they shared. How one was so eager to take the drug and yet wouldn't if his brother disagreed. How the other could see the risk and yet would not deny the blood-eye the chance at getting better. They remind me of Byrne and me and the protectiveness we hold for each other. I scowl at the thought. They aren't blood, look nothing alike, and one is a getic. It's strange and unnatural, yet somehow, after no more than a few minutes with them, no one would ever question their bond.

After they agreed and I no longer felt as if they would tear out my throat, I apologized for slicing him at Byrne's demand. I had to admit, it was a smart move. It was a show of good faith, but that didn't mean I enjoyed or meant it. The blood-eye nodded and accepted my attempt to make amends with a stoic face. The getic seemed composed, but I could see his brother angle himself to get between them should he decide to stop being so civil. I doubt he could do anything to me, but his glare managed to cut through the dense armor I've spent years building, rendering me weak and helpless. I looked away first, and it made my blood boil.

It took only an hour to convince them, but Byrne never made a move to leave. Instead she called the cook in and had her prepare lunch for the four of us. The brothers were hesitant at first and many heavy glances passed between them but after one bite of the tasteless food all their worries seemed to melt away. The brothers practically inhaled the steaming stew and fluffy rolls. My sister even gave them her untouched bowl, which the getic dutifully split between them. I wasn't hungry, especially for this watery stew made of leftover meat scraps from the night before, but I still ate the entire bowl. I almost gave it up to the brothers, thinking it some sort of punishment, but changed my mind as I watched them eat as if the food was a delicacy. When they finished, Byrne asked after their brothers and sister, and for the first time, neither looked in the least bit infuriated or doubtful. They seemed dejected... broken. They seemed to sink into themselves, leaving nothing but hollow shells. I wonder if they'd given up on their siblings and accepted they can no longer be a part of their lives?

We spent the rest of the day with them, learning of their childhood and family. I would have been quite content to leave after we got our answer, but Byrne stayed rooted in place. I asked her why when we finally cleared out of the house only an hour before having to meet Cassien at the Council building and she'd simply told me that they're only let out of the room for two hours a day. She kept quiet the rest of the way, but her pride was clearly written on her face. She had freed the brothers from a day in the darkness and was glad for it. I wanted to hate how we bent the rules, but in the end, I was enjoying listening to the brother's easy banter and was taken by the strangeness of their stories.

We step back into the Hael house as the sun sets over the horizon, the lady of the house bowing her head as she leads us inside. The Hael boys and their sister are all sitting in the kitchen, laughing around their elder brothers. For a long moment, we watch the way their grandfather leers at them with eagle eyes as the blood-eye bounces his sister on his knee, the child giggling madly. They all listen to the second youngest of the brothers, Antares, making a show of explaining a joke one of the students had played on their classmates. The student would have been taken to receive private punishment for misbehaving, but young Antares leaves that part out of the story. The eldest of the Hael boys, Altair, stands against the wall, smiling softly at his brother. I don't miss the confused glance he sends toward the blood-eye and getic, as if for a moment, he forgets who they are.

We step into the kitchen as the smell of whatever had been prepared for dinner wafts through the air. My mouth waters as the aroma of spices envelops me like a warm blanket. The elder Haels quickly round up the boys and rip Saiph from the blood-eye's arms before ushering them upstairs and dismissing the cook. The brothers watch their siblings long after they disappear through the door with sorrow-filled eyes, listening attentively to their footsteps as the children race up the stairs.

With the small wooden box still cradled tightly in my hands, I follow the brothers to their room. They sit shoulder to shoulder on a cot as their knees hit the bed across from them. Their physical differences stand out sharply in the light of the oil lamp Byrne sets down beside her as she takes a seat on the opposite cot. The getic's near ebony skin and dark eyes are stark against the blood-eye's too-pale skin and glowing silver eyes. Their only resemblances are their above-average height and stoic expressions.

A small pile of ripped strips of fabric is lying on the ground, some stained red with blood. Why would they keep bloody bandages?

The creaking of the old cots pulls me from my thoughts. "I struggle when I sleep," the blood-eye explains as he follows my gaze to the pile of material. By the Goddess, he had told me he needed to be tied down, but my mind had not realized what he meant. I swallow hard, uncomfortable with the weight of his truth. I carefully open the box and my throat tightens as I take in the contents. A glass and metal syringe filled with a metallic-black liquid sits in a neatly folded cloth. I pick it up and frown as I hold the syringe up to the light. The drug itself takes on a color so bright, it could challenge that of a cut ruby. The longer I stare at it, the more it seems to glow and cast a shadow simultaneously. Cael leans over with nothing but curiosity and takes the syringe in his hand.

"You have to inject it directly into the side of his neck," I say quickly as a lump starts to form in my throat. The blood-eye's mouth falls open as reality finally sets in. The getic sits straighter as Byrne leans against the wall, an unsettling feeling hanging in the air as we stare at the substance. My sister takes a deep breath and stands before taking my arm and pulling me into the kitchen. "We'll give you some space," she says to the brothers as the blood-eye's face turns ashen.

"Wait! Don't go too far, at least for a while. We don't have much luck with things going well and I'd rather Cael not be alone if something were to happen," the blood-eye pleads. It's the first time I've heard him allow fear to drive his words. They're foolish for trying this, but I nod all the same and take a seat at the cooking table. Byrne sits beside me as she fiddles with her hands.

"At least we won't have to hide in order to keep an eye on them," I mutter, staring at the wall. The blood-eye curses as the getic orders him to stay still from inside the room. Byrne flinches at the sound.

"What do you think will happen?" she whispers softly, her voice uneven.

"I have no idea," I confess, shaking my head. "The blood-eye could willingly be taking poison for all we know." My sister tenses and meets my gaze.

"The blood-eye has a name. So does the getic. They aren't difficult to remember." She pauses for a long moment, seeming less sure of herself. "Do you think Father would poison him?"

"No, I don't think so. Cassien kept him alive for a reason. There's something about them we haven't figured out, something Cassien knows." I glance at the now silent room. "Have you ever seen anyone with his markings, two bands around their code?" My sister shakes her head, pondering the same thing as her brows knit together.

"Blood-eyes have one band between their elbows and their numbers, not two. Maybe he's half blood-eyed and half gold-eyed?" she wonders aloud, mulling over the possibility. I scoff loudly at the thought.

"There is not a soul in this city who would willingly spend time with a blood-eye and by law it is forbidden. His eyes flood with blood like theirs do, there cannot be gold-eye in him." My sister goes strangely quiet as she wraps her hands around herself and sinks into the chair. The thought of our people mixing is revolting. No wonder she looks like she's about to vomit.

My mind wanders to what it would be like to live their lives, to run from everyone without a moment's peace. Sympathy rises out of my depths along with a strong wave of disgust.

Deep screams bounce off the walls as the sounds of struggle hit our ears. Byrne and I lock gazes, frozen in place. "This would be a good time to tell me you both stayed!" the getic calls, somehow breaking through his brother's screams. We jump out of our seats and sprint to the room, nearly getting caught in the door. The getic kneels over his brother as he tries desperately to tie a gag around his mouth and keep his flailing arm down on the cot. His legs and other arm are tied tight to the bed, but the material keeping them in place strains against him, starting to tear. Byrne lets her eyes melt gold and takes the blood-eye's arm. She reels as he fights against her, her face tight as she forces his hand down. His ankles and wrists are bleeding from pulling against the restraints and his lungs heave quick short breaths as he shakes. It's like he's being tortured, attacked by a force we can't see.

The getic finally gets a strip of fabric around the blood-eye's face, muffling his screams enough so as not to wake the rest of the household. Tears fall from his eyes as his back arches off the cot, desperate to get away from his own mind. His words come back to me in a flash. *I don't sleep, I die.*

"Wake him up!" I order frantically, looking to the getic as he jumps over his brother and lands on the cot between the blood-eye and the wall. He holds down his other arm, doing his best to keep it still.

"Don't you think I would have thought of that!" he snaps, fear sharpening his anger. We gave him whatever pulled his brother into this fit, and I can't help but feel responsible. "You can't wake him up once he's asleep. We have to wait it out."

The restraint around the blood-eye's ankle snaps and his leg lashes out. He kicks his brother so hard I hear the wind leave his lungs. He doubles over and lets go of the blood-eye's arm. His hand flies to his neck, scratching and prying as if someone were choking him. Blood flows from new scratches and broken stitches before the getic can stop it, the bandage protecting his neck torn away. The getic grabs his brother again as he gasps for air. I find the discarded fabric and press it to the leaking wound.

"Wake up!" I try, praying he'll snap out of it. As if in response, his leg flies to the wall and a loud pop sounds when it collides with the stone. The getic adjusts his position before taking the cloth from my hands, the shock of seeing the injury momentarily freezing me in place.

"Keep his feet down," he commands breathlessly, still struggling to fill his lungs. I do as he says, shifting the silver of my eyes to gold. Even with my senses sharpened and strength heightened, I have to lean all my weight on his legs to stop them from flailing. I try my best to steady his injured leg, but every time I get close to popping his knee back in place, his thigh juts out and pulls the limb in two different directions. My stomach churns at the revolting sight.

"Leo?" a sleepy voice calls from beside the door. It's strange to hear such a small voice twisting around with the muffled screams. The getic meets his younger brother's worried gaze and easily soothes the fear from his features. I have to admire how efficiently he changes his expression for the boy. The youngest brother, Castor, goes deathly pale as he watches the blood-eye struggle.

"Look at me, Cass," the getic says. Castor does as his brother asks, his eyes glazed with unshed tears. "He's fine, Cass. It's just a bad terror. Go back to bed and tell Antares and Altair not to worry." The getic's voice is soft and coaxing, but there is a string of tension lying underneath. Castor doesn't miss it.

"Leo doesn't yell," Cass says, craning his head to see past his elder brother.

"Cass, he's going to be okay. I need you to go back to your room," he urges evenly. "Go sleep with Altair or Antares. Leo will be fine in the morning, I promise." Cass nods skeptically, his eyes straying to the blood-eye's writhing body before he disappears. Sadness and guilt creep into the getic's gaze as he watches the door after his brother is gone.

I don't know how long it lasts, minutes... maybe hours. Suddenly, just as I begin to give up on the idea that he will ever wake up, the blood-eye pulls so hard on the restraints, the three of us can't hold him down. He leans over the side of the cot and retches all over the floor, convulsing violently. The getic lets out a relieved sigh and steps down from the bed, gently pushing past my sister. Byrne's face is as pale as moonlight, her eyes stuck on the waking blood-eye. We pull our shirts over our faces to try and keep out the smell, but the getic doesn't seem to notice.

"Cael?" the blood-eye scratches out roughly.

"I'm here, brother, catch your breath."

TWENTY-SIX

LEO

My throat burns like I've swallowed hot coal. My leg feels like it's been torn in half and the wound on my neck opens and pulls as I breathe, bathing me in pain. But worse than anything are the lingering wisps of terror. I can still feel the hands wrapped around my neck, keeping me from my family. I try to bleed my eyes, yearning for numbness, but the more I try to call on it, the more my head throbs. Panic takes hold as I grasp at a cold void just beyond my fingertips.

Cael helps me sit up, trudging through the remains of my dinner and not caring in the slightest. Elana and Byrne stare at me with more fear than I thought possible. I hold the piece of fabric to my neck, pressing hard to stanch the steady flow of blood. Cael stands by my twisted leg and inspects it with creased brows. I can still see the horror etched into his features, but my brother has a way of focusing solely on what needs to be done.

"I know what we saw was worse than ever. The physical

effects of the terror were… something I don't think any of us will forget," he says shakily, meeting my gaze as his hand subconsciously hovers over his stomach. I must have hurt him. "You knocked the wind out of me, that's all," he says dismissively, knowing where my thoughts had gone. His eyes go far away, as if he were remembering what happened. "You screamed, Leo." Goose bumps run down my arms as I breathe through clenched teeth. "What went on in your head?" my brother asks gently, pulling me from my train of thought.

I look at the sisters as I try to put the words together. It takes me a moment to register their glowing gold eyes as they sit watching me from Cael's cot. I push away the memories of my parents and sister, their eyes glowing the same mesmerizing hue.

"Leo?" Cael tries, bringing me back once more. I must have been staring because both sisters shift uncomfortably. Their eyes fade to silver as I pin my gaze to the oil lamp sitting beside them, throwing a buttery light around the room.

"You were there," I croak, my voice hoarse. "And Mum and Dad and the boys and Pleiades. You were all there." Cael shudders, sitting beside me as if he weren't sure if his legs would keep him standing. "The terror merged with my memories. They were torturing you. They killed Pleiades first, the same way she died. Then Dad and Mum, even Pollux. They strangled me, nailed me to the wall to keep me from moving. I've lived that particular terror dozens of times, but you're never—" Cael forces my knee back into its socket. I bite my tongue so hard I taste blood. I swallow the scream rising in my throat and press my head to the wall. I hear Byrne gasp as her hands fly over her mouth.

"Sorry," Cael mumbles. "I figured it was better if you weren't paying attention to what I was doing."

"I'm going to get you back for that," I wheeze. "You could

have at least given me a warning." My words hold no power as the fire running up my leg immediately disappears,.

"They ask me questions I don't know the answers to and punish me when I can't tell them, but they... you're never..." I scrub my eyes with the heel of my hand, trying to wash away the memories flashing behind them.

They stare at me with disbelief, but while worry lines my brother's face, the Cassien sisters look like they've seen Lady Death, their jaws slack and eyes wide. Cael steps closer, squinting his eyes as if something didn't make sense. He puts a hand over the bandage on my neck and presses much harder than he needs to. "Ow!" I jump and swat his hand away. "What was that for?" I demand through clenched teeth.

He stares at me strangely, tilting his head to the side. "Why aren't your eyes red?" he asks suddenly. I blink and try to pull the instinct into place once more. Nothing happens. Panic sets in at the same time as the vulnerability. I feel bare, exposed without the instinct acting as my armor.

"I can't. It won't... I don't know why, but I can't get my eyes to turn," I rasp desperately, looking to the sisters in hopes that they can give me an answer. Elana's expression goes coldly neutral. She's figured something out.

"You're most likely just reeling from being dragged through the terror," Cael says with less confidence than I would like. I nod, knowing I can do nothing else. Cael has to be right, because I don't want to consider any other possibilities.

It takes me all night to stop shaking. Cael stayed by my side, even while I knew he was being crushed by the darkness and pelted by waves of his past. I speak numbly until his breathing evens out, droning on until he falls asleep and no longer needs a distraction.

When the Haels come to let us out the next day, I stay curled up on my cot like a scared child. Cael tries to get me to come with him, but no matter what I tell myself, my legs won't move. He leaves the door slightly ajar, hesitating before he turns away. As I lie by myself, I try bleeding my eyes over and over. I become so desperate that I unbury memories I had locked away deep inside me, memories that make me cower with fear and shake in anguish. Nothing works, and with each try, I only fall deeper into oblivion.

The familiar, living instinct that usually sits within my reach, waiting patiently to be called upon, is gone. The space where it sits in my mind is dark and empty, left stagnant without the power. It feels like I've lost a part of myself. I brace myself against the wall and close my eyes as I try one more time.

Footsteps pound outside the room, pulling me out of the grueling memory I had been replaying. Cael and the boys must be back. I take a deep breath and finally manage to get myself standing through the grueling pain. I don't have the will to do anything but lie down and search the empty space in my mind, but I won't let the boys worry. Cael said Cass had come down last night. He won't believe I'm all right if I'm curled up in bed. My mood immediately darkens impossibly further as I step out of the room. My eyes narrow as I come face-to-face with two torturous stares. Saiph squeals as she tries to wrench her hand free from her grandmother's hold. Somehow, she manages to get away from the old crone and runs toward me. Her footsteps are so much surer than they were when we left Somereil. I scoop her up into my arms and hold her tight as I use the wall for support. She smiles as she wraps her hands around my neck before launching into a story about a yellow butterfly. I listen intently as I take in her improving dialect. She's grown up so much in the short time we've been here. Time I'll never get to spend with my little sister.

"She is under our care blood-eye. Put her down and let her return to us. You've had your moment." My eyes shoot up as the grandfather spits the words at me. The cook stills at the oven and lowers her head before hastily making her way out of the room.

"I raised her. She is my sister. I'm allowed to have more than a minute with her," I say as my voice rings with finality. I make sure to keep my anger in check for Saiph's sake. The Haels glare at me as bloodlust shines in their eyes.

"I will not tolerate you in my house if you do not abide by my rules, blood-eye. It's bad enough they have had to live with you monsters this long! We will not allow them to suffer any longer under your *care*," the grandfather all but snarls.

"We've raised them better than you ever could. Don't speak to me about what it was for them to live in our care. We did everything for these kids and always will," I say, my voice low and dangerous. I hold his stare as I nod along to my sister's story.

"We will rid them of the impurities you placed in their minds and raise them to be Haels. Raise them to be the image of what a proper gold-eye is expected to be."

"Are you going to raise them like you did your son? Because he turned out quite *dead* in the end." I hit a nerve. The grandfather lunges for me as his eyes flash gold. The empty space in my mind fills and the entity at the tip of my fingers takes form right in time for me to grasp it. My eyes bleed red and my entire body seems to sigh in relief as I easily dodge the attack. I hold his neck in one hand and Saiph in the other, turning her away from her grandfather. I pin him against the wall while my fingers dig into his throat. He sputters as I push harder, rage driving my actions.

"You are the monsters. You are the reason they will become corrupt. We will always do what is best for them. No one, not even you, will get in the way of that," I threaten softly, my voice a whisper in his ear. I catch a flash of gold as the grandmother moves behind me. I turn away from the grandfather as his wife throws her hand through the air, a blade clenched in her fist. I catch her wrist midair and twist sharply. Her hand opens involuntarily and the steel clatters to the floor. Fear clouds her expression as Saiph buries her face in my shoulder to escape.

A stern hand lays softly on my shoulder. Cael pulls me back, forcing me to let go of her wrist. I turn as the grandfather takes a seat on the same stool I sat on when I first arrived, wheezing and panting.

"You will never step foot in this house again. Ever!" he yells furiously between gasps. His wife walks to his side as she clutches her wrist to her chest. Cael takes Saiph from my arms and leads me out of the kitchen. I don't turn my back on the Haels until I'm out of the room and the door is closed behind me. Cael and I dart from the house, stopping as we meet the boys on the front steps.

"What was that?" Cael asks, his voice even. I would have expected my brother to be disappointed and worried about the consequences of my actions, but he seems relieved about what he witnessed.

"We're going to have to find another place to live for a while," I tell the boys as I watch the front door from the corner of my eye. Their faces drop. "Go grab your things, we'll ask Cassien where else we can stay."

"You mean the High Lord?" Altair corrects me hotly.

"Sure, whatever you want to call him," I dismiss,

wondering how I'm going to collect my belongings. A thought stops me. I have nothing but the clothes on my back.

"Why can't we stay with grandmother and grandfather? They're family and we finally have a good home. I don't want to leave. I want to go to the Academy," Antares complains as his bottom lip juts out. Altair and Cass both wear the same pleading expression. It melts me and angers me simultaneously. How could they want to stay here?

"We're staying in Wate, but we aren't welcome in this house anymore. Now go grab your things and Saiph's too, please," Cael says, his voice firm.

"I don't want to go. I want to stay here. Why do we have to go somewhere else when we're happy where we are?" Altair demands, his jaw clenched and feet set apart. Something flashes in his eyes: a shadow of real hatred. "Why can't you see we're happy? Why do you have to go around messing things up when we're *happy,*" he spits, a deadly venom lacing his words. I glance at Cael as my brows shoot up. Altair has never spoken to us like that.

"Altair, everything we do is to keep you safe. This is for the best. Leo isn't the reason why we left home last time, and Leo isn't the reason we're leaving now," Cael explains, trying and failing to hide his sorrow. Antares and Cass both nod and give us the barest of smiles.

"All right," Antares says softly, leading Cass toward the door.

"No. I'm not letting you drag me away from people who care about me. I'm not letting you corrupt me." I freeze, so completely taken aback by shock that my brain refuses to function. I look to Cael, but his gaze is pinned to Altair.

"What are you talking about? We care for you, Altair." My voice is no more than a whisper of disbelief. He shakes his head before stomping toward the door.

"They were right. Blood-eyes and getics only bring pain and unhappiness," he mutters under his breath, but we all hear it. Cael watches Altair go, no inkling of emotion visible on his face. Antares and Cass watch their brother disappear behind the door as their mouths move without sound.

"Why?" Cass asks. Cael shakes his head slowly, his expression tight as he reaches to spin the ghost of his ring.

"I don't know... I don't know."

Elana and Byrne lead us through the city with Saiph sitting in the crook of Cael's arm and the boys following a few paces behind us. Something is wrong with Altair, he hasn't spoken a word to us, scaring even Antares and Cass. His words cut us all deeper than I dare to quantify. He's barely glanced our way since he trudged back into the Hael house and has been ignoring our efforts to explain.

The sisters take us through the looming iron gates of the Academy and my stomach rolls as we step onto the wide dirt road. I keep my eyes down. I'm not up to facing the bitter glares of the people of Wate. Altair sputters as we stop in front of the puppet barracks. Elana and Byrne turn to face us.

Though I don't look, I can feel the stares of the students and instructors burning into the back of my head. They call out to their classmates to come see who will be taking up residence in the Academy. "There are five beds in the back. Boys, your schedule has not changed, and you are expected to continue your training as you did before. You may leave the premises after classes, but you must be back here by sundown when the gates are closed. You two," Elana says, gesturing to Cael and me, "will have to leave when the day begins and come back before the gates are locked at night. You are prohibited to be on the Academy grounds when classes are in session unless you are accompanied by the High Lord. You will also have to take care of your sister since the Haels have refused to have anything to do with you." I nod grimly, but I don't feel any regret. Altair glares at the barracks, his hands curling into fists as firelights in his eyes. "We'll leave you to get settled."

The sisters leave us without another word, Byrne giving us her best encouraging smile. We enter the barracks in silence as the contents of my stomach go leaden. The second we breach the building, the smell of decay and unwashed bodies hits me like a punch to the throat. Altair and Antares both go into coughing fits as we walk deeper into the wide-open room. They pull their shirts over their noses to block out the stench. We pass child after emaciated child as they bury themselves into their dilapidated cots, trying to disappear. The oldest is maybe a year older than Altair, but it's hard to tell with their jutting bones and swollen bellies. They look like they should be dead, but by some terrible miracle, their hearts still beat in their chests. Cael passes me a weary glance as my throat begins to close. Cass and Antares's faces are pale as they follow close behind us. The sight is overwhelming, even for me.

We set up at the back of the room, selecting five rusty cots with broken tables between each of the narrow beds. Saiph, Cael, and the boys lie down immediately, though I can tell it takes them a while to fall asleep. There is not a single moment when someone in the barracks is not awake, either having been thrust from their sleep by a nightmare or a coughing fit. How can they live like this? How could they allow children to live like this? The thoughts circle through my head in an unending cycle until the birds announce the rising sun.

TWENTY-SEVEN

LEO

Cael and I leave the Academy grounds as Saiph trots between us with her hand tucked tightly in my brother's. He seems agitated, jumping at every sound. When I ask him about his strange mood, he brushes me off with a wave of his hand, only deepening my worry. I don't push him again, knowing he'll speak when he's ready.

We walk through the streets silently, taking in the view of the taverns and shops selling everything from clothing to food to medications. I search for an inn or a boarding house, but not one appears. There had been dozens lining Somereil streets, usually packed to the brim with all types of patrons. I guess they would have no need for an inn here, but the notion that there are never travelers passing through unsettles me.

The avenues are cleaner than any in Tominay. The orderly streets aren't soiled with oil spills or filled with the stench of rotting garbage. There are no cramped buildings leaning on each other like old friends or barkers beckoning to the stream of natives and tourists alike. I almost miss the familiar bustle of Somereil's market streets.

We stop to sit at the beginning of a wide thoroughfare lined with carts and bright stalls. Daeta's market. The buildings rise higher and are much closer together than in other parts of the city. *This is where the lower class live,* I realize with a frown. It's still ten times more proper than most of the quarters in any city I've ever visited. The feel of the market basks me in a blanket of easy calm as the smell of cooking food and the sound of barter wafts through the air. I expect my brother to be as at ease as I am, but he looks like he's ready to jump out of his skin. His eyes track a man with white-blond hair and porcelain skin standing across the street. The man is tall and lanky, unlike the lady he speaks to. She could not be more his opposite with her rich-black skin and short stature, thick with bulky muscle. They pay no attention to the steaming drinks they hold in their hands. I watch the duo carefully, wondering why Cael would take such an interest in them.

"I'm going to go for a walk," Cael blurts as he scans the rest of the crowded market. "Why don't you see if you can get some food?" He lifts Saiph off his knee as he stands and places her on the ground beside me. He rummages through his pockets and pulls out a small embroidered pouch. Without so much as glancing my way, he takes out a few coins and drops them into my waiting hand.

My brother melts seamlessly into the crowd without another word, disappearing so completely it's like he turned to ash and floated away in the wind. My eyes wander back to the pale man Cael had been watching so intently. Our gazes meet for a fraction of a second before he throws himself into the current of people, discarding his drink on the first stall he passes.

I stand and pull Saiph up into my arms to stop her from getting swept away in the bustle of people. I immediately feel the burly woman's gaze pin me like the tip of a blade as her eyes track my every movement. As I merge into the crowd, the people quickly step out of the way with a gasp or a glare. I block them out and let the sound of popping oil and the smell of sugar and spices guide my steps.

"Leo," Saiph coos as she grasps at the air, pointing at a stall overflowing with multicolored sweets. I make my way over as I turn the coins in my hand. Pastries like these would cost a small fortune in Tominay, but the child ahead of us gives two coins over to the lady manning the table and runs off with a fluffy delicacy stuffed with jam and dusted in fine sugar. My mouth waters as I step up. Saiph scans the lines of goods with eager eyes. Wate can't be so terrible if they have food like this in the market.

"How much for one of the pastries?" I ask with a polite smile on my face. The lady takes a step back as her chin juts out and her eyes thin to slits.

"I don't serve blood-eyes," she says with disgust as her voice wavers.

"I can pay. I have money." I lift my hand to show her the coins. She flinches at my movement, watching Saiph in my arms with open concern. "It's not for me, it's for her," I try gently. The lady takes another step back.

"I don't serve blood-eyes," she repeats.

Every stall I try gives the same clipped answer, some sellers acting like they want to disappear while others glare at me like they'd enjoy beating me to a bloody pulp. I continue along and try one last stall filled with carved wooden toys. Dogs with moving feet and birds with flapping wings sit proudly on display. The vendor tucks his son behind him and doesn't even bother to answer my questions.

"Blood-eye!" a raspy voice calls as my patience starts to fray. I turn quickly in search of the voice. I catch the burly lady watching me closely from a nearby stall selling shoes as I scan the market. Confusion passes through me briefly as I realize I reacted to someone calling out "blood-eye." When did that become a name I respond to?

An old woman across the street waves me over with knobbed hands. I reluctantly walk over as unease pools in my stomach. Nothing about this woman feels right, but something inside pushes me forward. *You need to let people see you're just like them, then they'll accept you. You cannot fear them.* I stop in front of her table as Saiph goes still in my arms. This feels wrong. She pushes a paper cone full of meat skewers and fried potatoes into my hand.

"Thank you," I say, my brows knitting together as I hold out the coins. She shakes her head as if she were appalled at the prospect of getting paid. Maybe it's a custom here.

I walk back over to the spot Cael and I had scoped out and take a seat. I prop Saiph on my knee as she tries to take the cone from my hand.

"Hold on, I'll give you some in a second," I tell her, taking a bite of the meat skewer. I gag at the taste and immediately have to place my hand over my mouth to stop myself from spitting it out. It scrapes down my throat as I force myself to swallow. It tastes worse than the mixture Cael used to make to chase away the pain from my wounds, like burned, rotting metal. Saiph reaches for the cone once more and whines when I pull it away.

"This isn't for you, Saiphy. You won't like it," I say, grimacing as I dare to try one of the potatoes. Surprisingly, they're good, though the lingering taste of the meat killed off my working taste buds. I hand her the cone of potatoes as I force myself to eat what I can of the meat. I only manage half before I'm sure I'm going to throw it up. I hate to waste it, but I doubt even a starving animal would be interested. It's no wonder the lady gave it to me.

I catch sight of Elana and Byrne walking through the crowd, deep in conversation. Byrne spots me and her face lights up as she waves, pulling her stubborn sister by the hand. She says something clipped over her shoulder and Elana relents on her efforts to stay away as her forehead creases. As they get closer, Byrne's face drops as her eyes fasten on the half-empty cone.

"Do you want some?" I offer in way of greeting.

"Did you buy that or did someone give it to you?" Byrne asks tightly, ignoring my question.

"An old lady gave it to me; she didn't take the coins I offered." The sisters' eyes lock. Byrne's expression tightens with worry as Elana radiates concern at her sister's dismay.

"Come, we need to leave," Byrne presses urgently as she turns around and locks eyes with the dark-skinned woman that had been watching me. The woman fumes as she averts her gaze, the ground suddenly becoming extremely interesting.

"Why?" I start as I position myself to stand up, but my head starts to spin and my legs give out before I get the chance, sending me crashing back to the ground. Elana catches my arm and aggressively pulls me to my feet with a blank face.

I blink as the world comes in and out of focus. Byrne takes Saiph into her arms as Elana drags me along, her pace too quick for my feet. My stomach turns with every step. Within seconds my vision blurs and I am completely disoriented, leaving me helpless. My knees buckle under my weight, but hands catch me before I plummet to the ground.

I try to call on the instinct and fall into the familiar feeling to get me through, but it's not there. I stretch for it, searching for any part to grab hold of, but there is only a dark, stagnant void. My breathing picks up as panic sets in and my body starts to shake.

As we pass into the woods, I try my best to lift my feet over the roots growing out of the ground, but they feel like they're made of solid stone, dragging me down. I am lowered to the ground as the sounds of flowing water and muffled arguing float distantly around me. Hands push my back against a tree as I break into a cold sweat, my mind drowning in a fog of pain. The earth feels too hard, the wind too cold, and the air too sharp as it fills my struggling lungs.

Someone places a wet cloth over my mouth and nose, eliminating my access to the air. My throat burns with the lack of oxygen as my muscles revolt. I try to scramble away, but my body feels like lead, chained to the ground. I fumble desperately for any sign of the instinct. Tears swell in my eyes as dark shadows creep around the edges of my vision. Just as my mind starts to float away, I feel it, a whisper of power sitting at the end of my fingers. I grasp onto it and pull with all my might. My eyes bleed red and my muscles react without a second to waste, pushing the damp cloth away from my face. I turn over onto my hands and knees and spill whatever I had ingested at the market, coughing frantically as I regain my senses. When my breathing finally levels out, my stomach completely empty, I sit back down and lean my head against the tree.

"Are you all right?" Byrne asks frantically, breaking me from my trance. I nod as I meet her glare through a red haze. I hesitate before draining my eyes, afraid to let the numbness go. I swallow hard and force it down, the red curtain falling away. I look up to the stunned sisters. Elana holds a dripping piece of fabric as she eyes the vomit with disgust.

"How many times am I going to have to watch you retch?" she sneers.

"Did you try to drown me?" I breathe incredulously, ignoring her question. I stare at them as I desperately try to calm my thundering heart and speeding thoughts. Byrne bounces up and down as she tries to quiet Saiph's whimpering. I grab the tree and start to stand, my knees unsteady beneath my weight. Elana starts toward me as her face contorts into what can only be concern. I push her hand away and lock my knees, keeping a firm hold on the tree.

"Give her to me," I demand, my voice stronger than I expect it to be. Byrne reluctantly hands my sister over. The minute I wrap her in my arms, she quiets as she lays her head on my shoulder.

"It's all right," I whisper over and over, swaying slightly. My eyes stay locked on the sisters, but I don't dare ask anything, not until I can wrap my mind around exactly what happened. They knew there was something in the food the moment they saw me. They know, and they're still not telling me.

"What was it and why did it weaken me?" I finally ask, my voice low and dangerous even as a rasp. I intend it to be sharp and it hits its mark. Byrne grimaces uncomfortably as Elana stares, for once looking unsure of herself.

"The food was rotten. Minia, the lady who gave it to you, likes to give oblivious children bad food to make them sick. She thinks it's a game."

"I'm not a child."

"You are oblivious."

"That food wasn't rotten," I hiss. "Tell me or I swear by the stars on my back you will not step off of this riverbank."

"I saved your life!" Elana yells in disbelief, the gleam of worry that had appeared on her face nowhere in sight.

"By trying to kill me? You think trying to finish me off while I'm choking on poison is something I should be thankful for?"

She stares at me, her features trained into cool indifference as she reels in her rage. With a jolt, I realize I'm doing the same thing as I school my expression into an even plane.

"You don't know it was poison," she says coldly.

I scoff as I hold her gaze. "Do you honestly think me stupid? I've come close to death enough times to know when something is draining the life from me. Was it the same drug you told me would help me sleep? Ruby Tar?" Byrne takes a step forward and angles herself between us.

"That's enough. We can talk this out like civil people—"

"It is Ruby Tar then. The liquid metal you told me was a cure. You're trying to kill me." Byrne's expression saddens as despair wraps itself around my words. I laugh in hysterics as the hope that had dared bloom burns away.

"Stay away from my family. Do you understand me? I've killed hundreds in Tominay, your life won't weigh me down any more than theirs." I turn and walk away as my hands shake. After a long moment, Byrne runs after me, calling my name. I walk off the trail and hide behind a wide tree. She stops and scans the woods not far behind me. She seems hurt, and I almost feel bad. She has been kind to us, the only one in this wretched city who seemed to care. I hear Elana walk up the trail toward us a few minutes later. Byrne pushes her shoulders back and stares her sister down as she approaches. Elana walks ahead of her without a word with her hands fisted at her side. After a moment, Byrne reluctantly follows her along the path. Elana looks back before they disappear around a bend. Our eyes lock, and I know she's seen me, but she turns around without hesitation and continues on as if she had not.

TWENTY-EIGHT

CAEL

My attention narrows on one of the far stalls as I blend into the crowd. There is something wrong with this city and it's been eating at me since I arrived. It's not just the fact that Wates people seem like they would like to see me drawn and quartered, there's something bigger going on. I disappear easily into the wave of patrons all trudging sure-footed through the madness of Daeta's market. The white-haired man and dark-skinned woman have been stalking us for days. Anytime we go outside, I catch them lurking, watching from the corner of their eyes. They're shadowing us, and I don't like it.

I breathe easier as my mind goes quiet, the way it would in Tominay when money was spread so thin we had to resort to lifting food to survive. Leo has always been skilled at hiding, hunting, and killing in the darkness, silence and death his only friends. I, on the other hand, enjoy walking in the light, blending into the crowds and using my knowledge of mechanisms to open the old apothecary locks and take whatever supplies we needed to survive. I let myself drift to that life as the bustle of Somereil's streets comes back to me, my hands relaxed by my side.

I weave my way through the sea of people, keeping an eye on the white-haired man as he frantically scans the market and ruthlessly shoves patrons aside in his search. The stall I had been watching is different from the rest. It's covered in dark canvas on all sides with two soldiers dressed in black standing by the entrance, eyes dutifully ahead. I push through the crowd, feeling how it moves and flowing with it. The man turns in circles when he can't find me, his eyes sharp with panic. When he looks away, I take my chance and step out of the throng a few stalls ahead of him. I walk behind a busy cart with my eyes fixed to the ground and silently creep right up to the covered stall.

I flatten myself to the ground and lift a corner of the canvas. The tent is littered with crates marked with green circles painted on their panels. A short girl with upturned eyes and pin-straight jet-black hair cut just above her shoulders sits on the farthest crate, transforming it into a throne with her presence. Four soldiers dressed in black livery dig through the crates and wordlessly take stock of whatever lies inside. I bite my tongue as they begin to pull out weapon after weapon. Maces, long and short swords, daggers, throwing knives, axes, finger blades, and arrows. The girl grabs one of the sharp-tipped axes and takes her time inspecting it, reflecting light off of the steel.

"The getics' craftsmanship is disgusting," she sneers, her lips curling as she throws the weapon carelessly into an open crate. A loud rattling of metal on metal rings around the tent. Dread weighs heavy on my shoulders as I realize the crates must be filled with weapons. They should have no need for this type of armament in a peaceful city unknown to the rest of the world. Yet they train their children from birth to become heartless soldiers and are receiving crates of weapons.

The porcelain-skinned man barges through the tent flaps, his eyes crazed and hair disheveled. The moment he catches sight of the girl sitting on her throne of weapons, he straightens his back and bows his head, all emotion wiped from his face. He's our shadow, the one who's been watching us.

"Speak, Phantom," she says airily. The man winces and stiffens with fear. This girl is dangerous.

"Emila, I've lost track of the getic. He disappeared in the market." I can feel the tension rise in the tent as the others continue with their tasks.

"And why would this be of any concern? Go find him. He's a getic. He's probably gotten turned around and is weeping in a corner, lost without his poor brother to hold his hand," she mocks as she waves her hand dismissively. I block out the insult, letting it fly over my head. The snow-haired man swallows hard as unsaid words float before him. Emila's eyes narrow as she goes deathly still, all pleasantries dropping away. "You did not come here to tell me you can't do your job, Phantom. Spit it out before I cut the words from your head." He doesn't meet her gaze as his hands stick rigidly to his sides.

"The Cassien sisters dragged the blood-eye away after Minia gave him the Ruby Tar. We were unable to follow or watch its effects," he reports quickly, spewing the message in a single breath. Emila's expression darkens as she glares at him like a monster closing in on its kill.

"I ordered you to disregard the Cassien sisters, did I not? My word is second only to the High Lord's, and he has alluded to our working around the sisters. He will be displeased that we have not only lost eyes on the getic but have no information on how the Ruby Tar affects the blood-eye," she purrs as she stands from her perch like a predator playing with its prey. Emila stalks toward him slowly before flipping out a dagger and pressing it to his throat. "Why do you disobey orders, Phantom?"

"Elana is a Cassien. She is the rightful heir to Wate," he says evenly, suddenly interested in the canvas wall behind Emila. She chuckles softly, the sound laced with brewing violence.

"You fear her," she states slowly, tilting her head to the side as she pats his cheek with the flat side of the dagger. "You know full well the High Lord will not name Elana as his successor. I am his second. I will become High Lady when the time comes. Elana may be good with a blade, but she's soft with the love she holds for her sister and the love she yearns to have with her father. She is weak, and I am strong. You are under the command of a leader, my command. Do you understand?" she asks, her voice like honey on which the man is drowning. "You will fear no one but me." Emila tips her blade up under his chin and presses in, drawing blood. The man's hands begin to shake. "Where is Ceyana? She was tasked with the same assignment as you, correct?" He parts his lips to answer, but Emila stops him with a smirk. "I don't recall giving you permission to speak." She's trapped him. The pale man nods as she pushes the blade farther into his flesh. Emila watches intently, her grin widening as the man winces. He continues to nod until she takes a step back and returns to the crates turned throne. "Call her here. I want to speak with that phantom," she orders to one of the men who had been prying open another crate. He nods in acknowledgment and hastily takes his leave. "You are going to find the getic and report back. If you do not find him, please don't hesitate to let the current of the Vallan fill your lungs. Clean yourself up."

I let the flap of canvas fall and stand silently as my mind reels. I watch the tent as I retrace my steps and blend back into the bustle of the market. The man comes out with his hand holding the underside of his jaw, his eyes sparked with pain. My presence hadn't even been known, but Emila's words sent a sharp sting of fear into my bones. I keep to the densest areas of the market as I steadily get farther away from the tent. The second I clear the crowd and I'm sure I haven't been spotted, I burst into a run, the man's words sending a wave of panic coursing through my mind. *The Cassien sisters dragged him away after Minia gave him Ruby Tar.* I trust Byrne as much as someone like me can, but I'm not foolish enough to put it past anyone to try and get a shot at Leo. Not in this place.

I run through the streets, turning corners at random as I trust the senses I've depended on since my parents first shoved me into their cage. I stop at the northern forest edge. Someone is in there, walking quietly toward me. I strain my ears to listen as they approach. The gait is quick and the strides are long as one foot hits the ground in faster increments than the other. Leo walks out from behind a tree with slumped shoulders and Saiph cradled in his arms, her face red and stained with tears.

"Where have you been?" he pants when he comes close enough to keep his voice low. My brother looks like he's just visited Lady Death, his face pale and eyes glazed. I immediately take Saiph from his arms and put her down before looping his arm over my shoulder. He sighs in relief as I take the brunt of his weight.

"I had to see about something. Tell me what happened, and I'll tell you what I saw," I offer as I search for a suitable spot to sit. The gates of the Academy won't be open for a few more hours yet.

We find a secluded corner at the edge of the woods to sit. We are hidden enough not to draw any unwanted attention while allowing us a full view of one of the main thoroughfares leading to the Council buildings. I wait until the color returns to Leo's face before asking him to go through what happened. He slowly recalls the horrors of the past hour as he stares blankly down at his hands. I chase after Saiph, her laughter floating weightlessly through the air as she runs in circles around me with a wild daisy clutched in her hand as I listen. I couldn't feel more weighed down as Leo tells his story, the sentiment clashing with my sister's innocent joy. This is how we live, doing everything in our power to protect a perfect, peaceful landscape for Saiph and the boys while we face a roaring battlefield at their backs.

"If you don't mind, I'd like to hear what's going on inside your head instead of having to try and decipher it from your expression," Leo drawls once he finishes, crossing his arms with a false ease as he watches Saiph fall and right herself in the same awkward movement.

"I don't think they were trying to kill you. It seems more like they're... experimenting. Trying different doses and ways to administer the Ruby Tar." He gapes at me as if this were the first time the idea had crossed his mind. "You look like a fish, Leo," I point out dryly. His mouth snaps shut, his lips thinning.

"But why would they test it on me? It's obvious there are those among their own people who they don't treat with the same... kindness," my brother wonders aloud, images of the children in the puppet barracks flashing behind my eyes.

"You are different from them, Leo. I don't exactly know how, but you are." He nods solemnly. "Do you remember Tominay's flag?" I ask, redirecting the subject.

"Of course. A green circle around a hammer. When the Royals came to Somereil, they would fly a flag large enough to cover the width of the main thoroughfare," he reminisces as confusion crosses his eyes. "You don't remember?"

"I do, and that's the issue." The crease between Leo's brows only grows deeper as I explain what I witnessed in the tent. "The crates of weapons were branded with green circles."

"But there was no hammer?"

"No, but the part of the flag signifying the royals is the circle. The hammer represents Tominay and its all-mighty laws." Leo snorts.

"It's ironic seeing that Tominay is the most crime-ridden country on the continent. The royals love parading themselves around as the picture of civility though." The corner of my lip pulls up as I nod.

"Oh, definitely," I add sarcastically as my expression pulls into a frown. "Those crates were in the clearing the day we were attacked." The unsaid words hang heavily in the air. Leo rubs his hands over his face.

"The Tominese have a part in this too then?" I nod as the pieces refuse to fit together in my head.

"Could this have something to do with Elana not being High Lady after Cassien? The girl, Emila, didn't you say she was... plotting against her? Could she be using the Tominese as backing?"

"Maybe, but she said Cassien had already named her as his second, so why would Emila need to resort to force? And I doubt she would have been able to keep that plan a secret when half the city was in the clearing," I say near silently as I stare into the distance.

"Whatever's happening to Altair must fit into this as well," Leo murmurs, as if he didn't want to say the words aloud. We haven't acknowledged whatever's happening to our younger brother, but we both see and feel it. Altair has always been sympathetic, careful, and calm. He is not one for anger or rage and his regret was always overwhelmingly sharp and fast when he did something even remotely wrong.

"Do we have any idea why he's pulling away from us? When I first woke up, he was himself, then all of a sudden he's throwing blame and looking at us like we're strangers." Leo picks a little purple flower and hands it over to Saiph. She holds it out in front of her as if it were a thing of magic, capable of setting the night sky alight. "Maybe being here has made him realize he isn't truly safe with us. What he said was harsh but not far from the truth, Cael." I'm not sure how to respond. The boys know everything we do is for them, but I can't help but second-guess myself. I heave a deep sigh as I touch the ghost of my ring.

"Should we tell the sisters about it?" Leo asks as his expression clouds over.

"No. Chances are they are fully aware of what's going on. It's better if no one learns that we know as much as we do." He nods once, closing off the matter, though I doubt either of us will stop thinking about the happenings in this city for a long time.

TWENTY-NINE

CAEL

The sky is streaked with pink as we clear the Academy gates and head for the barracks. The grounds are silent except for the odd wandering student. I can't shake the unease weighing on my conscience since I saw Leo stumble out of those woods. The second we walk through the doors, all thoughts of what happened fly away. The kids are hiding behind their meager cots with their heads clutched between their knees. Altair stands at the back, looming over a small boy cowering in the corner. The boy's face is badly swollen and bruised, and his dull-red hair is covered in dirt. Cass comes running toward us with fear smeared across his face and Antares at his heels. He moves around Leo and presses his hand to his back. "He's hurting him," Antares says desperately, his expression strained with panic. I look up as Altair kicks the frail boy in the stomach, his back cracking off the wall.

"Hey!" Leo screams, his hands fisting by his sides as his eyes stay locked on our younger brother. Altair turns to us as blood drips from his knuckles. He doesn't move as he stares us down with fire in his eyes. He's almost my height now but seems twice as big as he stands in the dark corner. There is nothing in his gaze but raw anger. *He looks like Leo when he lets his monster take hold*, I realize with a jolt.

"Don't interfere," Altair spits at us before turning back to the boy. I can feel Antares fidgeting behind me as anxiety radiates off my younger brothers. Altair kicks the boy again, harder this time. The boy gives a pained cry as his head smashes against the ground.

"Altair!" Leo roars. "By the Lady step away *now!*" His voice is low and commanding. I straighten without thinking as he takes a step forward, his fists curling. I put a hand on his shoulder, keeping him rooted in place. Leo wouldn't lay a hand on Altair, but he won't hesitate to defend himself. That is a fight my younger brother would not win, but there's a violent glint shining in Altair's eyes that tells me he isn't thinking about how that brawl would end. He's not been himself since we came here, but he is still our brother, and Leo wouldn't forgive himself if he hurt him.

"He deserves it. He ratted me out for speaking," Altair fumes, a new venom bleeding from his words. He sounds cold, numb. Shivers run down my arms as his gaze meets mine. I don't see a sliver of my brother in those vengeful eyes.

"They would have whipped me if I didn't—" The boy wheezes from the ground, his words cutting off in a sharp gasp as Altair kicks him again, this time in the head. The crunch makes me cringe as the boy's eyes roll back. I don't stop Leo as he pushes toward Altair with shaking fists. I can feel the hot anger rippling off him in bursts as I walk beside him, my own composure worn thin by Altair's callousness. Leo grabs his arm and starts to drag him away, but Altair grabs Leo's wrist and jerks it at an unnatural angle. A stomach-churning pop sounding from the joint. The room falls silent around Leo's ragged breathing as his eyes bleed red. I stopped fearing him a long time ago, but it doesn't stop the unnerving feeling that comes with knowing how easily he could tear my heart out of my chest, and if he willed it, never feel an ounce of remorse.

Altair can't hide his fear. Leo positions himself between Altair and the boy still curled up on the ground. Leo hesitates, his stern expression cracking as he sees Altair's wide eyes. His regret becomes a tangible entity as he moves to step back. Before he's able to retreat, Altair swipes out a dagger from his sleeve and holds it in the air. I step back as I shake my head. My younger brother's forgotten the one thing that will write your death in the stars. This place has twisted him so severely, he's forgotten the unspoken rules of our family. No matter how enraged you are, you never pull steel.

"You're going to regret that," Leo snarls. He grabs Altair's hand and spins him around in one smooth motion, almost too fast to register. He holds Altair flush against the wall. Altair struggles against Leo's grip as he tries to turn his head to look at us. I pry the blade from his hand, the weapon feeling wrong in my grip.

"You're turning into something you should be afraid of, brother. You are allowing yourself to become the version of myself I fight to keep you safe from. Do you understand? You're losing your humanity, get it back!" Leo snaps in a cold whisper. He lets go of Altair, his face still taut with emotion as he turns to me. I open my mouth to speak as Altair pivots toward me with his intention clearly written across his face. Leo's jaw is clenched in resolve as he waits to see what decision Altair will make.

Leo turns and steps to the side a second before Altair launches at him, his fist meeting air. Leo elbows him square in the face as Altair stumbles past. I wince as the sheer force of the blow throws him to the ground. Altair's shaking hands move up to his face as blood gushes from his nose. His expression contorts in disbelief as he stares at me through tear-fogged eyes. Altair shrinks into his own skin, the power he thought he held bleeding away to fear. I move to help him with his wound, but he pushes me away and turns to the wall.

I stand back up and turn toward Leo. He looks like he's going to be sick, his face pale and breathing heavy. "Hold out your arm as far as you can." He does as I ask without a second thought. I place my hand around his wrist and pull. His shoulder pops smoothly back into place and rotates easily as he tests it out with a flat expression. He thanks me quietly before I step toward the boy on the ground. The boy's eyes are distant as I pick him up and lay him down on Leo's cot. I hold two fingers to his wrist and count his heartbeats as I watch Altair out of the corner of my eye. Altair stares back at me from his cot, blood, tears, and snot covering his face before turning away to face the wall. As I look around, a dozen starved eyes land on me. Some of the children are still cowering behind their beds while others have joined Saiph and the boys in the middle of the open space. Their stares dance between Leo and me, admiration and gratitude shining on their faces.

A fragile girl with dirty, ruddy curls walks up to us reluctantly and stops a few feet away. "Thank you," she says weakly as she wrings her hands. She gives me a small smile, the first I've seen from any of these kids. My heart twists as she watches the boy with big, sad eyes. I motion for her to come sit beside him. Her resemblance to the boy is uncanny. My chest feels heavy as I watch her take his hand, the boy smiling faintly at her presence. How many times have I been in the same position, watching my siblings helplessly as they struggle to stay conscious, pushing forward when all they want to do is close their eyes? How many times have I wanted to close my eyes?

We wished for this city to be a haven for our family and yet we are surrounded by misery. The children around us starve, Altair lies crying as he holds his hands over his bloody face, and Leo stares defeatedly at the wall as he gets lost in the tangle of his dark thoughts. This place is a curse that appears to the boys as a blessing. They sleep in this barracks and attend classes with these kids, yet they still speak about the city with reverence, like it's a miracle sent from the Goddess herself. I watch as the girl curls up beside her wounded brother on Leo's cot. The sight is devastating as tears roll down her cheeks, even in her sleep.

CHAPTER

THIRTY

CAEL

It's been a week since we've taken up residence in the puppet barracks, and Altair hasn't given us so much as a glance. Wate found a way to strip the humanity from his young bones and carve out his love for his family, and I don't know how to bring him back.

My mind swims at night with so many nightmares it's impossible to ever get any rest. But I'll take a million sleepless nights over being trapped in that suffocating room and reliving my past. Leo is fully aware of what's happening, and I can see the worry he tries to hide. I couldn't be more thankful for his ability to pull me from my thoughts, both of us poking fun at each other until we feel lighter.

I sit beside Leo as we lean against the tree we claimed as our spot after he was poisoned with the Ruby Tar. My thoughts wander to Emila and the Tominese crates. I look around and easily catch the tails shadowing us. The fair-skinned man with hair whiter than snow and the woman with thin black braids and rich ebony skin pound us relentlessly with their stares. Their constant attention is an itch at the edge of my senses, hard to ignore and completely distracting.

Cassien comes around the corner and strides toward us with Elana at his back. Four guards clad in their black livery trail behind them, carrying various blades shining in the sun. A muscle tics along Leo's jaw as his eyes shoot up to where the father and daughter approach. Leo and Elana have fought in the dome twice since Elana sliced him. He beat her both times, but it was always close. Thankfully, she has yet to pull another blade on him.

They stand before us, not a word slipping past their lips. We still won't rise for the High Lord, and it may be making everything worse, but it's one of the few things we can control. Neither Leo nor I are willing to give up the sliver of power we hold. We get up to follow only after they turn and start toward the Academy. We walk in silence as Saiph keeps pace between us, her hand held in Leo's. My brother picks her up as his expression darkens in time with our entrance onto the grounds. He hates this place. I share the sentiment.

Just as the domed sparring building comes into view, something catches my eye. An instructor and student walk parallel to us on the next street over. I crane my neck to get a glimpse of them every time we pass an intersection. It's Altair. The instructor with him walks with her chin held high and a pin-straight back, her pristine white cloak stark against the gray of the buildings. I watch them as they cut across a side street and merge onto the road directly behind us before disappearing into an alley. I shiver at the sight of my brother as my hands fidget restlessly.

Leo tenses as we pass under the arch of the dome, his movements tight and eyes sharp. Older students, who I learned are in their last years of training, spar brutally in chalked circles centered between racks of deadly weapons that line the curved walls. Leo smooths his expression into one of cool confidence as Elana glares at him from across the floor. I almost smile as I watch the swirl of emotion he hides under the mask of arrogance. I take Saiph from his arms and wait for the fight to begin. I register as someone checks Leo for weapons, a precaution they take even though it was Elana who pulled a blade, but my mind is elsewhere, distracted. I subconsciously turn myself to make sure Saiph can't see the chalked ring as they chant the words carved into the arch of the dome. *Never merciful.*

I try to pay attention to the fight, but the fray floats to the background of my thoughts. Elana dances on her toes as she searches for my brother's weak spot, hoping to find the crack in his armor. She won't find one, Leo's lived a life that did not allow for vulnerabilities. Leo was trained with the same techniques as Elana so the basis of their fighting styles are similar. But the time Leo spent fighting in Tominay's arenas and streets has given him more than technique and skill. I note Elana's movements and the catches in her breathing pattern, but the more I try to focus, the more my mind wants to break away. Leo is fully concentrated on his opponent, and so far, it seems like he has the upper hand. He'll be fine. I step away from the circle of onlookers and head for the arch. I check my shoulder before quickly sneaking outside. The only thing I can be thankful for in this dammed place is that they adhere to their class times so strictly. I push away the gnawing sickness growing in my stomach the farther I walk away. Leo will be fine.

"You need to stay quiet now, Saiphy," I whisper as I listen for footsteps. She doesn't make a sound, like she understands exactly what I'm about to do.

I make my way over to the alley where I saw Altair disappear. I hesitate when I see the sign hanging over the door marking the building as a laundry house. Through the window, I can see the racks of clean uniforms and bins of muddied clothes. Why would he go into a laundry house? I walk into the alley and stop in front of a thick metal door. I touch the lock, seeing the mechanism in my mind. It would be simple to pick with a pair of pins. I place my ear to the wall as I bounce gently to keep Saiph silent. A muffled, monotonous sound seeps through the crack in the door. It's no more than a droning mumble, but I would recognize Altair's voice anywhere. It sounds like he's repeating the same phrases over and over. I press closer, straining to hear more.

Saiph starts to fuss, and I immediately go still. She squirms, becoming uncomfortable with the tension hanging in the air. My brother's voice dies as I hear a chair scrape across the floor. I know my time has run out as Saiph's face starts to redden. I turn and run out of the alley, heading for the dome. I stop short when I sense footsteps coming toward us from inside the arch. I'm not supposed to be out of Cassien's line of sight. I panic as I rack my brain for a solution, an explanation...

I pin Saiph's hands to her sides, apologizing under my breath. She wails just as Cassien exits the dome with Elana behind him, her face bloodied and eyes shining gold. The smiles on the gold-eyes following them are victorious and proud, all but Elana's. For once, I can't read the emotion crossing her twisted expression. The people laugh and bare their teeth like animals as they pass. Thankfully, no one questions my being outside the dome as I try to calm my screaming sister. I let out a tense breath and let her arms free, but she doesn't calm. I plunge my hand into my pocket and pull out the embroidered pouch Byrne had given me. I shake it in the air so the coins clink together and Saiph immediately ceases crying, taking the pouch in her hands, and running her fingers over the elaborate design. My stomach twists as I watch the crowd walk away, the students whooping as they glance in my direction. My hands start to shake as realization dawns. Elana didn't lose.

THIRTY-ONE

LEO

I stare Elana down, her expression unreadable. I can tell she's trying her best to hide her distaste as I paste on an arrogant smile, taunting her. I don't want to fight her, even as the memory of the damp cloth pushed over my airway resurfaces.

Yellowed bruises line her face and her movements aren't as fluid as they usually are. Her arm is stiff, like it's been hurt and she's trying to ignore the pain. She's practiced at hiding injuries; the difference in the way she moves is so slight most would never notice. I push the thought aside as she starts advancing.

I block out the sound of the crowd's chant, knowing the words by heart even as my mind doesn't process them. I bleed my eyes as we circle each other, ready to get this over with. My gaze shifts to Cael, subconsciously checking to make sure he and Saiph are all right. He seems far away, his eyes slightly glazed as he meets mine.

Elana tries unsuccessfully to find my weak spot as I wait for her to leave an open passage. I land more than a few punches, hard enough that my knuckles crack under the force of the impact. They would break her bone if she didn't pull back. She kicks back fast, forcing me onto the defensive. We dance around the ring, blocking and dodging, attacking and spinning. She takes a shallow breath as she reels from a blow to the stomach and I strike, knocking her to the ground.

She scrambles to her feet as her raging eyes light with frustration. I take the moment to even out my heavy breathing and glance at the crowd. Many of the onlookers shake their heads, their disappointment and shame clear. I doubt they could do any better. My eyes land on the spot where Cael had been standing, but he's not there. My gaze roves over the crowd, but I don't see him or Saiph anywhere. Trepidation rushes through me as I scan the gathered faces again. They're fine, I tell myself, but Cael's not one to disappear.

I dodge as Elana comes at me, seeing my concentration slip. My elbow crunches into her jaw, but in the second it took me to collect myself and throw my arm, she attacks. It's strange, she doesn't hit me hard. She doesn't even hit me with her fist, but jabs at my shoulder with the knuckles of her pointer and middle fingers. My arm goes completely slack. I stumble as it hangs at my side, instantly rendered useless.

She pounces at me again with a new drive in her eyes. I block as well as I can and land a halfhearted punch, holding my own briefly before she gets the better of me. My head snaps numbly to the side with whiplash speed as her fist pounds into my face. Warm blood spews from my mouth. I struggle to take the reins on my panic as I try uselessly to sharpen my fear to steel. Elana floats around me, muting my blows and delivering her own. She manages to sweep my feet out from under me before spinning and throwing me to the ground. She takes a step back, and though her hands are still raised, she shakes her head ever so slightly, pleading for me to stay down. Everything in me screams to get up, but her expression stops me. She looks dejected, begging me to end this. Blood drips down her face and arm as deep-purple bruises stand out starkly on her jaw. The longer I stare at them, the more my head spins. I hit her hard, but those bruises shouldn't have shown up that fast.

I kneel in the dirt with my arm limp by my side as my lip swells. Cruel smiles appear on every face around me, except for Elana's. They cheer as Cassien calls her the victor, the sound bouncing around in my skull. Moments later, Cassien leads Elana out of the dome without so much as acknowledging me. They're followed by an onslaught of mocking smirks, congratulating Elana as they go. They aren't above kicking a downed man as they filter out, leaving me with a few extra bruises. I'm stunned as I try frustratingly to regain motion in my arm. I scan the empty dome. Two guards stand by the arch, left behind by the High Lord to make sure I leave. They watch me with smug expressions as they paw the swords hanging at their hips. Why did I let her win? I could have brought her down again. I could have tired her out. My face pulls into a sneer as I stand and my thoughts switch directions.

Cael isn't here. Why isn't he here? Dread pools in my stomach as I hobble to the arch. I don't get a step out of the ring before Cael comes barreling through with Saiph in his arms. He assesses me with a stoic expression. He seems composed, but his hands shake and his eyes fly over me with clear worry.

"Arm?" he asks, a bit breathlessly. I give him a shallow nod, not masking my hurt at his disappearance. He steps forward as he puts Saiph down and takes her hand to keep her from running off. "Can you move it?" I shake my head as he prods at my shoulder. "Can you feel it?" I stay silent, words too difficult to form. He sighs and pulls his hand away. "The feeling should come back in a minute." He stares at my bloodied knuckles, the skin torn and my right hand bruising. They decided it would be "more efficient" for us to fight without wrist wraps. "Would you stop glaring at me," he says flatly. "That's broken, Leo," he states as he tries to redirect the conversation by nodding to my hand. He takes a step back to meet my gaze and blows out a defeated breath as he touches the ghost of his ring. "Saiph was whining, and I couldn't stay in here."

"You're not the only one who can tell when someone's hiding the truth, brother," I say, keeping my voice low. He watches me for a long moment, weighing his options.

"I was the reason she got you, wasn't I? I left and when you realized, you lost focus and she got the upper hand." Genuine regret flashes through his expression at my nod.

"Let's go back to the barracks, we're already on the grounds," he says finally. His eyes are apologetic, and yet I know there's more to his story lurking underneath. I don't doubt he feels bad, but his mind still isn't all here and he's not getting away with such a vague excuse. Whatever's going on, it better be worth what happened.

As I sit on my cot, Cael hands me a wet piece of yellowed linen to wipe the blood from my arms and face. We went to get a bucket of clean water and encountered more hecklers eager to get under our skin. I tried to ignore them, but their taunts are starting to get to me. I wipe my hands and arms off slowly, staring at them blankly. Pale, ragged scars line both of my knuckles alongside the new cuts and bruising. I cringe at the thought that they might have gotten a chance to heal here if I was a true Hael. How naive I was. There is no place or peace for people like us, who have had to do the worst to survive and keep those we love alive. I finish with my hands and stare emptily at the rag, noticing faint smears of a dark-gold powder on the cloth. Elana must have been wearing it. I push the thought of her aside as Cael sits on the cot opposite me. Biting back the pain, I let the silver of my eyes show as crimson tears run down my cheeks. I wipe them away as my head pounds in time with my throbbing knuckles and tingling arm.

"It's only a fracture, you'll be fine in a couple days," he says quietly, holding my swelling hand in his. I suck in a sharp breath as he wraps it and sets my fingers straight.

"Where did you go?" I ask as he tends to a shallow cut above my brow. My brother doesn't miss a beat.

"I saw Altair go into the side entrance of a laundry house with an instructor. I couldn't stop thinking about it, so I went to look." I pull away to search his face, because there is no way that's why he left. He shrugs at my incredulous expression.

"You do know I'm supposed to be the reckless one, right? I jump off a bridge, you catch my foot before I plummet to my death. Or am I going to have to start warning you not to do anything stupid?"

"Leo, when have you ever heeded my warnings? You decide to jump off the bridge into a free fall. When I go, I tie a rope to the railing before throwing myself over the edge. I thought about this. There's something in that building worth knowing."

"So, you decided following our brother to a laundry house, the least suspicious place possible but one we are barred from going to, was a good idea? With Saiph? While I was fighting in a roomful of people who would love to see me dead? Because you had a bad feeling!?"

"When you put it like that it sounds— "

"Reckless, dangerous?" I scold, brows raised. "Oh, by the

Goddess, I'm becoming you. Look at me! I'm the mature one," I say, agitated, throwing my hands in the air.

"Very funny. Are we bringing up times when we acted irrationally? Because I have a few I'd like to mention. There was that time you thought you smelled fire, so you ran around the house sure as anything it was going to burn, when it was your clothes that smelled like smoke from cooking," he deadpans.

"You didn't have to go there." I grimace, starting to cross my arms, but wincing and deciding better of it. A small smile appears on his face as he goes back to his work.

"It was fine. I made sure no one saw us," he assures me, shaking his head as his smile grows. "By the Goddess I do sound like you. I need a cold swim in the Vallan."

"You do kind of stink." He steps on my foot, but I can still see the smile he tries to hide.

"You're one to speak." I scoff with mock hurt, my good hand going over my heart. It's stiff, but the feeling is returning and I'm able to move it again.

"Excuse me, I was recently in a rather brutal fight. I should be getting coddled and fed sugarcoated sweets for my bravery." Cael rolls his eyes as he shakes his head, but the grin stays put. "Next time don't wander off searching for nothing in a pile of dirty laundry without telling me, or at least giving me a signal. A bird call maybe?"

"Fine, but don't expect me to go around whistling and flapping my arms every time I need a break from you."

"Who would need a break from me?" I ask, genuinely curious. Cael rolls his eyes as an ease I haven't seen in a long time settles over his features. This is us at our best, dragging each other out of the dark after I've had my head knocked in. More nights than I can count were spent with him stitching me up while we poked fun at each other, keeping him out of the worry and nightmares and me away from the pain, old and new.

Antares and Cass walk into the barracks side by side a few minutes later as exhaustion pulls at their faces. They pause when they see us sitting on the cots, blood splattered across my clothes, and now, all over Cael's hands. The boys sit on Antares's cot across from where Saiph lies, deep in her nap. As Cael works, he asks the boys about their day to fill the silence. Antares gladly embarks on a tale as Cass nods along. We listen intently as he tells us about the technical sparring drills and their literacy and history classes. They smile droopily as they prepare for their final two classes of the day: strategy and mathematics. Cass is excelling at it all, while Antares seems to have a constant issue with sitting still, which isn't surprising. They'll both sleep well tonight, better than I have in years. I count the days in my head and grimace when I realize that this will be the third night since I've slept. I could try and convince Cael to let me stay up, but it would be hard with the dark bruise-like crescents blooming under my hazy eyes.

"Where is Altair?" Cael asks, bringing me out of my thoughts. I sit up straighter. Altair was the reason he left me in the ring. "Doesn't he usually have classes with you both?" Antares shrugs.

"He's with us in the morning, but he goes to a private class by the dome in the afternoon. He comes back at the end of the day before you meet us here," he explains while Cass nods along with his words. Cael's eyes go far away as his expression becomes unreadable. I pass him a questioning glance, but he waves me off as if to tell me not to worry. I don't believe him.

The boys head off, dragging their feet and promising to try and bring back bigger dinner portions for us from the mess hall. We don't bother leaving the barracks, not caring if anyone comes to drag us out. Cael forces himself to sleep because we all know he won't get more than a few hours tonight. He tosses and turns as I watch the frail puppets drag themselves through the door, tensing before they head outside. I thought my life was bad, but these kids would probably give anything to have what I used to. It's as if they haven't seen a good day in their entire lives. They were abandoned by their families because they weren't good enough and left to rot alone. How any of them get up in the morning and decide to go on is beyond me. I watch as two young girls whisper to each other in a corner, one waving her hands subtly through the air. How many times have we hid from wandering eyes and worn tattered rags to cover rumbling stomachs? And yet those are the moments I yearn for, the quiet fun and laughter of the times when we were all together. Those are the times I wish I still had.

Cael wakes with a start and jumps from his cot, his eyes wide with fear. It takes him a long moment to come back into reality as he watches the roof like it's about to come down. I try to calm him for several minutes, but it's as if the nightmare has him trapped and refuses to let him free. All of a sudden, it's like a switch flips and the tension melts away from his face.

"Are you all right?" He nods shakily as he rubs his eyes with his palms. I smile sadly and put a hand on his shoulder.

The boys couldn't have had better timing as they trudge in with two trays of lukewarm food. Well, if what they bring us can be considered food that is. It tastes all right but looks like it's already been eaten. It must be good for us though, because the boys are finally gaining some weight. I can't say the same for Cael and me, given that the boys only bring us what they're given: two plates of slop for dinner and three rolls between us in the morning. I eat my portion after giving Saiph enough to keep her full. Cael and I make sure to keep some to share with the puppets who can't get up to go to the mess hall.

The boys fall asleep quickly, Antares barely making it to his cot before passing out with his boots still on. I pull them off as Cael tucks Cass in and wishes him a good night. Altair still does his best to ignore us and has now completely isolated himself from Cael and me. I have no idea what's going on in his head. It's as if he's at war with himself, studying us like he's trying to remember why he's here.

"Good night, Altair," I whisper, wondering if he'll respond. All the others have silently crawled into their bunks. My brother stares at me for a long moment, confusion passing over his face before nodding and turning to face the wall. Cael sits on the cot beside mine as Saiph sleeps soundly under the covers.

"Ready?" he asks, pulling out the strips of thick material. I take a deep breath as I nod and lie down. My brother ties my feet and hands to the legs of the cot and sits back, careful not to disrupt Saiph. He still looks far away, uneasy.

"Is the nightmare lingering?" I ask as I turn my head to the side. He glances at me with a blank expression.

"You're about to dive into one much worse than mine." I watch him as he fidgets with his index finger and his foot bounces restlessly against the ground. He gives me a tight smile, setting off alarm bells in my mind. "I'm fine, just a bit shaken. It was... vivid," he says quietly. My expression softens at his words. I lie silently, giving him the option to tell me. After a long moment, he takes a deep breath, drawing my gaze back to him. "I was back in the room, digging my chains out of the wall. I could hear your voices, telling me they were coming, that I needed to hurry. I couldn't get the chains out, and then the door opened and they... they did what I heard they were going to do the day I got out." His words are thick with emotion, his back slouched and his head hanging low. Nothing I say will make him feel better, but simply getting the thought off his shoulders will help. No words can truly heal the monsters swimming beneath our skin, but a listening friend, someone who will sit by and take the weight you carry, is the only way to make scars fade.

"But you got out, brother. You're out now." He nods as a sad smile plays on his lips.

I stare at the ceiling and fill my head with thoughts of my siblings grinning like we used to. As I fall into the terror, they are my shield and armor, my sword and prayer. But even as I clutch to the brightest memories, I cannot be saved from my own demons.

CHAPTER

THIRTY-TWO

CAEL

I wait until Leo's asleep, listening to his breathing even out. Unlike most people, Leo's every breath becomes sharper and shallower as time passes, telling me he's gone into the realm of restless unconsciousness.

The nightmare shook me, badly. I haven't had one so vivid in a long time. I can still feel the dampness of the room, the shrill of my mother's voice as she argued with my father about the best way to get rid of me. But the nightmare wasn't the only thing on my mind. I promised Leo I would tell him before following my intuition, but he needs his sleep, and I'm not going to drag him into whatever this is. Maybe after all these years, Leo's finally rubbing off on me. If that's the case, I hope he's on good terms with Lady Death, because he may have to start bargaining for more than just his life.

I stand slowly and check Leo's bindings once more before I walk past the rows of sleeping souls. I pry open the door, wincing as it squeaks, and slip outside. A wave of relief washes over me as I scan the road and see that no one is lingering. I was sure they would have the tails they assigned to us stationed at the doors.

I stick to the shadows as Leo had shown me time and time again. Armed guards patrol the grounds, but they keep their eyes ahead, not noticing as I move beyond their line of sight. I can feel a group coming before I hear the drunken, heavy laughter echo through the street, giving me enough time to duck behind a wall. A guard comes running back toward the noise with an arrow nocked in his bow. The laughter grows louder, coming so close I hold my breath, as if the sound of air leaving my lungs might draw their attention. I'm running on time I don't have and even a second wasted could lead to disaster. Leo doesn't sleep long and leaving him alone is a dangerous risk I've never dared take before. I'm starting to second-guess myself.

"What are you doing out of your barracks, slayers? It's past curfew," the guards voice booms, sounding like he's trying to suppress a smile.

"Us? Oh goodness, we were just having a wee, little, tiny drink at the mess. A phantom brought in a whole crate of whiskey. Nothing to fret about, sir," a slurred voice says, hiccuping in between statements.

"You're not supposed to tell him! It's a secret, remember?" another scolds, the sound of bodies falling following the words. They laugh themselves hoarse, shushing each other as they go. I glance around the wall as the guard shakes his head. The slayers are so drunk I can smell the drink on them from here.

"You know the rules, I'll have to report you all for being out after—"

"Why must you ruin our fun? We're celebrating before those wretched little impostors take the oath. It's not often we get a chance at taking back Illena. Why not have a drink to celebrate the end of an era?" another chimes in, her voice high and light. "And while we're at it, why not spill some getic blood too? When they find out what the High Lord has planned, they're going to wish they had never taken their first breaths!" I tense at their howling laughter, dread closing in like hands around my throat.

"By the time they realize what's been done, they'll be in chains doing our bidding and the blood-eyes will be cowering at our feet!" They cheer at the gruesome words before starting to laugh once again. Everything in me recoils from the group, their words feeling like a rusty blade twisting in my gut. The guard sighs before telling them to follow him as he mumbles something about how their instructors are going to give them a beating when they can't perform tomorrow. One of the slayers falls over and retches right beside where I crouch. I close my eyes as my stomach rolls and hold my breath as he gets back up and stumbles after his friends. I wait there, trying to calm my frantic heart as the guard corrals them toward the barracks.

When I'm certain there is no one else around, I sprint to the dome, careful to watch over my shoulder. I don't encounter anyone else, but something seems off. This isn't breaking into an apothecary in Somereil's poor quarters. I'm in way over my head.

I retrace my steps and enter the alley next to the laundry house. I stand by the door and take a moment to listen. Not a single sound comes from inside. I pull out the forks the boys had brought with our dinner, three out of the four prongs broken off on each. I press them both gently into the keyhole and listen for the release of the tiny springs as I feel for the slight increase and decrease of pressure. I hear a satisfying pop as I turn the pins, the door jumping open quietly. I wait as my breathing seems too loud in my ears. It's in instances like these when I understand why Leo carries his blades like they're part of him.

The moonlight streaming through the door illuminates the wide room as I step inside. It's a lab. There are tables stacked with documents and glass vials lying in a neat pattern all over the room. I had heard of facilities like this in Tominay where they would do research to build new weapons and find medications. I always found them interesting, but this room is unsettling to say the least. I walk with silent steps, leaving the door open for light. The walls are covered from floor to ceiling with charts of bodies and brains, the smell of fresh ink and something metallic floating through the air. I walk up to a table in the middle of the room holding vials filled with a deep red liquid organized neatly in three even rows. Blood, they're vials of blood. My eyes go wide as I read the notes stacked neatly on the desk. It's all about Leo, or "the double-banded blood-eye" as it's written. Everything is documented, from his height to the color of his eyes to the way he fights. I shuffle through the pages as my breathing becomes labored, the air around me too thick. There are bone density tests, his healing speed, charts on his terrors. I don't know what he would have done if he were here and I don't want to think about it, nor do I want to imagine why they've done this.

The next table has files labeled with Altair's name. I flip through them as my hands shake. There, written in a precise script, are our lives, all documented through Altair's eyes. The oldest pages are clear memories, ones I remember well. When he used to climb the tallest tree to watch the sun set and played Hunters or sat by the fire at night. His nightmares and dreams, and how he loved going into the city on Saturdays to get bread pastries. He knew we had no money, but he didn't care because he had all he needed. I flip to the newest pages and swallow as I read the words. I squeeze my eyes shut, barely able to process what's written. If this is true, Altair said we did everything for our own gain and kept him prisoner against his will. He said as the eldest Hael, he stayed because his younger brothers and sister were still in our grasp. The memories written here are twisted. It says he used to climb the tallest tree because he was trying to find an escape. Farther down, it's written that Hunters was not a game, but his chance at freedom. He'd get close to escaping, but we'd always find him and drag him back. What did they do to him?

I tear my eyes away. I need to get out of here, out of this city. I stumble as I catch something glinting in the corner of the room. More vials line the back wall on a table beside a door. The liquid inside glows bloodred in the moonlight. I stand in the path of the light, my shadow projecting my dark outline onto the wall as the vials go black in the darkness. "Ruby Tar," I mutter to myself. Bile creeps up my throat as I turn slowly to take in the entirety of the room. I continue searching and find more pages with notes on our movements, what we eat, when we leave the Academy, everything. I knew they had tails on us, but this? My blood runs cold as I begin to turn, my hands shaking. I stop suddenly as the bite of steel pushes on my throat.

I slowly raise my hands. Everything around me disappears into a haze as my senses narrow onto the short sword pressed against my neck and the hand holding it. I move quickly, snapping my head back and smashing it into a nose. My head throbs as I spin, grabbing the sword and hitting my attacker square in the face with the butt of the blade. I don't wait for a scream before I run, my heart racing.

I'm not fast enough. Hands grab my arms and push me against the wall, my cheek pressed against cold stone. The blade in my hand is ripped away as people gather around, laughing menacingly as a dagger is pressed against my side. "And what do we have here? A curious getic. The High Lord is going to be pleased with us, and the entire people of Wate are going to be ecstatic you decided to misbehave. We haven't had a good show in a while." I swallow hard because I know that voice. It belongs to the man tasked to shadow Leo and me.

"Let me have a go at him before we bring him to Emila," a female voice snarls from behind me. She steps into my line of sight, breathing heavily with anger. She has blood smeared across her face and her nose is badly broken.

"Emila won't be happy, Serra. I'm not putting myself on the sharp edge of her knife again," the man says as his dagger slices into my side. I wince and he pushes it in farther, breaking the skin.

"We didn't beat him up, he resisted," she says lightly as what must be a painful smile spreads across her face. The man sighs behind me as the others around them grow restless.

"I'm not going to be able to stop you, am I?" he says flatly. Her smirk grows feral, reflecting the dangerous gold glint in her eyes. My stomach drops and my hands tremble madly as I fist them.

"Don't worry, Andreus. I won't smash his head in. Emila will get to end him, but I want to make sure he pays what's due."

CHAPTER

THIRTY-THREE

LEO

I wake with a start, struggling against the bindings trapping me to the bunk as the terror slowly fades. My ears ring as I fight away the nausea rising in my throat. I pull on the restraints, but they're tied tight, locking me in place. "Cael?" I rasp, the words scraping out of my throat. I get no answer but the heavy breathing of my sleeping brothers. "Cael?" I try again. I turn toward his bed and squint in the darkness. His cot lies empty but for Saiph, soundly sleeping under the threadbare blanket.

He's not here. Fear sinks its claws into my mind as my thoughts whirl. Cael's never disappeared while I sleep. He knows the dangers of leaving me alone. *But he did yesterday*. I force myself to take a deep breath as my lungs begin to feel too tight, like my ribs are collapsing into them. He promised he wouldn't do anything rash, and yet I remember the glint in his eyes and how he seemed distant. But he wouldn't, couldn't have left. I've broken through the restraints more than once, hurt more than myself. He is the smarter one of the two of us. He wouldn't leave unless he absolutely needed to, but... A storm of hurt, rage, and worry builds inside me as I stare at his cot like he'll appear out of thin air.

Locking my jaw, I look to the side and find Cass sound asleep in the bed beside me. At least he's the easier one to wake up. "Cass." He flinches at my voice, his face pulling into a frown. I call his name again—a little louder—and he jumps from his cot with glazed eyes. "It's okay," I whisper, pulling his attention to me. He studies me for a few seconds, like he's figuring out where he is. "Were you having a nightmare?" I ask gently as the hurricane of emotions ebbs inside me. He dips his chin slightly, his expression going slack. None of us ever gets a moment of reprieve. "Help me with the restraints, Cass," I tell him softly. He unties my hands quickly as his own shake.

I move to unbind my ankles when my hands are free as Cass stands silently by my side. I turn to him and open my arms as he falls against me. I hold him tightly as he folds in on himself. "It's all right," I say over and over. He presses his hand to Pollux's star map on my spine as a sob escapes him. I nod, resting my chin on his head as tears run down his face. "I miss him, too," I tell him softly as he pulls away just enough to look up at me. I can see the wall build back up inside him as he locks away the flood of emotion from the everlasting grief of losing his twin.

When I'm confident enough Cass will be all right, I tuck him back under the blanket, the worry for my other brother screaming at the back of my mind. "Do you know where Cael is?" I ask him as he settles. Cass stiffens as fresh fear builds in his eyes. "It's all right, he most likely just went outside to get some air. The dark was probably getting to him," I say quickly, keeping my voice light. Understanding flashes in his eyes, but he remains tense. "You want me to stay until you fall asleep?" I offer, knowing I should find Cael but unable to leave Cass's side. Cael will be all right. Cass nods pleadingly, taking my hand in his. He closes his eyes and his expression softens as the gnawing concern squeezes its way to the forefront of my mind. "Cass, I need to ask you a favor." His eyes open slightly as he watches me from under heavy lids. "If I'm not back by the time you're up, take care of Saiph until we come back, all right?" He nods as unease creeps into his tired gaze. "I should be back by the time you wake, but you know how much I love to get into trouble, right?" I ask playfully, putting on a charming smile. Cass smiles through his fear as his eyes droop shut.

"Good night, Leo," he whispers. My heart lunges happily. I don't think I'll ever get used to him speaking.

"Good night, Cass."

***

Cass falls asleep in a matter of minutes, but I stay by his side a little while longer to make sure the nightmares don't come back right away. I don't know what I would do if he couldn't sleep, but I wasn't going to leave. I walk out the door, racking my thoughts for an answer to where Cael could be. I back into the wall as people run past, calling for each other to hurry up. None of them notice me as they run with wide smiles toward the Council building. My stomach sinks as I watch them, dread closing around my throat. Every dark, gruesome fear my mind has ever concocted flashes in front of my eyes. I sprint after them through the dark, not caring who sees me or where they're going.

The wave of people slowly make their way to the Council

building to gather in the courtyard. The post towers over the crowd like a beacon, beckoning me closer. A bloodcurdling scream tears through the air. I know that voice, that cry of pain. I push through the crush of bodies laughing and hollering. I'm going to carve the grins from their faces. When the raised platform comes into view, my feet stop moving and my body goes numb. I'm going to throw up, then I'm going to slaughter everyone in sight.

Attached to the post at the center of the platform, Cael sways against the chains holding him up by his hands. They're clasped above his head, the only thing keeping him standing. Blood flows from his back in time with his shallow breaths as the cuffs shred his wrists. A short girl with shoulder-length hair and a dripping blade in her hand stands before my brother, eyeing her work. She presses it to his back and slowly splits his skin. Cael's body going taught, then completely slack as she lifts the blade to start anew. I can hear him pant as he moves in and out of consciousness.

I snap as Cael screams, the girl tipping the blade back to his skin to deepen an already gaping wound. I lunge forward, shoving my way through the crowd. "Stop!" The crowd goes silent as all eyes turn to me. An unrestricted grin appears on the girl's face as her gaze locks with mine.

"And why would I do that? You aren't even supposed to be in this square unless you're brought here in chains. That... thing, on the other hand, was dragged here by his heels," she sings, gesturing to my brother. Rage ripples off me as I continue to charge through the crowd. "Oh, do let him through. Let's see what the all-mighty blood-eye has to say for the getic," she says with disgust. The people around step aside to clear a path, watching me closely. They hiss and snarl like animals as I advance unflinchingly. Someone stands in front of me, but I push him aside with a strong elbow to the jaw. The laughter quickly turns to silence after that. A few others try to stop me and end on the ground, clutching an arm or a leg, while I finish with a dagger. Fury fuels my motions, sharpening an already deadly blade. The girl standing by Cael simply tilts her head as if this is a game to be enjoyed.

"Well, what a show. You do like to make an entrance, don't you?" she points out with raised brows. Cael moans in agony, trying and failing to turn his head. "I knew you would come, but I have to say I'm disappointed it took you so long. I have no problem with getics. Snooping getics, maybe a little. But blood-eyes, oh I've wanted to rip your heart out from the moment you walked into Wate. Or rather, the moment you were *carried* in. But I'm glad for your tardiness. I got to have so much fun." The people snicker around me, but I block them out as I size her up. She must have the keys to the cuffs keeping Cael from crumbling to the ground. I need to get them and get my brother out of here. I hold on to the ounce of hope lying at the bottom of my chest and tell myself Cael will be fine if I can free him. I need to free him.

"Let him go," I say, my voice low and commanding. She stares me down, smirking as if I had muttered a joke. She makes a show of thinking as she taps her index finger on her chin, eyes gleaming.

"No." She unhooks a long leather whip from her hip. "But since you're here, why don't we discover how fast a blood-eye can bleed out." Sharp metal shards hang off the end of the whip as she unwinds it and angles herself to strike. I realize what's happened after I've done it. My hand is outstretched and my eyes have gone bloodred. Gasps ring out from the crowd as they gape, astonished. Blood drips down my arm as I hold the end of the whip in my hand, the shards of metal cutting through my palm. I pull it toward me, no pain firing in my nerves. She stumbles forward with shock clear on her face.

In one swift movement, I take a step and grab her, trapping her arm behind her back and pressing the dagger to her throat.

"Here's what we're going to do if you want to keep your throat intact," I whisper with unnatural calmness. "You're going to tell me where the keys are to unlock my brother. Then I'm going to carry Cael out of here without another word from you." She swallows as hatred burns on her face. She tries to kick away, but my grip only tightens, the dagger pushing against her windpipe.

"Pocket," she grumbles without moving her lips. I grab them and let her go, but not before smashing the pommel of the blade into her temple. She falls back and hits the ground with a thud. Her hand flies to the blood trickling down her forehead. Her eyes flash gold as she begins to cackle.

"Oh, you're going to regret that," she swears. Goose bumps run up my arms, but I ignore the threat as I pull Cael up to unlock his left hand.

"Leo?" he breathes as his eyes flutter.

"I'm here, brother, can you stand?" I catch his arm as it slides away from the chain and prop him up as I throw it over my shoulder. He winces, his breathing ragged.

"I don't think so," he mumbles before slipping away again. I shake him gently, bringing him back with a tight wince.

"Stay awake, I'll get you out of here." He gives me a shallow nod. I don't care what I have to do, I won't let him die. "I swear if you take him, Death, I will kill you myself," I murmur, my voice shaking as Cael goes under again. I glance at the crowd as they tremble with resentment, calling for our blood. "On the other hand, if you're going to collect a life, let Cael live. You owe me for what I've given you," I beg, desperation quickly creeping in as Cael's breathing becomes shallow. I stand and pull him with me as he forces his legs straight, coming back for the moment. I start to carry him away but stop short as words bounce around the silent square.

"You will die, whether it be you and your family, or your entire kin, it's already carved into the wind by the blade of the Ash sword. Lady Death is coming, and she is not happy nor merciful. You will suffer," the girl swears, the wound on her head bleeding freely as she pushes off the ground, unsteady on her feet.

"Death is my weapon to wield. I kill for her so she lets me live and acts as my lever. That has been our deal since the day I was born. Don't think for one second Lady Death hasn't been creeping in my shadows. She is merciful, but I am not, so I suggest you take a second to think whether you value *your* life before you start spewing words you'll regret," I say, my voice lethally cold. Not a single sound comes from the crowd, even the wind ceases to blow.

"Lady Death serves no one," she says, more to herself than anyone here.

"Yet she gives her blessings to the Blood Prince," I say, dragging my brother through the crowd.

No one tries to stop me as I move through the corridor the people have parted to create. Someone catches my hand at the edge, stopping me for the briefest moment.

"Go to the opening in the forest line where we brought you last," Byrne's hushed voice whispers so softly even Cael couldn't have heard. I know where she wants me to go, but can I trust her? My heart pounds in my ears, every sound putting me on edge. I expect someone to come at me and shoot me through with an arrow, but they know Lady Death is hovering over us, just not whether she is here for Cael or for them...

Byrne's words bounce around in my head. There's nothing in it for her. I look at Cael, sweat dripping from his forehead as his eyes flutter, trying to hold on to reality. His skin is gray, the blood from my hand mixing with his as I hold his weight with my injured hand. I got him out, but I don't know how to heal him and he's already lost so much blood. I'm drenched in it, my clothes sticking to my skin. I take a deep breath and without another second of hesitation, turn toward the forest.

THIRTY-FOUR

LEO

Cael sees her before I do, pulling his eyes from the ground to the forest line. He pulls on my arm weakly, trying to get me to turn, but I keep on. He relaxes slightly when Byrne appears, wearing a long black cloak, her footsteps silent even in the brush. She runs to us, taking off the cloak and tying it around Cael's torso to stanch the bleeding. She throws Cael's other arm over her shoulder, making him wince.

"There's a small shack right behind where we brought you." Her words are clipped with worry and her face is tight with fear. "Elana's already there setting up supplies." I tense, and it doesn't go unnoticed as we heave Cael over a fallen tree in our path. "This place is ours and ours alone. No one knows it's out here. While you two are in this cabin, Elana won't say a word, and she's promised me she will do nothing but help." I nod, still not completely trusting Byrne's words as she pants under Cael's weight.

"Tails?" Cael mutters. Byrne glances worriedly at my brother before quickening her pace.

"I took care of them," she says, her voice strained. I meet her gaze over Cael's shoulders. "A rag drenched in Gyll oil made it easy." My eyes go wide as I watch her. Gyll oil was extremely expensive in Tominay. One drop can knock a person out in seconds and keep them unconscious for hours. Plus, it's untraceable and causes no clear side effects to indicate it's been administered. The victims simply look like they've fallen into a deep, dreamless sleep. I tried it myself years ago to get rid of the terrors. Not only did it not work, but it gave me a pounding headache.

I don't take notice of the lopsided wooden cabin until we're mere feet away. Vines crawl up the sides, making the walls and roof seem like nothing more than a cluster of mangled overgrowth. The only sign it's there at all is a faint light shining through a crack in the wall.

I realize how cold it is when Byrne props open the door and a wave of heat washes over us. Elana stands across the cramped space, her face stoic. She eyes Byrne worriedly, but says nothing.

"We could use some help," Byrne breathes through bared teeth. Elana nods and helps us get Cael onto an old wooden table covered in a thin, crisp sheet. Cael winces with every movement, letting out a weak cry as we move him. The sisters immediately get to work. Byrne hands me a vial of murky gray liquid that reminds me of the concoction Cael used to give me when I'd come home broken and bleeding. "Get him to drink it. It will lessen the pain and allow him to rest." I nod quickly, my hands shaking as I stare at my brother's ravaged back. "Leo." I look up at Byrne's voice. "Your eyes," she says softly, as if she were speaking to a child. I quickly drain them and the pain in my hand slowly grows. I struggle to open the vial as the skin on my palm pulls the wrong way. I push the thought of the pain Cael must be feeling away and crouch in front of him.

"You need to drink this," I say. He shakes his head.

"We need to leave, Leo. We need to—"

"We'll deal with everything else later. Right now, I need you to live. Drink." After an agonizing moment, he finally nods and gulps down the strange liquid, grimacing at the taste. It doesn't take long to kick in, my brother passing out cold in a matter of minutes. I stay crouched on the ground, counting his shallow breaths as they leave his lungs.

"Leo, help us, will you?" It takes me a second to register Byrne's voice. I glance up and find both sisters staring at me. "He'll be fine, Leo. He just needs rest and some clean bandages," Byrne says softly. The sad glimmer in her eyes makes me think she's lying, and something breaks inside of me.

Elana and I work on cleaning and packing the gashes across Cael's back as Byrne sees to a wound on his head. The bleeding from my hand slows as I work. The cuts are relatively shallow and clean, so stitching them up is straightforward, though extremely time consuming. I try to help, but Byrne orders me to keep track of the bandages without looking up from her work. A shape slowly starts to appear as the blood washes away from my brother's back, getting sealed off by the clean stitches. The sisters share worried glances as they work, the air growing tense.

"Where did you learn how to sew someone up?" I ask, noticing the deep-purple bruises lining Elana's jaw and the new cut over her brow. They exchange a quick glance as another silent moment passes between them.

"When you're prone to getting hurt, it's a useful skill," Elana says, a nonanswer.

"I don't think I'd have done a good job," I admit, needing to fill the silence. Elana shoots me a questioning glance; it's the first time she's acknowledged my presence without seeming like she wants to rip my head from my shoulders. "I'm the one who runs off and gets myself hurt. That's how our dynamic works. I distract, protect, make all the rash decisions, and end up bleeding. Then Cael patches me up, puts sense into my mind, and keeps me on task." I stare blankly at the reddening bandages as my heart squeezes in my chest. Neither of them says a word.

"What did she mark him with?" I ask, my voice low as I stare at the shape carved into my brother's back. It's a triangle with a line running from each of the three points across the opposite side. They both go deathly still. Byrne opens her mouth, then shuts it again, deciding against whatever words were playing in her mind. My stomach drops. "What is it?" I ask again, more forcefully.

"It's a symbol. One you don't want around," she says, avoiding my stare.

"What *is* it?" I repeat, shifting my gaze to Elana as she takes a long breath.

"It's a death symbol, a marking Illena uses to brand their traitors. But to have it etched into his skin..." We sit in silence as her words hang around us.

"What? To have it etched into his skin what?" I squeeze out.

"It's the worst type of condemnation. They branded the Death Dancers with it after the war. The ones they let live, that is. Even people who wish death on another wouldn't do it this way. It's said those who are marked with it will be turned away by Lady Death."

"Denying him the peace she provides in death," I breathe, barely able to say it out loud. She nods slowly.

"It's not something we take lightly. Even the worst don't

get branded with the tripoint and it is forbidden to discuss. There are few worse sentences," she says gently, her eyes softer than I've ever seen them. I bury my face in my hands, trying to get a hold of myself. Byrne finishes laying the linen after applying a reeking salve to lessen the chance of infection. Her skin takes on a green sheen as she stares at Cael, then at a pile of blood-stained rags overflowing from a bucket on the floor.

"Are you all right?" I ask her shakily. She grabs the bowl of red-stained water and makes for the door.

"I'll go refill this at the river," she says with a foot already out of the cabin. The door shuts behind her, leaving Elana and I alone. Gold rays of dawn flit through the cracks in the paneling. We stare at each other for a long moment. I try to feel what I did last time I saw her, knowing I should hate the girl standing before me. I shouldn't allow Elana in here with my brother. I try to pull the memory of her dry drowning me as the Ruby Tar took hold of my mind, the dozens of bitter looks and sharp words she's said, but I'm only met with a wall of desperation and gratitude. She picks up a clean cloth and brings over a bowl of water. She sits beside me on the cold ground, leaving a space between us.

"What happened to your hand?" she asks, her voice cold. She seems uncomfortable, not meeting my gaze. I lift it up to see it in the light. I forgot I was hurt.

"I caught her whip." Elana's brows rise in surprise and her sparkling eyes meet mine.

"You caught Emila's whip? With your bare hand?"

I nod as approval flashes across her face. Elana passes me a soaked cloth. It feels like a peace offering, one I'm willing to accept. I watch her for a moment, searching her face. Her eyes are the same as when I first met her—sad and broken—and yet, there's a glow to them, an ease that was not there before. She lifts her gaze to mine once more. Heat rises up the back of my neck under her heavy stare. I avert my eyes quickly, starting to wipe away the blood crusted on my hand. The cloth stains crimson as the sharp tang of copper floats through the air. So much blood. I'm covered in so much blood.

"Do you fight a lot?" I ask, needing to busy my thoughts. I see her tense beside me as she stares at the leg of the table. She stays silent for so long I give up on hoping she'll respond, focusing instead on cleaning the puckered flesh on my hand.

"You could say that," she replies quietly, startling me. "I protect Byrne from getting hurt, and sometimes that means taking the blow myself." I nod, knowing the feeling well. She looks up at Cael as her expression clouds over. Somehow, I feel like we're much more alike than either of us would ever have thought possible.

THIRTY-FIVE

ELANA

Before they walked through the door, I had prepared myself, steeled my thoughts against seeing his cocky smile hiding his sharp rage. But when the blood-eye barreled into the cabin, eyes crazed and his brother's blood soaking him through, he was a different person than I had met in the ring. He was the boy I had glimpsed on the roof before he knew I was there, no longer the confident killer holding the string of life in his palm. I had seen it when he was with his siblings too. He was lost, broken. How could a blood-eye be anything but a coldhearted brute? The worry and fear were etched so clearly onto his face. He was human, a helpless boy without a clue what to do.

I let myself pass a quick glance toward him as he stares hopelessly at his brother. I can see all the shattered pieces of his soul in his eyes, and it reminds me of my own. Byrne went to get Saiph from the Hael boys about an hour ago. They would be in class and couldn't take her with them. Leo had argued he needed to go see them, if anything, to let them know what had happened, but Byrne and I shut down the idea. We agreed that when she went to pick up Saiph, she wouldn't mention either brother, at least not until we get this figured out. People were still too riled up for Leo to show his face. I understood why when Byrne told me what Leo had done while retrieving his brother. I wonder if he meant it when he said Lady Death follows in his shadows and that she can be merciful? As I watch him, it's not difficult to believe. I touch my jaw, the bruises stinging under the slight pressure.

The door flies open as Byrne walks in with her hood pulled low over her face. She sets down a large basket then shakes off her hood, letting the light hit the dark waves of her hair. Leo shoots up to his feet, his expression instantly morphing from a stressed frown to a relieved type of joy. He takes his sister gently from Byrne's hands, shielding her from the sight of the getic's bandaged back. She smiles wide at him and throws her arms around his neck. My heart squeezes sadly at the sight. She's so young to have seen all she has, but the longer I watch him with her, the more I understand how the child can still smile. He takes the brunt of the pain, grief, and worry, all so his siblings can grow up properly and have a chance at a decent childhood. It's a lot to ask for people who have lived as they have.

He puts Saiph down and she stands on her toes to look at Cael.

"Cael!" she squeals, tapping his arm with her hand. He hasn't woken from the mixture Byrne made for him, and it's for the best. The cuts were shallow enough that he wasn't losing blood too quickly, but he was out there for a long time. The medication will have slowed his heart to keep him unconscious, but a heart can't pump without blood. I wouldn't be surprised if the drink is the only thing keeping him alive.

Leo crouches down beside Saiph, holding a little linen doll in his hand. I do a double take to make sure I've seen it right.

"Cael's having a nap, Saiphy. He's tired so we have to be quiet, all right?" The child smiles and puts a hand over her mouth. The corner of his lip pulls up, but the grin doesn't meet his eyes as he hands her the doll. The child's smile grows impossibly brighter as she crushes it into a hug. I had one just like it when I was young, so did Byrne. My mother made them out of bright fabrics, wrapping the strips around each other and tying several complicated knots to create a perfect little doll. She used to say she would teach me to make them if Byrne or I ever decided to have children. She never did.

"Where did you learn how to make a linen doll?" I ask, the first words I've spoken in hours. He continues watching his giggling sister with a sad smile as he leans against the wall. Leo meets my gaze, his eyes glazed as memories flash in his mind.

"My mother taught me when I was young, maybe five or six. I wanted to give my sister a birthday present, and she had lost the one my mother had given her when she was a baby. It took me a long time to figure out," he admits, laughing under his breath. I could swear happiness flashes in his expression.

"You had another sister?" I ask, biting back the question about his mother that floats in my thoughts. He nods sadly.

"She died a long time ago. That was the day we found out we could never be free in Tominay."

"They killed her?" He nods solemnly as his fists clench.

"They don't like our people. The majority of the population think we're myths, but the ones higher in the chain know the truth. They fear us for what we can do and the power we hold. Having gold eyes was reason enough to hang Pleiades," he says, his words clipped and cold. I swallow, watching him as he keeps his eyes on his brother. I'm not surprised that they killed her, but a country must truly be corrupted to kill an innocent child. There was a treaty signed after the war declaring if we wanted to live, we must stay in Illena. If we leave, our lives are forfeited, all because they're scared of what we were created to do.

"What about your... parents?" I ask, wincing as the words leave my mouth.

"My father died of a sword through the chest. He got in with the wrong people without learning how the... industry worked. My mother died giving birth to this one," he says, twirling Saiph around herself as a pained smile plays across his face. Watching them, the corner of my lip tips up subconsciously. I erase it quickly and lock my jaw as he continues. "Cass's twin, Pollux, died of disease." There's an old grief lacing his words, one I can tell he's buried deep enough to overlook. I didn't know he had lived through so much loss, and by the sounds of it, each death hit him harder than the last. He looks up at me with such cool indifference I almost flinch. I swallow the real meaning of the question I had asked, feeling it probably isn't the right time.

His eyes dart suddenly to the table, registering something that escapes my senses. Cael groans as he stirs. "Don't move," Leo throws out tensely as his brother's eyes flutter open, taking in his surroundings. "How are you feeling?" he asks softly, his gaze worried as he stands over him.

"Like I wish I could bleed my eyes," he rasps, wincing as he tries to smile. Leo lets out a short breath that could only be his best impression of a laugh. "How bad is it?" Cael asks, eyeing his brother warily. Leo stays silent for a moment as he glances at Byrne and me.

"Your back was carved with a knife, so not great," he deadpans. Cael seems to stare right through him, even in his state.

"What?" Cael pushes quietly, as if he knew Leo was keeping something from him. Leo rubs the back of his neck nervously. "What did she carve into my back?" he demands, his voice surprisingly steady. Even Saiph goes still.

"It's... It's called a tripoint," he stammers. Cael winces, whether from pain or his brother's words, I have no idea.

Leo closes his eyes, breathing deeply. "It marks you as an enemy to anyone who sees it, and it's said to bar you from taking Lady Death's hand in death."

Cael nods sadly, not taking his eyes off his brother. We stay silent for a long moment as Cael seems to sink into himself. "Well, then I guess I should be glad I have a few years left to live and anyway, I enjoy wearing shirts," he jokes, trying to lighten the mood. Leo plays along, giving him a sad half smile.

"Yeah, and I love the arenas like a second home." Cael huffs a laugh, grimacing at the movement. I shake my head and glance skeptically at Byrne. He has a symbol said to keep him from peace in death, and yet neither brother seems to care.

"You're both fine with all this?" Byrne asks him, her brows creased in confusion. The brothers share a look, showing nothing but relief.

"I'm alive, aren't I? And I don't have much of a choice concerning the wound or my fate. Worrying will do me no good," Cael explains heavily.

"And there's no way I'll be allowed a peaceful resting place, so we'll spend our eternity together," Leo says sarcastically, winking at his brother. Cael does his best impression of an eye roll as he smiles tightly.

"And here I was thinking I had finally gotten rid of you," Cael says lightly, though he shifts in discomfort. Leo shakes his head as he huffs a laugh, crouching down beside Saiph as she runs over to him.

"But," Cael says, his eyes meeting Leo's as his voice turns

grave, "there are more pressing matters at hand. We have to get the boys and leave now." Desperation and terror strangle his voice.

"Why?" I ask before Leo gets a chance, cursing my inability to keep my mouth shut.

"I found a lab inside the Academy. That's where they caught me." Fury creeps behind Leo's eyes, but he smooths his expression into a practiced evenness. Cael eyes him warily, seeing something I don't before continuing. "They have tails on us, which we already knew, but they've been keeping track of everything we do. There were pages documenting Altair's memories of our life in Tominay and they have your blood, and vials of Ruby Tar." We all go deathly still as the sound of the river falls away and the air floats stagnantly around us. "The worst part is I didn't have time to rummage through it all or check the back rooms. I only saw what was on the surface."

"Do they have notes on me?" Leo asks quietly, his voice strained.

"Yes. Like I said they have your blood and charts on your bones, sleep, terrors, healing time… They have everything," he breathes, his voice tight. The brothers stare at each other in a silent conversation.

"And the Ruby Tar?" Byrne whispers.

"It's not for terrors," Cael replies numbly. Leo's eyes shoot to me, confusion and hurt flashing behind them. I glance at Byrne, hoping for once she'll say something, but she seems to be praying the wall will swallow her up.

"We had no choice but to give it to you." I lift my chin in defiance, daring them to fight back.

"There's always a choice." Leo says, his face trained into an unnerving stillness.

"Then you were the best option," I respond, shrugging with an ease I don't feel. His hands shake as he holds my stare, his breathing becoming slightly ragged, but Cael shifts, a pained groan escaping his throat. Leo immediately forgets about me as he watches his brother and orders him not to move.

"This table isn't exactly comfortable, Leo," Cael says in an attempt to distract his brother. Leo shakes his head in response and murmurs something about how only he would be thinking of the table right now.

"You didn't know about any of this, did you?" Cael says, more of a statement than a question as he meets my gaze. I shake my head. The way he senses what goes unsaid is disconcerting. I wasn't aware there was any sort of lab here, and it makes me fume. A knowing glance passes between the brothers.

"They don't want you to succeed as High Lady after your father, Elana. That girl with the whip, Emila, said something about how everyone knew Cassien wouldn't be assigning you as High Lady, but her instead." The wind kicks out of my lungs and my head spins as violence awakes inside my bones. Emila has always hated me, and I wouldn't expect any less from her. She sucks up to Cassien like a dog, constantly working to win his favor. A clammy hand presses against mine, making me flinch. I didn't realize Byrne had moved to my side.

"They can't do that," I grind out, the words hollow. The only reason I ever stayed was because one day I could make things better. I would have the power to do whatever I pleased. I could send Cassien to live in Tominay, or better yet, to live with the blood-eyes in Arkezo.

"There is no rule against it," Byrne says gently. I hate it, but I know she's right. Emila is many things, cheat being at the top of the list, but she is not a liar. She scares people into giving her power but is known for her candor. So here I am, standing in the cabin I used to play in as a child with my little sister whose heart is too big, a half-dead getic, and a blood-eye that should have been slaughtered a long time ago, if he is who I suspect he is.

"There's also the fact that Tominay is supplying Wate with crates of weapons," Cael adds, deep in thought.

"Weapons? What do you mean weapons?" Byrne asks, taking her hand from mine to cross her arms. I miss the comfort of her touch the moment her skin leaves mine, and yet my muscles ease at the distance.

"Daggers, long swords, short swords, throwing knives, bows, arrows. Everything you could possibly imagine. They were hidden in a stall at Daeta's market in crates marked with a Tominese symbol."

"So that's what those were," Byrne mutters. She seems to remember we're here and clears her throat. "When I went to see you in the clearing, Cassien told me I was not to go until he gave me word. He knew I could deal with people and thought it might be a good idea to try to get information out of you."

"Did you?" Leo interrupts, his eyes sharp.

"No, none of you were in a state to be questioned. I told Cassien you wouldn't give me anything," she finishes, wincing as she rubs her jaw.

"You never told me about that," I say, worry and frustration creating a whirlwind of emotion in my mind. She straightens and pulls back her shoulders.

"You don't have to constantly take the fall for things, Elana," she says as she glances quickly at the brothers. They're watching us carefully and almost seem sad. I give myself an internal slap. This is not the time.

"What do we do now? Chances are the Council and half the people in Wate think Lady Death came to get you a long time ago," I say, changing the subject as I motion to Cael, who is clearly struggling to stay awake. Leo watches his brother with overwhelming concern as his frown deepens the grooves in his forehead.

"We can't stay here," Cael says, his words starting to slur together.

"We'll get the boys and head through the mountains to Anateya. Try to find a southern village and stay there for a while." Leo's dread is written all over his face as he runs a shaking hand through his hair. Byrne glares at me, and Cael doesn't miss it.

"What?"

"I've never left the island, but I know Illena is not composed solely of Wate. There are dozens of villages and cities, four of which are gold-appointed. Though, gold-eyes and blood-eyes are not allowed to be in the same place unless on official business, we share Illena's lands." If I could have frozen his expression in time, I would have. Leo looks as if he's witnessed me conjuring a miracle, his mouth hanging open and eyes wide.

"How? And you didn't think to mention there are other people like me? Either of you?" he questions incredulously.

"If you mean how are we separated, it happened after the gold-eyes tried to stage a coup. They wanted one of their own on the throne and ended up killing a crown princess in the process. The blood-eyes beat us back, but the relationship became so strained between the people the crown decided to confine us to four different cities across Illena. We are not allowed to leave unless under direct order from the king or queen."

"That's not what he meant," Cael says, blinking quickly to keep himself concentrated. An unwanted sense of sympathy washes over me as I watch him struggle to keep his eyes open.

"You never asked," I state simply, shrugging. Leo shakes his head, running his hands over his face.

"Then we go to one of the blood-eyed cities. We'll stay there until we can move again and find someplace to settle," he says, his voice showing his exhaustion even through the burst of hope flickering in his eyes.

"It's not that simple. It might be easier for you to show up and make some sort of life for yourself, but your brothers and sister are gold-eyed. Not to mention he's a getic," I say, nodding to Cael. "They will not take them in." We sit in silence as the air becomes heavy around us.

"I'll take them over," Byrne says quickly, taking a step forward as she wrings her hands, avoiding my prying gaze. "I... I know someone. He'll help if I ask." I stare at her in shock as everything else in the cramped room falls away.

"You've been over the river!" She flinches at my tone but gives me a tight nod. Disbelief washes over me. "And what if this *he* doesn't help? What if *he* reports you and has you killed?" I demand, my words coming out sharper than they had been in my head.

"He won't," she assures me with unwavering confidence. "He'll do as I ask... if I go with them." A hysterical laugh escapes me as I stare at her. It takes me a moment to realize she's being serious.

"You? Go with them? Are you insane?" She averts her eyes as the brothers wince in sync.

"You could come too, Elana," she offers quietly. My mind blanks.

"What? We just up and leave? One look at our eyes or the marks on our wrists and we will be sent back and killed as traitors. Or maybe the blood-eyes will have mercy and finish the task themselves."

"Elana, they did it! They all have bands on their wrists and have hidden them for years!" she says desperately, her voice begging me to understand as she motions to the brothers. I shut my eyes and pinch the bridge of my nose, trying to keep my outrage in check.

"It's more complicated—"

"How is it more complicated? What do we have left here, Elana? If anything, we cross the mountains and find people who know nothing about us. We can make new lives for ourselves. This is our chance to start over, Elana. To be free." I study her for a long moment as her pleading expression cracks my shield.

"You truly want to leave?"

"There is nothing waiting for us here but an early death." I swallow the bile rising in my throat because I know she's right. The way things are going now, I won't live to see the day the title of High Lord belongs to another. He won't let me.

I look up to Leo placing his hand lightly on his brother's shoulder, his demeanor serious. Cael must have passed out while Byrne and I were arguing. We all stay silent until Saiph runs up to him, babbling about how she'd named the doll Lynn. He crouches down and greets the toy as he would a new acquaintance with a hand still on Cael's shoulder. His expression clouds over as he speaks to his sister. *He's tracking Cael's breathing*, I realize. I don't know what we would do if he stopped breathing, but Leo keeps his hand there anyway. There is still hope inside him, a flame I can only envy. My fire burned out years ago, and it won't be long before his vanishes too.

CHAPTER

THIRTY-SIX

ELANA

I open the door and motion for Byrne while Leo speaks with the child, needing to be out of the confines of the cabin before I explode. She nods and quickly tells him we'll be outside. Once we get out of earshot, I turn on my sister as my rage slips loose.

"He?"

"Do you think Cael will survive?" Byrne asks, her voice strained.

"Don't change the subject," I snarl as my patience runs thin.

"I don't want him to die," she admits quietly, watching the cabin. "They're all so close, like pieces of one of nana's puzzles. If they lose one, they won't ever make the same picture."

"Their puzzle has been incomplete for far longer than we know," I say dismissively, crossing my arms over my chest. "Now spill." She takes a deep breath and forces herself to meet my gaze.

"His name is Emrys."

"That's very helpful Byrne, thank you," I say sarcastically as my frustration builds. "Who is Emrys, and how do you even know him?" I throw my arms in the air as my voice rises in pitch. She could be killed for leaving Wate, never mind meeting with a blood-eye.

"He came over on a trade ship from Arkezo. He wandered into the woods and I found him. I was curious, I wanted to see what he was like. We were told blood-eyes were vicious, but he looked the furthest thing from a monster. He seemed... normal, like any other boy from Wate. He caught me watching and I thought he was going to call his people, but instead he asked me my name."

"He caught you? Byrne, you're trained as a phantom!" I yell in disbelief, barely able to process what she's saying. Her lips thin into a line and eyes glisten as she stares, pleading with me to let her finish.

"I gave him a false name, to be safe, but he didn't try to turn me in, he only wanted to talk. He asked about simple things like our food and what we do in the summer. When the next trade came around, I went into the forest and there he was. We saw each other that way for... a while." My mind is racing. How could that be possible? Blood-eyes weren't allowed to leave the designated area when they visited Wate, but I have heard stories of them wandering in the forests to scare children playing in the woods or the fields on the far side of the island.

"How long has it been since you first spoke with him?" I spit, my words clipped and hot. Her hurt is plastered across her face. I don't care.

"Three years," she reveals. Only silence answers her as the words take too long to sink in.

"You've been seeing this blood-eye for *three years?*" I yell hysterically. She only nods in response. I feel my eyes go wide. My sister, the one person I trust with my life, kept this from me?! And it's no trivial matter, she's been meeting with a blood-eye for three years!

"We met each other that way for more than a year. I asked him if I could see him more often and he told me there was a place he could meet me across the river. It's a two-hour walk for me and a two-and-a-half-hour ride on horseback for him. I agreed and I've been seeing him across the river ever since."

"How often do you go to see him?" I grind out between clenched teeth. I don't dare say anything else, or I might explode into a ball of searing flames.

"Once every two weeks."

I lose it, chuckling darkly. I turn my back to her and scratch my nails down my face. I feel my eyes shift from silver to gold as the water of the Vallan becomes brighter and the leaves on the trees more distinct. She flinches when I spin back around. I don't know what to say to her, my sister, the daughter who followed the rules and played the good student, when all along she had been breaking the biggest one of them all.

"What did he tell you to convince you to go with him?" I ask, refusing to believe she could be so stupid.

"He's more than my friend, Elana," she whispers, as if saying the words aloud was something she was wholly unprepared to do. Everything around me feels too bright, the air too light, and the wind too sharp.

"We will help them get across the river, you are going to bring them to this Emrys, and then you are going to come back, and I swear by Lady Death herself you won't ever leave this island again!" I seethe. She stares me down with tears clouding her eyes as she slaps her hands over her mouth.

"Don't say that, Elana. Don't do that. You know as well as I do we can't stay here if we want to live. We have a chance to get out and find a home where we aren't beaten because Father's had a bad day. We have Leo. If they take him in, which we both know they will, they'll have to take in his brothers as well. If they take in four gold-eyes, what's two more? There are so many places we could see, Elana. So many things waiting for us off this damned island," she says, her own voice rising as she shakes her head. "Elana, we need to go with them. We cannot stay here." My teeth grind against each other. She looks up at the sun as tears run down her face. "Elana, not a day goes by when I'm not terrified of him. I can't escape him here. And you can't keep taking the fall for me." She shifts her gaze to mine. "He's going to kill you one day because I was hiding, or I was late, or I didn't make sugar tarts like Mama did or—" Her voice chokes off in a sob. The roaring fire inside me fizzles out, leaving a gaping cavern of cold darkness in its place. I step toward her and carefully wrap my arms around her shoulders as she shakes. I don't remember the last time she cried in front of me. I don't remember the last time I let my own flood gates open enough to allow my fear out of its cage. A tear rolls down my cheek as I force my eyes closed.

"They know what he does, but no one stops him. No one will care if he kills us." I pull her impossibly closer and take a deep breath.

"We'll go. I guess I understand why you were so nice to them in the beginning, huh?" She draws back and nods with red-rimmed eyes. All our people have the same dark-silver irises, but after living with them your entire life, you learn to see the differences. Byrne's are identical to our mother's, the swirls of silver giving them a soft, kind feel. Mine could not be more different, passed down from a man I wish to forget. "We'll take the chance, but if this doesn't work, promise me you'll agree to go north, even if that means leaving... what was his name?" She laughs, hiccuping in the middle.

"Emrys, Elana. His name is Emrys. And I promise, if something goes wrong, we'll leave without a second thought. Maybe my phantom training will finally come in handy beyond spying on people of status to learn all the gossip." I laugh as I gather her in another embrace and allow myself a single moment to imagine a life where I could breathe peace instead of fear before opening my eyes back up to reality.

THIRTY-SEVEN

LEO

I didn't dare ask the sisters what had happened while they were outside. They came in with tear-stained cheeks and swollen eyes, and I understood right away that whatever had gone on was not something they would share. Elana made quick work of telling me they had decided they would come with us. It was not up for discussion, judging by the glare she passed me, but I wouldn't refuse either way. They are the sole reason Cael is still breathing and I know they could have easily turned us over to Cassien. Strangely, my stressed mind eases at the thought of the sisters joining us.

I sit in silence until nightfall, Saiph running around the room and playing with her doll until she passes out from exhaustion. The sisters left to get information and supplies and came back in complete silence. I eat the barest amount, the nausea that had risen at the Council building still not settling. Elana tracks me as I stand up with Saiph cradled in my arms. Cael has yet to wake up again, but we changed the bandages and checked his wounds. To our surprise, the bleeding had subsided, and he wasn't showing any signs of infection. I thank Lady Death for our luck, even though I still can't tear my eyes away from the bruises darkening his burnt-umber skin.

"I'm going to see them," I announce as I meet Elana's gaze. The sisters freeze with their food hovering halfway to their mouths. My clothes are still stained with blood, but at least my hand is healing nicely. Byrne stitched it up after forcing me to show her the wound. She had scolded me for not taking care of it and then gave me a lecture about deep wounds needing to be tended to in order to heal correctly. I didn't bother telling her the flesh would knit itself back together in a matter of days and simply thanked her instead. The stitches will help it heal a little faster, and the Lady knows we need as much time as we can get.

The sisters brought me a fresh pair of clothes, nicer than anything I had ever worn. I didn't put them on, telling myself it was because if I was seen, they would expect me to look ragged and red-eyed.

After a long moment, Elana nods, accepting that I won't be kept away from my brothers any longer. With a heavy sigh, Byrne puts down her meal and stands with her arms outstretched to take Saiph. I hesitate out of instinct and Byrne doesn't miss it, but thankfully she doesn't seem offended.

"It's all right. I'll make sure she doesn't wake up," she assures me. I force a tight smile and hand her over. Byrne takes my sister as if it was the most natural thing in the world. "I used to help with the children at the medical center," she explains as she bounces slightly. I smile gently at her, my worries ebbing enough to allow me to step away. I walk out of the cabin and follow the same way we had stumbled along to get here. I push away the sound of my brother's shaky breaths as I spot a bloody handprint painted onto a tree. We'll have to clean that up or Cassien will have a path to the cabin drawn out for him. I rub my hands over my eyes until they sting. I need to make sure people believe I'm grieving my brother. It should be easy to fake seeing as the color disappeared from my face the moment I saw Cael on that post. I managed to sleep last night but seeing Cael lying unconscious tore open a wound I've been working to heal for years. Worried about not living up to the expectations, I pick up a handful of dirt, take a deep breath, and throw it into my eyes.

I fully regret the decision the moment the dust flies in the air. My eyes burn as I force them to stay silver, tears rolling effortlessly down my face. I lock my hands at my sides and force myself not to scratch them. This is a new type of torture, but from the near unrecognizable face staring back at me in the tranquil waters of a nearby stream, the dust does its job. Sometimes I can be utterly stupid, but at least it worked. I look like a ghost, with gaunt cheeks and tear lines painted down my dirt and blood-stained face.

I hang my head and slouch my shoulders, dragging my feet as I pull up memories I've prayed to forget. Those emotions I try to keep control of pull free, wreaking havoc on my mind. One after the other they play and all a sudden I'm reliving every heart-wrenching moment over again. I squeeze my eyes closed and press my forehead to a tree as I force myself to breathe. Slowly, concentrating on the rustle of the leaves and the sound of flapping wings, I lock the thoughts away until reality comes crashing down like a wave of freezing water. Banishing the rising swell of nausea, I push off the tree. My stomach somersaults in my gut as I continue forward, narrowing my focus to nothing but seeing my brothers.

I keep my gaze plastered to the ground, even as the urge to burn the whole place to the ground rages through me. No one walks the streets, but I keep to the shadows to be safe. The night will be a success if I can get away with sneaking in and out unseen. Inconveniently, my luck has proven time and time again to be unreliable.

I curse as the Academy comes into view. I know they close the entrance at night, but the thought had escaped me in the mess of the last few days. I survey the surrounding area for several minutes, trying to find a way through but come up empty-handed. Sighing defeatedly, I walk along the towering fences, staying alert for any wandering eyes. When I'm certain no one is watching me, I start to climb, my chest tightening as I push higher. I jump over the spikes capping the top and land hard on the grounds of the Academy, my ankles vibrating from the impact. I take a moment to gather myself. All there is left to do is head for the hellhole of a barracks my brothers call home.

I only pass two guards walking their rounds as I trace the familiar way to the puppet barracks. No one's out tonight, so different from the last time I was here. My mind won't stop circling back to the blood and raw fear when I saw Cael on the post. So much can happen in so little time. Your entire life can reset and go crashing onto another course in a matter of minutes, and we can't seem to catch a break. I push away the crushing feeling of helplessness creeping up on me, adding it to the ever-growing list of emotions I wish would stay trapped at the bottom of my soul under lock and key.

I open the door of the barracks and silently slip inside. The puppets sleep soundly in their beds, some shaking from cold, others from the nightmarish thoughts plaguing their unconscious minds. I pass the boy Altair had beaten and a rush of relief sweeps over me. He seems mostly healed, the lingering bruises nothing but faint yellowed spots. His breathing comes in deep sighing breaths, no longer the shallow wisps they had been. I walk slowly to the back of the open room and stop when I stand over my brothers' rusted cots. Cass shakes under his thin sheet as he tosses his head wildly. I sit on his bed and gently place a hand on his shoulder.

He startles awake, his eyes glazed from the nightmare that had taken hold of him. My little brother stares at me for a long moment as if he were trying to figure out if I was real. He throws his arms around my shoulders the instant he realizes I'm truly here. "It's all right," I whisper as I run a comforting hand up and down his back like our mother used to do. He presses a hand to Cael's star map on my back and I tense. I go back and forth with myself for a moment, deciding whether it's the right thing to keep them in the dark. But how could I burden them with that grief and sadness? Cass pulls away from me, his face pale with fear. He's a child, I can't condemn him to live with more pain than he already bears. I look around to the others sleeping on their bunks. This needs to stay as private as possible.

"Go wake up Antares and I'll get Altair. I need to tell you a story." His brows knit together as he studies me, the confusion and desperation clear on his face. "I'll explain, but I need you all to be awake." He nods once and pulls himself to his feet.

Antares jumps awake as Cass shakes his shoulders. My brows knit together as I wonder when he started sleeping so lightly. He scans the room quickly, wide awake in seconds. When his gaze lands on me, his hands go so still, something visibly tearing inside him. By the expressions on their faces, they've pieced together Cael not being here and the stories they must have heard during the day.

I don't realize Altair is awake until he's standing before me, staring me down like I'm an intruder.

"Is he dead?" he asks bluntly, making me wince.

"Like I said to Cass, I'm going to tell you a story." Antares and Cass listen expectantly as they sit on the bunk beside me. Altair doesn't move, seeming like he's seconds away from slitting my throat. *It wouldn't be the first time*, I think sadly.

"Remember the one about the fox and the rabbit Mama used to tell us?" I ask gently, earning a nod from Cass and Antares. "Well, the fox caught the rabbit and hurt him badly. A big blue bird saw what the fox had done and came to help the rabbit escape. The fox knew they wouldn't make it far, so he let them go. The bird brought him to a safe place to help him, far away from anywhere the fox might be. Do you remember how it ends?" I ask, hoping they do as I scan the puppets. Some are clearly awake, listening as they pretend to sleep. I changed the wording slightly to better explain what had happened, but the end is all that matters. The rabbit stays hidden in the bird's nest until the fox gives up his search and leaves. The rabbit then escapes to a new home once he's healed and *survives*.

Antares and Cass exhale deeply, their worry slowly melting away. A small smile appears on my face as they wrap their arms around me with a crushing strength that surprises me. Altair seems confused as he watches us, his eyes shifting from me to the boys. Does he not remember? It used to be his favorite story, the one he asked Mum to tell before he went to sleep. He would help her act it out with the shadows on the wall but would only do the bird because it was the only animal he could manage to create. *He must be confused at how Cael could still be alive*, I tell myself, dismissing the rising unease.

I stay with them for hours, whispering jokes, adventures, and old stories in the dark. It's strange to not hear Cael chip in, but it felt good to momentarily forget what was going on and to imagine it was a normal night with all of us together, talking before we forced them into bed. Well, forced Antares that is. It catches me by surprise when a faint glow starts to filter in through the windows and under the main door. I stand and promise the boys I'll come back soon. They look devastated, but nod nonetheless. Altair stares me down, confusion and accusation clear in his expression.

"Where are you going? Why are you leaving so soon?" he asks. The words seem innocent, but his tone is clipped.

"I'm guessing you heard what I did, Altair. People haven't exactly taken a liking to me, and I doubt after the show I put on they'll start now," I say, watching him carefully. Cass and Antares both wince as I speak, but Altair doesn't move, his gaze boring into mine. I drop my voice as I run my hands through my hair in frustration. "We're going to have to leave soon, but I need time to figure out how to do it safely." Antares and Cass's eyes light up. Altair passes them a sharp glance, making them step back.

"We aren't going anywhere with you. This is our home, whether you're both here or not," Altair fumes. Fury burns through me, and it takes all my will to keep my voice level. Beneath the surface, a current of pain runs deep, waiting for me to sink into its depths.

"That's fine, I didn't come here to take you away. You take care of them, all right? I'll be back as soon as I can," I promise. Saying the words in a normal tone seems like the most difficult thing in the world. "Keep an eye on Altair too," I say as I turn to Cass and Antares. Twin smiles adorn their faces. I've never asked them to look after each other when an older sibling was around. They stand a little taller and a small burst of joy courses through me. I hold on to the glimpse of happiness like a starving man would a bit of bread, knowing it will soon disappear, but guarding the thought that for a second, the hunger will cease.

THIRTY-EIGHT

LEO

My emotions are an unsolvable tangle of string as I leave the boys behind. The other students are waking now, rising with the sun. They file out of the phantom barracks and come to a screeching halt as they catch sight of me. I turn away and hurriedly walk toward the gates with my head hanging low and eyes trained on the ground. My heart races as I hear them follow and split into different groups. I continue on, keeping the instinct at the tips of my fingers. *I'm not in the mood for this right now.* I stop as a group of people around my age stand fanned out in front of me, blocking my way. They all carry a weapon in hand, whether it be a long sword, dagger, or sleek metal staff. Thankfully, none carry bows. The phantoms live up to their titles, being near silent as they position themselves around me to tighten their circle. The blade I swiped off Emila seems to sear the skin under my blood-splattered shirt as I look up. By the Goddess, I'm glad I have it.

"You are foolish to show up here after what you did, blood-eye," a girl says from directly in front of me. I shrug and continue walking as if I hadn't noticed the dozen people herding me in the street. Twelve highly trained, bloodthirsty, armed soldiers. I raise my eyes to meet hers, deciding this would be a good time to stop pretending to be naive. I paste on an arrogant smile, radiating an ease that makes the phantoms bristle.

"I should have the right to tell the boys, who my brother helped raise, that they won't see him again," I state simply, wiping all emotion from my face. A cruel smile pulls at the girl's lips.

"What a shame. Too bad no one will be there to tell your little brothers about you." I keep my attention trained on her, but years of fighting in the dirtiest arenas and darkest alleys teach you to detect things that don't seem right. I push away the strand of humanity I hold so dear and let the Blood Prince out. An idea flashes through my mind as a few gasps ring out from the circle. I tilt my head to the side, smirking to show the monster inside.

"Are you suggesting I'm about to die?" I ask, my voice filled with expectation.

"You said it," she sneers as her confidence cracks.

"Death would be a mercy," I say, straightening my posture as my hand hovers beside my hidden weapon. In the time it takes the girl to move away from the blade I launch at her head, I'm sprinting through two stunned phantoms and clearing their blockade. One of them catches the outside of my arm with her dagger, but it's no more than a scratch. I push my legs faster, but even with my head start, they're nearly stepping on my heels. I barrel through the narrow side streets and zigzag through the buildings, unsuccessfully trying to lose them in the grid of the Academy. Why couldn't the streets be dark, winding, and peppered with corners to disappear in like

Somereil's lower town? Another bad idea pops into my mind, but I know it's my only option. Grinding my teeth, I turn a corner and run for the barracks. I hear one of them laugh as they realize where I'm heading. Students and instructors emerge in force to watch, some even whooping like it was a show.

When the puppet barracks come into view, I catch sight of Cass and Antares as they poke their heads out to see what's gotten everyone worked up.

"Go back inside," I yell, my voice strained as I bolt toward the slayer's barracks. None of them stand outside, giving me free passage. I fly through the door, stopping as I realize that these barracks are nothing like the one designated for the puppets. I expected a run-down open room with rusting cots and bleary-eyed students, but this room is... clean. The walls are painted in a light gray to offset the dark upholstered settees set up across the room. A hall at the back leads to doors that must be connected to the bedrooms. More than forty pairs of eyes land on me as I still. The cards, games, and food held in their hands and strewn across marble tables are completely forgotten. I hear the door open behind me and all hell breaks loose. The slayers grab whatever weapon lies within arm's reach—which is a wide variety of shining blades and axes—as the phantoms come funneling through the door. They all launch themselves at me at the same time, working against each other as they try to trap me. I grab a dagger the size of my forearm and start fighting my way through the horde of people. I took a chance by leading them all into the confined space of the barracks, but after having watched the slayers, I knew there would be no order to their attack. The chaos is so extreme I can barely take a step without crashing into a body. I punch, slice, and shove my way through the mess, careful not to deliver deadly blows. When the door finally comes into my line of sight, I burst through it, hitting the cool air with a sigh. I don't have time to cherish the moment of peace, so I push myself back into a sprint and don't stop until I'm hidden behind a building, still clutching the bloody blade in my steady hand.

I take a second and focus my attention inward. I'll have a few new bruises and a cut or two, but no major injuries. I bleed my eyes and wipe away the crimson tears with the back of my hand. My bones ache and my head spins from having run for so long. I allow myself to rest and calm my racing heart before coming out from behind my corner. I find an empty weapons rack pushed up beside a wall in an alley, take a steadying breath and I climb up, using the height to jump to the roof. I run above it all, forcing myself to keep my eyes forward. I can hear a wave of people running in the opposite direction and snicker at the thought of how much trouble they'll be in. I pass a quick glance backward to the barracks, regretting it immediately as my stomach twists, the ground moving in and out of focus. I can't keep the smirk off my face as I watch the brawl down below. It seems to have gotten personal. Instructors and guards are desperately trying to tear students apart as the soldiers, slayers, and phantoms rough each other up. The puppets are the only ones who have yet to join the fray, grinning wildly as they witness the madness.

I walk through the door of the cabin feeling relieved, but I'm met with three burning stares as I step over the threshold. "What did you do, Leo?" Cael asks before I can close the door behind me. Elana shoots to her feet and takes a step toward me before freezing, her brows knitting together. I tear my eyes away from her and meet Cael's prying gaze.

"I went to see the boys," I reply impassively. Cael's expression darkens.

"What did you tell them?" All eyes turn to the bloodied blade I still hold in my hand.

"I told them the rabbit and fox story Mum used to tell us." As if on cue, Saiph comes running around the table, squealing as she sees me. I drop the dagger and pin it against the wall with my heel before it can hit the floor. I lift her up and hold her in the crook of my arm. Both sisters look at me like they're about to tell me not to pick her up, but stop themselves, their lips forming identical thin lines. I'm covered in dirt and blood, but Saiph has yet to understand what that means. *She would probably find it strange to see me without red-stained clothes*, I think darkly.

"So, the others in the barracks wouldn't understand," Cael says, nodding his approval. "Did they get it?"

"Cass and Antares knew what I was getting at, but Altair... to be honest I don't know if he did. He seemed confused." Cael's face goes stone cold as he stares at me.

"That was his favorite story," he whispers to himself. "He's changed."

I nod solemnly, wishing I could contradict him. The bonds in our family run bone deep because of the memories we share. You would need to erase his entire personality, reshape everything he is and everything he ever was in order to strip him of that love. It shouldn't be possible.

"What does any of this have to do with a story and could you explain why you are covered in blood?" Byrne asks, her eyes wide and tone incredulous.

"There was an old story our mum used to tell. It ends with the rabbit surviving after he had been hurt by hiding away in a bird's nest before escaping to a new home," Cael says casily. A heavy weight lifts off my chest as I catch his clear eyes. He looks so much better than he did yesterday. "But do tell how you ended up with a sliced arm and bruised face? I'm intrigued," Cael says flatly. I inhale slowly and gently let the blade slide to the floor before I give them the basic details of the story.

"So, to be clear, you ran into the slayer's barracks with a pack of phantoms on your heels?" Elana says with raised brows and wide eyes. I nod once, grabbing Saiph's hand before she can poke at a bruise on my shoulder. "It's a wonder you survived," she adds, shaking her head. I narrow my eyes as her gaze locks with mine.

"I make up plans so crazy they have to work. It's one of my best qualities, among others," I say, a half smile pulling at my face as I wink. She snorts and turns around, straightening our already perfectly organized medical supplies. My brother rolls his eyes so hard that for a second, I think he's passed out.

"I didn't know you had any," Elana mumbles, throwing a glance over her shoulder. Byrne not so covertly slaps her hand over her mouth, hiding her growing grin as Cael laughs outwardly. I can't keep the smirk off my face as I lean against the wall, placing a hand over my heart.

"Ouch."

Cael blows out a long breath as he passes me an exasperated glance. "Speaking of stupid plans, we have to figure out how to get out of here. You weren't followed, were you?" he asks, suddenly serious. I shake my head.

"I took the roofs all the way back. Then I hid out for a while in a back alley before heading into the woods."

"Good. The two phantoms who've been assigned to tag you, Andreus and Ceyana, would have been called in to help with the fight, so we don't have to worry about them either," Byrne says.

"They were mediocre in the Academy but managed to get

in with the phantoms," Elana adds, shrugging her shoulders. "Now that they know you've been to see your brothers, Cassien will have them followed at all hours. He'll most likely station guards at the puppet barracks as well."

"Then we need to figure out a way to get them at a time when they won't be monitored," I state as if it was the simplest thing in the world.

"Initiation. Your brothers will be there to witness the older students take the blood oath. It's sacred to the Academy. They slice open their hands and recite an oath, dedicating their lives to the High Lord and the gold-eyed people. Some people believe it's an oath to Lady Death," Byrne says, wincing as she turns up her palm to reveal a pale scar. Elana does the same before quickly tucking her hand behind her back as she catches me watching. "Your brothers are too new to take the oath, but they'll be present. It happens at night in the woods, so no one will notice if they slip away. I did it every year before I was sworn in." Byrne's eyes cloud over, her mind far away as she stares at her palm.

"Then that's when we take them," I say, putting Saiph down and crouching to look Cael in the eyes. After a long moment, he nods his head, however reluctant. I slide my feet out from under me and sit up against the wall, moving the dagger and handing it to Byrne to place on the little shelf out of Saiph's reach. "But I'm not leaving until I get rid of the lab." Cael grimaces and I know it's not from his injuries.

"Are you honestly insane? What are you going to do, burn it down?" Elana asks sarcastically, crossing her arms over her chest. I eye her closely, tracking her movements with a grin.

"That's exactly what I'm going to do."

CHAPTER
THIRTY-NINE

We spend days planning, sharing information, and discussing the best way to put Leo's plan in motion. I can't help but be excited to destroy something Cassien built. Over the past few days, Byrne and I have gone home and attended to our duties around the city so as not to raise suspicion. Leo tried to convince us we didn't have to go, but even as his words hung in the air, I could tell he knew he was wrong. I swear I saw anguish flash under his questioning gaze when he caught sight of the purple bruises blooming on my face and arms when I came back. He hasn't said anything about them yet, but I know he's catching on, and he can't know. I won't be seen as weak.

Leo went back to see the boys four more times since the last visit. Each time was a risk, but thankfully, he came back with nothing more than a grim expression, and I found myself fighting an unwanted sense of relief. There were locked back doors built into all the barracks and Leo had taken the time to find out what kind of locks held them shut. After bringing back an outrageous amount of detail, Cael explained exactly how to pop them open, going through the motions step by step. The next night, Leo spent hours with the boys and was so happy he wore a smile for the rest of the morning. He swore he got the lock open in five minutes and even bragged he might be better than his brother. Cael quickly proved him wrong, to my extreme amusement.

He's taken to wearing daggers permanently now, always having them within arm's reach or tucked into his belt. I understand why he does it. I do the same thing, even sleeping with a blade hidden under my pillow.

I've seen Leo sleep before, but my memory didn't do the experience justice. How has he done it? For years, he hasn't had a second of peaceful sleep and yet he gets through every day. I loathe the thoughts dancing around my mind as I try to fall asleep and the nightmares that wake me in the dark, but watching him struggle pulls at something deep inside me. Maybe it's pity.

Cael's walking now, even with Leo's constant pestering about taking his time. It's hard to comprehend the ease between them. They aren't blood, but they know each other better than Byrne and me. They worry for each other, watch each other's backs, bicker, and joke to keep one another from sinking too deep. It's calming, the normalness of it. Even their strained moments aren't truly tense. Leo's taken to hovering over Cael like a mother would to her first child. I said as much, and I don't think I've ever heard Cael laugh so hard. Leo rolled his eyes, but I could see the smile he tried to hide. "Cael's acted like the dutiful adult my entire life, it's only fair I now take on the parenting position," he had muttered sarcastically.

As I head out the next day, I look up and stop at the forest line. I managed to convince Byrne not to come with me after endless pleading and pulling at her defenses. I know she only agreed out of annoyance, but I could not have been more relieved.

I walk out of the trees after listening for a long moment, deeming there is no one here to watch me sneak out of the woods. The dagger I keep tucked at my back grounds me, filling me with the false confidence I crave. I walk with my chin held high and shoulders straight, hiding away my emotions as people watch from their homes. I take the less populated side streets and alleys to the house. I can't convince myself to move any faster, even knowing Cassien will be home in a matter of minutes.

I approach the house from the back to forgo seeing the guards standing at the door. I leave the window leading to my room unlocked for this exact reason. It opens easily, whining at my touch. I haul myself up and in, and my feet hit the floor with a subtle thud. I have to wash up and take my boots off or Cassien will know something is going on. I must always be home when he arrives. I'll make a show of how I've been around all day, then I just have to wait for his crystal bottle of liquor to come out of the cabinet. When the drink starts flowing, Byrne and I disappear, making a point to stay out of his way.

I pull my boots off and push them to the side of my undisturbed bed. I stare at it for a long moment, the downy covers calling my name. I sigh as I run my hand over the fabric. I wish I could lie down one last time and not worry, throw the covers over my head like I did when I was a child and imagine them to be impenetrable. I sneer at the memory. How naive I was.

I walk away from the bed, resisting the urge to bury myself in its safety. I step out of my room and freeze. He's here, watching me from his carved wooden chair with his ankle neatly crossed over his knee. *He looks like a predator,* I think gravely as I swallow the bile creeping up my throat. My stomach sinks as I catch the glimmer of the empty crystal glass in his hand and the shine of a thick-cut black ring sitting on his finger. He's been here for a while, and he knows I haven't.

"Father," I say by way of greeting, the words foreign in my mouth. This man is not my father. His bloodshot eyes track me as I move. My mouth dries as memories start to resurface. I push them away desperately, knowing fear only feeds his violence.

"Ella?" he asks, rolling my name around in his mouth as if he were trying to taste it. Anyone else wouldn't hear the change in his voice, but I do. The lilt of the monster he hides under his fine suits and power. The Council knows what he is, and they drink it up like Cassien does his liquor. They took the man who used to be my father and twisted him, *broke* him. They fed the monster inside until my father was gone, nothing but the shell of the man he used to be. My entire body goes rigid as his gaze travels from my feet to my face. The blade burns at my back, but my hands stay tight against my sides, under their own control.

"Where have you been? You look like you've had a run-in with a tree," he says dryly.

"Byrne and I went for a walk through the woods. She's gone to spar with one of the other phantoms," I lie smoothly, the deceit coming as easy as they always have. I beg my face not to lead him to the truth. He stands and I flinch. I know I'm dead the second he registers the movement. My life flashes before my eyes as panic takes hold of my mind, seizing my muscles.

"I want her here, Elana. Why isn't my daughter at home to take care of her father?" he asks, slowly pulling out the words. He steps toward me and stops a breath away. He's only two inches taller than I am, but I feel like a child as he stares down at me. His eyes cloud with terrifying intent, his thoughts clear to me after seeing that same glint so many times before. I don't know where the dagger comes from, but in seconds he holds it against my throat and pins me against the wall. I pray I'll vanish into the air as my blood freezes in my veins. "You will make sure she is here. You will always be here to do as I say," he whispers into my ear, each word another lash to my back. The blade breaks the skin over my throat and blood drips slowly down its edge. "You are more worthless than your mother was. A sly child who thinks the world belongs to her. I'll teach you what the world does to people who disobey their gods." He pulls away as time slows and punches me in the jaw, the onyx ring pounding against the already purpled flesh of my face.

The taste of iron fills my mouth as my head smashes against the wall. My knees shudder as I lock them straight, denying my body the choice to fall to the ground. I clench my jaw and my eyes water as I steady myself, willing them to stay silver. Cassien grabs my chin and forces me to meet his stare. "I own you, control your every move. People can say what they wish, but we all know they only give you their respect because of me. I suggest you step in line and bow your head, Elana," he snarls. My entire body begins to convulse. I'm going to kill him. He sees it in my gaze as I hold his glare, tears building in my eyes. "I said bow!" he screams as the monster finally snaps free. He bashes the pummel of his blade into my temple, knocking me off my feet. Not a single part of me responds as my knees buckle. My eyes flush gold as I lie paralyzed on the ground while Cassien kicks me again and again. I don't feel anything, my thoughts separating from my body as tears roll numbly down my face, watching the scene from above like a lost spirit. I curl into myself as his boot forces the air from my lungs. His glass shatters over my shoulder, showering me in shards of blood-stained crystal. I squeeze my eyes shut, blocking out everything but the memory of the wind as my father would throw me into the air all those years ago, telling me I could do anything, even fly.

My eyes flutter open, the throbbing of my head hitting me with so much force nausea rises into my throat. I stretch my jaw and my ears pop as the pain crashes me into darkness. After an agonizing moment of dizziness, I start to take in the light and color of the room again. I push myself up and wince as I sit against the wall. I shift my eyes and the pain immediately subsides. I touch the wound on my head and my hand comes away red and glistening. I curse under my breath as I pull myself up to my feet. The room is completely dark. It must be at least a few hours since I left the cabin. A snore rings through the air, making me jump as my eyes find Cassien cradling a flask in his hand, fast asleep. His dagger is crusted in my blood on the side table. I sneer at the sight of him, my mind a whirlwind of fear and revenge.

I pull out my blade, fingers curling around the hilt. I stride over to him, hovering the knife above his throat. I press it to his skin and hold up my chin, my lips curling back from my teeth. He doesn't move. My breath comes in short wisps as my bones ache and muscles scream. I beg myself to end it, to shove the blade through his throat and run. I haven't killed before, but I imagine this death to keep me sane. The sound of ripping flesh as I force the blade through his skin and the jarring feeling of hitting bone when it reaches his spine has played in my mind millions of times. I wouldn't weep or grieve him; I would take Byrne and make a new life for us. A life free of pain, free of him.

I push my weight against the dagger, but it stays in the

same spot, my hand keeping it still. I tell myself to do it, to finish him, but the steel continues to hover over his neck. I snarl at myself, dropping the knife from his throat and burying my face in my hands. I need to kill him. I'll be doing the world a favor. He won't be able to hurt me or anyone else. *Not yet*, a small voice whispers in my mind. *You won't do it.*

"I can," I say aloud. *But you choose not to.* I want to scream as I step away, pulling at the roots of my hair as tears fill my eyes. I could slit his throat so easily, and yet I take another step back, staring at him through a golden haze. The ring on his finger reflects the light as his hand twitches. It's the Hael ring. Cael used to wear it. I lean forward and carefully wrap my fingers around the smooth onyx. Cassien stirs, bringing my entire being to a screeching halt as dread builds inside me. I stand over him for a long moment, counting his reeking breaths. I close my eyes and pull the ring off his finger. I stay frozen, waiting for him to jump up and shatter my skull. He doesn't move, snoring soundly. I slip the ring onto my finger and quickly head for my room.

I clumsily slip on my boots before raiding the pantry and closets, filling a blanket with supplies and food. I tie the sack up tight and throw it over my shoulder. I stumble back into my room and climb out through the window, barely keeping myself upright. The cool night air feels like a lullaby to my racing thoughts. I keep moving forward with my ears open, stopping only when a guard passes on patrol. The woods seem so far away, but I will myself to take each step as my thoughts quiet to a murmur at the back of my mind.

***

I walk through the door of the cabin, my sight blurry even with the gold sheen of my eyes. They never fail to take away the pain, but my body can only be pushed so far. My head swims as I drop the blanket of supplies. I feel my legs sway and I start to collapse. Strong hands catch me and scoop me up before I hit the floor. I hear silent swearing as another pair of hands shake my shoulders. My body is lowered against something hard and cold and my head is propped up from the ground. Light sweeps across my eyes as someone holds a wet towel to the back of my neck, making a shiver run up my spine. "Elana? Elana, can you hear me?" a frantic voice calls from far away. I swim toward it. I know that voice, I grew up hearing it.

My eyes slowly come back into focus. I'm in the cabin. I blink fast, trying to straighten my clouded thoughts. Someone holds my head up, his eyes boring into mine as he lets out a long breath. A familiar hand cups my face and gently holds me steady as I try to sit up. I lean back into waiting arms. "What happened, Elana?" they ask. I hear the words, but can't discern their meaning, like trying to read an old text I can't decipher. Someone steps away from the wall and crouches down beside me, wincing as they approach.

"She's concussed, Byrne," they say, slowly moving their hand up to my face. I flinch as my heart races, recoiling into the arms of whoever is keeping me upright.

"It's all right. We won't hurt you." I feel the voice vibrate against my back, soothing my tightening lungs as a hand traces easing circles up and down my arm. I relax slightly, leaning against the solid body holding me up. My tongue feels heavy in my mouth as I'm handed a cup of water. I swallow it down and sigh before taking another. My eyes flutter shut as sounds muddle around me, old thoughts flowing freely through my mind as my shield falls. I see the memory again, the blue sky flecked with drifting clouds. I feel weightless, like I'm flying, then falling, plummeting toward the ground instead of into the safe embrace of the father I used to want to love.

LEO

"She's out," I say, holding Elana tightly against me. Her breathing has evened out at least, but the sight of her—cuts flecked across her face and bruises darkening her skin—lights a fire in my veins. I lift my eyes to Byrne who sits helplessly a foot away, her hands covering her mouth. "Who did it?" She meets my gaze, her eyes broken as she shakes her head defeatedly. Then it occurs to me. "It's him, isn't it? He does this to both of you." Her silence and glazed eyes are all the admission I need. Cael tenses beside me as his gaze clouds over.

"I'll clean her up. Can you get clean water, a cloth, and needle?" I ask gently. Byrne nods and pulls Saiph up into her arms. I place my hand on Cael's shoulder, making him jump. His eyes clear instantly. "Are you all right?" He nods, swallowing before standing up and leaving the cabin to get more water.

"What's wrong with him?" Byrne asks as she watches the door shut behind my brother.

"This brings up memories he'd rather forget," I say softly as I motion toward Elana. She looks over at her sister, her brows furrowing.

"Why the needle? I thought you weren't good at sewing. I can do it," she says shakily, wiping a stray tear from her cheek.

"I'm not, but there's glass in her cuts," I say. Byrne flinches as she drops a little box on the table. "And neither of you should be holding anything sharp right now," I add, eyeing her shaking hands.

"I'm fine!" she says roughly, wincing at her clipped tone.

"I know," I whisper, watching her trembling hands fumble with the box. She grasps the edge of the table so hard that for a moment, I think it might splinter.

"It's not usually this bad. Normally a few hits satisfy his need to feel powerful. But Elana never... She never..." Byrne trails off, squeezing her eyes shut. She takes a deep breath before she wipes her cheeks and lays out the supplies in front of me. Cael comes back in, his focus narrowed in on the bowl of water in his hands. He sets it beside me before pulling out a worn chair. He takes Saiph from Byrne and sits, his dark gaze fixed on the wall as my sister clutches her doll, Lynn, tightly in her hands. Byrne moves to the other side of the room and sits down on the floor.

"Byrne?" I call. She raises her head and meets my gaze. "She'll be all right." The only response she manages is a slight dip of her chin and I can't stop the surge of worry and rage coursing through me. I will get them out of here, both of them.

Cael and Byrne are both sound asleep on the floor with Saiph curled up between them. We set up a bed using all the blankets we had to keep Elana comfortable. My head snaps up as she stirs, pushing at the blankets.

"Elana? How are you feeling?" I ask, my voice sounding more frantic than I meant it to. She groans and opens her eyes.

"Like I've been bashed in the head," she moans before throwing a hand over her eyes. Byrne shoots up so fast she hits the table, startling my brother awake. She races to her sister's side, carefully grabbing her face in her hands. Elana swats her away, scrunching her nose as she tries to sit up. "I'm fine. It's just a scratch," she dismisses roughly.

"Elana, you've been out for *hours*! I'd be surprised if your brain *wasn't* bleeding." Elana leans back against the wall, trying to hide the wince she can't help.

"No one could ever truly hurt me, Byrne. You know that." She glances my way, nervousness flashing across her face.

"We know," I say evenly, hiding the fire burning inside me. Elana cuts a glance at her sister as Byrne's hands fly up in defense.

"They figured it out." She shrugs as she scans her sister with a tense expression. Elana closes her eyes and tips her head back as she smothers her face with her hands. She pulls them back suddenly, staring at the sparkling onyx ring on her fingers.

"Is that—" Cael starts, his words dying on his lips as he moves toward her.

"When I woke up, he was passed out and wearing it. The least I could do was take something from him after he stole hours of my life. He won't remember anything in the morning," she says to Cael, not realizing the significance of what she's done. She pulls the ring off and extends her hand as my brother and I gawk disbelievingly. He takes it from her, his hands shaking as he slips the ring over his finger. He sputters, his mouth opening and closing when he can't find any words.

"Thank you," I breathe, voicing the words for my brother. "You have no idea what this means to him." Cael nods as he spins the ring around his finger, grinning faintly to himself. I almost choke on the air entering my lungs as I catch Elana smiling back at him—a real, genuine smile, lighting her eyes and softening her face. I force my gaze away, fidgeting with my hands as I watch Saiph.

"We're even now," she says as she touches the crooked stitches above her brow, gesturing to my brother before shifting her gaze to Byrne.

"Actually, it—"

"It wasn't an issue. He's fixed me up a million times. It's about time he helped someone else," I blurt out, gaining a strange look from my brother. Elana glances at me, nodding sternly before turning her eyes back to Byrne. I stand up and move to sit beside Saiph as my thoughts spin, wondering why all of a sudden the room seems too warm.

FORTY-ONE

LEO

Elana and Cael are both back to their old selves, though they haven't been without their bad days. We removed Cael's stitches, which took an extensive amount of time. Elana is doing fine, besides the lingering bruises, healing cuts, and her solemn mood. She tried to go back into the city, and it took everything in me not to force her to stay. Even if I told her not to go, I think she might simply do it to spite me. In the end, Byrne did convince her and I managed to limit my input to a nod.

I push the thought out of my mind, concentrating on the task ahead. When I said I wasn't leaving without dealing with the lab, I meant it. The initiation is getting closer, hanging over us like a bad omen, and we've been running on borrowed time for so long that waiting is no longer an option. I left for the city early this morning and I've been lying on this corner of the roof across from the lab since dawn, waiting for the dark to return. I touch the blade I took off the phantoms and the extra one

Elana and Byrne gave me to ground myself as the sky starts to turn a soft pink; it's a beautiful night. Those are always the best days to work. When people have a good day, they never expect it to end in flames. I take out the dagger the sisters gave me and run my finger along the edge. An overwhelming sense of longing fills me as I turn the blade in my hands. My father's weapons had been special to me, perfectly worn to my hands and made with steel that sliced through anything like it was air. I take a steadying breath and force myself to focus.

Darkness falls over the city like a warm blanket, the day's heat lingering in the air. I crawl to the back of the building and jump down, bending my knees to make sure I land silently. The pressure on my lungs eases instantly as the fog of fear recedes. I watch for any people lurking around the street before slipping into the alley and stalking over to the laundry house. The door is right where my brother said, beckoning me closer. I take out the two lock picks Byrne procured for me and get to work. The lock is different from what Cael had described. After a long ten minutes of meticulously maneuvering the mechanism, the lock finally pops open with a click.

I wait and listen for a long moment. Two people came in this morning and two came out this evening. It must be empty, but something feels wrong. After getting broken into once, no one would leave the place unguarded. It's in our nature to protect valuable things, yet all they did was change the lock? It doesn't seem right.

I push the door open and step over the threshold as my eyes flush bloodred. A small candle burns on one of the tables near the back, gently lighting the room with its dancing orange flame. I walk forward reluctantly, taking in everything laid out in front of me. Cael told me what I would find, but it's different seeing it for myself. Chills creep up my spine as I look around at the notes, the vials of blood, the Ruby Tar, and the endless drawings and diagrams depicting everything from our whereabouts to my body composition. I walk over to the vials and have to stop myself from smashing them against the ground. I watch the candle throw my shadow against the wall, the glow making everything seem more ominous. I move closer as the wax drips slowly down the smooth sides and falls onto the table beside a red fountain pen on a page half filled with script. My heart drops.

I whirl toward the door at the far side of the room as footsteps sound from behind it. I drop to the floor, hiding under a table draped with papers and maps. I watch, barely breathing as a set of boots stop at the threshold after the door swings open. A crisp light-blue coat hangs above them, cutting off before the ankles. Thank the Lady I closed the door behind me after coming in. The man sits down and returns to whatever revolting work had been strewn across the desk. I push the maps aside, getting a full view as the man buries his nose into a book. I back up slowly, making sure to keep myself well hidden until I hit complete darkness.

I push to my feet, watching the man in blue with an uneasy stare. He continues his work obliviously, reading his notes, then jotting down another. He shifts, sneezing and then groaning as he stands. He turns back to the door with a hand covering his nose. It closes as he disappears into the connecting room, and I take my chance. I hurry and stand behind his desk with my back flush against the wall. He walks back into the room, wiping his face with a cloth as he sits down. It amazes me how unaware some people can be. They walk around, work, and eat without constantly worrying someone is holding a knife at their backs. By the Lady, they can sleep without worrying someone will forbid them from waking the next morning. Longing and pity fill me as I watch the man return to his studies. Living with those luxuries is a gift I will never be blessed with, but I accepted that a long time ago.

I step forward quickly and wrap my arm tightly around his throat as I clear my mind of my conscience. There is no room for worry or sympathy in situations like these. You must act without thought or reproach, jump when the chance is given and turn off the empathy and thoughts of life and family. There is no other way to stay sane.

He responds immediately, his hand searching under his coat. My body moves before my mind has time to react, finding his dagger and dropping it to the floor before kicking it away. I cover my hand with my sleeve and place it over his airways, cutting off his oxygen. I move the arm at his neck to his shoulders, keeping him pinned to the chair. He struggles, scratching at my arms and kicking out his feet. He tries to twist away, but I push my hip forward, trapping him against the desk.

His arms finally go limp and his head drops onto my arm as I pull my hand away. His breathing comes back in short gasps, his lungs desperately trying to keep him alive. I take a deep breath as I step away, letting my thoughts back in. Sympathy pricks at the back of my mind but I force myself to ignore it.

Fury builds in my veins as I pick up the candle from the desk and try to understand how this man is here. He's either been inside for a while or there's another door. I watch him for a moment, slumped against the table. This was supposed to be in and out, no one gets hurt.

I cross the room and open the door the man had come through just minutes before. A narrow hall lined with doors lies on the other side. I look through the thick square pane of glass at the top of the first door and jump back. I lean forward and squint to get a better view, not believing what I'm seeing. The room is lined with shelves of jars filled with strange liquids. Shivers run down my spine as I move to the next door, nausea rising.

The next room is eerily similar to a cell. The walls are painted a shining white, reflecting the light of my small flame. In the middle sits a table with two chairs opposite each other. For some reason, this room bothers me more than the last. For a moment I swear I catch a glimpse of Lady Death's black, bottomless eyes staring back at me through the small window. Nothing good can come of her being in that room. Then I understand the unsettling feeling in my stomach. It feels like pain and *death*. This room is used for no sane purpose, and it sets me even more on edge.

I continue down the hall and stop cold to glance at whatever lies beyond the next door. A large pile at the back of the room is covered by a wide sheet. The tip of a blade pokes out from underneath, reflecting the candlelight back at me. I push on the door, but it's locked. I sigh, take a step back and angle my shoulders downward. I charge into the door and smash it off its hinges with a bang. I freeze as the sound bounces off the walls. I wait for a long moment, expecting the patrols to burst in and drag me away, but no one comes.

I walk quietly over to the sheet and lift the fabric away. My breath hitches at what I see. My weapons. My prized possessions. They're all here. My slayers, my dagger with the copper wire, my light throwing knives still tucked into the navy leather bandolier, the one knife missing at the end. I never replaced it after I got Altair out of the military compound in Somereil. I don't think I'll ever want to. As I scan the pile, I realize even the boots and clothes I had been wearing when we were in the clearing are here, lying in a discarded pile. I pick up the blood-stained shirt and my stomach sinks. There are more holes in it than I can count, some from having been in the woods for so long, others from my last stand in the clearing. I touch the scar at my side. I don't think I've ever been so close to death. A cold shiver runs down my spine as I drop the shirt back onto the floor. My boots are here, still crusted in mud but they seem as good as they once were, beaten in just like I remember them. I check the sole of my left boot and find the blade still hiding in its compartment.

I glance around the room and notice our packs neatly lined up against each other. Grief hits me as I realize I can't bring it all back with me. I dig through the bags, discarding the dirt-stained blankets and threadbare clothes. I grab Antares's ball, and an old shirt that belonged to Pollux for Cass. I scrounge through my things, my hands shaking as I find the letters. Blood is soaked through a corner, but they're still intact. I release a ragged, sob-like breath.

I tuck them all gently in my pocket before picking up my blades. Something eases in me as I hold the weapons that have brought me surety in the most uncertain times. A half smile pulls at my lips as I strap them on, sighing in relief as a small weight lifts from my shoulders. Some people may have an old portrait or relic to bring them courage and peace, I have these blades. I can't believe I ever thought I could live without them. They take me back to when Dad used to spar with us out in the yard. The grueling tasks of training always led to endless laughter out of the sheer exhaustion from hours in the blazing sun or freezing cold.

With my head held a little higher, I walk to the last door. It isn't like the rest, made of a weathered, older wood. I push it open and a slight gust of wind rushes over my face. This explains how the blue-coated man got in.

I stride back over to the man still slumped on the desk and haul him over my shoulders. I walk outside and drop him on the opposite side of the alley, praying no one decides to pass by. I stop myself as I start crossing his hands on his lap. *He's not dead*, I remind myself, but the weight of my weapons and the stillness of his body brings back old scars I try so hard to forget. I outran the Blood Prince; I am not him anymore, and the still-beating heart inside this man proves it. The memories push against the wall I built deep inside myself. All those nameless faces. The people Vela wanted rid of. By no means were any of their hands clean, but there's always a story behind blood-soaked pasts. I shake off the thought, moving my head as if I could physically remove them from my mind.

I walk back inside and take out the small piece of flint I brought with me from the cabin, careful not to spill the other items in my pocket. I hit the edge of the blade Elana gave me over the flint and throw sparks over the inked pages. After three tries, the paper catches, a small flame surging to life. I carefully pick it up and ignite pages all over the room. Smoke stings my nose as I spread the flames into every part of the lab. I pull my shirt over my nose as my eyes start to water, the heat singeing the air as the fire takes to the desks. I run to the back door and take a moment to watch it burn. If they want to become monsters, so be it, but they should know there are those of us who have lurked here much longer.

I run out the door and lock it tightly behind me before making my way around to secure the side one too, leaving the man propped up against the opposite wall. He'll be confused and have a headache when he wakes, but he'll live. I sprint away with the sound of screeching voices and devouring flames filling my ears. A vengeful grin pulls at my lips at the thought of what I have prevented. Cassien can try and take our freedom, but no one steals from me and gets away whole.

FORTY-TWO

ELANA

He did it. I catch sight of Leo as he runs toward me through the darkness, blending in seamlessly with the shadows. I can see the flames licking the cold night air from Daeta's market where I wait behind an old stall.

"You are crazy," I tell him dryly as he stops beside me, panting slightly. The soot and smoke clinging to his skin makes me cringe. It takes me a second to realize he's armed with weapons I've never seen before. The sheaths and bandolier are made of a navy leather so dark it's closer to black. The closer he comes, the more detail I notice. The harness is intricately decorated with spirals and stars; every corner covered in subtle detail. His eyes light up when he sees my expression. He tilts his head to the side with a playful grin.

"How did I convince you I wasn't?" The glimmer in his eyes clouds over. "I'm glad it's gone. There were things in there I don't want to talk about, and it reeked of death. But at least I found my weapons," he says, losing the seriousness as he waves a hand over his torso.

"How? I mean... Those are... impressive?" I stammer, fumbling over my words. They're beautifully made, better than anything I've ever seen in Wate. I had taken him as one to steal a knife and keep it close, but these are impressive blades. He pulls one out of its sheath and lobs it through the air. I catch it easily, my eyes going wide as I flip it in my hand. It's simple, the hilt a smooth wood inlaid with copper wire, but it's the most balanced dagger I've ever held. The edge is sharp and thin and the handle fits perfectly in my hand, creating the exact amount of friction to allow it to move without compromising my grip. I turn my focus back to Leo as his past becomes a little clearer in my mind.

"They belonged to my father. My parents kept them hidden under the floorboards for years. Cael and I found them when we were young and all I remember wanting to do was stare at them. I'm sure Dad knew because we made so much noise trying to put the board back in place, but he never said anything. My mother gave them to me on her deathbed," he recalls, sadness and joy spinning in his voice as he lays a hand over the fine leather.

"I guess you knew they would be yours," I say, tossing the dagger back to him. He catches it smoothly and places it back at his side. He looks more at ease than I've ever seen him, the tightness he usually carries melted away. He nods as a half smile plays on his lips, making my stomach flutter.

"I guess I did."

He starts loosening the many buckles fastening his blades to his body as I wet the cloth I had brought and hand it to him. He takes it along with a flask I offer him. His hands still as he raises a brow.

"I didn't know we were celebrating," he jokes, the smile still stuck on his dammed face.

"It's water," I state evenly, prohibiting myself from letting loose the quipped reply my brain had formulated. His eyes shimmer as he washes away the soot from his face. He downs the rest of the flask and strips off his ruined shirt before throwing it to the ground. I feel myself smirk as I remember it's Cassien's shirt lying in a ruined heap in the dirt. It's small, but it still feels like I'm fighting back, chipping away at his control. I have to do a double take as Leo wraps his knives up in the shirt and tucks them carefully under a pile of ripped canvas to hide them from sight.

Scars line his entire back, wrap around his torso, and run down his arms. Some are straight and fine while others are twisted and gnarled, all of them only distinguishable by a faint discoloration of his skin. I should be intimidated, but only empathy and anguish rise to the surface of my mind. I saw the wound he had on his hand and how quickly it healed. You can barely see a mark now. Bile rises in my throat as I imagine the severity of the injuries to have caused those scars, wounds so much worse than the one to his hand.

While the ghosts of his injuries were what first caught my eye, it's the column of circular star maps lining Leo's spine that captivates me. Some are slightly deformed from the scars, but they're still beautiful. Something about the imperfection suits him, like the design runs deeper than his skin to reflect his soul.

He catches me staring and a flush of heat runs up my neck. I turn my gaze back to the bag I brought with me. "I was upset the first time I was injured and the scarring messed up my tattoo. I was sullen for days, as Cael can attest. But as time passed and I fell deeper into a place I could not climb out of, I realized they were better tainted. My family has been through horrors worse than you can imagine, but we survive and continue on. I get hurt, but the ink remains, even if it's different than it once was," he says so softly, I can barely hear him. When he meets my gaze, his eyes tell a different story. They're filled with pride. I wonder how much his loyalty has cost him.

He slips on the clean shirt I hand him and dips his chin. "We aren't done yet. I left a man unconscious out the back of the building. If you make it look like you saved him, it might give us an extra little bit of breathing room." His lopsided grin begins to fade, the smile he wears now one of necessity, not joy. His eyes don't light up like they do when he's truly happy. I scold myself at the thought. When did I start noticing these things? I exhale a long breath and clear my mind. "Go be a hero," he drawls, staging a terrible bow.

"Monsters don't get to be heroes," I say, the words slipping out before I can think better of them. His expression drops, his eyes dark as my words hang between us.

"We all have our monsters, Elana. It's our decision to fight them or let ourselves become them."

"And if we've already become one?" I whisper, not sure if I want to know the answer.

"Monsters don't realize what they are. Only good people can see the bad inside and make the decision to fight it," he says confidently as his eyes bore into mine. "I've seen many monsters, Elana. You are not one of them." I nod, not knowing what to say. I close my eyes and swallow hard before pushing past him, leaving his words behind.

I start yelling as I push myself into a sprint. "Fire! Fire! Fire in the Academy!" People come flying out of their homes half dressed and bleary eyed. I run to the Cassien house, barreling past the guards and through the door as I train my face into an emotionless mask. Cassien is dead asleep on his carved wooden throne, snoring in a way that makes me sneer. I slam the door against the wall so hard the whole house shakes. He jumps up from his chair, his piercing eyes glazed. Before he can tear me apart, I walk over to the table and grab his ring of keys. The iron is almost as heavy as the glare he pins to me.

The pressure in my chest eases as I race out the door. The guards are no longer here, most likely waiting to be let into the Academy. I push through the crowd gathering at the gates and start shoving keys into the large lock. Thank the Lady Cassien is as paranoid as he is and keeps the keys with him instead of giving them to the guards. Finally, the third key slips in and turns with a click, unlocking the gates to a tidal wave of frenzied, half-asleep people.

I can't help but be impressed, though I don't dare show it. Leo did his job perfectly; the entire building is engulfed by the blaze. Nothing will survive this. The students and instructors are haphazardly throwing water onto the flames, running in a panic. I sigh and start barking out orders, quickly soothing the rambling chaos into a working unit. Once I've dealt with the scrambling crowd, I tell one of the high-ranking officers I'm going to search for survivors. He eyes me skeptically, either because he fears me or thinks me insane for suggesting I go into the blaze.

I pull my shirt over my mouth and take a handful of water from a passing bucket to drench it through. I push my legs into a slow jog and shift my eyes as they start to tear up from the billowing smoke. People yell to get back, but no one tries to stop me. Most likely, they simply don't want to deal with telling Cassien his daughter went into the flames and never came out. I smile at the pain I would cause him should I die, but would he be upset? Would he even give me a second thought? My mind spins faster and faster as I try to find the answer and wonder if I even want him to care. I come up empty-handed and quickly force the thought away.

I round the building as more people flood in to help. Why no one noticed the man slumped against the wall across from the laundry house is beyond me. His face is covered in the dark soot and ash falling like rain from the burning sky. I can barely breathe as I run over to him. The oxygen feeds the fire as the heat burns my wheezing lungs. I can feel the flames on my skin through the wall, singeing my clothes and boiling the air. I make quick work of lifting him over my shoulders and carrying him around the building. At the sight of me, a frail old medic comes running. My chest heaves as I force my feet forward.

I drop to the ground in a coughing fit and it takes me several minutes to regain my breath. Once I do, I scan my heated skin, making sure there are no serious burns. I look up in shock as the entire building collapses into itself; soot, smoke, and ash erupt in the air with a blast of heat. I turn away and shield my face as I hear others scream, getting hit by burning debris. We all watch in silence as the building slowly disappears.

By the time Cassien shows up, the flames have died down significantly. I'm on my feet again, laying out orders as far as my raspy voice will carry them. I still as he moves toward me and stands by my side. He's staring intently at the lab, his expression cold and unreadable, but his eyes are burning brighter than the smoldering embers before us. "What happened?" he asks evenly, pushing out his hand. I unhook the ring of keys from my belt and place them in his waiting palm.

"We don't know. I saw the flames and ran here. By the time I opened the gates and the people filled the buckets from the wells, it was too late," I explain, forcing indifference into my words.

"Any casualties?" He speaks of death like it's nothing more than one of his daily reports. Maybe it is.

"I found one man out the back, passed out on the ground. He was covered in ash so I couldn't tell who he was. No one has been reported missing and there were no signs of anyone being trapped inside." I twist false relief into my voice. He doesn't so much as glance my way, simply staring ahead as he takes in the exhausted, injured people being cared for by the medics. The sight of their bubbling burns is so horrible, I have to look away.

"Where is he?" Cassien asks, his voice making me straighten. Rage pools in his darkening eyes.

"We have reports of seeing him watching the flames from Daeta's market. I can confirm that they are truthful," I say, staring straight ahead. Please let him be blind to my lies for one last time.

"Are you telling me this is not of his doing?" he seethes as his anger snaps loose. I close my eyes, my entire body seizing as my mind slowly starts to blur around the edges. If this were an ordinary building, Cassien would not have cared. We would have rebuilt and moved on, but there were countless invaluable things in those rooms. Research, experiments, and weapons that will not easily be recreated.

"No," I tell him, focusing on a dark point beyond the dying flames. I don't want to think of what he'll do if he sees through me. His glare stays fixed ahead, the tic in his jaw and darkening eyes the only evidence of his displeasure.

"No one saw him coming or going?" he asks. I shake my head as I fist my hands to prevent them from trembling. "He has climbed the gates before, Elana. He's slid in and out while being chased by some of the best phantoms the Academy has ever created. Do you truly expect me to believe that this is not of his doing?" he questions, letting a sliver of his controlled expression slip. I flinch at the feral glint in his eyes. I shake my head again as if confused and straighten my shoulders. I can't let him see my fear.

"Why would he want to burn down this building? I would think others would have brought him more... pleasure." I fake a scowl, continuing my charade as my entire body goes rigid. He turns away abruptly as his hands tense at his side. I know full well the only reason he isn't beating me into the ground is because he can't let me think anything of value was lost. If word got out, not only would I have more sway, but it could bring the blood-eyes marching. He walks away from me without another word, and my breathing immediately evens out, knowing he'll be deep in his drink tonight and I won't be there. He'll likely destroy half the house and pass out before I get back to the cabin. Meanwhile I'll be one step closer to getting off this island, ridding myself of the demon crawling under his skin.

***

The sun starts to peek over the horizon by the time I make my way back to the cabin. The man I dragged around the lab was Doctor Hemar. He did work for the Council and was a celebrated man all around. His wife found me before I left the Academy. I could see the tears welling in her eyes as she spoke of him, but she didn't let one fall. To cry is said to be a sign of giving up among the gold-eyes. It is considered a weakness to yield to pain, emotional or physical. She informed me her husband had woken up without a single memory of the fire. The medics said he would be restored to his usual self in a matter of days, but I didn't really care. Even the woes of the woman couldn't shake the disgust I felt toward what he had been doing. She handed me a small, wrapped package as thanks for saving her husband and scurried off, not daring to spend another second away from the poor man. Maybe he had been forced to work there, the ways of our society branded into his mind as they are in mine, but it makes no difference, he still deserves no empathy. I wonder if I'm the same? If that's how the brothers see me? I am what Cassien created, and I'm finding it harder and harder to understand how I ever believed the atrocities they painted as honorable thoughts.

I walk through the cabin doors with the small package tucked in my hand. Byrne's asleep, sitting in a chair with a blanket pulled up to her chin as the brothers speak softly so as not to wake Saiph sleeping between them. All three of their heads shoot up as I walk in, Byrne coming out of her sleep so fast, she almost falls off her chair. "How did it go?" Cael asks hesitantly, spinning the onyx ring around his finger. I'd noticed the habit before, and it makes much more sense with the band in place.

"We're good," I confirm as an involuntary smirk lights my face. The air itself seems to lighten as they all let out a relieved breath. Leo tilts his face up to the ceiling, murmuring to no person in this room. "And," I continue, pulling their attention back to me as I hold out the package, "The Goddess bestowed us with a reward." Leo's brows shoot up at the sight of it, exchanging a look with his brother as he places a hand on the dagger at his hip. I don't know how it can be comfortable for him to sit with the slayers crossed on his back, but he doesn't seem to mind them.

"What is it?" he asks, pulling my gaze to his.

"No idea." Byrne lunges for the gift and steals it from my fingers. She quickly unwinds the fabric and a sweet smell fills the room.

"What is that?" Cael repeats. The brothers practically salivate as they move closer.

"It smells amazing," Leo adds, eyeing the small pastries cupped in Byrne's hands.

"Sugar tarts," Byrne and I say simultaneously. Wide smiles grow on our faces. In her hands, my sister holds four of the most delicious pastries you can get in Wate. They're a staple treat, filled with amber sugar surrounded by a flaky crust. When we were growing up Byrne and I used to steal them off kitchen windowsills while they cooled. We burned our hands more times than I could count, but it was always worth it.

She passes them out, one to each of us. I can't stop the sigh from rumbling out of my throat as I bite into it. It tastes like joy. Sweet, sugary, gooey happiness. Cael and Leo stare at their tarts as they hold them carefully in their hands, pained expressions dawning across their faces. After a long moment, Leo breaks his in half, wrapping it back up so Saiph can eat it when she wakes tomorrow.

"Everything okay?" Byrne asks, the last piece of her tart hovering in front of her mouth. She's got the sugar filling smeared across her cheek. The brothers exchange a tense glance, Leo finding his pant leg extremely interesting.

"It's just... We didn't have anything like this in Somereil. And the boys aren't here..." he says, smiling sadly. Leo's shoulders hunch as his jaw tightens.

"I'll make more of them when we're all together," Byrne promises, eyeing the last bite of her tart. I nod, wanting nothing more than to finish mine as well, but feeling uncomfortable as Leo passes Cael a tight smile.

Leo raises his eyes to meet mine and finally, they take reluctant bites. The minute they do, Leo's head falls back as a huge smile grows on his face. It catches me by surprise, the realness of it. It isn't the half smile I've glimpsed so many times, but a fuller, lopsided grin that fills me with warmth. He makes a show by moaning and throwing his arms in the air as he takes another bite. Cael shakes his head as he watches his brother, not able to keep the smirk off his face, the skin around his dark eyes crinkles as he tries not to laugh.

"I think this is the best thing I've ever eaten," Cael admits, slapping Leo on the back of the head as he starts to lick his fingers clean. Leo passes him a confused look before shoving the rest of his fingers into his mouth. Cael chuckles as he leans his head back against the wall and contentedly accepts defeat.

"They're good, but no match to the ones our mother used to make. Elana and I begged her to make them so often she would tell us if we spoke another word of a pastry, she would put away her apron for good," Byrne recounts, the memory replaying in my mind as I know it is in hers. Both the brothers' jaws seem to drop, Cael pulling Leo's hand out of his mouth like an overbearing parent.

"I don't believe you," Leo says, placing the same hand over his heart. "This is the best thing I've ever eaten, and I don't think it's possible anything could be better."

"I don't think there's a child in Wate who hasn't gotten stuffed on sugar tarts," Byrne says, the disbelief clear in her voice. "These are one of the best treats, but there are so many others that are better." The brothers shrug in unison, though I can see the doubt in their eyes, like children discovering the world and not quite believing it's real. It's eerie to witness how their thoughts line up.

"We only ever had enough to get by. These types of things weren't something we could afford in Tominay. Even if there was sugar to buy, I'd have to work a lot of jobs to even think about buying a handful," he says as the happiness drops from his face. Cael puts a reassuring hand on his shoulder, his lips thinning to a tight line.

"But weren't you, I mean, weren't you—"

"A mercenary?" Leo finishes for Byrne, voicing the word my sister could not. His gaze is sharp as he lays his fingers over the blade sheathed at his thigh. I swallow the lump forming in my throat as she nods. "The man I worked for paid me enough to survive and not a mark more. He held information over us instead, a more secure currency. Vela knew where we lived, about Saiph and the boys. He knew what I was, about every murder, and the laws dictating that under no circumstances was I to be left alive on Tominese soil. He knew everything. Vela could easily have led the king and his army straight to our door, but he wanted me at his disposal. So, I did whatever he asked." Leo's expression melts into indifference like a mask falling over his face. Most would probably have been convinced by his charade of apathy, but I don't miss the way he shrinks into himself.

"To protect them," I murmur, startling myself. I didn't mean to say it out loud. Leo shifts his gaze to me, his eyes searching mine. Cael seems far away, as if he's reliving the past in his mind. "Well, here's to a future where we need no protection," I say, lifting my chin.

"To being safe." Leo repeats. "And to more of those sugar tarts," he adds eagerly, the ease returning as quickly as it had vanished.

FORTY-THREE

CAEL

My back still hurts like hell, but the dread gnawing at my stomach keeps my thoughts busy. At least the stitches are gone and the gashes are healing, but any wrong movement feels like it could tear them open again. I sit on a chair around the table with Saiph propped on my knee, playing with the Lynn doll Leo made her. We've been going over the plan for days, deciding on the best course of action. I don't like any of it. First, Leo and I will get close enough to the initiation ceremony to catch the boys as they filter out. Then once we have the boys, the second part is easy: get to the rowboat where Elana and Byrne will be waiting with Saiph and leave this cursed place behind.

As long as nothing has changed from when Elana and Byrne went through their initiations, there will be no guards on patrol. The only problem is the Council and all of their best fighters will be there to bear witness to the event. We'll have a matter of seconds to pull the boys away, and a single hitch could mean the end of our freedom. It's an impossible feat, so of course Leo loves the plan. But what surprises me is the sisters are on board, putting me on the losing side of a three versus one.

After the fire, I did a double take when Leo walked into the cabin with his blades strapped on. I could see confidence he used to wear once again blanketing his features, his shoulders held higher and eyes shining. I felt the same thing when Elana brought back my ring. The band brings me no protection, but it provides me with a sense of comfort, a grounding familiarity.

"And you're sure we can get a boat?" I ask as I bring my eyes up to meet Byrne's. Though she assures me that she can, we're talking about needing a craft that will have to stay afloat with all eight of us in it. She nods nonetheless, nothing but certitude depicted on her face.

"It might take some time, but we can take one of the rowboats from the other side of the island. We'll have to lug it through the woods, and it will be heavy, but it should be easy to steal," she says, nodding to herself. I've seen the boats she speaks of and I'm skeptical. I look over to see Leo scowling in his seat, likely thinking about having to carry the boat through the woods.

"Then that's it, today we get the boat and three nights from now, we get out," he says, his voice steady with conviction. We all nod, ready to throw ourselves off the edge of a waterfall and hope there are no rocks waiting beneath the surface.

I talked Leo into trying to get some sleep, but I could tell his nerves were on overdrive because he barely got a few hours. I tried lying down as well and though I can usually block out the bad thoughts, last night my skin crawled when I closed my eyes as devastating outcomes flashed vividly in my mind.

Leo and I walk in complete silence as the sun starts to rise. I can't keep the chill off my skin even in the warm air. Leo left his blades at the cabin, though I could tell he was hesitant to part with them after just getting them back. Instead he carries one of the daggers the sisters gave him tucked into his belt, as I have one tucked into mine. "This is going to work," Leo whispers to himself. It doesn't help my churning stomach when I glance his way and catch the dread twisting his expression. I nod as I pull my shoulders back and banish any wayward thoughts from my mind.

"What's different about this?" I ask, not entirely wanting to know the answer. My brother is one of the most daring people I know. By the Lady, he ran into the sharp end of a blade for years because we needed the money, and not once did he hesitate. He shakes his head slowly.

"These people... They aren't fools. They don't look at me the same way the Tominese did: like I was an anomaly they thought they could best for glory. These people know exactly what I am, and they loathe it. They want to kill me because of what I am and it has nothing to do with the things I did or what I made myself. This all feels wrong, especially putting the boys in the cross fire," he says as he runs a hand through his hair. I had noticed the difference in him when we walked the streets here compared to Somereil. He seemed more on edge, and as he explains, it all makes sense. I watch him for a moment, knowing if the boys weren't a part of this, his mind would be much more at ease. If something does go wrong, he'll give himself up. I can see the sliver of fear etched in his expression and buried in his movements. Not for himself, but for us.

"We'll be fine, Leo. We always are. We're running like

we've been for months. This time we're just adding two sisters, a city of people who think I'm dead, and a river," I reassure him with mock indifference, trying to lighten the air. His gaze locks back on mine as his shoulders slump.

"That does not make me feel better. I'd take a year's worth of arena fights if it means we could stop running," he says. His face immediately blanches as he shakes his head slowly. "I take that back; I don't ever want to step into another arena."

"We'll be fine. The boat has been hidden and ready for two days, and Saiph and the sisters are already waiting. We'll be out of here before we know it." Leo stops abruptly and stares at me intently. I won't look away, defying my brother for no other reason than to show him this is no time for worry. After a moment, he turns away, sighing as he rubs the back of his neck.

"I'm going to win a stare off one day," he vows as the corner of his lip tips into the beginning of a grin. I scoff and roll my eyes.

"In your dreams. Call a medic for me the day I submit to your weak glare," I say as he throws his hand over his heart like he's been hurt.

"Come on, brother, my glare is as strong as the king's word."

"Yes, and trees have ears," I say casually, but Leo stops, his eyes widening as his hands fly over his mouth.

"Shh! They'll hear you," he whispers, a half smile settling on his face as he points timidly to the trees. I shake my head, grateful for the distraction, knowing the moment we get close to our destination, there is no going back.

Something hits my face and startles me awake. It's completely dark. I must have fallen asleep. The moon is the only thing allowing me to see where Leo sits perched on a branch a few trees away. I think about throwing something back, but the expression on his face stops me cold. He points to the ground and folds his hand over his mouth. I follow his gaze downward. Out of nowhere, a raging fire erupts between our perches. Two dozen people stand in front of it on a stone platform, their gold armbands glinting in the light as they stare into the woods.

I hear their footsteps before I see them. Students come streaming in with the same instructors I've seen walking the Academy grounds by their sides. They line up, staying completely silent. My eyes immediately land on Cass, Antares, and Altair, my youngest brother's hands shaking as Antares steps closer to him, sensing his unease. Altair seems oblivious to their unrest, his shoulders pushed back and chin raised as he watches the men and women standing in front of the bonfire. One of them pulls out a curved dagger and steps forward. I look back to Antares and Cass. They're by far the youngest here.

I pull my eyes away from my brothers and my gaze locks with Leo's. The contents of my stomach turning to lead as I realize who's holding the blade. I know Leo sees it too, as his expression changes from dread to furious. Cassien. Leo shifts silently to his feet, sitting in a crouched position on top of the steady branch.

"You are here because we have deemed you ready to be sworn by blood to the gold-eyed people. We have seen the potential you hold in the protection and liberation of our people. We are thieves of blood, people of gold. We are never merciful," Cassien says, voice booming. The students watch him with wonder and reverence, all but my two youngest brothers. They don't move, but I can see the fear building as Cass reaches for Antares's hand.

"Altair Hael," Cassien calls. My heart stops. My brother steps toward him and time stands still. This isn't right. Elana said they wouldn't initiate them because they were too young, too new. "Draw your blood to save the lives of the gold," he orders as his face flickers in the firelight. Altair takes the dagger Cassien hands him without a sliver of doubt. My mind whirls as I try and fail to find a way out of this.

Altair runs the blade across his hand, spilling blood to the ground. The breath punches from my lungs. "I will give my life for the protection and liberation of the people," he says, his words strong and sure. I raise my eyes back to Leo and just when I think nothing can get worse, his expression proves me wrong. I know what he's going to do the moment I see his eyes bleed crimson. I shake my head, begging him not to do it, to stick to the plan. But Leo can't let this go on, and I'm powerless to stop him. He hesitates as he catches the dread and fear flashing in my eyes. Cassien calls Antares's name, and my little brothers clutch to each other with pale faces. A hooded man comes up behind them and yanks them apart. I can't breathe as every fear my mind had created comes to life and Leo drops to the ground.

FORTY-FOUR

LEO

Embers dance through the air as I plunge to the ground, rolling to mute my fall. My bones ache as I straighten, immediately feeling numerous startled and furious gazes pin me in place. My vision snaps to my brothers. Cass shakes uncontrollably as Antares pushes him behind his back. Altair stands to the side as blood spews from his hand. His expression remains blank, as if he were feeling nothing at all. I would expect him to be surprised or relieved or even mad, but my brother stares at me like I'm a stranger.

"Leo?" My eyes land on Cass as his head peeks over Antares's shoulder. The fear in their eyes brings the world crashing back, the weight of what I've done firmly settling in and adding to the unending list of deeds that will someday tear me apart. Maybe that day will come sooner than I thought.

"Run," I breathe. Someone lunges at me, then another and another. In a matter of seconds, I'm fighting off multiple attackers. Screams bounce off the trees as I fly through the brush. My mind banishes everything but the concentration needed to stay on my feet and flow from strike to block. I catch sight of Antares and Cass running as a shadow pulls them away. I know the moment I see the relief in their faces, it's Cael.

I need to get away, but there are fists and knives flying at me from all angles. I can barely defend myself, let alone attack as they pounce on me in a perfectly timed rhythm. My first slip comes from a four-man attack when I'm forced to move to avoid being skewered. I miraculously avoid three of the blades, but the fourth rips through my flesh and embeds itself deep in my side. I don't feel the pain, but my body begins resisting my orders to move as blood quickly soaks my shirt. Swinging fists push me backward as I lash out with my own dagger, slicing through flesh and hitting bone as howling screams fill the air. I only stop when I feel the cold bite of steel at the back of my neck, pressing so hard it slices my skin. If I take a deep breath, the dagger will push right into my windpipe.

"You should have stayed in the woods with the getic's corpse." Cassien tsks as he places a dagger to my spine. I hear the smile in his voice as I see Lady Death's black, depthless eyes watching me from the dancing flames of the fire. "Did you think I would keep all our Ruby Tar in the lab?" His blade disappears only to be replaced by something being stabbed into the side of my neck. It's not sharp, more like a dull needle forcing its way deep into my flesh. I suck in a breath through gritted teeth as a burning feeling slowly starts to spread through me like vines crested with thorns, suffocating my movements. I freeze as terror takes hold. I can feel the numbness fading as my side begins to throb and my head starts to spin. I scramble to keep a hold on the instinct and my eyes flushed with blood, but the feeling slips through my fingers. My eyes water as the pain of the fight hits me head-on, the Ruby Tar pushing me to my knees. Cassien lets out a vile laugh, something an old crone would let loose to scare children. He steps away as I stumble to the ground.

I press my hand to my side to stanch the bleeding, breathing through my teeth as my eyes come in and out of focus. I try unsuccessfully to pull myself to my feet as my head sinks deeper and deeper into a whirlwind of panic and pain. I manage to steady my vision and stand up, clutching the bloodied blade Elana gave me as I turn on Cassien. The others who had braved fighting me are either injured or lined up behind him, Altair among those still standing. The High Lord waves a hand and two of his minions stalk to my sides, grabbing my arms and kicking the backs of my knees. I can't take my eyes off my brother, the betrayal slicing through me as I hit the ground. Cassien takes his time as he crouches in front of me. He looks nothing but smug while I struggle to keep my head up and see one High Lord instead of two.

"Unrefined Ruby Tar," he reveals as pride flickers in his eyes. "Our tests have shown only a small dose is fatal. To most it acts like a strong poison, killing in a matter of minutes, but it won't kill you. It will simply render you completely human, meaning those wounds won't heal like they usually do and you'll experience a great deal of pain. Maybe Lady Death will do us a favor and take you herself."

I stare up at him and will myself to give one last push, one more burst of energy to snap his neck. It's cleaner than he deserves, but I don't care. As the seconds pass, the sharpness of the world fades to a dull blur and the sound starts to resemble garbled slurs in my ears. That's when they start the real beating.

Fists force the air from my lungs and cut up my face. I'm

helpless as they hold me up, blood dripping from my mouth and running down my forehead.

When they finally start to drag me away, I can no longer tell where I am. Their laughs bounce around in my head as I shake with grueling pain, blood and mud soaking me through.

They drop me without care when we reach our destination. I hit the cold floor so hard my eyes flutter. I beg them to bleed red, but the instinct has disappeared, the place where it usually floats a dark void. I hear a lock click shut as a fit of tremors rolls through me. The pain sears through my bones as I curl my knees to my chest, lying in my own puddle of blood. Memories flash behind my fogged eyes, seizing my chest as the devastation overwhelms me.

Mum's strong hug. Dad's smile. Antares's energy. Saiph's squeal. Altair's confidence. Cass's silent joy. Pollux's ridiculous stories. Pleiades's grace. Cael's jokes. Silver eyes like raging oceans. Water fights and sunny days. Midnight fires and hushed laughter. They all melt together and rip apart, fading to a place I cannot follow.

A slight gust of cold wind folds over me, rustling the still air. My eyelids feel like they're made of stone, my head too heavy to lift. Sure hands shake my shoulders, but I only curl in tighter, the movement sending shock waves of pain to my head. *Take me. Take me and let them live,* I beg silently into the dark. *Let them survive.*

The hands leave my shoulders and not a moment later, ice-cold liquid meets my lips. It takes me a moment to piece together what it is; water. It dribbles down my chin and throat as I force myself to swallow. The smooth liquid feels sharp as I drink. I choke as more water rushes down my throat. Whoever is helping me doesn't give up, repeating the cycle until my jaw fuses shut and every breath becomes too much.

My body shakes furiously as my shirt peels away from my side, my mind comprehending a string of what sound like curses. Cold hands touch the tender skin around the wound, making a fresh ripple of pain sear through me. The same process repeats itself over each wound, no matter how small. Cold hands, blinding pain, and a salve being spread over the cuts and bruises. More water trickles down my throat, and for the first time, the shaking subsides.

I don't know how much time passes between visits, but they happen regularly. When I feel a gust of warm air, nothing happens, but with a cold breeze that sends goose bumps up my arms, the person comes in with water and a salve I've started to crave. Someone sits beside me now, a presence on the edge of my senses. I can't figure out who it is. My mind is barely coherent enough to make out the meaning of the sounds they whisper. I dread the moment they leave, the only anchor I have to this world pulled away, plunging me back into the dark as the cold wind becomes not a sign of hope but a reminder I am still trapped.

I must have fallen asleep because a new pain burns through me as moments of my terrors flash behind my eyes, the lasting images the clearest my mind has concocted in a long while. I tell myself to open my eyes, and to my dismay, they do, though sluggishly. I force myself to breathe. Hunger and thirst hit me so swiftly my head spins as I squeeze my eyes shut again.

Cautiously, I stretch my hand out and run my fingers along smooth tiles. I move each of my hands, then my feet. Even moving my toes sends a searing blast of pain through my side. I gather all the strength I can muster and flip onto my back, grunting as my entire body seems to light itself on fire. I try to bleed my eyes, but they stubbornly stay silver, denying me the much-needed reprieve. I watch the clouds skim across the sky through a small skylight carved into the roof. I force my head to turn to the side to take in the bookcase-clad room. It's small, so the wall isn't too far from me. I can move three feet. I take a deep breath and flip myself onto my stomach, a strangled scream bursting from my throat as I press my forehead to the cold ground. On second thought, three feet seems like wishful thinking.

I move painfully over to the wall, using a crawl-slide technique that makes me doubt my need to sit. I shift agonizingly until I've propped myself up with my back resting on a bookcase. The jutting edges of the shelves dig into my back, only furthering my discomfort. Sweat gathers on my brow as I force my eyes open and take in the small room from an upright position. Hundreds of thick tomes line the walls and the tiles are worn in a way you can tell they used to be bright. As my thoughts continue to clear, I wonder why—of all the places in Wate—Cassien stuck me in a library? It's unsettling, considering I learned rather quickly that the High Lord of Wate always plays at a deeper game. I see it in every move he makes, like we're all pieces of his puzzle, awaiting his hand to be assembled.

For as long as I can, I force myself to keep my eyes trained forward and my hands away from the wounds on my side, but gruesome curiosity wins out. I slowly lift my shirt up, the pain so intense I might as well be peeling away my own skin. I suck in a sharp breath as I look at the festering wound. The flesh is gaping open, the skin green with bright-red edges. My head spins anew at the sight. I've never been sick or suffered from infection before. My hands shake as I place my shirt back down before taking in the multitude of other lacerations and bruises across my skin. I touch the cut at my throat and wince as pain shoots up my neck.

After I manage to push past the worst of the pain, I lift my arm as much as I can and run the pads of my fingers over the leather-bound spines at my back. They feel... old. I grunt as I pull one out, the book dropping to the floor with a thud. I curse at the weight as I slide it over my lap and flip it open. Inked names, titles, and dates of births and deaths mark each page. Under each name is a short description of their lives: children, families, status, awards, accomplishments, and crimes. He put me in a records room.

The walls seem to close in on me as I scan the books. There are thousands of lives captured in here, thousands of ghosts and souls printed onto these pages. I close the book with shaking hands as death hangs heavily in the air. The spine catches my eye as I push the tome aside. The leather is embossed with an *E* underlined by three horizontal lines. I open it again to look closer. The last names all start with an *E* and the log is organized by date of birth.

I push the book aside and scan the room for the books embossed with an *H*. Within seconds I find them, as if the pages were calling to me. I crawl over slowly as my lungs wheeze, taking more time than a child learning to walk. Grasping the ledges in front of me, I pull myself up and rip the tomes from the shelves. They clatter around me as I fall back to the ground. I quickly grab a book and scan the pages as my entire body convulses. I stop cold when I find it.

Kerin Hael
37001197

Born - 179 AGW. Date of Death -

Bile rises to my throat as I stare at the empty space beside the *Date of Death*. It should say 218 After the Great War, but only my family could have known that. There was so much blood that day... A burst of pain startles me out of the memory, rooting me back in reality as I curse. I wait for my vision to stop spinning and continue reading.

Kerin Hael was the first and only son of Killian and Amory Hael and husband to Ada Cazidey...

My mind races as I read the page again and again. I never knew Mum's name was Cazidey. I turn my eyes back to the page, roving over it without absorbing a word until I see the last lines.

In 204 AGW, Kerin Hael disappeared with his spouse. Upon investigation, Kerin Hael was charged with treason by the High Lord of Wate, accused of aiding a valuable prisoner to escape. The warrant for his arrest remains outstanding. If Kerin Hael returns to Wate he is to be remanded into custody and prepared for trial in front of the Council of Wate.

My heart sputters in my chest. *That's why we didn't come back,* I realize with a jolt. My mind races as I set out to find the books engraved with *Cs*. I drag myself across the room and start pulling each book out. I rummage through the pages until I find her, Ada Cazidey. My eyes scan through the information. There are mentions of her time at the Academy, her career, and the same heavy words describing her supposed crimes, but my gaze catches on one sentence.

... In her youth known affiliations of Ada Cazidey include Dahlia Kizova, prisoner sentenced to death in 204 AGW...

Something about the name speaks to me. "Dahlia Kizova," I whisper as goose bumps climb up my arms. Faded memories gather at the edge of my mind, just out of reach. I grit my teeth and make for the books marked with a *K*.

It takes me a moment to start pulling the tomes from the shelf, breathing hard from the exertion of having dragged myself across the room. *The Ruby Tar is taking its toll,* I think to myself, sneering. I take the last book from the shelf and sort through the hundreds of names, stopping only when I find what I'm searching for.

Dahlia Kizova

43203578

Born – 180 AGW. Date of death – 204 AGW.

Most of the page is blank. I run my fingers over the numbers on my wrist; the first three digits written on the page are identical to mine. My stomach flips as I force myself to read on.

Dahlia Kizova was charged with conspiring with the enemy, contravening the Separations of the Peoples law of Illena and endangering the gold-eyed people of Wate. She was found guilty with the supporting evidence of the blood-eyed numbers and band her child carried on his wrist. Dahlia Kizova was granted leniency for her prior deeds and was permitted one minute with her son before execution. The child was awaiting execution before disappearing two days later from the holding cells in the east wing of the Council building.

I stare at the book for a long moment, daring myself to connect the dots. Silence rings in my ears, bearing down on me like a hammer. I lift my wrist and stare at the two bands. The blood-eyed band between the numbers and my elbow and the gold-eyed band circling my wrist. The forbidden son of a gold-eye and blood-eye. The son of Dahlia Kizova and a blood-eye. My mother's friends took me as their own and left their home because they knew I would be sentenced to death. I take a deep, shaky breath and lean my head back against the shelf. I killed my mother. I forced those who raised me to leave their home. I'm the reason Saiph and the boys have lived a life of running and hiding. I'm the reason why they have seen so much blood. I'm the reason Pollux, Pleiades, Mum, Dad, and Dahlia are dead.

The thoughts spiral for hours behind closed eyes, circling my mind like a pack of snarling wolves. The pain is unbearable. I feel the cold breeze brush against my clammy skin as I shake. When did I start to shake? I realize I don't care. The door opens and I feel the tears falling down my face. I've begged Lady Death to take me before, but it feels useless now.

"Leo?" a voice I would know in my sleep whispers. I don't open my eyes, clenching my jaw as I will my mind to stop, to leave me to die in peace. "Leo?" it says, hysterics working their way into the fading word. My hands shake harder as I squeeze my eyes shut. *Stop it. Stop it, stop it, stop it.* Cold fingers grasp my wrist as the memories I've buried and thoughts I've banished crash down on me. But this time, as I feel myself drowning, I don't try to swim. I let myself sink.

FORTY-FIVE

LEO

I open my eyes with a gasp as I choke on bile lodged in my throat. "Don't move," a voice says frantically. I blink as my mind slowly clears and I realize the voice belongs to Cael. I'm lying on my side. Someone holds my head as Cael checks the pulse on my wrist. All I want to do is curl into the floor, but my body won't let me.

"Leo?" asks a strong but distressed voice from above me. Elana. I groan as I try to roll onto my stomach, needing to move and get out of my sinking mind. They both sigh in tense relief.

"Can you speak, Leo?" Cael asks. I grunt something that sounds roughly like a *no,* earning a strained laugh from my brother.

"Check the wound on his side, right under his ribs. Help me flip him onto his back," Elana says with a false calm. Cael does as she says, and after a moment of burning pain and whispered apologies from my brother, I'm lying flat on my back, breathing hard.

Cael slowly peels my shirt away and the smell hits me first, sending a wave of nausea through me. Cael's face twists as he sees it and Elana recoils as she averts her gaze. I manage to mumble another disgruntled sound, to which Elana sends me a questioning glance. Cael pushes my shoulders up as I vomit the contents of my stomach, which happens to be nothing but yellow bile. Elana jumps to her feet, barely missing the mess as she grumbles about having to watch me puke again.

"Thank you," I manage, the words burning my throat as I take quick, shallow breaths. "Help me," I rasp as I try to sit up. Cael opens his mouth to tell me to stay lying down, but the glare I pin on him makes his mouth shut tight. He stands and lifts my back, propping me against a bookshelf.

"How did you understand any of that?" Elana asks as her gaze roves between Cael and me. My brother shakes his head, as though he is tormented.

"I just... did. I know things sometimes, and those words were something I knew," he says as he passes me a metal bottle. "Can you hold it?" I take a second to try to move my arm, the pain starting off sharp but slowly subsiding as I swallow half the contents in a single gulp and sigh gratefully.

Elana crouches down to look me in the eyes, then presses the back of her hand to my forehead. Her expression grows concerned as she pulls it away. "You're running a fever," she says, passing a glance at Cael as he winces.

"I'm fine," I say instinctively.

"You are most certainly not fine. You've got a stab wound that's green and smells like rot, at least a dozen other festering cuts, you're painted in bruises, you've had a seizure, and there's poison running through your blood. There was foam coming out of your mouth Leo, you are nowhere near fine," Cael says, his desperation clear.

"Can you bleed your eyes?" Elana asks with a pinched face.

I avoid her prying gaze, giving her all the answer she needs. Cael studies me for a long moment.

"What's making your mind sink?" he asks softly. By the Goddess, my brother knows me too well. I take a deep breath, taking my time to accumulate enough strength to share the story.

"My mother," I say simply, numbly. Elana freezes, seeming stunned. I nod to the open book lying on the floor. Cael reads the open page with a frown, his eyes slowly growing wider as he reads. I quickly fill them in on the other two books that lead me to Dahlia Kizova's page. I can tell Cael is skeptical, but a glance at my wrist and all his doubt disappears.

"It's not your fault. The blame rests on the High Lord who ordered her death," Cael says, his jaw ticing as he spins his ring. I don't think I realized how much I needed him to say that until my mind processes the words, even if the weight on my back remains.

Elana hiccups and then slaps a hand over her mouth, obviously trying hard not to laugh. Cael and I look at her with identical quizzical expressions as I wonder if the sight of my injuries have made her go crazy.

"Is something funny?" I ask gruffly, my voice wobbling before I clear my throat. The laughter falls from her face in time with her hand.

"No... I... I didn't think... I thought I was insane," she mumbles to herself, shaking her head in clear disbelief. When she sees our confusion, she continues. "When Byrne and I were girls, Cassien would tell us a story of a blood-eyed prince who fell in love with a gold-eyed girl. It started out as a fairy tale for the girl. She was falling for a *prince*. He planned to bring her to his castle so they could live happily ever after, but the girl found out she was going to have a child before she could be with him. The people of her town worried for her and said she had been bewitched by the prince, because there was no such thing as a blood-eye who was capable of love. The girl wouldn't believe them. She screamed and tried to run to her prince, but they locked her up. After she had the child, they said she died of a cursed heart. When the prince finally came for her, the story goes that he didn't wear the face of a royal but of a monster, dripping in blood with crimson eyes and claws of steel. The people managed to capture him and put him at the mercy of Lady Death. They said he did not scream but wailed for days as he died," she whispers, her voice faint as she reminisces.

"What happened to the child?" I breathe.

"That's where the story veers in different directions," she says, pulling me from my thoughts. "Cassien used to say the prince killed the child simply because he *could*. But I've heard others say the infant disappeared like he was made of dust, carried away by the wind... or saved by a couple who loved the child's mother." Elana stares at my wrist and I have to fight the urge to tuck it behind my back. Her expression is full of wonder as she meets my eyes. My heart speeds up as I hold her gaze, pounding inside my chest.

"I don't think it's a fairy tale," Cael says, shaking his head as he pulls my attention away from Elana.

"No, I don't think so either."

Cael fixed me up as best as he could without making it obvious they had come to see me. I can barely move, but seeing their faces pushes me to keep my eyes open. I can't sink again. I have too many things to live for, people who are living for me. Elana put all the books back, her face blanching as she stared at some of the names. I understand why Cassien put me in here now. I was already physically destroyed but finding what I did left me dangerously close to being shattered mentally too. I can still feel the water rising around my ankles, there one second and gone the next as I blink myself back into reality.

The days pass in agony, but at least I'm able to think straight. Every morning a guard opens the door and throws me a half-spoiled bowl of mush and a murky bucket of water. Elana comes at night to give me real food, medicine, and clean water. Cael joins her sometimes, but it's much harder to sneak in two people, especially when my brother is supposed to be dead. I find myself waiting for her to open the door, watching the sky shift above my head like a ticking clock. She brings me news of Cael, Saiph, and sometimes the boys. Byrne goes to see them every other day, soothing their worries as well as she can. Her updates simultaneously ease my thoughts and make me want to throw up.

I'm staring at the skylight with the book embossed with the *K* held tight in my hands when the door creaks open. The sun isn't directly overhead, making my pulse spike. I push the book back onto its shelf and cross my arms over my chest, waiting with a raised chin. I paste on a mask of bored indifference because it's better to put on a show of strength than reveal weakness. Cassien walks through the door with two others, a stout man with a long beard and a stone-faced woman with hair in long thin braids, gold leather shining around their arms. Soldiers dressed in the black of the High Lord's guard stand in the hall behind them.

Cassien studies me with slitted eyes as he scrunches his nose in disgust. I've never wanted to rip his throat out more. "You smell like a rotting carcass," he says, scanning the room. I tilt my head to the side.

"You've kept me prisoner in here for days with festering wounds and no way to bathe. How am I supposed to *smell?*" I ask sarcastically, waving my hand through the air as I bite back the pain. They stare at me like I've lost my head. I probably have, seeing that I'm speaking back to a group of armed soldiers who would love nothing more than to see me buried six feet deep.

"We've come to see if you're well enough to stand against the pole. The people don't like it much when you can't fight," he says as a smile pulls at his face. He means to scare me, but he's using the wrong life as bait. I raise a brow and force an easy grin.

"You think leaving me in here to rot is going to make me heal? I'm quite sure I'll be gone by the end of the week," I drawl. I haven't decided if I believe it or not, but the way my body is currently shutting down, I'm afraid my time is finally running short. Cassien isn't ruffled in the slightest as he stands above me.

"No, you won't. I've known who you are since the moment I saw your wrist. By the way the books are misplaced, I'm going to assume you do now too." I huff a laugh, shaking my head as I lock onto his overpowering gaze.

"I never pinned you for one to keep track of the details," I drone, wanting nothing more than to pummel his face. Seeing Cassien's expression after knocking him to the ground would be well worth a visit with Lady Death.

"You're showing your inexperience, blood-eye. You've been living on borrowed time since your selfish mother conceived you." My blood freezes over as the breath catches in my throat. "I was a good friend of hers. For a long time, she was a good girl. Worked hard, kept her head down and followed the rules. I was the one who found her creeping in the woods with the blood-eye. I was the one who caught your father. He screamed for days on the post, but not for himself. No, he cried for you. We didn't take Dahlia's body away, so he could spend his last moments staring into her vacant eyes. Of course, we never let him see you, even when he begged and cursed and prayed. The little Blood Prince destined for such great things. I knew your father, knew who he was the second I stuck a dagger in his stomach and he kept breathing. I was never going to kill you, you're too valuable to be wasted. Even without bleeding your eyes, you'll die much slower than the rest of us," he says, his eyes flashing as a lump forms in my throat. My skin crawls with hatred as he turns away from me and heads toward the door. "Your brothers though, they aren't much use to me now that I've figured out how to... sedate you."

Time stops. He's going to kill them. "Do you care for your daughters, Cassien?" I blurt, needing to stall him. Elana might kill me, but I can't let him leave. He tenses, freezing with one hand on the door. He whispers something to his companions before they leave the room, closing the door behind them. My heart stutters in my chest as he turns to me, the picture of calm composure.

"Why do you ask, blood-eye?" If a snake could speak, it would sound like he does in this moment, cold and calculated, baiting its prey and biding its time to strike.

"I doubt you do. No father who loves his children would beat—" I don't finish my sentence as his hand clasps around my throat.

"I *discipline* my daughters when there is a need for it," he seethes, squeezing tighter. "I will not be looked down upon by a blood-eye." His face is inches from mine. I try to speak, but it comes out as a strangled squeak as the edge of my vision begins to darken. I manage a nod, sucking in a deep rush of air as he lets go and wipes his hands on his pants like he had dirtied them by touching me. His cold demeanor returns in moments as I pant, pressing my head against the bookcase.

"My daughters submit to my word, and it won't be long before you do too."

"No," I croak, fighting against my swaying mind as my eyelids become heavy.

"No? Well maybe we should bring in some incentive. I'll find the little girl—"

"What about we play a game?" I blurt, my thoughts suddenly aligning. Cael's not going to like this. "We play a game of Hunters. If I win, you swear to provide my brothers and sister with care and proper housing and you leave them alone. If you win, I'll do whatever you ask without complaint. You can keep Saiph and the boys as collateral to make sure I stay in line," I say weakly, my voice cracking. I know that risky plans are most often the ones that work, but this is teetering close to perilous. The High Lord turns to me, the corner of his lip turning up into an unsettling grin.

"Hunters?"

"It's a game we played as children. Each player has to find the others and pin them to the ground. If you get pinned, you're out. We play with two teams. Your best fighters against myself and my siblings. The last one standing wins," I explain, praying he won't see the fear curling behind my eyes.

"You want to compete with your siblings, including the young one, in Wate's forests, against my best fighters?" he questions as he folds his hands behind his back. I nod, clenching my fists until my knuckles turn white.

"I'll carry Saiph and go in with the boys. Weapons aren't allowed other than what you can create in the woods, meaning no steel. You pick four fighters. We set off first, then your people join and whoever is left standing at the end wins."

"Why do you want this, blood-eye? You must know there is no way you can win," he asks, his curiosity sounding genuine. I force myself to swallow the bile rising in my throat.

"This gives me a chance and I've learned to take what I've been given." He watches me closely, as if he were weighing my words. They are sincere, so he won't find a hidden lie.

"Why do you think I would agree to this when I already have you trapped?" he asks with a raised brow.

"Because I will fight you using every weapon I have until the day I am free if you don't, and I promise you that I will get away by whatever means necessary. You need me alive, and I have nothing against death." He thinks for a moment, scanning me with slitted eyes.

"In five days, we'll bring your siblings here," he declares. "We'll deliver the official rules to you before the game." He walks out without another word and locks the door behind him. I lean my head back on the shelf and close my eyes, unsure of whether I should feel relieved. Letting out a long breath, I push myself to my feet and start walking.

CHAPTER
FORTY-SIX

ELANA

I crack open the door of the archive room, checking behind my shoulder for the guard who is supposed to be on duty. One good thing about the Academy is you're forced to learn everything about your opponents and it's just my luck Bastien's on night duties. He was in my year at the Academy and has an ego the size of the Vallan. He hated getting stuck with guard duties because he thinks his gifts are wasted on "standing around and watching the clouds move across the sky." He is a terrible fighter, but he has a way of abandoning his posts without ever getting caught. It's a good thing too, because drugging a guard night after night isn't something even I could get away with.

A chill runs up my arms as I step inside the moon-lit room. The stale air inside feels like death and it makes me want to crawl out of my skin. I have no idea how Leo is enduring it.

I almost stumble as I turn away from the door and catch Leo standing against the wall. He crosses his arms over his chest as he meets my startled gaze. "You're looking better," I remark, because at first glance, he does. But the longer I watch him, the more his exhaustion becomes apparent. There are purple shadows under his eyes and tension bracketing his mouth. It seems like he might shatter if he moves too quickly.

"As you know, I usually heal quite fast," he says easily, eyeing the pack slung over my shoulder. His face darkens as I pull out the bottle of water and a package of hardtack. "I'm guessing you heard about the little arrangement." I nod tensely as I hand him the food. He thanks me with a small lopsided grin as one corner of his lip turns up in its usual fashion.

"I don't know how you managed to do it," I say, shaking my head. Cassien is as solid as a stone. Trying to get him to listen is like trying to convince a frog to fly. I've never been able to influence him in any way.

"I used you." I freeze. "I don't mean it like that," he says a bit frantically as he pushes off the wall. He goes to take a step toward me but catches himself, standing awkwardly in the middle of the floor as he rubs the back of his neck. "I asked him if he cared for you. Then when he and I were alone in the room, I brought up how he... did things no father should do."

"How he beats us?" I snap. I don't know if my anger is directed at Leo or Cassien, but he averts his eyes as he nods, clearly thinking it was for him.

"I needed to get his attention and I knew bringing you up would snag him," he confesses, his face going stone-cold as his arm drops to his side. I clench my jaw as my hands curl into fists.

"You had no right." I mean to say it loudly, yell it even, but it comes out as a whisper. His sad, empathetic eyes stare into mine and it fills me with burning rage. "Don't look at me like that."

"Like what?"

pasting on the arrogant smile that makes me want to wring his neck. My hand tightens around my blade as I shake my head. The smile falls from his features, instantly replaced by deep, pleading eyes.

"I'm not going to pull a blade on you, Leo. You can barely stand." I watch him incredulously while I spin the dagger in my hand. I bend my knees in a way to make it seem like I'm shuffling uncomfortably. He goes to rub his neck again, his eyes falling to the ground for the first time. I take my chance. He catches me right before I can do any vital damage, deflecting my blow. He's sluggish but still manages to block and turn away before I can get my knife near any flesh. It takes less than a minute before he's panting, his breath coming in short bursts. I keep pushing, every strike harder and swifter than the last. He stumbles, his eyes wild as he tries to regain his balance and defend himself at the same time.

Suddenly, it's like he's become another person. His breathing changes and he fends off my attack before perfectly placing his own, throwing off my concentration. He stops fighting abruptly and lets me pin him against the bookcase with my blade pressed tight to his throat. He looks more alive than I've seen in a long time. He flashes a half smile, the red film covering his eyes giving him a strange, almost deific appearance. "Thank you," he breathes. I feel a wide smile bloom on my face. He slips out from my hold in one smooth motion, spinning around to pin me against the shelf with his body flush against mine. I bark out a laugh as I push the edge of the blade closer.

"Hold on a minute, are you... laughing?" Leo's eyes light up as he throws an arm in the air. "I made the great Elana Cassien laugh. I think I deserve an award," he gloats as warmth floods through me.

"I am capable of being human, Leo Hael," I note as heat warms my cheeks.

"Are you sure? I'd bet money you wear a scowl to bed." He grins, leaning in.

"Watch what you say about me, I'm the one with your life in my hands," I sing as his eyes darken.

A click makes us both jump. Our eyes shoot to the door as the hinges begin to creak. Leo pushes me forward, sending me shuffling behind the door as he tosses me my bag. I stick to the wall and hold my breath, but I can't seem to close my eyes. Leo slides to the floor and tilts his head back against the bookshelf. Bloody tears run down his face for a moment before he quickly wipes them away. He looks sick, halfway to death. I almost step away from the wall to help him, but his eyes open slightly and lock with mine, demanding I stay hidden.

"What are you doing in here?" the voice calls, clearly frustrated. I recognize the voice; it belongs to Bastien. He must have been close enough to hear us. Leo lifts his head slowly before staring him down. My heart squeezes at the pain in his expression.

"Trying not to die," he rasps, the strain in his voice making me grimace.

"You were making lots of noise," he says, the sneer visible in his tone. Bastien isn't happy about having to leave whatever he was doing to pass his time, most likely playing cards and losing his week's pay. Leo stares through him.

"I tried to get up a few times," he admits painfully as he bares his teeth, but he looks weak. So, so weak. Bastien lets out a barking laugh. Leo turns his head away and glues his eyes to the wall.

"You blood-eyes make yourselves up to be so strong and you can't even stand? You're pathetic," he mocks. "Enjoy your last moments." My stomach curls with rage as he laughs, but

Leo's determined expression stops me short. He shoots to his feet as the door clicks shut. "Are you all right?" he asks quietly as he scans me from head to toe with a frown. Why would he be worried about me? He was the one who dealt with Bastien.

"I'm fine, but Leo..."

"Are you sure? You're pale as death and your hands are shaking, Elana. Maybe you should sit down," he offers, reaching out his hand as worry strains his expression. I raise my hands and as it turns out, my fingers are curled into fists and, indeed, trembling. I release a long breath and force myself to uncurl my hands before relaxing them by my side.

"Leo..." I start, the overwhelming sense of regret and embarrassment filling my mind. His concern seemingly evaporates as he suddenly turns serious.

"Don't. You don't want my pity; I don't want yours. People say things in accordance with what they're taught. That guard hasn't been given the option to think the way he does. He needs to be shown how wrong he is, then if he makes the decision to continue, I'll deal with it differently," he says more as a reassurance to me than anything else. He takes my hand and meets my gaze as he runs his thumb in circles across my palm. My senses narrow down to the contact, my breath hitching.

"I'm sorry," I blurt as guilt overwhelms me. He hesitates as his thumb freezes in place. "For treating you that way. And... and for slicing you in the throat," I say sheepishly, trying to gauge his reaction.

"You already apologized for cutting me," he says, visibly trying to smother a smile as his thumb returns to its comforting circles. I look away as heat creeps up my neck.

"I didn't mean it. Byrne... made me say it," I confess. He stays silent for a long moment and I start to worry he's still holding it against me. I wouldn't fault him if he was. His free hand gently guides my chin upward. My concern melts away as I see him struggle to hold back his amusement, his eyes twinkling. It doesn't work. We both lose ourselves in silent heaves of laughter, the kind where tears gather and you smile even though you can't breathe. As the giggling subsides, I notice something different flash in his eyes, a glint of emotion I've never seen before, paired with a smile that makes the outside world disappear.

FORTY-SEVEN

LEO

They should be here any second to drag me away. Cael, Elana, and I straightened out the plan and went over every detail and possibility, but still my mind reels. Cassien unsettles me and I don't trust for a moment this is going to be a fair game. I could tell Cael feels the same, but Elana has assured us that because we have surprise on our side, this is going to work. Plus, both sisters will be there to help from a distance. Apparently, Byrne is the best shot Elana's ever seen and I believe her.

The door flies open and a swarm of hands clasp chains around my wrists before pulling me to my aching feet. The infection has cleared up, though the wounds are still angry and throbbing. At least Elana stitched them up last night, deciding it was worth the risk of discovery. I allow them to drag me away as I hang my head, internally snickering as the two guards carrying me grunt a stream of complaints about my deadweight.

The slip of paper tucked in my boot rubs against my shin. I ripped the page out of the records books after Elana left. I couldn't bring myself to leave behind the only information connecting me to Dahlia. I hope Cael took the time to make sure Mum's letters and the rest of our few possessions are safe and waiting in the boat. My thoughts wander to my blades and the intricately embossed leather sheaths. Mum told me they belonged to my father, but I never imagined he was anyone other than the man who raised me. I remember what she said like it was yesterday. *They were your father's. They're the only things I can give you from your family, Leo. I'm sorry I have nothing else.* I couldn't have understood what those words truly meant; that I wasn't the son of the only parents I had ever known.

My handlers throw me into the mud at the edge of the woods, my face scraping across the ground. I force myself to sit up and wipe the dirt from my face. Cass and Antares come barreling toward me and tackle me back to the ground as they wrap me in their arms. I wince as Antares accidentally knees my side, oblivious to my pain. By the Goddess, I've missed them.

"We thought you were dead. We thought you were gone," Antares mumbles against my shoulder. Tears spill down his face as Cass nods in silent agreement.

"I'm fine," I murmur. "I'm okay. Nothing bad happened, and nothing bad is going to happen." They pull back and stare at me with red-rimmed eyes. "But you have to trust me, and do as I say, all right?" My brothers nod in unison as their eyes light up. A guard clad in black unlocks my hands from behind me, allowing me to fold my arms around my brothers as they lean in. I don't care who's watching, these are the people I'm fighting for.

"Cael is waiting for us on the northern riverbank. We're going to meet up with a friend who'll bring us somewhere better," I whisper. "Now make a show of helping me stand." The boys lean back on their heels and nod once with tight smiles before helping me up.

My blood freezes as Altair starts toward us with Saiph squirming in his arms, trying her hardest to break free of his grasp. The relief I feel upon seeing him is quickly cut short by his withering glare. My brother used to be so caring with Saiph, his eyes growing soft whenever she was around. Now, walking toward us, he carries her like an animal, holding her at arms reach by her underarms. Her face is red enough to tell me she's about as happy about how he's carrying her as I am. "Put her down," I grind out through gritted teeth. I bend down slightly to beckon her over as Altair lowers her awkwardly. Saiph runs to us, steadier on her feet than I've ever seen her. "Hi, Saiphy," I say, scooping her up with a grunt. She starts babbling almost immediately and her speech catches me off guard. Her words are clearer and her sentences more coherent than when I last saw her. I hold on to her a little tighter as pride fills my chest.

Altair, who is noticeably taller, stands like a soldier guarding the entrance to a vault, his back pin straight, eyes trained forward, and hands tucked behind his back. "How have you been?" I ask, testing the waters. He stares at me as if he can't figure out what to do or how to act. The brother I knew would have had a smile plastered across his face with bright eyes to match. This boy with a stern expression and weary gaze is not him.

"What are you planning?" he demands bluntly with an unfaltering flat expression.

"Nothing, Altair. I just want you all to be safe." I sigh. I don't try to hide my sorrow as I look at him. My brother remains unmoving, bored.

"Why did you have to bring us into it? We're safe here, with our people. What are you planning?" he pushes. The way he says "we're," I have a feeling I'm not included, and it drives a blade clean through my gut. I shake my head in defeat and take a step back. We'll figure out what happened to him when we get out. Right now, I can't be worrying about this too. I bury the sadness and slip on a mask of disinterest.

"We're playing a game of Hunters. If we win, then Cassien has to provide you all with a proper house and keep you out of harm's way," I drone, aware of all the listening ears surrounding us.

"We already have a safe home. Why did you include us in your plan?"

"Why do you keep asking me about my plan?" I ask as I tilt my head to the side. Most people in Tominay would cower at the glare I'm giving my brother, but Altair doesn't even blink. I'm about to say more when Elana steps in my path, blocking Altair from my view. My stomach flutters at the sight of her, but I keep my expression flat, indifferent. She leans away from me as if she were disgusted to be standing so close, and even though I'm sure it's an act, it pulls at something deep inside.

"You have ten minutes to run after the High Lord calls, then our hunters will join the game. They understand the rules, no one will be killed unless otherwise provoked," she announces sharply, making me wince. I catch the apology as it flashes through her eyes and I shake my head slowly to tell her I know she is simply playing the part she must for this to work.

I don't say anything as she stalks off, her dark hair tied in two tight plaits and twisted into a knot at the base of her head. *Unless otherwise provoked.* This is going to be exciting.

Four people—two men and two women—walk toward us, each clad in fitted dark-green leather armor adorned with a gold band circling their upper left arms. One of the women with silver hair pinned up in a tight knot whispers something to her companion. The second woman, who is at least a foot shorter with blazing red hair, dips her chin in a shallow nod. The men are nearly identical with their lean builds, hooked noses, and vile expressions. The sheaths built into their armor are noticeably empty, but that doesn't take away from their intimidating appearances. Both men bounce on their toes in anticipation, their smiles feral as they roll their shoulders. The women stand stone-faced beside them, missing nothing with their sharp eyes and straight postures. A sense of foreboding washes over me as I watch them walk with stealthy footsteps, practically floating above the ground.

Cassien steps away from his group of gold-eyed mercenaries and personal guards after sharing a few words with the fighters, making their eyes gleam with delight. I know what it looks like to be out for blood and all four of these predators are dying to get off their leashes.

"You have ten minutes to run before my hunters are released. The entire forest is in play until you reach the fields to the east." The High Lord booms. "Thieves of blood. Heirs of gold."

"Never merciful."

***

The ten minutes are almost up. I stop running and the boys slow beside me. They're in much better shape than I am; they've barely broken a sweat while my bones are quaking. I bleed my eyes and my breathing immediately evens out as the throbbing pain recedes. All three of them gasp at the sight, but as Cass and Antares slowly start to smile, Altair's forehead creases with a deepening frown. "Did you think I would let us do this if I wasn't in perfect fighting shape?" I ask him as a smirk pulls at the corner of my lips.

"You couldn't get up before!" Antares puffs, his grin spreading wider. I shake my head as I huff a laugh.

"Remind me to teach you the art of acting. But that's beside the point. If we get split up, head to the northern bank. There will be a rowboat waiting to bring us across."

"Why do we have to leave?" Altair presses as his face grows angry.

"The list is so long we don't have time to discuss it," I clip, watching him over my shoulder.

"Try," he demands dryly as we walk.

"They killed my mother and father a long time ago, forced Cael to live in a meat cellar, used me as a test subject for their drugs, tried to kill me, threatened to kill all of you... Do I need to go on, Altair?" I demand through clenched teeth, staring him down.

"They like and accept us," Altair huffs.

"No," Cass contradicts timidly.

"Altair, we're family. We help and protect each other," Antares says, his eyes pleading.

"Have you thought that maybe it was because Cael was snooping around, and Leo burned down the laundry house and *fell* into the initiation that people don't like you?" he asks tightly, his voice rising. Cass takes a step toward me.

"I didn't want to be there," Cass admits softly. My heart wrenches in my chest as I place a hand on his shoulder.

"I don't care what you want, it's what you *need*," Altair seethes, turning his rage on Cass who hides himself behind me.

"Stop!" This time Altair has the good sense to flinch. "I don't know what they've put in your head Altair, but you don't turn your back on family. Not when they would do anything for you and have done nothing to lose your trust." None of them speak as Altair averts his eyes. "If any of you hear anything, you climb into the trees, do you understand?" I get three consecutive nods before pushing us all back into a steady run.

Perched in a tall, leafy tree, we hold our breaths as two sets of near-silent footsteps move through the brush. Antares sits the highest in the tree with Saiph held tight in his arms as Cass clutches the branch below him. Even Saiph seems to recognize our dire situation and stays completely silent.

I catch the man stalking through the foliage and my stomach sinks. I can hear two pairs of feet, but I only see one man. I recognize the ploy in a moment. He's a decoy, making himself seen to lure us out. I look up to the boys and point at him, then hold up two fingers. Antares, Altair, and Cass acknowledge as their gold-eyes flash. I'm still not used to the fact they can pull on the same instinct I can, my heart jumping every time I catch a glimpse of gold.

I drop to the lower branches, taking care not to rustle the leaves more than the slight wind rushing through the air. The other fighter is out here somewhere, I just need to lure them all out. I grab the stones I had stashed in my pockets and take aim. I throw one several feet away, rustling the brush as it hits the ground. The man whirls toward the sound, crouching low. Out of the corner of my eye, I catch a glimpse of silver hair sinking back behind a tree. There she is. They move in a perfect rotation, both stalking the spot the rock had landed. I wait until the silver-haired woman walks underneath my branch and drop from my perch.

By the time she realizes I'm there, she's crumbling to the ground, blood flowing down her forehead courtesy of my elbow.

"Thena?" the man calls as he pivots toward where I lie behind a thick shrub. He can't weigh much more than me, but he's at least four inches taller. He scans the area through slitted eyes as he bounces on his toes. He doesn't seem so confident as fear slowly creeps onto his face. He advances toward me with his hands curled in front of him as he moves around the bush. His eyes land on me in the same moment I sweep my leg out and hit his ankles. He barely catches himself, reeling as he tries to regain his balance. I jump to my feet and in one motion my fist contacts his jaw.

We dance in a hurricane of lethal strikes, dodging and blocking for our lives as we slowly distance ourselves from the boys. He pummels me in the stomach, then sends a jab hurtling for my head. I manage to pull back enough to stay standing, but I can feel my brain bounce around in my skull as my vision begins to blur.

"Leo!" Antares calls frantically through the woods, sending a spike of fear up my spine. The man stumbles at the sound of my brother's young voice. He hesitates long enough for me to gain the upper hand, attacking ruthlessly until I land a particularly nasty blow to his throat. He hurtles to the ground with his neck clutched in his hands. I catch a flash of silver streaking through the air toward my heart and duck out of the way. The blade set for my eyes embeds itself in my arm. The man lies on the ground, staring up at me with wide golden eyes as I dislodge the steel from my muscle.

"Don't like to follow the rules, do you?" I spit. He flinches at my tone. My hand wraps around his throat as he squeaks, trying to call for help. After a pitifully short moment, his eyes roll back in his skull as his arms lie limp on the ground. Panic seizes me as I pull a long dagger from the sheath at his side, the grip the same leather as his suit. My blood races as I run for the tree where the boys were hidden, the world seeming to shake under my feet. When I get there, I look up at nothing but branches.

"Hello, blood-eye."

I spin as my grip tightens around the daggers. Tears run down Antares's cheeks as the last man holds a dagger to his throat. He clutches Saiph in his other arm with a hand over her mouth. My entire body coils tight, waiting to be set off. This one is going to die.

"They're children," I say, keeping the quiver from my voice. The hunger in his eyes only grows as he pushes the blade tighter against Antares's neck. His desperate whimpers rip through my soul.

"People are easier to control when they have something to live for," he purrs. I raise my blade slightly, rotating my grip, but I don't dare take a step in his direction. He presses the dagger closer to Antares's neck, his eyes twinkling as my brother shakes. I take a deep breath and zero in on him. In a motion too fast to see, I launch the blade through the air. The man gasps and drops both my sister and the dagger as a terrible gurgle escapes his throat. Antares grabs Saiph right before she hits the ground and hurriedly moves toward me.

I run to my brother and sister and fall to my knees before them. I take Antares's pale face in my hands, quickly assessing him. "Did he hurt you?" I ask frantically. He shakes his head, holding Saiph tightly. I wrap my arms around them as my heart shudders in my chest. I pull away, my thoughts suddenly clearing. "Where's Cass?"

"I told him to run. He went toward the shore." I push myself to my feet, ready to carry them to the boat if I have to. I rip a piece off my shirt and quickly tie it around my arm to stanch the bleeding. "Leo, Altair went looking for the other hunters," Antares pants, dread clear in his eyes. "He wasn't going to try and hunt them. He went to get their help. That's why he didn't kill us right away. He was waiting for Altair to get backup." It takes a moment for the words to sink in. I swallow the bile rising in my throat and suppress a scowl as I march over to the still drowning man and yank the blade out of his windpipe. He makes one final gasp before going still, Lady Death having come to take him away

"What way did he go?"

Antares points south. Why did he have to go south? "Antares, I need you to bring Saiph to the boat. Cael will be waiting with Elana and Byrne. I'll get Altair. I need you to tell Cael to leave as soon as you're all there. If I don't make it back in time, tell him we'll hide and find a way over two nights from now. Do you understand?" My brother straightens, wiping the tears from his face as he sniffles. He nods solemnly, his eyes glistening.

"I don't care what you have to do..." I pick up the dagger that had held him captive and slap it into Antares's hand. "Get on that boat." I turn away before he can answer, praying they'll make it alive.

CHAPTER

FORTY-EIGHT

LEO

I run as fast as I can down the path Antares had pointed out, following the footprints stuck in the dirt. Rage blinds any feelings still holding on to my sinking conscience. When I get my hands on Altair, I'm going to kill him myself. I stop when I hear hurried footsteps coming toward me. I crouch behind a tree and watch as my brother advances with the ruby-haired woman by his side, a curved blade clutched in each of her hands. The blood-soaked dagger held in my fist seems to ice over. She stops and scans the trees with razor-sharp eyes.

"He's not here. I told you Jesper had a blade to Antares's neck. Leo won't risk my brother's life for anything," Altair assures, pushing through the bushes with a steady pace. My blood curdles in my veins as I coax myself into complete stillness. She searches the woods for another minute before deciding it's clear. How wrong she is. I wait until they come closer, then take my shot.

The woman sees me coming and sloppily blocks my blow.

Altair staggers away, his golden eyes wide with fear. I focus my rage into a cold concentration, hitting her over and over with the force of ten warriors. She stumbles as I hook my foot behind her knee, giving me the perfect window. I run my blade through her stomach, pulling a scream from deep in her throat. I leave the blade embedded in her torso, not caring as she falls to the ground and blood seeps from her mouth. If she's smart enough to leave the dagger in, she might survive if a medic finds her.

I turn on Altair, his face ashen as he stares me down. He turns and runs without direction. My brothers don't run from a threat like scared children, we fight when there's no way out. "What did they do to you?" I breathe, shaking my head as he flees. He throws a look over his shoulder and trips over a root, flying forward. Altair hits the ground so hard I wince. I jog up to him, panic seizing my lungs as I realize he's passed out cold. I put my hand in front of his mouth and sigh with relief when I feel him breathe. I haul him over my shoulder and push myself back into a run, heading for the north shore.

I don't let my guard down until I feel the cold breeze of the Vallan skitter across my sweaty, blood-doused skin. The blinding brightness of the water's reflection is such a relief my knees almost buckle. Cael stands on the shore with his back to me as he throws a thick rope inside the rowboat. He turns before I've cleared the forest line, relief clear on his face, but his expression deepens with dread as he sees Altair slung over my shoulder. He rushes toward me, meeting me on the rocky beach.

"What happened?" he asks as we hurry toward the water, tearing his eyes from Altair to glance at the knife in my hand.

"Altair tried to help them," I force, keeping my gaze forward. "Are Cass and Antares here?" Cael stops a step behind me, his expression slack and face turning a slight green. Relief washes through me as I see Antares sitting with Saiph nestled in his lap. Byrne sits on one of the wooden planks with two heavy oars in her hands. I move forward and lay Altair down between them.

"Is he all right?" Byrne asks as fear clouds her expression.

"He'll be fine," I snap through clenched teeth. I turn back around to Cael. "Where are Cass and Elana?" My breathing turns shallow as my heart races.

"Elana went looking for you both. We told her to stay but she said it was taking too long." My heart stops as I watch the dread build on his face. *Both.* "We thought Cass was with you," he says, his voice low.

A bloodcurdling scream pierces through the woods a moment later. It's a sound I've heard so few times I go numb when it hits my ears. We all turn to the tree line and try to peer through the thick bush. Cael starts running before I see the small form barreling toward us through the trees. Arrows rain down beside him as a pack of black and dark-green-clad soldiers chase after my little brother. I'm quick on Cael's heels, my heart humming in my ears as Antares frantically calls out Cass's name. A man with a bright-gold band catches the back of my brother's shirt as I bare my teeth and force myself to move faster. Cael yells something from beside me as he grabs me, but my mind doesn't register it.

I try to rip my arm away from Cael's grip, but his face stops me short. Broken, he looks hollow. I shift my gaze back to Cass as a bright-crimson spot grows on his shirt and his mouth hangs open. I hear myself scream as I fight to go to him. Cass's eyes slowly drop down to the spot of blood as tears fill my eyes. His small hands come back stained red as the world starts to sway. The man pulls back, a dripping short sword cradled in his hand. Cass drops to the ground in a broken heap.

More hands grasp my arm as the group heads our way.

Time slows and my heart beats backward in my chest as the clouds zip by. I can't leave him. We can't leave him.

Cael stumbles as he lets go of my arm, an arrow shaft protruding from his shoulder. He pushes himself up and reaches for me again. He stands in front of me with tear-stained cheeks as he pushes me backward. Byrne frantically joins him in trying to hold me back as I fight against them. They're doing everything in their power to keep me from massacring the people standing around my little brother's body.

"I'm not losing two brothers, Leo. Move!" Cael begs, his voice cracking as he shoves me toward the boat. I let myself get one last look at Cass before turning around, my soul shattering into a million pieces. Someone kneels beside him and scoops him into her arms. Elana meets my gaze, so many emotions written in her sorrowful eyes.

I help Cael and Byrne into the boat and start pushing us out, the current slowly becoming stronger at my feet. Byrne pulls out a quiver of arrows and a bow and starts releasing them on anyone who steps onto the beach. I haul myself over the side, taking one oar from Cael and rowing with all the strength I have left. I push Antares down beside me as a few archers manage to send arrows our way, missing us by mere inches as they embed into the sides of the rowboat.

We let the current help us down the Vallan as people start to gather on the beach, Elana clearly absent from the crowd. Without some type of raft, no one will be able to follow. The shallows of the Vallan are safe, but the depths are known to swallow anyone it wishes. We're out of range of their arrows now, so all I can do is watch them, eerily still on the faraway bank.

We sit in silence, listening to the splash of the oars and falling tears. We left our brother, our youngest brother.

I jump over the side when we near land and pull the boat onto the rocky shore. No one speaks as we unload our supplies, desperate to get as far away from Wate as possible. Byrne tells Cael to sit so she can take care of the snapped arrow sticking out from his shoulder. We exchange a tense glance before turning to watch the opposite shore where people still linger, stalking its length. They're no more than specks on the horizon from this far away, but I can still feel their glares burning my skin.

"They won't cross, not even in rowboats. There are laws even Wate's people won't break," she whispers, staring at her abandoned home.

"And if they do?" I ask dryly, incapable of feeling anything other than the roaring grief screaming in my head.

"Then we head toward Arkezo. They might have the courage to follow us onto these shores, but they won't chance running into any blood-eyes living in the forest or the surrounding area." I swallow hard and close my eyes to try and retake the reins on my spinning thoughts. My mind refuses to stop replaying Cass falling to the ground, his scared eyes weighing on my conscience.

Altair stirs in the boat and groans as he sits up. He freezes as he takes us in, pausing a long moment over my bloodied face and the arrow shaft sticking out of Cael's shoulder. He stands up slowly and steps out of the boat.

"You're alive," he rasps, his eyes wide as he looks at Cael. I walk over and shove him so hard he falls to the ground, hissing as his hands scrape across the rocks. "You dirty, helpless child! You're the reason he's dead! If you hadn't run off and led Cassien's men back to us, he'd be alive!" Tears run down my face as he crawls backward, desperate to escape.

Cael steps in front of me, one hand stanching the blood from his shoulder. "Don't. I don't care what the hell happened.

Cass is gone. We can't do anything to change what happened and I'm not going to let you kill Altair because of it," he says as his face crumbles. His words ringing with finality, rooting my feet in place. Altair tenses behind us.

"He's dead?" Altair asks, his voice full of uncertainty and confusion. Cael turns on him as his control slips.

"Just because I'm not letting Leo beat you into the ground doesn't mean I don't want to. You have one chance," he says, carefully articulating each word. "Tell us you didn't have anything to do with what happened. Tell us what we're all thinking isn't true." Tears creep into Altair's eyes as he swallows and angles himself away from us.

"They weren't supposed to kill Cass," he croaks. Cael jumps for him, but I hold him back, barely containing my own fury.

Byrne stands behind us, holding Saiph tightly in her arms. She turns herself away to shield my sister from reality like I've done so many times before. Antares stands unsteadily at her side. "I'm sorry," she says, tears running freely down her face. I slowly take my arms away from my shaking brother, overwhelmed by a storm of pain, sadness, and anger.

I stare into the tree line, a shell of my younger brother collapsed on the ground and the memory of another hanging over us. I say a silent prayer to Lady Death, begging her to bring Cass to his twin. We gather up our packs and head into the protection of the trees without another word, hoping we've finally found a place we can be free, even though I feel more chained down than ever.

EPILOGUE

LEO

It's been four days since we crossed the Vallan. I strapped on my blades in the first hour we spent on this side of the river as Byrne pried the arrowhead out of Cael's shoulder. I don't think I can handle hearing another scream as my mind scrolls through our last moments on Wate's shore. We left Elana and Cass. I squeeze my eyes shut and banish the thought away. I made the trip to where we left the rowboat nine times over the first few days, waiting for any sign of Elana. Byrne barely spoke and I knew it was because her sister was facing her father alone. On the third day, Elana rowed across to us. The relief we all felt was palpable as she stepped onto the rocks, but her expression was somber as she avoided our eyes. For a reason Cael and I could not fathom, Elana decided to stay in Wate. I wanted to scream at her for the decision, but Byrne beat me to it. We left them alone for hours as they went back and forth. When the yelling finally stopped, Byrne told us Elana was going to stay in Wate and nothing we could say would change her mind. Elana assured her they could meet every two weeks, but it did not appease her in the slightest.

Byrne hadn't said anything more until a few hours ago when she announced we'd be meeting Emrys tonight and so we had to move to their normal meeting point. Now, we all huddle together in the darkness, Altair the only one fighting the cold by himself. Other than Cael, none of us have dared to speak a word to him, and even then, it was only to ask if he needed anything. Saiph and Antares are both sound asleep between Cael, Byrne and I. Our clothes are torn and smeared in blood, our efforts to clean them useless. At least Cael's shoulder has yet to show signs of infection. It's the only good thing that's happened in days.

Cael's head snaps up as he hears something in the woods before the rest of us. A branch snaps, sending my brother and I flying to our feet, a slayer already tucked into my hand as Antares stirs on the ground. Byrne stands up slowly and steps around us as she pushes my blade down with a calm sweep of her hand.

A tall, lanky boy walks through the tree line with an easy smile plastered on his face. His dark-blond hair is cropped short to his head and his long face lights up when he spots Byrne. His expression changes quickly when he sees us, a dagger appearing in his hand as he reaches for Byrne and pulls her behind him.

"Emrys, these are friends of mine," Byrne says calmly, pushing around his arm to look him in the eyes. He studies us, noting everything marking us as different and dangerous. His gaze flits to Cael's eyes, to our wrists, then to our tattered camp. Antares is now awake and holding Saiph in his lap as she tries to stand.

"They're covered in blood, Byrne," he argues, angling himself protectively around her.

"We had some trouble getting out. We didn't all make it," she whispers. Emrys's face softens at Byrne's raw emotion. My stomach sinks, but I straighten my spine, pushing away the flood of sadness threatening to break free.

"So you brought them here?" he asks, and though his tone is gentle, I can tell there is a battle raging inside of him. Byrne nods once, holding his stare. "Why?" he questions quietly. I can tell he already knows the answer, but he asks her all the same.

"Because you can help. We've spoken about getting me out before, what's a few more people," she pleads. He closes his eyes and wraps his arms around her, not caring that we're all watching. He takes a moment to really look at us, his gaze lingering over my face as his brows knit together. Byrne steps away from him and motions toward us. "They need help, Emrys." He nods stoically.

"I don't know how I'm going to hide five gold-eyes and a getic. Especially when three of you are children." He sighs, rubbing his face with the heals of his hands.

"Four gold-eyes. He's a blood-eye," Byrne points out, nodding to me.

I bleed my eyes and Emrys gasps. "What?" she asks him, worry weaving through her voice.

"Dirix Matteus?" He squints at me as if he was trying to see through me. His eyes land on my blades and he blanches. "You are Dirix Matteus," he says breathlessly, with wide eyes.

"Dirix Matteus?" I ask in confusion.

"You... He disappeared almost two decades ago. Those are his sheaths. His Blades. You look exactly like the portrait." I drain my eyes and take another step forward. These blades were my father's.

"Who is Dirix Matteus?" I press, my mind buzzing.

"He's the eldest and only child of the late King Elora," he

replies. I blink, holding my breath as Cael gapes at me. "Dirix Matteus is the Crown Prince of Illena."

THE END

Subscribe to my newsletter to be notified when the second book in the trilogy will be released!

Acknowledgments

Writing a book has been one of the biggest, most rewarding challenges I've ever taken on. Creating Tominay and Illena and every character from Saiph to Elana has been a journey I will cherish forever, and I couldn't have done it without all the support from the amazing people in my family, my friends, and team. Mum, without your help, I would still be stuck on stage one. Dad, you always asked how my book was progressing and that means more to me than you can know. Calum, I know you hated that I never had time to watch a movie with you, but I always secretly loved when you said you would be my manager. I promise I'll watch a movie with you now. And to the rest of the fam jam who, from the first time I said I was writing a book but couldn't explain a word of what it was about, had complete faith in me, I am more grateful than I can put into words.

Leah, you were the first person to ever read one of my manuscripts, and even though it needed a lot of work, you still read the whole thing and let me talk to you for hours about what I planned to do. Though you never knew it, I figured out more than a few plot twists while I was with you and without them, I think Leo's story would be a heck of a lot more bland. Through everything, you were always by my side, the first person to ask how my writing was going and to tell me I could do it even when I was frustrated, and for that, I can't thank you enough. To all my friends at school, who were even more excited than me about this project, you made it all feel that much more real and made me believe in myself and the work I created, and I am so thankful for your support.

Speaking of school, I can't forget the teachers that made me love English and gave me the skills to write this book. Thank you for everything.

A thousand thank yous to the team of people who helped me straighten out this story and bring it to life. To the amazing artists, you took the words I spewed into emails and somehow created the perfect replicas of the thoughts that had been bouncing around my head for years. You are so talented and I am eternally grateful for the designs you created for me. To the editors who helped me make this story flow, you've taught me things about writing that make me a better author, and for that I will forever be thankful.

Last but never least, I can't end this book without saying the biggest thank you to Laura, who gave me this opportunity. Without your help I would have been completely lost and would never be where I am today. You made my dreams come true, and there are not enough synonyms of thank you to tell you how truly grateful I am for everything you've done for me.

About the Author

Ayla Marie is a Canadian high school student whose love for fantasy started when she was twelve and hasn't dulled since. She will read any book you put in front of her—textbooks do not count—especially when they have action packed storylines and a romantic subplot that makes you want to read as fast as you can, while wishing it would never end. Though writing, reading, and studying take up most of her time—or all her time according to her younger brother—she always manages to find space in her schedule to play some soccer and hang out with friends and family. Her goofy dog and two cats are her biggest fans, and though she could have done without the constantly interrupting barks and meows, she loves their annoying presence very much.

The Blood Prince is her debut novel, but she plans to write many more, deepening her love for writing and literature with every page.